# THE LORD OF THE LABYRINTH

## THE SPECIAL EDITION

EMMA CASTLE

# An Important Note from the Author

This story is a love letter to the 1986 movie *Labyrinth* starring David Bowie and Jennifer Connelly.

The movie is about a sixteen-year-old girl who accidentally wishes her little half-brother away to the Goblin King. When she realizes her mistake, she must journey to the Goblin King's world and find her way through the labyrinth to rescue her brother.

If you're like me, this movie creates a wonderful sense of nostalgia. We have a girl struggling to find out who she is in the world and what power she possesses as a woman and an adult to define her life. And then of course you add in David Bowie in those tight pants and a billowy blouse, crooning his songs and enticing Jennifer's character, all while the threat on her brother's life hangs in the balance. It is a story involving more than just one kind of awakening for the heroine.

When I set out to write a more adult *Labyrinth* retelling, I knew it would be an intense experience. I have so many emotions tied to this movie because I grew up watching it. And like many things that you rewatch (or reread) over time at different ages, you gain new perspectives on how it made you feel, what it made you think as you were younger and then later on as you grew older. I wanted to really capture the magic of the story by mirroring the character journey as best I could in certain ways. Before you read the story, I want to explain a few choices I made as the writer and why I felt they were important to discuss before you dive into this adventure.

Firstly, this is an adult romance novel. It contains descriptive sex scenes between the hero and heroine. Unlike in the movie where the heroine is sixteen, my heroine is eighteen. I know many readers roll their eyes and go "ugh" when they think about an eighteen-year-old young woman and a thousand-year-old Fae hero. But for me, part of the charm of the movie is watching the movie heroine, Sarah, discover her first true sexual attraction and her own self-worth and power. I wanted to capture that same journey with my own story, but have the heroine be a legal adult, that way we can finally enjoy love scenes between two consenting adults.

As of the day I write this note, I am thirty-nine years old. Eighteen feels like a lifetime ago, but I do remember that when I turned eighteen, I realized I was suddenly, for the first time, truly in charge of my future. That my choices would reflect my life's path and that I was the person I needed to rely on. Becoming an adult can be exciting, it can be terrifying, and it can be a mixture of both. There are dozens of "first" experiences in those years after graduating high school. And in some ways that series of "firsts" and the choices a person makes can define who they are for years to come. It's the point where we start to truly discover ourselves. It is the beginning of a grand journey that will last many, many years.

With my heroine, Kate, I want you, the reader, to feel what it's like to be that uncertain eighteen-year-old, to wonder about your future and feel that first spark of true adult female attraction that's more than just a crush. I want you to go back in time and relive that period of initial self-discovery with Kate as she navigates through her adventures in the labyrinth.

While this is in a way a retelling of the movie, there are parts that differ from the movie. I relied heavily on fairy research. I read extensively on the history of fairies all over the world. Each creature you read about is based on real fairy lore. The two ruling courts of the higher classes of Fae, the Seelie and Unseelie, are based on Scottish and Irish mythology, with the Seelie being the light Fae and the Unseelie being the dark Fae. The idea of the fairy courts of the Seelie and Unseelie have existed for hundreds of years, and many romantasy and fantasy authors have relied on such lore to create their own fairy worlds. Jim Butcher in his *Dresden Files* was the first author to really use fairy courts in modern-day fantasy writing more than twenty years ago, and many authors since then have been inspired by his concept of seasonal courts.

For my own story, I wanted to draw the distinction between morning and twilight as my two courts because so much of my created lore relies on the fairies being connected to either sunlight or twilight and moonlight. Unlike the original movie, my hero is not a Goblin King but actually a *Sidhe* (pronounced "Shee") or Shining One, one of the original ancient Fae peoples that possessed immense powers, according to existing world lore.

While most of my story concerns Kate's journey through the labyrinth and her time with Roan, the dark Fae King, there is an additional storyline concerning Roan and his tensions with the Seelie court led by his cousin Culan. I chose not to spend page after page involving expansive battles or court-related dramas. I wanted it to feel more like a fairy tale where the story focuses on the adventures of a limited group of characters. I also wanted the focus to be on Kate's personal journey and her romance with Roan, where I believe it's the most rewarding and the most fun! Just like in the original movie, Sarah's journey was episodic, and while she was dropped into a vast world, she only discovered parts of it through her adventures, and I wanted it to be the same for Kate.

There is a small cast of secondary characters that I hope you will enjoy. For fans of Hoggle and Ludo from the original movie, I've created a grumpy kobold named Patch and a female troll named Magda. They become Kate's friends and help her discover her self-worth and her courage, as well as show her the power of having friends who truly support you, even when you feel you are in your darkest hour.

I hope you enjoy Kate and Roan's story.

All my love to you, dear reader,
Emma Castle
June 2025

# PROLOGUE

*Once upon a time...a wish was whispered, weaving a spell of sweet longing and moonlight. No dark king could resist such an enchantment as a mortal woman's wish . . .*

—Anon., *Tales from the Twilight Court*

The barn owl that was more than simply an owl ruffled its feathers as its gaze swept through the darkened bedchamber. Layers of purple shadows stretched over the room, except for a single beam of moonlight that illuminated the figure of a young woman curled on top of the covers of a bed against one wall. Her soft weeping altered the vibrations in the air, keeping the owl that was not an owl on edge. He shuffled his clawed feet on the carpeted floor of the woman's bedchamber.

The owl's eyes funneled the scant light and allowed him to survey this new world through a predator's sharpened gaze.

He stretched a wing out until pain forced him to pull it back against his body. A soft screech escaped him. He had come a long way from the portal in the woods, and his injured wing still needed time to mend.

The woman on the bed stopped crying. The owl that was not an owl buried his face in his feathers, going still.

She sat up and looked around the room, her eyes trying to adjust to the darkness. He peered back at her through his shield of feathers. Her gaze finally settled on him, and a strange sense of destiny tugged at the core of his being, as though each breath this mortal woman took bound him more and more to her.

A life saved meant a life owed. But he was clever, and the payment of his debt would not come in a way this mortal would expect.

"You okay, Handsome?" Her dark hair fell around her shoulders, and the tracks of tears on her face shimmered like liquid moonlight over her cheeks.

Human tears. Did she not know the power they possessed? He could cast an enchantment that would last for centuries with a single tear from this beautiful woman. His eyes missed nothing as he studied her in the half dark.

*Oh, little mortal,* he thought as he ruffled his feathers. She slid off the bed and came to him, her slender bare feet peeking out from a loose pair of satin trousers she'd worn to bed.

"I hope the vet was right and that you'll be all right after a rest. You're too beautiful not to be flying out in the night." She knelt beside him and reached out a hand to him. He opened his beak and gave a little nibble on her finger, making her smile through her tears.

"You'd never hurt me, would you?" she asked.

Her tone told him that she didn't mean that he wouldn't claw or bite her. No, it came from somewhere deeper, somewhere darker in her soul. This woman had been hurt, and yet she dared to trust him.

*Oh, but, little one, I am darkness. I harm those with light within, even when I do not wish to. It is my curse . . . it is my nature.*

However, that endless black abyss within him that roared with rage and demanded blood went eerily quiet when this human was near. Each time she held out a finger to him or caressed his feathered head, a sense of peace he'd not known possible overtook him, quieting the raging storm inside him.

Could she be filled with a light he'd never seen before? A light that made pale the very essence of the Shining Ones like him? Surely not, for this woman was *mortal.* She had no ancient blood, no connection to his realm.

Her brown eyes, like honey shot through with amber, watched him intensely, just as he watched her.

"I wish I knew what you were thinking," she mused. "It must be quite serious, because you look like you're frowning." Her lips curved up in a half smile.

*A wish...yes.* He needed her to make a wish. The owl that was not an owl wanted her to speak the words that would give him the power to claim her, but for that he needed her to make a wish. But how could he make a human utter the words that would give him power over her?

The owl moved a step closer on the carpeted surface of the floor toward her. She stroked her fingers over the top of his head as he continued to look back at her, unable to tear his gaze away. Pleasure rippled through his body, and the ache in his injured wing faded to the background of his mind.

Had this mortal cast a spell on him instead? Such a thing was not possible.

"Are you hungry? Thirsty?" she asked.

He chittered softly, and she grinned. His breath caught at

the dazzling sight. It was like the glamour he could cast upon others, yet he saw no visible magic.

"Very well. I'll be right back."

She left the room. After a moment, the door opened, but it was not the young woman who entered. It was the little boy he had seen when the woman had first rescued him and brought him here. The boy couldn't have been more than ten or twelve mortal years. His mop of blond hair and blue eyes made him look desperately innocent. This was the sort of child who would have been welcome in his realm, for the Shining Ones adored beauty in all its forms.

"Wow. You're so cool." The boy knelt on the floor and reached out for him with a gentle touch, just like the woman's. "Kate's amazing. Of course she'd rescue you. I bet by the time she's done taking care of you, you'll be better than ever."

*And who is Kate to you?* the owl wondered silently. He'd spent so little time in the world of men. This modern age had left his kind overshadowed by bright lights and frightening technology that weakened magic.

"I . . . I think she really needs a friend right now," the boy suddenly confessed. "I'd love to be her friend, but she doesn't even want me to be her brother." He paused, his face tightening with pain. "But I'd do anything for her. *Anything.*"

A little brother. A loyal one. That was something the owl understood. Loyalty was a treasure to be cherished and protected. Even for a creature of darkness and mist, he craved loyalty and—foolishly—love.

*Perhaps I am not so different from these mortals.* He chuckled at the ridiculous thought. He was the king of twilight, the lord of silver and night. What did he have in common with humans?

"I better go. She'd get upset if she knew I came into her

room." He offered the owl a secretive smile. "So take care of her for me, okay?"

Then the boy was gone. A few minutes later, Kate returned and sat on the floor at the foot of her bed with a small bowl of water and a parcel of brown paper.

"Here you go." She set the bowl down. The owl that was not an owl bent forward so that his beak could dip into the water to drink. He had been thirsty, and the cool water was a balm to his injured body.

"Now, try this." She opened the parcel and began tearing something into small chunks. "I bet you'll think it's tasty." She offered him a small piece.

He humored her and tasted it. It was meat. Finally, a proper source of sustenance. He clicked his beak and moved closer so she could feed him several more bites. Once he felt satisfied, he moved away from her a little. She wrapped the meat back up in the parcel but left the bowl on the floor while she disappeared from the room again.

The food had not been the kind he was used to; it held no healing powers, yet he felt stronger. In a short while, he could return home.

"Feeling better?" Kate asked when she returned. He closed his eyes halfway and fluffed up his feathers in a show of contentment.

"I have to get to bed. It's Christmas tomorrow, and I need to sleep if I have to deal with Sandra." She reached out once more and trailed her fingertips over his uninjured wing. The caress was delightful, and he despised how much he enjoyed it. The woman thought him some common woodland creature and was treating him like a pet. But damned if he could lie and say that her touch didn't stir dark, delicious things within him.

"You know, I think it was you who saved me tonight," she whispered. "I don't know where I would've ended up if you hadn't crashed into my window. I might have kept driving in the dark and gotten lost. Or worse."

*Lost in the dark.* It wasn't a fate a creature full of light like this woman deserved.

He was forever lost in the shadows. It was his burden, his fate.

"I'll see you in the morning," she whispered to him. She then returned to her bed, this time climbing beneath the sheets. She let out a sigh of contentment that filled the room with new vibrations that called to him.

He watched.

He waited.

He wondered . . .

Once she was deep asleep, the moonlight burst into stardust above her head and her dreams played out before his eyes. Mortals always failed to shield their dreams, and now he had a glimpse into her world. He watched with rapt attention as the magic of her mind moved through countless images.

Figures made of glittering dust danced before him, playing out a private opera of whispered words and bittersweet music. But soon the sweet words changed, and her dreams were consumed by the phantoms of her nightmares.

*"Selfish creature . . . never listens . . . have to do something about her . . . Send her away . . ."*

The owl's eyes slanted as he spread his wings, filled with rage. Kate stirred, her dark dreams disrupting her so violently that even in her sleep she began to weep.

The owl let out a hiss and took flight, landing on the woman's bed. He hopped close to her and pressed his beak against her cheek, clicking softly. Her eyes opened, and she stared up at him in shock and wonder.

"How did you get up here? Did you fly?" she asked, wiping her eyes. He bobbed his head, his eyes tracking the sight of her tears, his dark heart pounding furiously. She sat up and carefully scooped him into her arms, burying her face in his feathers without fear.

"I wish I could leave, that you could fly me away from here . . . I wish I could forget everything."

*A wish . . .*

She had spoken a wish he had the power to grant, one that would let him own her body and soul. The strength of her desire infused her wish with power, and his magic was strengthened by it. If there was something that mortals possessed that the Fae envied, it was the power of their wishes. Creatures like him did not make wishes.

*Yes, little one, yes.*

He could take her away. He possessed enough power now. And once he took her to his world, she would be his and he could study the strange effect she had on him for as long as his dark heart desired.

Releasing his hold on his wild shape, the barn owl transformed into his true Fae form. Now towering over the young woman, he wrapped his arms around her. She stiffened in his hold as her face tilted up and she saw him without his glamour.

Her lips parted in shock, but it was too late to change her mind.

"Your wish is granted, little one. You're mine, now and forever. I shall steal you away by twilight." He spoke the claiming words that would bind her to him forever. Patterns of moonlight and shadows whirled around them as he opened the space between worlds and carried her into the darkness with him.

*Beware the deep, dark woods. Men have been lost within the birch and poplar branches. But should a woman venture forth, the rowan and ash will show her the way. Their boughs will bend and their leaves will murmur to the twilight king . . . his bride has come.*

—Anon., *Tales from the Twilight Court*

**A** *few hours earlier*

"HE'S NOT MY FAVORITE, KATE. STOP ACTING LIKE A CHILD AND BE more respectful to your mother."

"*Step*mother," Kate Winslow corrected her father as she desperately tried to control her temper. The only time her stepmother ever called herself Kate's mother was when she was trying to win an argument or shame Kate into something in front of her father.

Robert Winslow glared at her from across the kitchen island, arms crossed. Her stepmother, Sandra, stood beside him, lips pinched in a sour frown. She continued to cut a bunch of carrots into small chunks for the Crock-Pot for tomorrow. Sandra's brown eyes met Kate's, a dark glint in them, warning Kate of the poison she was about to spread in Robert's ear.

"I'm not a child!" Kate snapped. "I'm in college, for God's sake. Stop treating me like some spoiled brat." She couldn't understand why her father believed anything Sandra said about her. It was all so clearly untrue.

"Then perhaps you shouldn't act like one, Katherine," Sandra said as she set her knife down. "Caden doesn't act like this, and he's eleven."

Caden. Her half brother. The son Sandra had given Kate's father. The perfectly adorable kid whom Kate loved, but Sandra used him as a wedge to drive Kate even farther away from her father. And now that she'd officially moved into the dorms two hours away, that emotional distance between them had only intensified. She hadn't known how unhappy she'd been these last few years until she'd seen how other people on campus behaved with their families. Many had blended families like hers, but none seemed as miserable as she was.

She almost hadn't come home for Christmas. When her roommates had asked her about it, she'd felt a terrible sense of dread at the thought of having to face Sandra again. And worse, she would disappoint her father just by being here, just like she was now, even though all she did was speak the truth. Kate had no value to Sandra, to the woman who could have been a second mother to her, if only she had wanted Kate just a little. But she never had. From the first day she'd met Kate, Sandra had made it clear that Kate was only in the way.

Unwanted. Even at eighteen, when she was moving on with her life, it *still* hurt.

Tears stung Kate's eyes. She *wasn't* a child. She was earning a business degree and studying French. She had talents, skills, and intelligence. She had earned a full academic scholarship, which had made her father proud until Sandra said it was only to be expected given the private schools they had sent her to. As if Kate's grades had been purchased and her years of hard work meant nothing.

Before Kate's mother, Amber, had died, she'd told Kate that a child was born into the world with love, that they didn't need to earn it. But her mother had been wrong. Sandra had made it clear love had to be earned, and Kate could never do enough to please her. Somehow, that wounded Kate beyond words, knowing that her mother's wonderful ideas about the world weren't true.

*How can she make me cry all the time? It's like she knows just what to say to make me look like a child.*

"You know," her father said, his tone firm but gentle, "I think it's time you went to see someone about your issues."

Kate gripped the edge of the white granite countertop. "My *issues*? The only issue I have is being a part of this family." The moment she said the words, she regretted them, but she'd be damned if she took them back. A look of satisfaction lurked behind the shocked expression on Sandra's face. A black pit formed in Kate's stomach. She'd played right into Sandra's trap. *Again.*

"Kate," her father warned. "This is why you need therapy. You need to understand how you fit into this family. Not every-thing is about you. Your mother taught you better than that."

*Your mother . . .* Those two words cut Kate's heart like a knife.

"But I don't fit," she said, almost in a whisper. She wanted to leave, but her body was frozen to the spot, unable to move. "That's what *she* wants." Kate glanced at her stepmother. "Isn't it? Driving me away so you get everything?"

Sandra's eyes lit up. "See, Robert? She just wants her inheritance. This little stunt is about money."

The evil woman had turned her own words against her. A metallic taste filled Kate's mouth. She swallowed, but her throat felt like it was coated in broken glass.

"That's it. I'm done." Kate turned to leave.

"Kate, come back. We aren't done talking about this," her father said.

*I am done,* she thought bitterly. *Done with everything.*

She stormed through the house, stopping only when she reached the stairs by the front door. Christmas lights covered the bushes outside, and a tall Christmas tree filled the entryway with its lushly decorated greenery. It was beautiful, but none of this was real. She wanted the old Christmas back. She wanted to have her mother's hand-sewn stockings on the fireplace mantel and randomly collected ornaments that carried special stories for their family. Sandra had stored them in the attic and replaced Kate's childhood with glitzy store-bought stockings that held no Christmas memories.

Christmas music drifted from the kitchen again. It had been paused when Kate interrupted them. Somewhere along the way, this had ceased to be Kate's world. Sandra had conquered it and controlled it, just like everything else in Kate's life.

This wasn't home. Home wasn't anywhere anymore. Her once beautiful world was now a frozen palace of ice in a land far out of her reach.

Kate stared at the family portrait above the fireplace. It held only her father, Sandra, and Caden. Sandra had scheduled the photo shoot on a day when Kate had final exams in high school, and she hadn't been able to sit for the portrait. Sandra was doing everything she could to push Kate away from her father. She kept pitting Kate against Caden, and Kate despised that even more. Caden was a sweet kid. She loved him, but seeing how her father glowed when he looked at his son compared to how he looked at her . . .

She shivered as a fresh layer of ice frosted her heart.

*Stop thinking about what should be. Think about what is.*

That was what she had to do. Her mother was dead. Her father had moved on. It was stupid for Kate to cling to her past and pathetic for her to wish for an impossible future.

Rather than go up to her room, Kate grabbed her purse from the side table and headed for the front door. She had to get out of here. She had no idea where she'd go. She only knew she needed to find a place where she could breathe and think. Something had to change in her life. She just had to figure out how to move forward.

"Kate?" Caden's voice halted her as she put her hand on the doorknob.

The little boy stood at the top of the stairs, wearing buffalo plaid red-and-black pajamas. His blond hair was a mess, and his blue eyes were wide with worry.

"Yeah?" she said softly, not wanting Sandra or her father to hear.

"You really think Mom has favorites?" He said *Mom* so innocently, as if he didn't understand that Sandra didn't want to be Kate's mother.

That's what hurt Kate more than anything. That she felt so unwanted when she would have been glad to have had a second mom. When her father had first gotten remarried, Kate had been open to the idea of a new mom. But from the moment she met Sandra, it had been clear the woman had no desire to have Kate in her life.

"I . . ." She swallowed past the lump in her throat. "Don't worry about what I said. I'm just mad." She could tell that he heard the lie upon her lips.

Caden came down a few steps on the stairs. "You're leaving? But tomorrow's Christmas."

"Then you should go back to bed so Santa will come tonight. He can't visit if you're awake. I promise I'll come back." He must have heard the uncertainty in her voice and came down the rest of the way.

"Kate, I'm eleven. I know Santa isn't real," Caden said politely. "You promise to come back?" He put a hand on her arm. "Please? You're my sister." His blue eyes were full of a pleading that tore at Kate's heart. She really loved her little brother, but so much of Sandra's cruelty involved him, and it created a bleak ache in her chest whenever she was around the boy.

"Promise me," he said again, his fingers tightening on the sleeve of her sweater. He could tell she didn't want to come back, that this place was a dark abyss of pain for her.

Her throat tightened. "Okay, I'll be back tomorrow. I promise."

Caden released her arm as she opened the door. Rain was coming down in thick torrents, matching her grim view of her future with her family. Caden gave her a small, helpless wave as she closed the door. She rushed to her car in the driveway, shielding her face with one arm.

The rain moved across the lawn and driveway in waves, the drops hitting the ground so hard they formed a layer of mist.

She wrenched open the driver's side door and threw herself in, half soaked by the time she slammed the door shut.

Kate started the engine but sat in the driveway for a few minutes, watching her headlights light up the garage door. She rested her head on the steering wheel and closed her eyes, fighting off more tears.

"What the hell am I doing?"

She couldn't just drive away from her family on Christmas Eve. But that was exactly what she was going to do. Drive somewhere. Anywhere. Just get away for at least a few hours.

She raised her head and, with renewed determination, backed out of the driveway. The rain pounded against her windows, making it impossible to see more than a dozen feet ahead of her, even with her headlights on and the windshield wipers working like mad.

She turned down the road that would carry her away. Despite the rain, she could make out the silhouette of the dark woods ahead that bordered the housing development. Only a thin strip of asphalt separated the dark wood from the suburban neighborhood she had just left. Her mother would have called that a liminal zone. A place *between*, not quite one thing or another, but somehow a hint of both.

Kate slowed as she passed the woods and thought of her mother and how much she missed her. Her mother had loved to read her fairy tales, myths, and legends. She had often warned Kate never to venture into the woods, unless she was strong enough to fight off any wolves that might come after her. Kate used to imagine an enormous wolf pursuing Red Riding Hood, but as a grown woman, Kate knew that other dangers lurked in dark places, in those strips of the earth that lay between worlds.

Suddenly a flash of white and silver streaked through the darkened woods.

A gust of wind exploded, bending trees violently in her direction, and her car swayed as the wind buffeted it. The passenger window exploded in a shower of glass. Kate screamed as the car rocked on its wheels and something soft and white smacked into her body. She covered her face, gasping. The wind howled like some childhood nightmare, and wild flashes of light broke over the car in spirals, blinding her through her closed eyelids.

Then, everything went silent. Even the rain suddenly stopped. A strange hum filled her ears—half felt, half heard—deep in her chest and inside her head, a tone that sent her pulse racing before it dropped into a slow, steady rhythm. In the tomb-like silence that followed, she dared to open her eyes and look around.

It took her a moment to adjust to the darkness again. She stared at the shattered passenger window and the creature crumpled on the seat. A barn owl splayed its wings out and stared back at her as it struggled to stand up. Its right wing didn't seem to move the way it should. Its heart-shaped face bobbed and swiveled around, looking at her and the car in confusion. The owl let out a piercing screech.

Kate had no idea what to do. One of its wings was bent, and several feathers seemed out of place. Its body quivered, possibly from shock.

She calmly moved to grip the wheel and let out a slow breath. "Okay . . ." She wasn't afraid of the owl, but she was afraid it might hurt itself more if she spooked it.

Thin red slashes on her forearms dripped with blood. She was only now becoming aware of the pain. She wasn't sure if the scratches were from the glass, the owl, or both. She examined the cuts and winced, but they didn't seem too severe. What mattered was the owl. It could be badly injured, and she couldn't let it suffer.

There was a veterinary ER nearby. They might let her have some antiseptic wipes and bandages while they checked on the owl. She prayed they could fix its wing and that it would be able to fly again.

"Okay, little guy, I'm going to take you somewhere to get you help." She started driving again. Thank God the rain had stopped.

She headed for the veterinary hospital a few miles away. The owl's unblinking gaze was fixed on her the whole time.

"I promise you'll be okay," she said. "Just don't claw me when we get there? I just need to make sure you're not hurt so we can get you flying again. You want that, don't you?" If she'd been able to fly, she'd never want to touch the ground again.

Kate stopped at a red light and looked down at the owl. Its one wing was still a mess of white-and-gold feathers, while the other was tucked securely against its side. The owl swiveled its head to watch the bright lights of fast-food restaurants and coffee shops along the street. Then it swiveled its head back to look at her. It slowly blinked, its dark eyes luminous.

"You're beautiful," she whispered.

Kate didn't feel silly talking to the owl. She loved animals. Before her mother had died, her family had a golden retriever, Macintosh. She'd loved to bury her face in his fur and talk to him about everything she'd done that day. That was one of the many things she loved about animals—the quiet ability to exist on the earth and to accept others with such patience. They listened and let humans be themselves. It was a gift that people often took for granted.

They soon reached the veterinary ER. The bright red-and-white sign of the building glowed above them, the mist from the storm creating a halo around the letters.

She considered the problem of safely handling the owl, then spotted her gym towel in the back seat. That might do the trick. Kate retrieved the towel and got out of the car.

"Just remember, I'm not going to hurt you." She approached the passenger door, then cautiously raised the towel with one arm while she opened the door with the other. The owl pressed itself flat against the seat when he saw her advance, which made it more difficult. But after some careful prodding, she managed to wrap the cloth around the little bird and swaddled him like a baby, making sure his talons couldn't hurt her.

"See? That wasn't so bad." She ignored his disgruntled hoot and grabbed her purse with her free hand before she entered the building.

The woman at the check-in desk wore a cheery Christmas sweater and was watching a Christmas movie on the big-screen TV in the empty waiting room.

Kate cleared her throat, making the woman jump. "Hi. This owl crashed through my car's side window. I think it injured its wing."

The woman's lips parted in shock. "We don't see wild birds here that often." She stood and came around the counter. "Do you have it secured?"

"Yeah, he's wrapped up. His talons are in the towel."

"Okay, great. Let's get you into an exam room, and I'll have the doctor come straight in to look at him."

Kate took a seat in the first exam room, the owl still bundled up on her lap. She stroked the top of its head, and it tilted its head back to look up at her.

"Now we wait—" Her whispered words were cut off as a middle-aged woman in green scrubs and a white coat stepped into the room. Her gray eyes lit up with wonder when she saw the owl.

"Janice said you had an owl, but I honestly didn't believe her. Let's set it up on the exam table so I can get a better look." The vet held her hand out. "I'm Dr. Coburn."

"I'm Kate. Thanks so much for looking at him." Kate set the towel-wrapped owl down on the exam table.

"I'll see if he wants a little meat treat before I start messing with his wings." The vet opened a little Ziploc pouch of treats and offered one to the owl. He stared at the vet's hand and the treat with a look of effrontery.

"Oh come on, just try it." Kate stroked the owl's head, and then it opened its beak and took the treat, swallowing it.

The vet carefully unwrapped the towel around one side of the bird. The left wing seemed to be okay, at least from what Kate could see as the vet carefully stretched it out and moved it around.

"Huh," Kate murmured. "His wings looked worse just a few minutes ago when I first found him."

"Well, this one looks all right to me. Let's check his right side." Dr. Coburn covered the left wing and exposed his right wing. The owl clicked his beak in warning as the vet gingerly stretched his right wing out from his body.

"I know it hurts. You're a brave little guy, aren't you? No one is going to hurt you." She ignored the hiss the owl threw at her.

"Hey, she's not gonna hurt you," Kate whispered as she stroked the owl's head. "It's a boy?"

"Oh yes. Male barn owls have paler white-and-gold feathers, while the females are darker gold with hints of brown to blend into wooded areas while they nest. This fellow is a boy, aren't you, handsome?" Dr. Coburn stroked the owl's head with a gloved finger, and he made a little cooing sound, his eyes half closed.

"He seems to like that," Kate giggled.

The vet nodded. "One of my colleagues once said that owls have bird hardware but are downloaded with cat software. They love to be petted but can nibble a little when they're feeling playful or anxious."

"Is his wing going to be okay?" Kate asked.

"It seems to move all right. I think it's just tender. I'm going to try to reset some of these bent feathers. Just give me a moment." The vet prepared a large syringe with hot water and used it to heat up the feather shafts, then straightened out the bent feathers. As Kate adjusted her hold, the vet noticed the scratches on Kate's arms.

"Ouch, did he do that?"

"I'm not sure. It was either the broken glass or him. I meant to ask if you have any antiseptic wipes I could use?"

"I'll do you one better. Let me get him taken care of, then I'll see to you." Dr. Coburn reset the remaining bent feathers and removed two that weren't fixable, then tended to Kate's scrapes.

"They don't look deep, but keep an eye out for infection. Go straight to the doctor if they start looking too red. Now, about this little guy—I know a rescue group that handles wild animals if you want them to take him in. Once he's healed, they'll set him free. I can get you the info sheet." The vet left the room, while Kate continued to stroke the owl's head. He made a soft twittering sound and settled deeper into the towel as she cradled him.

"That's it. Just rest, Handsome. You've been through a lot lately." Kate had decided to name the owl Handsome.

When Dr. Coburn returned, she put the info sheet in front of Kate. "Now, we're a bit short-staffed right now, but you can leave him here until the holiday is over if you want; that's when I can send him to the rescue group. Or I can leave you some care instructions if you want to hang on to him until the rehab center is open on Monday."

Kate looked down at the owl's gold and white head. Handsome looked straight at her, unblinking. For a second time, the dark fathoms of the owl's eyes seemed to make the world around her vanish. Spirals of silver light seemed to form within those dark, mysterious eyes, and she couldn't look away.

"Miss Winslow?" The vet's voice was distant, as though it came through a deep tunnel. Kate shook herself back to the real world.

"What do you want to do?" the vet asked. "I don't normally let people keep wildlife in their homes, but under the circumstances, I think he'd be okay for a few days with you."

"I'll take him home for a few days. Can you call me when the wildlife center opens?"

"All right, if you're sure. Just remember, he's a wild animal. Don't treat him like a pet. I'll print out some info on how to care for him while he's with you. If you have any trouble keeping him until after the holidays, just bring him back here and I'm sure we can make room for him."

"Thank you."

Kate once more looked down at the owl in her arms. "You hear that, Handsome? You're coming home with me."

CHAPTER

# TWO

*O*nce the path is set, you must move forward, never back. For to look back is to welcome the haunts of goblins and trolls or the will-o'-the-wisp to lure you into the dark. Do not chase the false lights for they will lead you to your doom.

—Anon., *Tales from the Twilight Court*

It was easier than Kate expected to smuggle an injured barn owl into the house. She slipped in through the front door, the owl still wrapped inside her gym towel. Her father was singing Christmas carols in the kitchen with Sandra while they prepared the Christmas meal for tomorrow.

Kate cuddled Handsome close to her and crept up the stairs, wincing when the third step from the top creaked. She paused outside her bedroom and eased the door open. A shaft of light illuminated the hallway as a different door opened behind her.

"Kate?" Caden whispered.

"Yeah?" she whispered back, trying to keep the owl hidden from her little brother.

"You weren't gone very long. Where did you go?"

"Uh . . ." She'd never been able to lie easily, especially not to Caden.

Before she could say anything, he was at her side peering at Handsome.

"Is that an owl?" he asked, his eyes going wide.

"Yeah. It smashed through my passenger-side window."

"Is he hurt?"

"He should be okay. His wing just needs time to heal."

Caden tried to move closer. "Seriously? Can I see him?"

"You have to be careful," Kate warned. "His talons are dangerous, okay?" She let her half brother see the owl's face, which peeped out from the towel.

Handsome looked annoyed, his eyes half closed. But Kate could be misreading a simple warning signal. Lots of animals changed their features to look more intimidating or threatening. She'd seen a video on social media of a northern white-faced owl who could change its facial appearance entirely by slanting its eyebrows and flattening its ears, which made it look more fierce when facing a predator.

"Don't tell Sandra or Dad, okay?" She kept her voice low as she spoke. "I'm only keeping him until the rehab center opens after Christmas, but they may force me to take him back to the vet, and they're pretty full right now."

Caden met her gaze in confusion. "Isn't rehab for people with addiction?"

She smiled at her brother. "It's a different kind of rehab.

This place works with injured wild animals. When the animal is healed, they can release it back into the wild."

"So cool," Caden said, grinning.

"You can't tell. Promise me."

"I won't," he vowed.

"Good. Now go back to bed. It's late. I'll let you see him tomorrow. Our little secret, right?" She rubbed her free hand in his blond hair and he grinned.

"I'm glad you came back," he said.

"So am I." She was only glad to see Caden, though. Not her father or Sandra. And that thought only made the ache in her chest widen to a vast chasm of pain.

Once inside her room, Kate settled Handsome on the floor near the edge of her bed, where she made the towel into a nest. The owl's eyes were shut as it settled deeper into the towel. She was a little surprised he didn't try to escape. It wasn't normal to see a wild animal be so cautious and docile, especially injured. But then, she didn't exactly have a lot of experience with wild animals. Maybe this was normal for owls, or maybe it was still in shock.

She left him alone to change out of her wet clothes and into her favorite pajamas and hide the bloody sweater in her laundry hamper to deal with later. Then she pulled back the covers of her bed and climbed in to sleep, but she was too anxious to settle.

After a few frustrated minutes, she got up and went to her desk, opening a little music box that held her jewelry. The box had a pair of dancers in the center who spun to the musical notes. She turned the silver crank on the bottom to wind it up and then watched the dancers move. A simple melancholic melody filled the room, reminding her of the day her mother had given it to her. She'd been only five years old, but the memory was still so vivid. She'd just seen *The Nutcracker* with her parents that afternoon, and they'd come home to open presents on Christmas Eve. A rare snowfall had turned the whole world white. Kate remembered pressing her face to the windows of the family room to watch the gentle snowstorm sweep over the landscape.

Her mother had sat beside her and held Kate's hand. She had felt safe and loved. That little girl hadn't known that her mother would be gone two months later.

*Will I ever feel that way again?*

Possessed by a wild longing for the childhood that she'd loved so dearly, she searched her bookshelves for one of her mother's old books. A collection of fairy tales from England and Scotland.

When she found it, she settled on the bed again, turning the pages and taking in that old-book smell, reliving the memories of her mother that she'd buried so many years ago.

*"Do you know what your prince will say?"* her mother teased.

*"What?"*

*"Kiss me, Kate."* Her mother placed a kiss on Kate's brow. *"That's how you'll know he's yours."*

*Kiss me, Kate.* It was silly, but those words had clung to her deepest dreams. None of the boys she'd dated had ever felt like "the one." They'd been nice and fun to hang out with. But when her mother had talked about love, she'd said it was something that changed you forever.

But how would Kate really know? She couldn't imagine feeling changed forever by anyone.

Her mother's words echoed in her mind once more. *"Love is like a path in the woods. Once you begin, once your foot touches the earth, you must move forward until you reach its end, whatever it may be. And you will find yourself in a very different place than when you started."*

Kate set the music box down on her desk, its music

winding slowly to a stop. The owl's gaze followed her as she turned out the light and returned to bed, pulling the covers up around her. After a moment, tears escaped from her eyes. Her body quaked with sobs that she didn't try to fight. A soft chitter came from the owl; it sounded almost a question. She wiped her eyes and sat up to check on her feathered companion.

"You okay, Handsome?"

The dark eyes of the barn owl stared at her as if peering into her very soul. Kate left the bed and knelt in front of the owl.

"I hope the vet was right and that you'll be all right after a rest. You're too beautiful not to be flying out in the night." She smiled as he nibbled gently on her finger.

"You'd never hurt me, would you?" she asked Handsome. "I wish I knew what you were thinking. It must be quite serious, because you look like you're frowning."

Handsome shuffled closer, and she brushed her fingers on the top of his soft head.

"Are you hungry? Thirsty?" The owl chittered in response, and she grinned. "Very well. I'll be right back."

She crept down to the kitchen, glad to see that her father and Sandra were no longer there. She filled a bowl of water and grabbed some raw hamburger meat before she returned to her room. The owl was still sitting where she had left him.

"Here you go." She set the bowl down and let out a sigh of relief when Handsome dipped his beak into the water and drank. "Now, try this." She offered him a pinch of ground meat. "I bet you'll think it's tasty." He took it reluctantly, but after he swallowed it, he clicked his beak excitedly as if pleased. She fed him piece by piece until he seemed satisfied. That should be enough for a few hours, she hoped.

She returned the leftover meat to the fridge but left the

bowl of water on the floor in case he needed to drink. When she got back to her room, she found the owl all puffed up, his feathers fluffed and eyes half closed in contentment.

"Feeling better?" She chuckled. "I have to get to bed. It's Christmas tomorrow, and I need to sleep if I have to deal with Sandra." She couldn't resist touching the owl one more time. Once he was at the rehab center, she might never have a chance like this again.

"You know, I think it was you who saved me tonight," she whispered. "I don't know where I would have ended up if you hadn't crashed into my window. I might have kept driving in the dark and gotten lost. Or worse."

The owl's eyes opened wide, as if he understood. But that was crazy.

"I'll see you in the morning." She got back into bed, and the weariness she had carried all evening finally overtook her and she slipped into dreams. They were not happy ones.

Then something soft and smooth brushed against her cheek, and a clicking noise pulled her from her nightmares. She came face-to-face with the owl.

"How did you get up here? Did you fly?"

The creature's head bobbed and swiveled, studying her room from this new angle. She sat up and scooped the owl into her arms, burying her face in Handsome's feathers. She remembered a moment later that she was hugging a wild animal, but thankfully he didn't hurt her. He let her hold him and take comfort in his soft white-and-gold feathers.

"I wish I could leave, that you could fly me away from here . . . I wish I could forget everything."

She'd had similar thoughts before. Dreams of escape, of freedom. But she had always held back, thinking about her future, about school, about Caden. But right now, she had never meant anything more in her life. What a gift it would be to have the wings to fly far away from all the pain and the loneliness.

*Take me away,* she wished silently. *Let me forget. I can't hurt if I can't remember.*

Feathers fluttered against her cheek as the owl slipped out of her hold and dropped from the bed, only to rise. She gasped, because it was no longer an owl that stood before her.

It was a man.

She stared into the face of a beautiful stranger. Sharp blue eyes cut through her. His smooth lips were the only thing soft about the hard but angelic lines of his face. He was dressed in a black tunic and trousers. Pieces of shining armor covered his shoulders and arms, seeming to reflect the dark more than it did the light. Before she could speak or even summon a scream, the man grabbed her by the shoulders, pulling her flush against his hard body.

Kate couldn't move, couldn't breathe. When he spoke his tone was low, dark, and it intoxicated her senses.

"Your wish is granted, little one. You're mine, now and forever. I shall steal you away by twilight."

The broad swath of moonlight entering her bedroom window suddenly shattered into swirling beams like a kaleidoscope.

"Don't fear, I have you." The man's arms tightened around her body as the world she knew vanished into shadow. They flew through the night, but it was not any night sky she recognized. Even the air had vanished. She tried to suck in a desperate breath but couldn't. Her lungs screamed until she slipped into unconsciousness.

Roan Arun, king of the Twilight Court, burst into the vast expanse of space between the human realm and his own. His arms were locked tight around the mortal as he barreled through stars and galaxies. The dust of a universe's lost dreams clung to their bodies with their shimmering essence. Whispers of ancient worlds, stories older than the stars, teased his ears as they traveled faster and faster. He only prayed that he would reach his home without interference from the warriors of the Morning Court.

Flashes of white and silver lit up in his periphery. Damn, they had found him. He'd hoped they wouldn't have been watching this path, but they must have known he'd been in the mortal world rather than his own.

Tapping into the dark magic within him, he cast a glamour around himself and the human woman. It was one of the strongest he could manage and would trick even the Seelie fools, if only for a short while. To them, he would appear as nothing but a flash of light. He had only to make it a little farther to reach the safety of his kingdom.

Just then, the mortal woman started to slip from his hold. Her hair whipped at his arms and her sooty lashes fluttered. With a roar, he pulled her away from the retreating tides of time that now tugged at her.

He would not surrender her, not now, not to anyone or anything. From the moment she'd touched him, colors and sensations had intensified for him, and he was hungry for more. Her warm body fit to his in the most perfect way. Roan had granted her wish, to free her of the place that had trapped her, and now she belonged to him, this beautiful little mortal with mournful eyes whose dreams made his chest ache in a way it never had before.

*I will give you everything, little one. Everything. So long as you are mine.*

With a final burst of strength, he penetrated the last barrier into his realm, along a Fae road that only he could follow. The wind carried him and his prize toward the distant palace of the Twilight Court.

The Seelie warriors dared not follow him into the dark woods. Not even their light shone bright enough to let them find a way out of the forest that covered his lands, and the closest they had dared to appear was upon the tallest of the Black Hills.

Roan careened toward the ground like a meteor, silver-and-blue flames trailing in his wake. If mortals knew that shooting stars were traveling Fae, they would never look at the night sky the same way again. Roan landed in a low crouch, the mortal woman cradled safely in his arms. Dust billowed out along the stone floors of the Twilight Palace, and the male and female Fae in his court fell silent at his abrupt entrance.

Dozens of Fae knights gripped their swords, and more than one female courtier reached for her hidden dagger. Though they hadn't been at war with the Seelie for many years, the peace between them was tenuous and Roan's people were always prepared for battle.

"Brother?" His younger sister, Eudora Moondove, rushed toward him. Her dark hair was pulled up and threaded with blue ribbons. Her purple-and-gold court gown made her stand out among the courtiers. Her pale seafoam wings fanned out behind her, leaving a trail of glittering sparkles like motes of dust catching the sunlight.

Eudora halted at the sight of the woman in his arms. A

murmur rippled through the court, then silence fell again as his people saw that he carried a mortal with him. He wished he could shield her body from their view, such were the possessive and protective instincts that surged through him. He wanted to guard her against their inquisitive stares, for the Fae were ever curious about the world of mortals.

But that was not what worried him most. In front of all these witnesses, he had just broken one of the most important laws his people had made since the Arthurian wars.

It was forbidden to take mortals from their world.

"Roan," Eudora gasped. "What have you done?"

But he knew what he had done, just as everyone in his court knew. Yet he did not care. The mortal woman was *his*.

He glanced down at the woman in his arms, and that deep, unfathomable peace filled him yet again.

Without looking away from the mortal, he said, "I may have doomed us all."

CHAPTER

# THREE

*"To look in the face of the dark king is to die, but oh what an exquisite death it shall be," said the bride as she stood before the throne carved of night and obsidian and the lord who would own her soul forever more.*

—Anon., *Tales from the Twilight Court*

R oan parted the crowd in the vast throne room with a single shout. "Rath, to me!"

Rath Ender, his First Lance and most trusted friend, stepped forth, his silver cloak billowing behind him as he fell into step beside Roan. Eudora kept pace with Roan on his opposite side as they left the throne room together, still concerned about the human he'd brought to the Twilight Court.

Rath's dark eyes swept over the woman in Roan's arms as he walked with them. If Rath hadn't been so madly in love with Eudora, Roan would have been tempted to banish his friend from his presence so that he could not look upon his prize. He was oddly possessive of the human woman in a way he never had been before with any female.

"It's been a while since you've had a pet," Rath mused with a dark chuckle. "Are you bored with battling the Seelie? I thought that was my task, to kill those sunny bastards."

"As my First Lance, you should be focused on protecting anything I care about, whether it's my new little mortal or my sister." He cradled the human woman closer to him.

"I've been demoted to a human pet-sitter?" Rath chuckled.

"Rath, this is serious." Eudora shot Rath a cold glare, which he answered with a hot look of lust. Eudora tossed her head and she raised her chin in challenge to the Fae knight.

Roan ignored the tension between his sister and his oldest friend. They had danced around each other like this for a thousand years, and it was beginning to bore him. Like everything in the world of the Fae, nothing ever changed. Not like the woman he held in his arms, a woman who would in a brief span of time age and die, unless he kept her here in his world with him.

He'd broken the laws of his people by bringing her here, but the woman had saved his life. She'd tended to him without knowing what he was or what he could give her in return for her kindness and compassion. She'd even been hurt when he'd entered her car. Her bleeding because of saving him was one of the ways his people could bond to another creature. It had deepened his life debt to a blood bond, a thing considered sacred to the Fae.

When she'd held him in her arms and whispered her wish like a fervent prayer, he'd been compelled to grant it. Not only because he owed it to her, but because he'd wanted to *keep* her.

If he brought her to his world, she could be his forever, and he would see that she wanted for nothing.

Roan moved through the black-and-white marble halls until he reached his private chambers. Rath opened the door for him, and a pair of tiny brownies paused in their cleaning of the room, their scrunched, goblin-like faces frozen in fear. One of the little Fae creatures quickly swept off her brown cap and bowed deeply to Roan.

"W-we d-didn't expect . . ." the female called Babbitt stammered, her sharply pointed ears flattening back a little in alarm.

"Leave us," Roan barked. The pair vanished with a soft pop. Roan stepped into the room with his sister and Rath, who closed the door behind him.

"Roan, what is the meaning of this? What do you mean to do with her?"

Eudora caught his sleeve. Roan winced and sucked in a breath. Her fingers came away covered in blood, which had soaked through his black tunic sleeve.

"What happened?" She forgot all about the human, focused instead on the crimson blood glistening on her slender fingers beneath the starlight lamps. It had been a long time since his little sister had seen him injured.

"The Seelie happened, dear sister," he replied as he set the human female down upon his vast bed. The enchantment he'd cast over her continued to work, weaving a beautiful dream that spun in stardust patterns above her head.

As he took a step back from her, he felt strangely untethered, as if he might be carried away by the southern breeze that drifted through the open windows. The weight of her in his arms had felt so right, so natural, but he couldn't fathom how that was possible.

Now the pain of his arm returned to him, stronger than it

should have been. It seemed this human woman somehow made everything he felt more intense. His lips formed a grim line as he knew he owed his sister and his friend an explanation.

"I was attacked, and I landed in the mortal realm during my escape. I was in my owl form and hit this woman's vehicle. She rescued me, and as such, I owed her a life debt. I chose to fulfill it by granting her wish."

"She wished to come here?" Surprise colored Eudora's tone.

"She wished to escape her world."

Roan leaned over, brushing her hair back from her face, his fingers lingering over her smooth, pale skin. The journey through the realms hadn't been easy on his little human, and it may have drained her of energy for a time. It had indeed been a long while since his people had traveled with mortals, and he'd forgotten how delicate they could be.

"And as I returned, the Seelie attempted to follow me on the Fae roads into our lands."

"The Seelie were *here*?" Rath growled, his eyes sharpening.

"No, I was in the borderlands of the Black Hills when they attacked. The dwarves had warned me of a sighting there, and I wished to investigate." Eudora took his arm again, despite his protests, and rolled up his sleeve to examine his wound.

Crashing through the vehicle's glass had not harmed him. His injuries had been delivered sometime before by Seelie weapons. As an owl, they had manifested as a sprained wing and some broken feathers, but in his true form they were now bruises and a deep slash from an elfin blade across his forearm. It was one of the few weapons that could do him real harm. There were, of course, Fae species that could injure him or kill him. But when it came to the other Shining Ones, those of their own species, they needed enchanted poisons or blades forged under the waxing light of a harvest moon.

"Eudora, let it be," he rasped, looking once more at the human who lay in his bed. He wanted to be left alone with her and he wanted time to think things through. He'd never acted so rashly in his life and needed to understand why this woman affected him.

"Don't be so stubborn. I will not allow my skills to be ignored if they can heal you." Eudora covered the gash with her hands and closed her eyes. The room filled with the smell of blooming night flowers, and a gentle warmth ran through his aching arm as his sister's magic did its work.

"Better?" She arched a dark brow at him.

He smiled indulgently at her. "Yes, now I am famished, and I need to bathe."

"But what about . . . her?" Eudora whispered as she nodded at the sleeping human.

He met his sister's gaze, ready for a fight over the words he was about to speak. "She is mine. I shall keep her and she will amuse me."

"Roan, it is forbidden to keep human pets. Ever since . . ." *Guinevere*. The name was not spoken aloud, but everyone knew of whom she spoke. "Merlin went to war against us over her, and we were already warring with the Seelie. We lost too many lives because of our father's obsession with a mortal woman."

"This woman is not the consort to the once and future king. She will cause no war."

"How can you be certain?" Eudora fisted her hands in her silken skirts and shared a worried glance with Rath. "It has been ages since we have kept up with the mortals and their kingdoms. They could have renegotiated their alliances with the wizards and witches of their world. She could be—"

"Eudora, I *have* kept up with the world of humans."

"You have? Why?" His sister tilted her head, her dark-blue eyes seeking answers he was reluctant to give.

"I have my reasons." He couldn't tell her that out of all the worlds he could see, the mortal one held his heart in a way that defied explanation. He feared his father's blood was in him after all, because his father too had been enchanted with humans and it had cost their people dearly.

"Then tell us what you know of the mortal world," Rath asked quietly.

"Magic is all but gone from their world. The age of wizards and witches is over. They have no shrines to the trees, make no offerings to the sea. They have turned their backs upon the magic of the earth in favor of metal, wheels, and wire." Roan had watched the humans for years through his scrying crystals. It fascinated him how they used science in place of magic. It was how he'd known of their electric vehicles called cars. It was impressive and terrifying how humans had used science to both improve their lives and destroy them in equal measure. The devastation of the two recent wars that had stretched across the entire earth still left him with dark worries.

"But why bring her here? Why risk the Seelie finding out? They could try to take her from you or start a war like they did with Father when he brought Arthur's queen here."

Roan chose his next words carefully. "This mortal woman saved me. I owe her a life debt, Eudora."

His sister opened her mouth, but Roan raised a hand before she could speak.

"Her wish was to leave her world." His voice was as hard as steel. "She was not desired in her world, nor in her kingdom, not even by her family." He thought then of the little boy, the child who had beseeched Roan to be a friend to his sister. That child was alone in his affections toward her, and that knowledge created a storm of emotion inside Roan that he could not explain.

"But a mortal in the Twilight Court? Roan, you know it will give others an advantage if they wish to take your throne. She would be at risk," Rath argued.

He shrugged. "Not if I make it clear the consequences someone would face if they dare to even touch her." He would see that she was protected as well and would appoint a body-guard for her. However, the true threat to her would not be from his people, but from the Seelie. If there was one thing that unified his court, it was their distrust toward the other Fae.

He had never cared about the plight of mortals before. They breathed but for an instant, and then they were gone and forgotten soon after. But this woman would be his for centuries once she tasted the honeyed breads of his lands, and so long as she stayed here with him she could live a Fae life. And he would spend those centuries untangling the puzzle of why she, out of all mortal women, held him in such a thrall.

Rath politely intervened, sliding his arm around Eudora's waist. "Come, Eudora. Let's leave Roan to bathe. He stinks of the Seelie, and you can put those healing hands on me instead."

Eudora smacked Rath's shoulder but let him escort her to the door, which he opened. She paused in the doorway, her gaze once more beseeching as she looked his way.

"You are the lord of the dark woods, king of the Twilight Court. But even you can be blinded by the beauty of mortality, brother. Tread carefully."

Roan nodded at his sister's warning. Then he shut the door behind them and, with a wave of his palm, sealed the lock. He did not wish to be disturbed, nor did he wish for his little mortal to wake and escape while he bathed. The Twilight Court was not a place for mortals to run about freely. His sister was right about that. Another man might claim this woman for his own—or worse, use her to harm Roan. Roan waved his hand, and the windows in his bedchamber closed and sealed tight.

After a moment, he retrieved his dark-blue coverlet from the foot of his bed and spread it over Kate. His realm was temperate most of the year, unless he wished it to be otherwise, but she carried the chill of traveling between worlds and needed the warmth.

As king, he could control both the skies and the earth. But sometimes, a simple blanket was the best solution. Once he'd seen to the woman's care, he turned and stepped into the moonlight that filtered through the glass of his balcony doors. The moonlight always gave him strength, and for a time he absorbed its soothing rays, his eyes closed.

Beyond the bedchamber, his private dressing room contained a large marble bathing pool that could hold a dozen naked dryads. The memories of past pleasures should have made Roan smile, but right now his thoughts were dark, turbulent.

He thought back to the attack he'd suffered moments before crashing into the mortal realm and, soon after, this woman's car window. Roan had to figure out how the Seelie had come to his land without him sensing it. He'd always been able to sense them before, but not this time. It was both puzzling and disturbing in its implications.

The Seelie had appeared at the edges of the hills, violating the ancient treaty his father, Bahden, had made when he had taken Thalia Moondove, the Seelie princess and sister to the old Seelie king, to be his queen. The union had put an end to centuries of feuds between the two Fae courts. But the old Seelie king had passed, and his son, Culan, the new king, hated the idea that his aunt had spawned Roan and Eudora, giving them access to the magic of both the light and the dark Fae.

It wasn't unheard of to have unions between the members of the two courts in order to produce children. It was the fact that those children were directly in line to the thrones of *both* courts that had provoked the new Seelie king into action. Culan wanted to destroy the Twilight Court and wipe out every last dark Fae.

Roan clenched his fists as he turned his back to the sleeping human woman, this distraction that he should not allow yet couldn't resist. He needed to focus on the war that would soon be coming, not bedding the mortal.

With a frustrated growl, he stepped into the bathing chamber and whispered a spell. Water sprites answered his call, forming a sudden waterfall at the edges of the large marble bath. Through the open bathing room windows, dryads sent petals from their sacred trees. Once they touched the water, they would dissolve into a healing nectar.

The pink-and-white crystals that grew in patches along the edges of the windows drew in the moonlight and glowed like frozen candles, making the room shimmer as he stripped out of his clothing. He set the clothes on the floor, knowing that Babbitt, the brownie who oversaw his quarters, would retrieve them and see them cleaned.

He eased into the hot water until he was chest-deep in the fragrant bath, a slow groan escaping him as he felt the healing start to work. He allowed his head rest on the edge of the pool and moved his arms and legs through the hot water, letting it sluice over his arm, which was still tender. If he could stay in this bath a thousand years, he would. The feeling of being utterly naked as his muscles soaked up the healing magic of his land was a bliss only second to taking a woman to bed.

As he bathed, he ran through a list of things that he must

do. Rath would want to scour the Black Hills for proof of the Seelie's incursion, but that was not wise. As Roan's personal guard, Rath should remain in the palace. His priority was to protect Eudora, though she was trained for battle and did not appreciate the special treatment.

Rath would remain vigilant, however. Culan would have no qualms about kidnapping Eudora to use as a bargaining tool, and he might even kill her if it suited his purposes. Roan suspected the man would not care if her capture cost him more than one of his Seelie warriors.

Outside the window of the bathing chamber, a star lark sang, its soft song filled with wonder and mystery. He loved the birds and the beasts of his lands, even those that were dark and dangerous. Roan let the lark's song soothe him for a time, until he turned his thoughts back to the Seelie problem.

Roan should send for Hagni, the head of the Shadow Guard, to search the Black Hills. Hagni had served with Roan's father in the Arthurian wars. He was one of the few aside from Rath that Roan could both trust and know he was capable of defending himself should the Seelie attack while he was on patrol.

Settled on the matter, Roan flexed his injured arm in the bath, testing the healing his sister and the bath had performed. Aside from a slight twinge, it felt as good as new. His thoughts then turned to the mortal in his bed. A slow, wicked smile curved his lips as he imagined just how much he would enjoy introducing her to the world of pleasure in his arms and in his bed.

THE DAZZLING DREAMS OF ICE PALACES AND OWLS FLYING IN THE night sky faded, and the cloak of deep sleep slipped away from Kate. She yawned and stretched, feeling the satin against her skin. She sighed in heavenly pleasure at the silky sensation.

Then she froze.

She didn't own satin sheets.

Kate's eyes flew open. A ceiling mural of moonlit woods with dancing women in translucent gowns met her startled gaze, bordered in silver-and-gold crown molding. Her eyes swept down the walls, which were made of white-and-black marble. Tapestries hung in the center, depicting battles between silver-winged men and women.

Her lips parted as she struggled to breathe.

She tried to keep fear from clouding her mind as she took in her surroundings. This wasn't her home. It wasn't like anywhere she'd ever been in her life. It was like something out of a dream. Only she was awake. Wasn't she?

The faint sound of splashing caught her attention. The door opposite the lavish bed she lay in was half open, and the faint shimmer of light reflected off water could be seen on the ceiling.

Kate pushed back the dark-blue coverlet and slipped out of the enormous bed.

"Miss-triss." A whisper came from beneath the bed, making her jump.

"Who's there?" she hissed, crouching a safe distance away from the bed, trying to glimpse what was underneath.

"Be not afraid, mistress."

This time, when Kate peered into the darkness, a pair of golden eyes stared back at her.

"Shit!" She scrambled back in a panic, then ran toward the tall gilded door. But the silver handle wouldn't budge.

*Oh God, where the hell am I?*

Was this one of those dreams where she had woken up into another dream?

A light popping sound came from under the bed, and the golden eyes beneath the bed frame vanished. Kate didn't move for a long moment until she felt certain that whatever had been beneath the bed was gone. Then she studied the bedroom again.

It was very large, with the biggest bed she'd ever seen. The white wood of the headboard was intricately carved with detailed figures. She took a closer look and gasped. The figures were slowly moving, as if she was watching a play. Men and women in elaborate clothing danced in swirling patterns of white and silver. The wood itself was *moving*.

"I'm definitely dreaming," she whispered to herself.

The sound of water drew her focus again. This time, she crept on bare feet toward the half-open door where the sounds were coming from. She peered through the space between the door and the frame to glimpse the glowing moonlit room beyond.

"I know you are there," a deep, sonorous voice said to her. "Come in."

With no way out and no point in hiding, Kate summoned her courage and pushed the door open. She'd expected this to be some sort of bathroom, but nothing could have prepared her for what she actually saw.

A man sat in a large marble bathing pool, the water rising to the middle of his broad chest. The man was not unfamiliar. She had seen him for a brief moment in her bedroom when the owl she'd rescued turned into an impossibly tall man with silver hair. The water he lay soaking in was strewn with red and white petals that looked like they were dissolving slowly in shimmering trails over the water's surface.

A dream . . . definitely had to be a dream. Owls didn't

simply turn into terrifyingly beautiful men in the middle of the night.

The heady scent of flowers filled the air, making her slightly dizzy. Could you smell in dreams? Or was it the sight of the naked man that affected her? Kate couldn't look away from him. His silvery-white hair was partially pulled back by a black leather tie and the rest cascaded down just past his shoulders. Despite the color of his hair, he didn't appear to be any older than thirty-five. His eyes were bright blue, the color of cloudless winter skies. But they also held a hint of ice, as though he never smiled. His features were beautiful, yet masculine in a way that did not seem possible. The muscle and hard lines of his body seemed one moment away from turning him into a wild beast.

It almost *hurt* to look at him, because whoever this man was, he could *never* be hers. A dream could not love her back. The deep ache inside her grew. She would never know this man in the light of day, would never feel a true kiss from his lips. When she woke, he would be just another half-forgotten dream that would leave her feeling empty inside.

"Awake at last." The man's deep voice caressed the air, made it vibrate, and sent tremors of desire through her body.

In that moment, she realized she'd never really known what it meant to *want* a man. The sweet kisses stolen by the boys she had dated meant nothing compared to the long, caressing look the stranger now gave her. It was a wild, dark feeling. She wanted to touch his skin, to feel his lips, to know what it meant to give her body, even her soul, to him. She'd never wanted that with anyone before, but right now, she wanted it more than her next breath.

Somehow, she found her tongue and spoke. "Who are you? What is this place?"

She continued to focus on the water that formed beads

upon the man's skin. There was a faint smattering of dark hair on his chest and light scars upon his body. He seemed bigger than life somehow, filling the room with a presence that wasn't simply physical.

"I am Roan Arun," he said, drawing her focus to his lips. "I am the lord of the dark woods, master of the labyrinth, and king of the Unseelie. You are in my home, the palace of the Twilight Court."

She tried to understand what he'd just said, but it made no sense. Who were the Unseelie? The word felt familiar, but she couldn't quite remember where she'd heard it. He slowly stood up, and the water poured in silvery streams down his body, over enticing grooves and down to the V-shaped muscles that pointed to his . . . Her gaze jerked back up to his face, and she saw the man's smirk.

Kate swallowed hard. She'd never actually been in the same room with a naked man before. She'd never even had sex, and now all she could think about was this man tossing her onto the nearest bed and pinning her beneath him. The mere thought sent a wild, erotic flush through her entire body.

"This is a dream," she said in a whisper. It had to be.

"In a way," the man agreed as he climbed out of the bath. "All that we see or seem is but a dream within a dream." He turned away to grab a white towel that sat on top of a neat stack on a stone shelf, then wrapped it around his lean hips, giving her a glimpse of his muscled ass before he covered it.

"Have you read Edgar Allan Poe?" she asked, confused and curious.

"*Read*, my dear mortal?" He snorted as if offended. "I am the one who gifted Edgar's words to him."

Roan turned back to face her as he walked around the edge of the bathing pool, coming toward her. She backed up out of instinct, her body pressed flat against the now closed door behind her.

*When did it close?*

"You are not wrong, who deem that my days have been a dream; yet if hope has flown away in a night, or in a day, in a vision, or in none, is it therefore the less gone?" He recited Poe's poem, stopping just inches from her as he braced one forearm above her head.

The smell of those strange and beautiful flowers drifted off his skin, along with a scent that made her think of mahogany and amber. He smelled like the woods at night, as if a fire had just burned somewhere nearby and the woodsmoke had left a tantalizing haze upon the leaves. Her body responded, her nipples hardening against her button-up pajama top. Her lips parted and she drew in a quivering breath. The presence of this man, this king, was impossible to explain. She felt like she was being pulled toward him like a moon dragged in by a planet's gravity. He leaned closer. He was tall . . . so very tall, easily towering over her by a head and a half.

"I am what you would call one of the dark Fae. Do you know the name?"

Fae? That was like a fairy. But they weren't real, or this big. "I thought fairies were small?" She couldn't help but think of Tinker Bell from *Peter Pan*, but Roan was massive, muscled and terrifyingly attractive. Even in stories she'd read of tall, human-sized fairies, they' all be slender and delicate. Roan was built like a warrior with broad shoulders and muscles *everywhere*. Her mouth ran dry as his cruelly beautiful lips twisted into yet another smile.

"Fairy," Roan chuckled. "Such a quaint twisting of words. But no, pixies, brownies, merrows, kobolds, dwarves—they are small. I am one of the Shining Ones. Everything about me is big." He trailed a fingertip down the side of her neck, his glowing blue eyes holding hers. "*Everything.*"

"What is a Shining One?" Kate's thoughts were still muddled by the heat of his body and the way he had trapped her against the door, caging her in.

"The Shining Ones are the most ancient of the Fae. We were once gods in your land, in the time before time. We ruled the night and the day, the seasons, the flora and the fauna. All was ours to command. Your people called us the *Sidhe*." He pronounced the word *Sidhe* as "shee," and she recognized it from her mother's book of fairy tales.

She breathed out a sigh of relief. "I *am* dreaming."

Roan's eyes still glowed. "What you think of as reality is but a veil between your world and mine. Dreams are but an instant when the cosmic winds disturb the veil in between, letting you glimpse this place."

*Was this another sort of reality, then? Was that what he was saying?* Kate's head ached as she tried to understand the immensity of his words.

"Wait." She lifted her face a little, daring herself to eye him more boldly. "You never explained why the *Sidhe* are called the Shining Ones."

"Because when we let our magic show, we *shine*. Even the darkest of us."

"Shine? How?"

Roan was still smiling, but the expression turned almost sinister.

"To show a mortal our shine would be to destroy them. You cannot bear the light of one such as me."

"Try me," Kate replied. She wasn't afraid of light.

Roan's eyes narrowed. "No. I have no desire to see you destroyed, not when I have plans for you."

"You can't even show me a little?" She reached up to touch

his chest without thinking. The moment her palm touched his skin, Roan closed his eyes. His features softened briefly as he let out a low growl of animal-like pleasure. He drew in a deep breath, as if breathing in her essence. Kate's heart kicked into a mad rhythm as her own breathing sped up. Roan caught her wrist with his free hand, holding it against his skin as he finally opened his eyes.

Gray lightning lit his blue eyes as he began to shine like a distant star, and moonlight shimmered around him like mercury, outlining his body as a pair of iridescent pale blue wings materialized behind his shoulders, trailing stardust as they moved. An instant later, the beautiful shine and those mysterious wings were gone.

"Was that enough for you, little one?" His low, rough voice sent delicious shivers through her.

"Um . . . yes?" The shine had enhanced the hard lines of his jaw and cheekbones, and she wondered if perhaps the Shining Ones might have once been mistaken for angels in her world.

Roan loomed over her for another long moment, the scent of night blooms wafting around them as his gaze lowered to her lips and his eyes closed as if he was lost in a dream himself. His fingers left the door and teased along her throat before closing on her neck in a gentle hold to keep her pinned against the door. He opened his eyes again, and she was captivated by the brilliant blue of them. His thumb stroked her pulse point, and Kate's body responded. Heat flooded beneath her skin and her heart raced madly. She should be terrified, he could crush her throat with a single squeeze, but he didn't...and she wasn't afraid. She was...turned on. Her clit gave a hard throbbing pulse in response to this man's controlling hold on her.

"What a sweet little pet you will make," he purred as his lips touched hers, in a hint of a kiss. "I might have to forge a collar under silver starlight to put around your delicate little neck," he whispered. "Would you like that, little one? To wear my mark of ownership on your body?" Then he slanted his mouth over hers, assaulting her senses with the mastery of his kiss.

Stars burst before her eyes as his lips moved over hers. Kate clutched his shoulders, her fingers digging into his skin. She'd never felt like this, like a kiss held the power to take her life simply from the sheer intensity of it. He tasted sweet, like something she felt she should be able to name but couldn't. His lips entreated hers to open, and she gasped as his body pressed fully against hers. The feeling of being trapped between the cold wood behind her and the hard, hot body of the man in front of her made her legs tremble. There was hardly anything between her body and his. She felt the press of his cock against her belly, and the overload of sensations and lust was overwhelming.

His kiss demanded dark, delicious things from her. Her mind spun with wild, erotic visions of his naked body and hers entwined in the satin sheets of his bed. Of her wearing nothing but a silver collar and him holding a delicate chain attached to it, wrapped around his fist while he made love to her... *owned* her.

"*Yes,*" he whispered in her mind. "*You're mine now.*"

A flash of clarity broke through Kate's mind. She shoved at the mountain of his shoulders. He backed away, his eyes still glowing bright blue, and licked his lips as if savoring her taste. He reached around her to open the door to his bedroom. She scrambled back from him, but rather than continue his pursuit, he walked past her to the tall silver-and-gold armoire set against one wall. He dropped the towel from around his hips to the floor, and she spun around to avoid staring at his naked ass again.

"You will lose that mortal modesty in time, little one," he

said. "Someday soon you will greet me in nothing but your pretty skin, begging me to take you."

*Little one* . . . He kept calling her that. He didn't know her name, did he?

"My name is Kate Winslow." She couldn't believe she was correcting a naked Fae lord. This was one hell of a dream. And apparently...a very kinky one. She'd never known she'd fantasied about a man putting a collar around her neck and calling her his pet. She hated how much it turned her on.

"I am aware of your name. You gave it at the doctor's office, if you recall," he replied with an amused chuckle. "*Little one* is a term of endearment. And to be fair, you are *quite* smaller than me."

"*That's* an understatement. How tall *are* you?"

"By your standards? Seven feet." He shrugged, as if that was quite normal.

She heard a rustle of cloth as he spoke, which meant he was getting dressed. She turned back to face him when he'd finished. He wore black boots and black leather trousers that fit his long legs and showed off his strong thighs. The white tunic he wore was unlaced at the throat, along with a dark-silver vest that he left unbuttoned. His silver hair hung down past his shoulders, no longer wet at the ends.

*Magic. Definitely magic.* She would have killed to have the ability to dry her hair in seconds.

He retrieved a long silver sword from the top of the dresser. It held a luminescent moonstone in the pommel. The blade itself was etched with a flowing script. It was a thing of lethal beauty, and she wanted to ask a thousand questions about it. Roan strapped it to his side, and she realized he was leaving.

She ran after him. "Wait! Where are you going?"

He halted at the door and faced her. "I have a war council to prepare for and orders that must be given. You are to remain here. Strip off your clothes, bathe, eat the food the brownies bring you. When I return, I shall take my pleasure with you." He leaned in, his mouth lightly touching hers with a sultry promise of deeper kisses yet to come. Then he raised his head and opened the door.

She started to protest, but he exited the room and locked the door behind him before she got even a word out.

"Take my pleasure with you?" she echoed in bafflement. *What in the actual hell?* And why did it sound both amazing and terrifying?

Kate jerked on the handle of the locked door and muttered a curse. It didn't budge, not that she had expected it to.

But if this was a dream, she could get control of it. She was familiar with the idea of lucid dreaming, even if she didn't know the details of how it worked. She just needed to change the rules of the dream and get herself out of this room or find a way to wake herself up. Because as interesting and tempting as it might be to explore what Roan meant when he said *take my pleasure with you*, she wasn't going to let him be in control. This was her dream.

She had to wake up.

"You are mine, mortal bride. Do you accept your fate?"

The bride stared at the king of the dark woods. All she saw was the taunting laugh of the will-o'-the-wisp in the shadows beyond, luring her to a place she should not go, to the man who would own her.

"You have no power here," said the bride. "I will take the path to its end."

The dark king bowed, his gleaming silver crown sharp with roses and thistles. "Then you will find me there waiting for you."

—Anon., *Tales from the Twilight Court*

KATE GAVE UP ON THE LOCKED DOOR AND INSTEAD SEARCHED THE bathing room. The windows, which had been open when she first encountered Roan, were closed now, and moonlight filtered in through the stained glass. She had no idea how much time had passed. Of course, in a dream, time could pass very quickly or very slowly.

And this was a dream, wasn't it? It had to be, because if this *wasn't*, Kate would probably have a mental breakdown.

She pressed against the windows, but they didn't budge. The faint blurry shapes of something far below stretched out across the landscape. Was it a forest? She couldn't quite tell through the beveled glass.

She looked around, searching for anything that might help her escape. The bathing pool took up the majority of the room and dipped into the floor. It was huge and looked like a small swimming pool. The water still looked hot, judging by the steam coiling from the surface. Pink-and-white crystals grew out of the marble walls near the windows, making the place feel like a cavern. Then her gaze settled on the scented petals still floating in the water. As they slowly dissolved, their essence made glittering patterns.

Their heady scent reminded her of the scorching kiss between her and Roan. Her fingers touched her lips as she closed her eyes, and heat blossomed along her mouth. She'd never been kissed like that before in her life. His lips had moved so softly, yet expertly, over hers, before he'd parted her lips with his tongue. It had felt like he'd kissed her a thousand times, as if he knew her mouth and the way to move by memory. He'd conquered her resistance in that moment, and she'd forgotten everything but the sensation of his mouth on hers. A stranger had made her feel more alive than she'd ever felt before, and it made no sense.

Then he'd had the gall to tell her to strip naked and wait for him in his bed. She shivered, because her body wanted to do exactly that. It seemed only her mind was determined to escape this place.

"Focus!" she commanded herself, returning to Roan's

bedchamber. She dug around the drawers of the large dresser, and at the bottom of the second drawer something sharp pricked her finger.

"Ow!" She jerked her hand back with a yelp. A bead of blood rose on the pad of her right index finger. She hastily put her finger into her mouth, sucking the blood away, then applied pressure with her other finger for a moment to stop the bleeding.

*What the heck had done that?* She carefully moved the perfectly folded silk shirts aside until she found the culprit. A slender dagger with a ruby in its hilt lay on the bottom of the drawer. The tip of the blade gleamed menacingly. She grasped the dagger carefully by the hilt and removed it from the drawer. Dream or not, she'd been brought here against her will, and it made sense to have some sort of weapon to defend herself.

"In an unknown land, it is better to be armed, isn't it?" she asked herself.

"It is indeed!" a chirpy voice agreed behind her.

Kate shrieked and spun around. A short creature about half her height with olive skin stared back at her with golden eyes. Her features were scrunched, like she was perpetually confused. She was wearing dark-green trousers, a little gray vest, and a brown cap on her head. Long black hair was tucked over her shoulder in two braids.

"Mistress," she murmured to Kate, giving her a polite curtsy.

Kate, still clutching the dagger to her chest, stared at the creature. "Um, hi." She considered hiding the dagger, but it was too late for that. The creature would've seen it. But she didn't *seem* hostile. If anything, she was friendly. Maybe she should try to befriend her.

"I'm Kate." She held out a hand. "What's your name?"

The goblin-like thing shook her hand with a happy smile. "Babbitt, mistress. I'm Babbitt."

"Babbitt. Um, please don't be offended, but . . . what are you?"

Babbitt blinked her golden eyes. "I'm a brownie, mistress."

"A brownie? Like a fairy?"

Babbitt nodded eagerly. "Yes, mistress."

"So this really is the land of the Fae?" she asked the brownie.

"Yes, mistress. Are you hungry?" Babbitt asked.

Kate put a hand to her stomach as it rumbled. "Actually, yes, I'm starving." No longer feeling threatened, she set the dagger down on top of the chest of drawers. "I could also use some better clothes. I'm still in my PJs."

"Peejayss?" Babbitt echoed uncertainly.

"Pajamas—you know, clothes that you sleep in?" Kate added.

"Lord Arun does not wear clothes to bed," Babbitt supplied.

Lord Arun . . . that was Roan. Kate remembered *Arun* among the slew of names and titles that he'd tossed out when she'd stared at him naked in the bath.

Kate tried not to picture the tall, dominating, bossy Fae king who'd kidnapped her sleeping naked in that huge bed . . . and failed. The mental image was too irresistible to avoid.

*What is wrong with me? I've never been fixated on boys before.*

But Roan wasn't really a boy, was he? He was all man, in a way that Kate had never really considered before. But seeing the hard planes of his bare chest, feeling the heat of his skin when she'd touched him, it had all lit a fire inside her that she didn't know could burn.

"Mistress?" Babbitt interrupted Kate's dangerously wandering thoughts.

"Right, pajamas. Listen, Babbitt, I can't walk around the palace wearing these."

Babbitt nodded, then snapped her fingers. A tray of food materialized on the enormous bed in front of Kate.

"Eat up, mistress. I will make you suitable clothing."

"Oh, really, I don't want you to go to any extra trouble—"

"No trouble, mistress. I love to help." Kate had a vague memory of her mother telling her that brownies loved to clean things and care for homes with happy families in them. If this was a dream, it was the most elaborate and coherent one she'd ever had. Usually by now, the dream would have shifted entirely into something else.

"Eat up. There's more where that came from if you like it, mistress." The brownie nudged Kate toward the bed and pointed at the food.

Kate sat down on the bed and pulled the silver tray toward her. There were slender slices of bread drizzled with what looked like powdered sugar and honey on one gold-and-silver plate. Next to it was a goblet of sparkling blue liquid with small petals floating in it. A soft sort of smoke drifted up from it, but when she touched the goblet it was cold, not hot.

"What kind of food is this?" she asked the brownie, who was busy folding the long blanket at the foot of the bed.

"Ambrosia bread with lavender-infused honey, and moon-flower juice with stardaisy petals."

Kate lifted one of the slices of bread and took a small nibble. The taste exploded on her tongue—sweetness first, then the tartness of a lemon, before it settled into the soothing flavor of the lavender honey.

This was incredible. She reached for the goblet next and took a sip. It tasted like sweet, sparkling water and made her tongue feel warm.

Suddenly, the sweet taste soured in her mouth. She felt a

chill as she remembered the tales her mother used to read to her. Eating food or taking drink in the fairy realm meant you were trapped there. Forever.

"Um, Babbitt?" Kate swallowed hard and stared at the food that had moments ago been such a welcome relief.

"Yes, mistress?"

"If a mortal—a human, I mean—were to eat the food or drink here . . . Does that mean I'm trapped here forever?"

*This is just a dream,* she reminded herself. *God, please let this all just be a dream.*

"Trapped? No, not this food, mistress. Now, the *Seelie* food, yes, that could trap you here. They like their mortals. But the Twilight Court is forbidden from taking them. This food here will heal you, mistress. Give you strength."

The brownie stepped into the bathing room and a moment later reemerged with her arms full of clothing and towels.

"I will return in a moment, mistress," Babbitt said. Then, with a pop, she vanished right before Kate's eyes.

Kate's mouth was still agape when Babbitt reappeared again.

"Now, how about a pretty gown?" The brownie snapped her fingers and pointed at the bed, where a silver-and-white gown appeared next to where Kate sat. Yards of fabric spilled off the side of Roan's bed, filling her vision with gleaming pearls and shimmering embroidery. It was something a princess would wear, not a human woman from her world.

"It's beautiful, but maybe you have something more practical? Like some blue jeans and a sweater?"

"Blue jeans?" the brownie echoed. "What are blue jeans?"

"They're a type of pants that women wear in my world, and—"

Once more, the brownie vanished on the spot.

"Okay," Kate whispered to the empty room.

When the brownie didn't immediately reappear, Kate devoured the rest of the breakfast, staring at the gown the whole time, debating whether she was going to try it on.

Babbitt reappeared with a giggle. "I know what blue jeans are now." She snapped her fingers and pointed at Kate. The pajamas on Kate's body vanished, and she was suddenly wearing blue jeans and a khaki-colored sweater, complete with a matching pair of khaki suede boots. Kate stared down at herself in shock. She hadn't even felt anything but a faint breeze as her PJs had vanished and these new clothes replaced them. She even had new panties and a bra. What she wouldn't give to have the ability to snap her fingers and change clothes like that.

"Do you like it?" the brownie asked.

"It's perfect!" Kate said honestly. "Thanks, Babbitt. Now, how do I get out of here?"

"Get out of where?"

"Here. This room. The doors are locked and I can't leave."

"Oh . . ." Babbitt's smile vanished. "Lord Arun wishes you to remain here."

"He may *wish* for that, but I sure as hell don't. He is keeping me here against my will." She strode toward the balcony doors and yanked on them.

*Locked. Shocker.*

"Babbitt, can you unlock the balcony doors?"

The brownie frowned slightly. "I suppose, mistress. Lord Arun would probably wish for you to get some fresh air." She pointed and snapped her fingers.

Kate, her hands still on the silver door latches, felt the locks click and she opened the doors. She stepped out onto the balcony and gasped. She was easily four stories in the air, and the brilliant moonlight lit up the ground below which spiraled out in a chaotic maze of hedgerows that seemed to go on forever.

"What's that?" she asked the brownie, who'd joined her at the balcony's stone railing.

Babbitt shivered. "That's the labyrinth, Mistress Kate."

"The labyrinth?"

Babbitt's golden eyes were wide with fear.

"Why does it scare you?"

"No one passes through the labyrinth. No one except Lord Arun. He is the only one who knows the way through it. That's what makes it dangerous. You think it's easy to understand, but . . . it never is. Even if you could find a way, there are dangers in the dark. The most deadly kind of Fae dwell inside the labyrinth. It is our greatest guard against the Seelie. They cannot reach the palace unless they make it through the labyrinth. Lord Arun sees everything in the labyrinth, and he would kill the Seelie if they tried to come to the palace."

There was that name again. *Seelie.* Kate remembered fragments of the old stories her mother had told her of the Seelie and Unseelie courts. Weren't the Seelie supposed to be the good fairies? Maybe these were different. "What exactly are the Seelie?"

"The Seelie are the Fae who dwell in the land opposite ours. They live in the land of the sun. We, the Unseelie, dwell in moonlight. We are two sides of the same coin, but we are enemies."

"So you never get sunlight here?" Kate judged that the moonlight was bright enough that if they never had sunlight, it was easy enough to see.

"Oh, we do, but it isn't as bright as the land of the Seelie, nor do they have strong moonlight in their world."

Kate studied the vast network of winding passages that made up a seemingly endless maze. "The Seelie never come here?" She wondered how big this world was. Was it on a full planet like her world or on some other kind of plane of existence entirely? Admittedly, she was fascinated, but she wasn't sure if asking Babbitt would give her the answers she needed.

"No, Mistress Kate. But there's talk that they've been sighted in the Black Hills, which are just beyond the edge of the labyrinth. The Black Hills divide our lands and theirs. Lord Arun was attacked when he visited the hills to search for them." The brownie pointed to a distant set of mountains that looked dark and forbidding.

"When was Lord Arun attacked?" Kate asked.

"Yesterday," the brownie replied. "I heard from the guards that he was injured in the fight and ended up in your realm trying to escape."

"The owl," Kate gasped. "Roan can turn into an owl? I thought perhaps that I'd dreamed it up. Is that . . . normal? For Fae to turn into animals?"

"For him it is," Babbitt said. "The owl is his wild Fae form. His sister, Lady Eudora, turns into a white cat, clever and fierce, and Lord Rath Ender becomes a large black dog, a dark guardian who will fight to the death to protect others. Not all Shining Ones have the wildness in them, mind you. Some have the gift of song, others the gift of dreams, and some the gift of enchantments. The gift of wildness is very special, very rare."

"Wait, who are Lady Eudora and Lord Rath Ender?"

"Lady Eudora is Lord Arun's younger sister, high princess of the Twilight Court. Lord Rath Ender is Lord Arun's closest friend and First Lance."

"What's that?" Kate asked.

"The First Lance is both a bodyguard and a confidant."

Kate tapped her fingers on the railing, studying the brownie. "You know everything about this place, don't you?"

"I have to, mistress," the brownie said with a ready grin.

"Then you can tell me how to get out of here and go home, can't you?"

Babbitt realized the trap Kate had set and began to shake her head. "No, no, Mistress Kate. You are Lord Arun's special guest, and I cannot interfere."

"Why not?" Kate pressed. "This isn't my world. I don't belong here."

The brownie removed her cap and held it awkwardly in her hands. "Lord Arun is my king. I cannot go against my king's wishes."

Kate fought off the sudden frustration that swamped her. Even in her dreams, she had no control. It wasn't fair. But that didn't mean she couldn't figure something out.

"I'm sorry, Babbitt, I didn't mean to upset you. I don't know anything about this place, and I'm going to make a lot of mistakes."

Babbitt sniffled and nodded in understanding.

"Can I get you anything else, Mistress Kate?" Babbitt asked.

"No, I suppose . . . Wait! Could you give me a very long piece of thick rope? Something that has knots tied in it every two or three feet down the length of it? Make it about seventy feet long?" Kate held her breath, waiting to see if the brownie could actually do that.

"A rope?" Babbitt's nose wrinkled. "I don't know why you would want one, but I can do that." She snapped her fingers, and the rope appeared in a coil piled on the floor at Kate's feet. It looked like the climbing rope she used to have to climb in gym class.

"Thank you, Babbitt. Um, I guess you can go now, if you want. I don't want to keep you busy when you have things to do for Lord Arun." She didn't want to make it look too obvious that she wanted Babbitt to leave, but she couldn't very well escape with the brownie watching her.

"If you need anything else, just call my name and I will come to you, Mistress Kate."

The brownie picked up her pile of laundry and vanished with a pop.

Chuckling, Kate grabbed the rope and dragged it toward the open balcony railing.

This was going to be easy.

B*eware the pools clear and deep, for morgens will sing thee to thy sleep.*

—Anon., *Tales from the Twilight Court*

ROAN SAT BACK IN HIS CHAIR AND LISTENED TO HAGNI, THE HEAD OF his Shadow Guard, explain how the Seelie had been known to test borders before launching a full-scale attack.

Roan and his war council sat at a large circular table made of obsidian. Roan had one of his legs thrown over the arm of his chair, lounging comfortably as he stared into the distance. His mind was miles away from the discussion of ancient battle strategies. It had been so long since the last war, it was ridiculous to think they would use the same tactics as before.

He kept replaying the moment he'd been fighting the Seelie warriors and one of them had slashed his forearm. Their numbers had been too great and the wound too deep and sudden for him to continue the fight. The only thing possible was to escape, but he knew better than to open a path on the Fae roads when his enemies were right behind him. If they were close enough, they could follow him and have a straight line to the palace. It was better to lose them between worlds, and that meant leaving his own. He had called on his powers and had his wild Fae form come forth. He'd immediately sank deep into his animal instincts, seeking escape so desperately that he shot like a cannon blast into the mortal realm. He'd lost his attackers in the *in-between*, but his miscalculation had sent him straight into Kate Winslow's arms.

He relived the moment he'd first seen his little mortal's face, the way he'd felt the instant he looked at her, something he hadn't felt in a thousand years.

*Alive.*

But why now? Why her? She was but a young creature who'd only begun to see the world with aging eyes, whereas he had seen empires rise and fall time and again. He had seen stars born and perish. He'd commanded armies in battles so ancient they no longer had names.

So why then did this mortal woman create such a peace within him that he could think of nothing but her?

"My lord?" Hagni said politely, breaking through Roan's thoughts.

Roan dropped his leg off of the chair arm and leaned forward. "My apologies, Hagni. What did you say?"

"I believe we have time yet before Culan and his warriors strike. He is more warlike than his father, but he fears you. That will buy us a little time. I would like to set traps at the foot of the Black Hills to catch any Seelie troops who may be scouting the area."

Roan nodded. "And what of our allies?"

"The dryads of the dark woods and the dwarves in the hills

will follow us into war if we call them to our aid. They are as concerned by this encroachment as we are and are providing what information they can."

Roan nodded again. Hagni knew their allies the best, having served with them in wars long before Roan had been born. He trusted the head of his Shadow Guard to do whatever was necessary to protect the people of Roan's lands.

"See it done."

Hagni stood and bowed, leaving the room with his lieutenants. Only Eudora and Rath remained, sitting on either side of Roan. He could feel the silence settle uncomfortably around them. His best friend and his sister shared a look before Eudora cleared her throat.

"Have you eaten anything yet?" his sister asked. "You're still pale, and I meant to send you food. I—"

Rath cleared his throat. "That is my fault, Roan. I distracted your sister."

Eudora blushed and sent Rath a look that warned him not to speak another word on the matter. The two were excellent at having silent conversations whenever they were in the same room. Any other time it might have amused Roan, but right now he wanted nothing more than to be back in his chambers, exploring the way the human woman had somehow made his world . . . brighter, softer . . . and more real than he'd ever imagined it could be. He wanted to recapture that feeling of comfort and love he'd felt when he'd been nothing but an owl in her arms, listening to her whisper her worries against his feathers. That moment lingered in his mind. How he had felt needed, and she had protected him, cared for him, and he had given her comfort in return.

Roan shook his head. "I will eat when I return to my room. See that I'm not disturbed."

"Of course," Rath promised.

Roan rose from his chair. As he passed by his sister, she reached out and caught his hand in hers.

"Be gentle, Roan. She is young and mortal. Do not frighten her."

"I will not," he promised. He had no desire to frighten her, only to seduce her. Would he corrupt her with his dark passions? Yes, that was unavoidable.

As he headed toward his rooms, he passed by a number of courtiers in the hall. Beautiful women in glowing gowns and gentlemen in black trousers and waistcoats the color of midnight. Each of them stopped whatever they were doing to pay their respects. He answered each with a brisk nod. Several brownies appeared out of thin air to see to some errand and just as quickly vanished. Dwarves and goblins were in deep discussion on matters of business and paid him little heed. The dwarves sold metal from the Black Hills to the palace and to the goblin blacksmiths who made the armor for the palace guards.

The Twilight Court was no mere palace. It was a vast city built upon the pale stones of an ancient mountain whose roots reached the firmament of creation. Its spires glittered like diamonds in the sunlight. At night, as the majesty of the moon moved overhead, the crystals that grew from the stones everywhere turned the palace into a beacon of soft, alluring light.

Roan wondered if Kate would appreciate the beauty of his world and fall in love with the twilight hours and the passing of midnight just as he had when he'd been a young boy. Sunlight was powerful and fierce, it was true, but the moon—ah, the moon—she was the mover of tides, the secret keeper, the mirror of the sun's light, softening it for the eyes of Fae and mortal alike.

He'd been given a choice on his one hundredth birthday,

just as Eudora had, to join the Seelie Morning Court, but they had both loved this place more.

Roan would convince Kate to see the wonder of his home. He would start by showing her the pleasure she would have for the rest of her life with him.

That single kiss he'd taken still lingered upon his lips. Her sweet taste, the touch of her soft skin beneath his fingers, the warmth of her eyes, and the rapid beat of that racing mortal heart had been intoxicating. He wasn't certain how he'd managed to stop from going further. But something about not rushing this conquest of her made each encounter all the more intense. How would it feel to explore her, to kiss every inch of her body and learn the secrets of her soul as he stole kisses from her lips?

He returned to the west wing of the palace and whispered the spell to unlock the door to his chambers. When he entered, his blood heated in anticipation, expecting to find the mortal naked in his bed.

But his bed was empty.

"Kate?" he growled into the silence. He strode toward the bathing room and jerked the door open. It too was empty.

Where was she?

He cursed softly and saw the chest of drawers had been left open. When he searched through his shirts, he noticed one of his spare daggers was missing.

So, his little mortal had escaped, and she had taken a weapon. This was not good. By the look of the empty tray on his bed, she had eaten, so at least something had gone right. She'd consumed food from the Fae realm, which would give her strength and would heal her wounds for a day or so. More importantly, it bound her to his land for a time. She would be safe—well, safe enough—until he was able to recapture her.

However, there was still the matter of *how* she had escaped . . .

"Babbitt!" he snarled.

The brownie appeared in the blink of an eye. "My lord?"

"Where is Kate?"

"Um . . ." The brownie glanced around, eyes wide. "She's not here?"

"Did you let the mortal woman leave?" His blue eyes turned gold as the wild form within him stirred with rage.

"No, my lord!" Babbitt replied without hesitation. "She asked to be set free, and I told her you wished for her to remain here. I was very clear about that. She was most under-standing."

Roan closed his eyes and rubbed his temples. "And *then* what did she do?"

"Well, she asked me for rope." The brownie smiled. "So I gave her one. A very long one." Babbitt, the little fool looked all too pleased with herself.

"Rope." He uttered the word with a dark scowl. "You gave her rope?"

"Yes, my lord. You said to see to her every need but not to let her leave your chambers."

When a faint breeze tickled his skin, he spun to face the balcony. The doors hadn't been fully closed.

"And you unlocked the balcony doors?" he added.

"Well, yes, my lord. The balcony is part of your chambers, and it's not like the mortal can fly away, can she? And we're far too high up for her to jump, so you'd need to have an awful lot of ohhhhh dear . . . I might have made an error in judgment, my lord. Please don't be angry..."

Roan's eyes narrowed as he flung the doors open. A stout rope was tied around the stone railing and dropped down out of sight. Roan peered over the edge, terrified that he would see the mortal woman's body smashed on the rocks below.

Instead, he glimpsed a feminine figure about twenty feet from the ground, slowly working her way down the rope. He didn't want to admit to being impressed, but he was. He climbed onto the railing and then leapt into the air, changing into his wild form. As an owl, he flew down in a slow spiral to the ground beneath the rope and then transformed into his normal self. He crossed his arms and stared up at Kate's bottom as she continued to scoot down the rope inch by inch, unaware that she had been discovered. He could hear her mutterings as her voice bounced off the rocks around her.

"Stupid idea . . . *Ouch* . . . What the hell was I thinking? I mean, I reach the bottom, great. Then what? Catch a bus back to Earth?"

When her boots reached the top of his head, he cleared his throat. She looked down at him and then shrieked, losing her grip on the rope. Roan caught her easily in the cradle of his arms. She was warm, and the sweet, faint scent of her sweat teased his nose. Her arms wrapped around his neck, purely on instinct, but he couldn't resist squeezing her just a little tighter to him.

"Dammit," Kate muttered. Her lovely brown eyes, the color of the tree trunks of his forests in the summer, stilled that racing madness in his head as he looked back down at her. She didn't take her arms away from his neck, and he felt that was a small victory.

"Kate," he said in light admonishment. "Did you really think you could escape so easily?"

Her eyes narrowed in challenge. "It was worth a shot." He did not normally like being challenged by anyone, but he found it oddly charming when this woman *ruffled* his feathers, so to speak.

Roan narrowed his eyes at her. "Surely you realize you cannot leave."

Her nose wrinkled. "Why not? This is your world, not mine. I don't belong here, Roan."

"You are mine." It was that simple. Why couldn't she understand?

"I am not—"

"If I wish to reorder the planets or birth a new star in the sky, such is my power." He felt her tremble as the words left his lips, and he tightened his hold on her before continuing. "You are *mine*. I will reorder time itself and break every rule for you, if you but ask me to. Consider it. Anything you wish will be yours. Any pleasures you wish to seek shall be found. In this land, there is no limit to your desires. You may have anything."

Her eyes flicked up to his with that word, and he could feel the heat that flushed into her skin. His fingers dug into the fabric covering her thighs, his body hardening and his lips quirking up slightly. She licked her lips, her lashes fluttering. "Anything?"

"*Anything*," said Roan, "but your freedom."

Her head snapped back. "Roan, I have to go back! My family—"

"Your family does not care for you," he said cooly.

The pain in her expression made him regret his words but not the truth of them. Her family had no interest in her, but he did. He was a king with vast power at his command who could have anything, and he wanted *her*.

"No one here cares for me either," she said, her tone quiet.

"I want you," Roan replied.

She turned away, her gaze looking toward a land he could not reach. "Wanting someone isn't the same as caring for them."

For one so young, she had moments of wisdom that many would not see in their entire lives, Fae or mortal.

The distance cleared from her eyes as she looked back up at him.

"Fae like to make bargains, don't they? You get me for one night, and then I get to go home the next day." She bit her bottom lip as she waited for him to reply.

"I may only want you, Kate. But my desires would not end after one night. My appetites can last a millennium. I offer you a chance to forget your old life and take this gift—to live in the land of the unchanging. To live well past your human lifetime, to do whatever you desire, so long as you belong to me."

"But what about my brother? I can't leave him. He needs me. Sandra will ruin him. I have to go back."

"No," Roan said simply, carrying her toward the path that would lead back up to the palace. "Forget your brother, forget those who would forget you—stay with me. I will show you such pleasures you will fear you will die from them."

He lowered her to the ground, keeping one arm around her waist while his other hand cupped her chin. Roan leaned down and kissed her, softly at first, then roughly, letting her taste the passion he held in check. Her soft lips parted beneath his, and his tongue delved into her mouth, seeking its mate. Kate made a kittenish noise at the back of her throat that drove his hunger for her even higher. He let his magic wrap around his body and hers, as he painted a future for her to see within her mind.

*"A consort to sit at my side, nights of sweet ecstasy in my bed, adventures and magic are yours."* Kate trembled as he spoke within her mind.

He backed her against the rock wall, gently pinning her there with his body as he continued his sensual assault on her senses with his kiss. He sent her a vision of him kneeling at her feet as she sat on the edge of his bed, naked, as he kissed his way up her inner thighs, to explore the taste of her. The Kate in his vision fell back onto the bed, drawing him up her body until he covered her with his own and sank into her welcoming heat. He rode her until she screamed his name and the stars in the sky fell to the earth at the force of their lovemaking.

As the vision faded from her mind, Roan brushed his lips along her jaw to her ear and then down her neck as he caressed one of her breasts through her sweater. She pressed closer to him with a moan, and he wanted to howl in triumph at her answering need. *Yes. Good.*

He gripped her bottom and slid his hand down the back of her thigh until he reached her knees, to lift her body up so she wrapped her legs around him. He rocked into the cradle of her thighs, letting her feel his desire for her.

"Roan . . ." She breathed his name, her nails digging into his shoulders.

"Tell me you belong to me," he encouraged. "That is all you must say." He was on fire at her touch, at her single utterance of his name. He'd never wanted anyone or anything as much as he wanted her, and it stunned him.

But rather than promise herself as his, his words brought the rebel back into his little human.

"Put me down! This isn't real. This . . ." She kicked and almost dislodged herself, but he tightened his hold.

"It's real, little one. Very real," he assured her. His gaze hardened as he watched her struggle with that truth.

Her eyes widened. "If this is real, and not some fever dream, then I really do have to go home. I *have* to. I can't leave Caden."

He paused. Now he understood what must be driving her need to get free. He'd already violated the ancient treaty about mortals once. What more could he suffer if he did it a second time?

"If you wish to be with your brother—"

She stopped fighting. "You'll let me go home?"

Roan closed his eyes. "That is not what I promised you."

An instant later, he and Kate appeared in the palace dungeons. The cells were empty at the moment. He set her down on her feet, and she glanced about in bewilderment. The dungeons were made of cold iron, one of the few places in the palace to have the wretched metal because it kept most of the Fae imprisoned and weakened, except Roan, who was too strong to be contained by iron. Lit wall sconces illuminated the grim place. It was empty and clean, but not at all welcoming.

"What is this place?" She glanced around the large iron-barred cell they stood in, clearly confused.

"My dungeons. Since you cannot be trusted to sit still in my bedchamber, you will wait here until I return." He stepped back a few paces and then waved his hand, sending the iron door slamming shut between them, containing Kate in one of the large cells.

"Roan . . . Wait, what are you doing? Don't leave me here!" she called out as he turned his back on her and walked up the stairs to exit the dungeons. Once he was outside, he traveled back to Kate's realm and retrieved the child she seemed to care so much about. It was an easy enough thing for him now that he was healed, and the child would not be missed because time passed far more quickly in his world than the mortal world. Ten years could pass here before even a minute would pass for Kate's human realm.

Roan reappeared once more in the dungeons, the child at his side in the cell next to Kate's.

"Caden!" Kate gasped and ran to her brother and caught his arms through the bars where their cells connected. The boy, still wearing his red-and-black checkered pajamas, looked around, confused and scared. Roan wanted to tell the child he had nothing to fear, that this was only to motivate his sister to acquiesce to Roan's wishes, but he held his tongue for now. Kate had to learn that he was in command of her future now. This was his realm, and he was no hero to rescue her. He was the king of the dark woods and lord of the Twilight Court.

"Kate? What is this place? I'm scared."

Kate held her brother through the bars and shot a furious look at Roan that almost made him smile. Her fire was a thing of beauty. He opened the door to her cell, ready for her to comply now with his desires, but his little human glared at him.

"Send him home!" she demanded. "Can't you see he's terrified?"

Roan crossed his arms and shook his head. "Not until I have what I want."

"You—" She charged him, fists raised. Roan grabbed her wrists, pinning them easily behind her back, holding her still so he could clasp her chin with his other hand, forcing her head to tilt back to look up at him.

"I suspect asking you to wait naked in my bed for me is an order that you will never obey. So perhaps I need to play a game that will help you understand the rules of this land?" He brushed the pad of his thumb over her bottom lip. Fury flashed beautifully in her eyes.

"Just let us go home," she begged, contrasting with the defiance in her expression. "*Please*, Roan."

He didn't grant her request, no matter how wonderfully erotic it was to hear her beg and say his name like that. Instead, he leaned down, feathering his lips over hers in the ghost of a kiss.

"You wished to bargain with me, little mortal, remember? Here is your bargain. Starting at dawn in an hour's time you will have a month to solve my labyrinth. If you do, you and your brother may leave. But each night, I shall come for you at twilight and you will give a part of yourself to me in whatever way I desire. And if you do not solve the labyrinth by the month's end, I will own you . . . *forever*."

Then he slammed his mouth over hers in a fierce kiss to seal their bargain as he sought to conquer that wild spirit that challenged him in a way that made him feel alive, made him feel changed in the land where *nothing* ever changed.

When their lips parted, he smiled softly at the dazed look on her face. At least his kisses had some effect on her. Yet something was missing . . . like a piece of an intricate clock out of place. If all the cogs and wheels weren't where they should be, the clock would not chime the midnight hour. The kiss he'd taken had left him wanting . . . aching . . . empty. And still, as he held her in his arms, he could feel that warmth, that promise of something yet untamed, unconquered within this human woman that drew him like the warmth of a fire on a winter's night.

*How can I have her, yet not have her?*

The desire in her eyes didn't fade, but he saw steel in her expression. This was a mortal who possessed the determination of a Fae queen.

"Thirty days?" Kate said. "I'll finish in a week."

He sighed softly. "Ah, to have the unfounded confidence of mortals." Roan chuckled. "You are no match for the labyrinth." *And no match for me,* he silently added.

But the labyrinth was dangerous, and he didn't want her to face the nightmares within. He simply wanted her to agree to be his, to let him show her what pleasures she could have as the love thrall of a Fae king. What mortal wouldn't wish for such a thing?

Her brown eyes hardened. "I may not be able to reorder the planets or turn into an owl, but I can solve your labyrinth."

He quirked one dark brow at her. "Be careful to presume you know what something is. Remember, to you I was merely an injured owl, and now you know I am far more. You must trust nothing in the labyrinth, not even yourself."

Kate opened her lips to speak, but he waved his hand and opened a Fae road built upon the westerly winds. His little mortal was pulled from his arms, out the nearest window, and carried upon the air as quick as he could breathe, until she stood at the entrance of the labyrinth far away from his palace . . . from him.

Already the distance between them made his chest ache and his hands clench and unclench as he wrestled with these unfamiliar feelings.

Caden, the young boy, grabbed the bars and stared at Roan in terror. "Where did my sister go?"

"To the entrance of the labyrinth on the far opposite side of my lands. She must learn that *I* control this world, not her. She must learn that she belongs to me now."

Caden's eyes filled with tears. Then he raised his voice to shout, "Good luck, Kate!"

"She cannot hear you," Roan said to the foolish boy.

"I know she can't. But she'll solve your labyrinth. You'll see," Caden declared confidently.

Had Roan been a kinder king, he would have set the boy free for his bravery and returned him to his home, but Caden was the key to Kate's obedience. Roan would use whatever advantage he had to make Kate obey him.

"We shall see," he said. "We shall see."

CHAPTER

# SIX

*"**G**ive me your lips, that I might taste the history of you in a kiss," said the dark king.*

*"Just a kiss?" his bride replied. "Or would you take my soul with it?"*

*The dark king smiled in the way of all clever Fae. "A decent kiss should do nothing less than steal one's soul."*

*—Anon.,* Tales from the Twilight Court

KATE TRIED TO CLOSE HER HANDS INTO FISTS AND WINCED.

"This isn't a dream." Her hands were red and raw from her climb down the rope. She'd been hurt in dreams before, yes, but she'd never actually felt any pain. Now her hands were in agony.

She tried to distract herself by studying her surroundings. The dungeon was gone, and so was her little brother. A forest lay behind her, so heavily crowded with trees it looked almost black, and a forbidding chill ran down her spine. She definitely didn't want to go that way.

Ahead of her was the entrance to Roan's labyrinth. It was made of stone, and it was beautifully carved with the most intricate patterns that looked like Celtic knots. Stunning but unfathomably complicated. The walls were impossibly tall, making her feel like an ant standing before a sycamore tree. And far beyond, almost out of sight upon the horizon, was the distant shape of the palace, which glittered in the pale sunlight that was just cresting the horizon. She lifted her face to the sky, seeing the weak light of the rising sun.

"There's more than just moonlight in this world as Babbitt said," she mused. But this sun was nowhere near as strong as the one back home. It was more like when there was a layer of cloud that filtered it so you could almost stare directly at it.

Kate tried not to think about Caden in that dark, barred cell and how scared he was. Surely Roan wouldn't keep him there forever . . . Would he? This was a man who had commanded her to strip naked and await his return, who had robbed her of her senses with a single kiss. He was used to taking what he wanted and not being refused.

"Please, just let Caden be all right."

The wind tugged at her hair before it whispered through the trees behind her. For a moment she thought she heard a woman, or perhaps several women's voices murmuring. Kate turned to look at the trees but saw no one.

"Is someone there?" she called out.

The trees stilled, and the wind faded.

*Focus,* she reminded herself. *You've got sunlight you can use to navigate the maze.*

She studied the shadows from the entrance. It was just now dawn, assuming the sun here rose in the west and set in the east. She could keep watching the shadows, and once the sun passed overhead at noon, then the shadows would stretch in the opposite direction. A labyrinth was just a complicated maze, right? She had solved a corn maze in middle school by keeping her right hand on the wall and following it to the end. She'd only run into two dead ends and corrected her course before she finally found a way back on the path.

*This must work the same. It has to.*

She wasn't going to let Roan win, and she wasn't going to let Caden down. Whatever Sandra might think of her, Kate would do anything for her little brother. She wasn't going to leave him in the dungeons of a Fae king.

With a deep breath to clear her head, Kate entered the labyrinth. The ivy-covered walls stretched up more than twenty feet on either side. She studied the glossy leaves of the plants, and inspiration struck. She ignored the pain of her rope burns and dug her hands into the foliage, grasping stems. She tucked one foot into the crevice of the plants and pulled herself up. If she could reach the top of the wall, she could see her path and find her way to the palace. If the walls were wide enough, maybe she could walk along the top the whole way!

Halfway up the wall, Kate was grinning. Her plan was working. This was easy.

Something sharp bit her hand and she gasped, jerking away from the ivy.

"Ow!"

She checked her palm. A little red dot formed, with a thorn jutting out from it. Before she could pull the thorn out, a new pain stabbed her other hand.

She tried to grab a different part of the plant, but thorns kept sinking into her hands each time. In her panic, Kate lost her footing and fell, landing hard on her side. Pain throbbed through her body as she tried to catch her breath. After a long moment, she rolled to sit on her backside and plucked the thorns out of her hands one by one.

The ivy had *attacked* her. She stared at the beautiful leaves that rippled innocently with the breeze as if nothing had happened.

Climbing was out.

"Can't blame me for trying," she muttered. The red welts the thorns left were another nuisance, but she could power through it. She had to. Roan was clever. It might not have occurred to most people to just climb the walls, but apparently he'd thought of it and prepared for it. And if the walls were lined with thorns, what other traps might she run into?

Kate got to her feet, brushed herself off, and held up her right hand, but she was careful not to touch the wall this time. From what she'd seen of the castle in the distance, it would take her a day walking straight through, which meant it was going to take too long to walk through the labyrinth's twisting paths. She needed to speed up. Kate's body ached from her fall, but she could at least jog. She was in decent shape and if she moved faster, she could get through the maze quicker.

Kate jogged for what felt like an hour before she took a break to walk and catch her breath. The labyrinth was starting to feel monotonous. The hedges seemed to go on forever in slow curves or sharp twists, yet they were somehow the same. Her own footfalls and her breath seemed to match the ripple of a breeze that moved along the walls of ivy, like the labyrinth was breathing with her. She knew logically that wasn't possi-ble, but it didn't stop her from thinking that the labyrinth was somehow connected to her.

The farther she moved into the maze, the taller the walls seemed to get, and the more the ivy would overhang the gap, which meant less of the pale sunlight could reach and warm her. Was she going underground? Or were the walls somehow growing above her? She couldn't tell. She studied the sky and had the eeriest sensation that she was being watched, but she saw no other creature near her or above her. She shivered and rubbed her arms. At least Babbitt had dressed her in warm clothes.

*Keep going. Don't stop. Just keep moving.*

She was still jogging when she burst around a sharp corner and barreled into somebody who was bent over.

"*Oof!*" a deep voice grunted as the person she'd collided with fell flat on his face, spilling a bag of rocks that sparkled in the muted light.

"Sorry!" Kate tried to catch hold of herself against the wall.

"Oi, what in blazes are you doing here, girlie?" the creature she'd crashed into demanded, his dark eyes narrowed in suspicion.

She tried to figure out what he was. Some kind of goblin, maybe, or a very tiny troll? He was only as tall as her shoulders, though taller than Babbitt back at the palace. He had a mass of dark hair that fell past his shoulders and a bushy black beard.

"I'm solving the labyrinth," Kate said.

A harsh laugh escaped the creature. "Are you, now? No one solves Lord Arun's labyrinth, foolish girl. No one 'cept Lord Arun himself."

"I'm not a girl," Kate said, holding her temper in check.

The creature snorted as he looked her over. "Ah. You must be Lord Arun's human pet. I've heard the pixies chitter on an' on about you."

"The pixies?"

"Oh, aye, little bastards won't stop yammering," the creature grumbled. "Of course, anytime the king does something, the pixies *have* to have their say, don't they?" He sniffed and looked her up and down. "Well, who are you, then, girlie?"

"I'm Kate, Kate Winslow." She held out a hand to the creature after he bent over to retrieve his small leather bag from the ground and collect the last of the sparkly stones, which he dropped inside the bag. He slung it over his shoulder and glared at her, but he didn't take her hand.

"Name's Patch. Well, off you pop, then." He turned away and started to leave.

She gently tapped his shoulder, and he looked back at her. "What is it?"

"Forgive me, Patch, but do you mind if I ask what kind of Fae you are? I don't know anything about this place. I only just met my first brownie. And Roan, of course."

"Oh, *Roan*, of course," he said in a high-pitched girlish voice. "You humans. Lord Arun is the most powerful Fae in the realm, and you call him *Roan*." He shook his head, muttering something about young'ins and a lack of respect.

Kate didn't want to call Roan by his title. It felt like calling him Lord Arun would give him power over her, and she desperately needed to keep him on the same level as herself.

Patch snorted. "I'm a kobold. I work in the royal mines."

"The mines? What do you dig for?" She was genuinely curious.

"Treasure. What else would you dig for? You humans sure are daft." He started walking, and since it was in the direction she wanted to go, Kate kept pace with him.

She ignored his insult. She needed to learn as much as she could about Roan, this place, and the labyrinth. "Do *you* know how to solve the labyrinth?"

Patch's boots slapped the earth in a rhythmic march as he walked. "Only the way back. I live on the outskirts. Only safe place to be in here. Go any deeper and you run the risk of being eaten or killed."

"Eaten or killed?" Kate's stomach gave an anxious flop.

She'd been told the labyrinth had danger, but she hadn't considered that something might eat or kill her.

"Trolls, basilisks, the baobhan sith, and hundreds of other creatures. They all roam the labyrinth. They feed off of any Seelie scouts and spies foolish enough to find their way deep into the labyrinth." He shot her a dark grin, as though the idea of Seelie being eaten was amusing. "It's how Lord Arun protects us. The Seelie fear this place, and the only way to reach the palace is through the labyrinth."

"The *only* way?" Kate hesitated. "Why can't they go around it?" So Roan's labyrinth wasn't designed to torture poor humans like her, but rather to keep his people and the palace safe. As little sense as it made, she preferred to think of Roan as a protector, rather than the man who'd kidnapped her because of some silly wish.

Patch shot her a look as if he questioned her sanity. "Because the labyrinth has no end, girlie. It goes on forever and a day on either side, like an endless wall between us and the Seelie kingdom. You can never find the center unless you already know the way."

*An endless wall?* Kate couldn't imagine such a thing was possible, but perhaps here she'd have to do as Roan said and never make assumptions of what was possible or impossible.

"Wait . . . what do you mean, find the center?" She'd been trying to find her way through to the other side where the palace was.

Patch arched a bushy black brow. "It's a labyrinth, not a maze, girl. You go to the center, not to the other side."

Kate felt like the wind had been knocked out of her. She'd wasted hours going about the puzzle all wrong. How could she have forgotten the story about the labyrinth and the Minotaur from the island of Crete? The goal was the center, not the other side, whereas mazes were about reaching the other side.

"I'm an idiot," she muttered.

Patch chuckled. "Well, don't blame yourself. Lord Arun made this impossible to solve. Unlike most labyrinths, which always lead to the center, albeit in the longest way possible, he's put up dozens of dead ends and ways that lead back to the beginning."

"Is the palace at the center?" Kate didn't want to think about how vast the labyrinth was if the distant palace was at the center of it.

"No, the palace faces the sea on the other side of the labyrinth and is protected from the sea by more enchantments."

"If I'm supposed to reach the center of the labyrinth and the palace isn't at the center . . . then how does that get me to the palace?" Kate tried not to let her disappointment show as she focused on her new goal. Reaching the center of the labyrinth.

"Don't know. Never been myself." Patch didn't clarify if he meant the center of the labyrinth or the palace, but Kate had a suspicion he hadn't been to either.

"You said there were trolls, basilisks, and . . . What is a baobhan sith?" She knew what trolls and basilisks were, at least from mythology and lore.

"The baobhan sith are Fae, pretty ones who will lure you into a dance. When you are exhausted from dancing, they will drain your blood." He hesitated and then gave her a nudge. "That blade you're wearing is made of iron. It would kill a baobhan sith."

"My blade? Oh!" She'd almost forgotten the slender dagger that she'd tucked into her boot. "How did you know I had it?"

"There's a gem in the hilt. Kobolds can sense the presence of jewels, just like dwarves. 'Tis why we mine." He tapped his bulbous nose. "We can sniff them out."

"Wait, I thought fairies didn't like iron. Why would Roan have an iron blade?"

Patch smirked at her. "You don't become king of the dark Fae unless you're strong, girlie. Roan is from the purest Seelie and Unseelie bloodlines. He carries the magic of the wild from his father, and there are rumors of other powers he's taken from his mother's lineage. A Fae like that will be uncomfortable around iron but not weakened like the rest of us."

"Roan is both Seelie and Unseelie?" That was something she hadn't expected.

"Aye. As is Lady Eudora, Lord Arun's sister. It makes the Seelie king blinding mad, it does."

"Why?" Kate asked.

"Why? Because to have the power of both worlds? Culan would kill to have that power."

"Culan? Is he the Seelie king?"

"Aye, and he's Lord Arun's and Lady Eudora's cousin. Culan's father was Lord Arun's uncle. When he died, he left a power-hungry son on the throne in the Morning Court."

Kate walked with Patch and remained quiet for a long moment as she considered her next words carefully.

"I thought . . . that the Seelie, the light Fae, were . . . the good guys?" She bit her lip, hoping that Patch wouldn't be offended by the question.

The kobold snorted. "Light and dark are only a reference to a Fae's source of power, girlie, not an indication of what lies in their heart. Are we dark Fae more prone to giving humans nightmares or tempting them into danger? Of course, life wouldn't be fun without a bit of danger, eh?" He was chuckling to himself now as if at some private joke. "I suppose if you want to get down to particulars, the Seelie might overall be more appealing on the surface, but trust me, Kate of the Winslows, you'd be better off with Lord Arun than the likes of

Culan. At least when Lord Arun seduces you, he will give you all that you desire. We are the court of dark, delicious pleasures. The Seelie love to play their harps and sing their merry songs, but us . . . we embrace our hungers and our vices in equal measure. You'll have no shame here, not if you become his consort."

"Consort?" Kate had heard the word before but only in the context of marriage to a royal person.

"Aye, some might call you a human pet, but Lord Arun would certainly take you as his consort, to care for you all your long-lived days." He hummed softly then, a little tune that was part mystery and part melancholy. "You wouldn't know the ballad of the Bride of the Dark Woods, would you?" he asked, clearly convinced he already knew her answer.

She shook her head.

"Didn't think so. Humans always forget the best stories we tell them. The bride was one of you, a human girl who was brought here by one of Lord Arun's ancestors when she made a wish. She became the king's consort, his queen."

"She married a dark Fae king?" Now Kate was enraptured. That was a story she'd like to read. "Could you tell the story to me?"

Patch huffed. "I'm no bloody bard, girlie. Besides, we've got to keep our wits about us. If I start trying to tell a story, we'd get eaten."

"Oh . . ." The sting of disappointment faded when she remembered what he'd been telling her about the labyrinth and its dangers. He was absolutely right—getting lost dreaming about fairy tales would only get them both killed.

"So how do I kill trolls and basilisk?"

Patch let out an aggrieved sigh, as though her questions were starting to annoy him. "You need only *run* from a troll.

They are slow, stupid beasts. Just don't stand too long in one place, so they can't strike you with a club."

"And basilisks?" She kept at his side as they walked along the path.

"Assuming you avoid staring at one or getting bitten, you need to have your blade soaked in its own venom to kill it." Patch shot her pitying look. "If you see a basilisk, you're probably done, girl. Done."

Kate shivered as a knot of dread welled up inside her. If she was remembering her mythology, a basilisk was a serpentine creature that was sometimes said to have a lion's tail or a even a rooster-like head, but was definitely snakelike. She wasn't afraid of snakes, at least not the ones who weren't venomous. She even liked holding ones that weren't dangerous. But a basilisk wasn't just a poisonous snake. It was a legendary one. One that could kill her before she could even blink. If she got herself killed, Caden would never get to go home.

*Oh, Caden . . .* She wanted to cry, wanted to go back home and just convince herself this was all some wild dream. But it wasn't. She sniffed, trying to fight off the burn of tears. If her mother was here, she'd tell her to buck up, to keep her focus on the goal.

"Well, I can't just give up, Patch," Kate whispered. "Roan has my brother in the dungeons at the palace. If I can solve the labyrinth in a month, he'll set us both free."

"Is *that* what Lord Arun said?" Patch looked unconvinced. "You're in the land of the Unseelie, girl. Every bargain has a price, every wish comes with a sacrifice. 'Tis the way with all Fae. We can't be trusted."

"Even you? You've been really helpful," Kate reminded the kobold. She had already learned quite a bit about this world, thanks to him.

The kobold gave her a look of reluctant surprise.

"If I was, I didn't mean to be," he grumbled and resumed walking.

Kate still had more questions, and she hoped the grumpy little Fae would keep answering them.

"Why would Roan bring me here? I mean . . . I'm not exactly fairy consort material." She was just a girl. She knew she was pretty, but she wasn't "bride of the dark Fae king" kind of pretty. She wasn't experienced, she wasn't worldly, she wasn't . . . anything Roan should be interested in. So why had he brought her here?

She didn't want to think about the way he'd kissed her in the bathing room, because if she did, she would have to acknowledge that some small part of her wished she had done exactly what he had asked her to do: strip naked and climb in his bed. That girl wouldn't be facing trolls, Fae vampires, or basilisks. She'd be having sweaty, mind-altering sex with a Fae lord.

But Kate had never had sex, had never done anything more than make out with a boy. Roan was all man, everything that frightened and excited her in ways she barely understood. She'd been hoping that in college she'd find a guy she liked and trusted, and then she'd take that step into exploring sex, but she was a long way from her college campus, a long way from that life she had been looking forward to.

Her previous life seemed strangely distant, as though another person had lived that life, and who she was right now . . . this was the *real* Kate. A woman stuck in a labyrinth with a grumpy kobold.

"You wished for him to bring you here. At least, that's what the pixies said. He only did what you wanted," Patch said.

"But I *didn't* ask him to bring me here, I—" She stopped dead in her tracks, her mind replaying her whispered plea into the barn owl's feathers. Into Roan's feathers. "That . . . that wasn't a wish," she protested.

Patch glanced over his shoulder. "A wish is a wish if you truly want what you wished for. That means you wanted to leave wherever you were. And no, Lord Arun has never done this before. Now his father, Lord Bahden Arun, *he* liked human women a bit too much. When he stole that human queen . . . er . . . What's her name . . . ?" Patch muttered as Kate ran to catch up to him. "Gwendolyn . . . Wandavere?"

"Guinevere?" Kate suggested.

Patch snapped his fingers. "Aye, that's the one. Well, that started a lot of nonsense in the human world, it did. Got 'em real upset."

"Guinevere was real?" Kate's heartbeat jolted with excitement. "You mean Guinevere as in King *Arthur* and Guinevere?"

Patch grumbled. "Of course I do, who else? Have you not been listening to a word I've said? Things here are *real.* You must stop thinking like a mortal, Kate of the Winslows."

"It's just Kate Winslow." She wasn't sure why she was correcting him. She kind of liked being Kate of the Winslows. It sounded . . . epic, like she was up to the challenge of the labyrinth. And God knew she needed some fun added to this whole nightmare of a deadly labyrinth.

He stuck his tongue out at her before continuing. "You are in *our* realm. You need to think like a Fae if you mean to make it to the center of the labyrinth."

"So there *is* a way to the center. You said there wasn't, but now you say it's possible." She couldn't stop the grin that curved her lips.

Patch adjusted his bag on his shoulder and let out a weary sigh.

"Is that heavy? I'd be happy to carry it for you," she offered. It did seem to hurt his shoulder.

He halted, a little reluctant, before he held out the bag to her.

"But you'd better not run off with it, girl," he shot her a warning glare beneath his dark, bushy brows.

The bag was heavy, but she had strong shoulders thanks to being a member of the swim team in high school, so she swung the bag up and let it rest on her shoulder.

"Nothing is impossible here, but if anything came close . . . it would be the labyrinth. Lord Arun is the only one who knows the way through it without magic. He allows his soldiers and any others in his realm safe passage so they can reach the dark woods and the Black Hills, but that won't help you."

"Why not?"

"Because he sends them on the Fae roads."

"What are the Fae roads?"

"Pathways on the wind. Only the Shining Ones can create them. And as the strongest of the Fae here, Lord Arun is the only one who can counteract the enchantments above the labyrinth to create the Fae roads for the dark Fae to travel when we need to."

"Patch, I thought Roan created the labyrinth. He said it was his. Why doesn't he simply undo the enchantments to let his soldiers travel through it?" She and Patch walked together as the sun sank lower and lower into the sky until it was almost beneath the tops of the ivy-covered walls.

They took another turn in the walls covered in greenery, and Kate kept her right hand slightly lifted toward the outside wall so she wouldn't lose her way.

"No one knows who created the labyrinth. It simply appeared here one day, and only Lord Arun was able to find a way through it. It wasn't always so . . . big. In its early years, it was smaller, simpler, but it's changed and grown over the centuries. Many others from the Twilight Court in the early days believed they could find their way to the center, and *they* were never seen again." The kobold looked up at her.

"I know Lord Arun has your little brother an' all, but why would you care to leave our realm? You might find that what he desires, you desire too. The pixies say that those who are loved by the Shining Ones are blessed with pleasures untold."

"If the pleasures are untold, then how can the pixies tell you about them?" Kate smirked when Patch frowned at her clever twist of his words.

"You don't want to be the lover of the king? Foolish, that's what I said when I first saw you, girl. Foolish."

"It's not foolish to want to be free to make my own choices, Patch." Kate bit her lip, searching for the right words. "Ever since my mom died, I've been told what to do and what was expected of me. This was the year that was supposed to change. I was going to college to be free, *really* free. But being here, a slave to Roan's desires, that's worse than being at home. At least at home I could go back to the dorms and escape." Here she would be in a gilded cage, and yes, dammit she liked the way Roan kissed, but that didn't give him the right to just . . . *own* her.

She curled her hands into fists. The raw pain from the rope had faded, and the red spots from the thorns were almost gone, both healing much faster than she ever expected. It was a small relief.

Patch chuckled ruefully. "No one ever escapes being controlled by others. That's life. Someone is always above you giving orders. What you can control is how you react. Take me, for example. I have three brothers, Grim, Gull, and Pinch. We kobolds are born to mine and quest for treasure, but I didn't want to spend my life underground. So I carry the gems my brothers find to a spot where folks from the palace treasury will collect them. I'm free in the open air and not beneath the dark earth with my brothers. Got to be clever, eh?" He tapped his temple.

"Yes," Kate murmured. "We've got to be clever."

She had been clever sneaking out of Roan's rooms. And by the look on his face when she'd seen him waiting below, he had found it amusing. Of course, he'd nearly kissed the life out of her, then carried her off like some barbarian warlord. A flush of heat rolled through her as she remembered the way he'd held her so possessively, as if she weighed nothing, and the way his blue eyes had swept over her face. She'd sworn she'd seen affection beneath the cool exterior of his expression. But he couldn't *like* her. He didn't even know her. She was just a possession to him, and all she did was run away from him. Wouldn't that make him furious with her?

With an inner frown, she pushed thoughts of Roan away and studied the sky. The sun was overhead now, and she noted the changing shadows. They were starting to lean in the opposite direction.

As they turned a corner, a beautiful waterfall appeared out of the rock wall, framed on either side by ivy. It poured into a vast pool lined with shallow stones. Lily pads as wide as Kate was tall covered the surface. The crystalline water coming down out of the rocks looked cold. Kate licked her dry lips and started toward the water.

Patch snatched her wrist, halting her. "Drink from the waterfall itself, *not* the pool."

"Why?"

"You might wake the morgens," he whispered.

"What are the morgens?"

"Pretty things with shiny tails and long hair." Patch waved a hand at his own tangled mess of hair. "If you hear them sing, you'll get close enough that they can grab you. Then they'll drown you. Before you die, their song will show you your favorite memories, to soothe you as they steal your last breath."

"Like sirens?" Kate asked.

Patch nodded. "But sirens aren't carnivorous by nature. They don't always try to drown you. Morgens, however, love to kill and will eat you."

But Kate was so thirsty, part of her wanted to rush over and plunge her hands into the quiet pool to drink.

"*Only* drink from the waterfall," Patch reminded her.

They skirted the stone-ringed pool and approached the rock wall carefully. Patch cupped a hand and filled it with falling water, bringing it to his lips. Kate set Patch's bag down on the ground and used her hands to cup the water and drink.

Then she heard a soft splash, and she turned around to see a morgen watching her from the ledge of the pool. Her orange tail swished playfully in the water. She brushed her wet blonde hair away from her face and smiled warmly at Kate.

"Don't move, and plug your ears!" Patch hissed.

*Too late.*

The morgen opened her mouth. The kobold plunged his fingers into his ears, and Kate tried to do the same, but slowed . . . and stopped.

The sounds she heard were like honey upon Kate's ears, making her feel warm and safe. Her body longed to take a step closer to the beautiful creature. The song reminded her so much of her mother. How could such a beautiful Fae possibly harm her? She was certain that this creature would wrap her in her arms and care for her . . . love her.

But something didn't make sense. Why would she love her? It . . . all of it was wrong. The song's intensity wavered, and her vision began to lose the golden glow that had haloed around the morgen.

Kate gasped, struggling to regain control of her own mind. *Caden. Think of Caden.*

She held on to the image of Caden as he grasped the bars of his cell, his frightened face as he called her name. The tremor in his voice, the darkness of the dungeons, and her desperation to free him. The truth that her brother needed her outweighed any pretty lie a song could weave in her head.

Patch's hand lowered from his ears, and he began to walk toward the pool in a trance. The morgen ran her fingers through her hair like a comb, still singing her deadly song.

"Patch! Stop!" Kate lunged forward, but she missed the kobold and almost fell in the water. Patch leapt toward the morgen, who held out her arms to catch the little Fae creature as he jumped over the lip of the stone pool's edge.

"No!" Kate screamed.

The morgen plunged into the water with Patch, vanishing beneath the lily pads.

Kate sprinted toward the edge of the pool and peered into the water. She saw the morgen swimming down into the darkness far below, Patch still in her arms.

"Oh, hell no!" She wasn't going to let some evil mermaid thing take Patch. Kate kicked off her boots, jerked off her sweater and jeans, and plunged into the pool, wearing nothing but her bra and panties. She swam with powerful strokes, gaining on the morgen, who didn't seem to be in a hurry. Once she was in reach, she grabbed hold of Patch's arm and jerked.

Patch slipped free of the morgen's arms, and the morgen twisted in the water and slashed at Kate with clawlike fingers, raking her arm. Blood clouded the water, and Kate tried not to cry out in pain. She kicked the morgen in the chest, using her as a springboard to push her and Patch toward the surface. Stunned, the creature swam away into the vast deep below.

Kate struggled back to the surface, an unconscious Patch

wrapped in one arm. The flickering circle of light above her seemed desperately far away, but she had to keep going.

At last she broke the surface and pushed Patch onto the stone ledge. He jerked, coughed, and sputtered water all over the ground. Kate breathed a sigh of relief, still clinging to the stone wall, then pulled herself up on shaking arms.

Something slithered around her ankle, and a second later she was jerked back under the surface, her scream choked by water. Two morgens were holding her ankles, tugging her back down to the dark depths, toward death.

*No . . . can't . . .*

She tried to swim, but with only her arms free, she couldn't fight the two powerful morgens. She had no breath, and her lungs screamed in agony. An eerie, beautiful sound echoed in the water like a whale's song, wrapping her in its beauty. The chill in her limbs turned warm and comforting. Her eyes closed and suddenly she was *home.*

*Kate was curled up by the fire, her mother's arms wrapped around her shoulders as they read a story and drank hot chocolate from their favorite mugs.*

*"Mom," Kate said uncertainly, too afraid to believe that somehow she'd been transported back in time. But she'd been in another realm, so wasn't anything possible?*

*Her mother's eyes were soft, sweet, full of that brown fire the Kate sometimes saw in her own eyes.*

*"I'm dreaming," Kate guessed.*

*Amber Winslow shook her head. "You're dying," she corrected Kate gently. "But it's all right. We can stay right here, in this memory, together." Her mother squeezed her waist and kissed her forehead.*

*Stay here with her? Kate wanted that, wanted to stay in her mother's arms. "Forever?"*

*"Yes, my darling," Amber said softly and stroked her hair. "Just like this."*

*Kate shook her head. No. Her mother was dead. This couldn't be real. She couldn't stay even if she wanted to. She had to do something.*

The vision of her mother vanished, and once more her eyes sought the ring of bright water far above her. So far away . . . The view of the sky above began to fade back into the comforting sanctuary of her mother and the warm fireplace.

Then she glimpsed a figure blacking out the sun and plunging into the water, shooting toward her like a falling star as it began to glow with a light that was beyond words. It made her think of Roan. She reached out her hand, wanting to touch that figure wreathed in light. But it was too late. She couldn't take it anymore, and in a desperate gasp, her lungs filled with water.

It all went quiet. All went dark.

CHAPTER

# SEVEN

*The bride knew that she was losing herself bit by bit to the path in the dark woods. But in losing herself, she discovered a new self, one who was unafraid to face the monsters. To find her way forward, she had to leave her fear behind.*

—Anon., *Tales from the Twilight Court*

The human child clutched the bars and stared at Roan with wide, innocent eyes through the gloom of the dungeon. Eyes that called Roan back to the moment he'd first met the child, when he'd whispered a hope that Roan would be the friend his sister needed. That request had stirred something in Roan's chest, settling beneath his skin as he'd considered the child's devotion to his older sister. He had liked the boy instantly for that love and loyalty to Kate.

A pixie flitted through the air, distracting Roan momentarily. The pixie hissed, leaving bright little green sparks above his head before it shot up the stairs. The human child jumped back in shock.

"What was *that*?"

"A pixie. They won't hurt you, unless you try to pet them," Roan replied dismissively. He had no intention of discussing pixies at present.

The vicious little creatures were always watching him and following him about. Nosy little things, always getting into everyone's business.

With a sigh, Roan waved his hand and the iron bars vanished, which left the child standing there confused.

Roan turned to leave. "Come with me." He heard the child's footsteps behind him, hurrying to catch up. Roan took the twisting staircase out of the dungeons and stepped into the light of one of the palace corridors. It was mercifully empty of palace courtiers or other creatures. He did not have time for their nonsense.

"Babbitt!" he called out.

The brownie materialized in front of him and curtsied. "My lord?"

"Take this child to Eudora," he instructed the brownie. He glanced down at the boy, feeling a little unsettled by this situation. He had no intention of being cruel to the child, but he had no time to sit around and watch him. Roan had to plan for the eventual hostilities with the Seelie, and he needed to make sure that Kate was safe in the labyrinth. If he could keep her in the outer edges of the labyrinth, she would face no real danger.

"Lady Eudora?" Babbitt blinked in surprise.

"Yes. Tell her that this is the mortal woman's brother, and see to it that he is fed, clothed, and watched over. Do not allow any harm to befall him."

The child seemed to relax a little at that reassurance.

The brownie nodded, her eyes serious as she looked over the human child. "Yes, my king."

"Sir?" The boy tugged on Roan's tunic sleeve. Roan glanced down at the child. "What *is* she?" he whispered as he pointed at the brownie. "And where are we?"

Roan was unaccustomed to explaining his world to mortals. He drew himself up a little and arched a brow at the child as he spoke. "To answer your second question first, you are in the realm of the Fae, boy. *Babbitt* is a brownie. I would strongly advise you do not point at her, or anyone else for that matter. It might be seen as rude, and rude can be dangerous here. Babbitt will answer your questions."

The child stared at the brownie, who gave an eager-to-please smile. Babbitt and the boy were of similar height.

"Fairies . . . *wow*," the boy murmured, still in shock but not as frightened as before. That was good. Unlike some of the courtiers in his court who relished their dark gifts, he was not a Fae who thrived on fear and darkness. His father had said he had too much of his mother in him.

"What's your name, little human?" Babbitt asked in a chirp, holding out her hand.

"Caden." The boy shook the brownie's hand, and the brownie led the child away.

Roan smiled at the thought of his sister playing nursemaid to a human child. At least it would give her something different to do with her days other than tease poor Rath.

He returned to his bedchamber, and with a twirl of his wrist, he conjured a glowing orb the size of an apple, which soon grew larger than his head. He let it hover in the air, milky-white smoke spiraling off the orb in illuminating tendrils.

"Show me Kate," he murmured.

The smoke filling the orb vanished, and he glimpsed the girl jogging through the labyrinth. It amused Roan to watch her futile efforts for a time. She was still on the outer edges of the labyrinth, far from its dangers. If she stayed along the fringes, she would come to no harm. He would be able to visit her nightly and take what he wished from her. He waved his hand, and the orb vanished. The girl was safe, and that was all he needed to know for now.

There were more pressing matters to attend to. It was time he visited the Black Hills and met with Hagni to assess the strength of their alliance with the dwarves and the dryads.

Roan walked to the edge of the balcony, spread his arms wide, and leapt off. He embraced the wild Fae within him and once again became a barn owl. He flew high over the labyrinth, letting the wind carry him on the Fae roads toward the distant entrance of the labyrinth and beyond. But as he passed over Kate, he couldn't resist seeing her again.

He flew well above where Kate's human eyes could see him. He tracked her progress as she ran run through the labyrinth. If she continued on her current path, she would spiral around the outside of the maze for days.

*Then she will be mine forever* . . . The thought filled him with a dark delight. To have her all to himself, to own her thoughts, her heart, her body, even her soul. She would be his to kiss, to take to his bed, to explore and pleasure until they both were too tired to move. It had been too long since he'd allowed himself to have such a creature at his beck and call.

Taking one of his courtiers to bed was never wise. Everyone expected him to take a queen consort, and many of the Fae females vied for his attention. But their naked ambition left him cold and unmoved. He had eyes for none of them. The games and power struggles that went on in his realm were predictable, tiresome, and boring. But Kate, Kate was new. She was interesting. She didn't do what he expected.

Perhaps that was what fascinated him about her. She

defied him at every turn, even when it would make far more sense for her to comply with his wishes. She was always herself. He wasn't even angry when she continued to defy him. Rather, it heated his blood and made him want to catch hold of her and kiss her senseless.

Confident she would get into no trouble for a time, Roan was about to leave when he saw her crash into a kobold coming from the gemstone mines on the eastern border of the labyrinth. Roan flew down to the top of the wall and observed what Kate would do with the kobold.

To his surprise, she seemed to befriend him, and the two traveled together for a time.

Roan flew along every few minutes and perched on the wall to keep pace with them. The meeting with Hagni and the dwarves could wait. He focused on Kate and the kobold and silently chuckled as Kate questioned the little creature for information about the labyrinth. The kobold was one he recognized as a gem deliverer from the mines. He would know to stay away from the dangerous areas of the labyrinth. If Kate stayed with him, she would be out of danger.

*You will find no answers from him, little one. The puzzle cannot be solved by anyone but me.*

Content with the knowledge that Kate would be distracted by the kobold, who would keep to the outer edges of the labyrinth, Roan settled down to rest, his feathers warm beneath the soft Fae sunlight. Being near Kate made him feel so calm, so at peace, that his natural restlessness just faded away. He actually dozed off and only woke to the sound of a scream several miles away. With a frantic flutter of wings, Roan took flight, his keen animal eyes seeking the source of the cry.

It was Kate.

She was at the morgen pool. Surely the kobold had warned

her not to drink from the pool? Roan bobbed his head, his eyes seeking any sign of the kobold, but he was nowhere to be seen. Had he already been taken by the vicious morgens?

Kate stripped out of her clothes and plunged into the water. For a long few moments, nothing moved beneath the surface. Roan prepared to transform, ready to dive in after her. Then Kate burst out of the water and shoved the kobold onto the stone ledge surrounding the pool. She struck the creature's back, making him cough violently, and water poured out of his mouth. The kobold lay still, but he was alive.

Roan released a tight breath. She just *dove* in to save the kobold's life! Foolish woman, she could have been killed over someone she didn't even know.

Kate gasped as something jerked her back beneath the surface of the water.

"Kate!" Roan roared, shifting back to his natural form faster than he ever had before. There was no one around to save her, no one—except *him*.

From high on top of the wall, Roan dove, arms stretched over his head. The momentum carried him down farther and faster than the morgans could drag their prize. The shafts of sunlight wavered and dwindled as he descended into the bottomless pool. Strands of the morgens' song traveled through the water, reaching his ears. He ignored them for as long as he could. Deep in the dark of the cursed waters, he glimpsed a flash of pale skin. *Kate.*

Roan swam on, his fairy shine intensifying as he let go of some of his glamour. His shine illuminated the morgen that held Kate's unconscious body, baring her pointed teeth at the intruder. Despite their pleasing appearance, these were little more than beasts. A second morgen slashed at him to protect their prey, but Roan grabbed her wrist with one hand, while grabbing her throat with the other.

The morgen tried to enchant him with song, but he snapped her neck, silencing her. The morgen's body drifted into the dark, out of sight. He spun toward the other beast, which held Kate in her arms. The creature's clawed fingers slashed across Kate's stomach. Blood drifted in a cloud around them.

The creature sang louder, the water around Roan vibrating with the power of her seductive spell, and for a moment, just a moment, he fell into enchantment . . . into a memory from nearly a thousand years ago.

*The bright summer night was awash with the colors of blooming flowers as he and Eudora chased each other across the silky grass of the palace gardens. Eudora toddled on her little feet, giggling and squealing, her rounded little wings shooting sparks of magic. Roan laughed as he waved his wooden sword in the air and pretended to fight Rath, his best friend, in a battle for Eudora.*

*"Children!" Queen Thalia Moondove's laughter was clearer and purer than any bell. She waved Rath over to her. "Your mother is waiting for you." She gave the little child a kiss before she sent him on his way.*

*"Mother!" Roan dropped his sword and ran to his mother, fisting a hand in her skirts. She bent down to press a kiss to his cheek. Her blonde hair, the color of spun gold, bounced in soft curls against Roan's face as his mother kissed him. Eudora joined him, giggling as she held out a moon flower to their mother.*

*"Eudora, did you grow this?" Thalia asked Eudora.*

*The four-year-old princess nodded eagerly.*

*"Well done, my darling." She bent down to squeeze her daughter in a fierce embrace before she turned to Roan and put an arm around him in silent warm welcome.*

*His mother always welcomed him. She seemed to know how much that mattered to Roan, who was only seven years old. To be loved, to be cherished. King Bahden had no interest in his offspring, but the queen? Her heart was full of sunlight and love, especially for her children.*

*Thalia tilted Roan's face up as she met his gaze. "You are loved, my dark little prince. You are deeply loved. Never doubt it. You carry my light within you, and it will always be right here." She tapped a slender finger on his chest right above his heart. "Do not be afraid to shine in the darkest night."*

The memory was ancient, yet he'd lived it so fully and clearly in his mind and his heart. Now she was lost to him.

Roan left the memory as easily as he had slid into it. His anger rose. This morgen had tried to take what belonged to him and him alone. And now it would pay the price. Kate was unconscious, which meant she would not be harmed by his light, and he could not afford to wait another moment.

Roan let the full might of his shine explode from his body. The morgen screamed in agony. Its eyes turned red and then cloudy white as it went limp and died. Roan swam forward and grasped Kate's hand, wrapping an arm around her waist and kicking them both toward the surface.

As he broke through the ring of bright water, he sucked in a breath. He pushed Kate over the ledge to safety, and she lay still on the grass near Patch. Roan dragged himself out of the pool and knelt by her side. He gently rolled her onto her back and pressed his ear to her lips. She wasn't breathing.

He cursed and placed his mouth over hers and summoned the water in Kate's lungs toward his lips. Then he drew back, allowing the water to escape her mouth. It formed a shining orb above her body. With a wave of his hand, the orb shot away and splattered on the ground.

Kate suddenly coughed, her body spasming. Roan turned her onto her side as she coughed a few more times, then let out a raspy sigh as she calmed. As her eyes opened, she stared up at his face in confusion.

"Roan?" she whispered. The pleasure of hearing his name sent a jolt of joy through his dark soul. He stroked tender fingers over her pale cheek, glad to see a tiny blossom of color return to her skin.

"Lesson one of the labyrinth, Kate. Never drink from the still pools," he chided.

She shivered a little and glanced around. "No, wait, where is he? I need to save him—"

"The kobold? The fool is alive. You *did* save him, but at unnecessary risk to yourself. *Never* do that again," he warned. "You're mine, Kate. Your life belongs to *me*. You cannot throw it away on another."

She narrowed angry but weary eyes at him. "I wasn't going to let him die. He's my *only* friend in this place."

Roan helped her sit up and settled her on his lap. She raised a half-hearted protest, but he ignored her. He needed the comfort of holding her in his arms. To think he could have lost her over such a foolish thing.

"*I* would be your friend, if only you would accept that you belong to me. If only you obeyed me, my rebellious little mortal."

Kate burrowed her face against his chest, as if to seek his body heat. Though they were both soaking wet, he was by far the warmer of the two. He liked how she turned to him, even if it was for warmth and not comfort. She had offered him such comfort when he'd been wounded and weary. He wished to could the same for her now.

"Friends don't order each other around," Kate said.

Roan chuckled, wrapping his arms tight around her. After a moment, she lifted her head, her lips accidentally brushing his jaw as she looked up at him. Heat shot through his body at her lips touching his skin, but he held still. Her brown eyes were full of pain, a pain not of the body but of the soul.

"I saw something when the morgen sang to me."

"What did you see?" he asked.

Kate paused, a tear rolling down her cheeks. "My mother." That tear gleamed like a frozen dewdrop upon her skin.

He reached up and captured the tear, imbuing it with a silent healing enchantment, then stroked it across the scrape on her cheek.

"It must have been a memory I'd forgotten. I was so young when she died, and my dad remarried so soon. It felt like I just blinked and my mom was gone, and Sandra was in our lives. That memory . . . it was so clear." Fresh tears clung to her lashes like diamonds. "Tell me that it was real, Roan. That somewhere deep within me I still have that memory, and it wasn't just an illusion?" Her plea trembled in the air, and her distress made him restless.

Roan brushed the backs of his knuckles over her now healed cheek, wanting to soothe her.

"The morgens' song can only unlock true memories, Kate," he promised. "Whatever you saw while under their spell was real. That memory may be very deep, but it's there. Sometimes our oldest memories are our strongest."

Kate pressed her cheek against his chest again and remained quiet. It seemed she needed time to process all she had been through. One of her hands rested on his chest, her fingers stroking his skin.

"Did you see anything when they sang to you?" she asked after a long moment.

"Yes."

"What did you see?"

He saw no reason not to tell her. "I was playing with my sister and my friend in the gardens when my mother came to greet me and my sister. I was but seven years old, and it's one of my favorite memories."

"Did you lose your mother too?" Kate asked.

It amazed him that she could deduce such a thing when she had no knowledge of his world.

"She did not die, if that is what you mean. Fae rarely do. But my mother could not stay. My father's darkness was too great, even for her light. She journeyed into the mists of time. I may never see her again."

"The mists of time? That sounds like a metaphor for death." Her fingertips stopped moving in small patterns on his chest.

He shook his head. "Time can be distorted, even reshaped. Much like a summer storm, the boundaries of time can be charged with energy and become an actual storm. When such a storm ends, it will often leave a fading mist behind for a time. People who travel into it are often not seen again."

He thought of the storm that had raged between her realm and his. How time had fought to claim Kate and take her away from him, and the tides of time had almost succeeded in pulling her out of his arms. Roan stroked a wet tendril of hair away from her face.

"Are you hurting anywhere else?"

She started to shake her head but then winced. "My stomach burns."

How had he been so distracted by talking to her that he had forgotten the morgen's slashes! Roan stood, Kate carefully held in his arms, and walked away from the pool. The sun had disappeared far beneath the walls of the labyrinth now, and he would claim his prize from her after he healed her.

The magic in his blood answered his call. At the nearest bend of the labyrinth, a bed grew out of the white ash trees. Ivy crawled up the four posts, and purple wisteria formed a canopy along the upper railings that draped down over the top of the bed. He pulled back the covers he'd conjured up and laid Kate down on the enchanted bed.

"Let me see." He pulled her hand away from her stomach. The slashes looked painful, but thankfully they were not deep. Crimson blood smeared her fingertips. Roan cursed himself for not noticing it sooner.

"It really hurts," Kate said in a wavering voice. Her brown eyes were full of tears as she looked up at him.

"Close your eyes," he whispered.

She flashed him one of those adorable, rebellious glares of hers that he was surprisingly charmed by, but this wasn't the time for her to argue with him.

"You're still being bossy," Kate whispered, but her eyes softened.

"It is for your own good. I need to heal you. Remember what I said about my magic? The shine is dangerous. You must trust me."

She lifted her lashes up as she continued to gaze at him, and then he saw it, that gentle slide into the direction of trust. Her lashes lowered and fanned across the pale skin of her cheeks.

"Keep them closed until I tell you it's safe."

She did. Roan released his glamour, and the shine of his magic grew brighter than the sun.

"Be still, little one," he soothed, and let his magic pour into her skin.

EVEN THROUGH HER CLOSED EYELIDS, KATE WAS ALMOST BLINDED BY the bright light. A searing heat burned in her stomach, but it grew less as the seconds passed, and she couldn't help the tears that escaped her closed eyes. When the pain finally ebbed away, the light pouring through her eyelids dimmed.

"You may open your eyes," Roan said.

When Kate opened her eyes, she saw the dying light of the sun creating striations through the canopy of wisteria high above her. Beneath her were cool, clean bedsheets and a soft mattress. The pain within her body was gone. She was tired rather than exhausted. In that moment, she felt as if she could be carried away upon a light breeze.

A black-and-purple butterfly flitted among the wisteria blooms, and Kate was mesmerized by its fragile beauty. Her lips parted as she took in such a simple but beautiful thing.

"What do you see?" he asked her.

"That butterfly. It's so large, so vibrant . . . We don't get butterflies like that in my world . . . not anymore. They're dying out." She thought of all those delicate butterflies that were slowly going extinct because of the destructive lives humans led. Nothing felt sacred or safe anymore, and she never felt that more strongly than she did now, watching a butterfly in the land of the Fae whose life was not challenged or threatened.

Roan sat down on the edge of the bed. "Now you begin to see." His gaze was not on the butterfly, but rather on her.

"See?" She slowly pushed herself up. Cool air danced across the bare skin of her stomach, and she glanced down. Impossibly faint scars stretched across part of her belly, right above her navel.

"*Oh God!*" She was practically naked. She snatched the bedsheets to cover her body. She forgot she'd had only her bra and panties on when she'd dived into the pool. At least they were dry now. She guessed that was Roan's doing.

He chuckled softly, then his eyes darkened. "You are starting to see the beauty in mortal things. I see a creature who is doomed to live a life as brief as a candle, but the light within it is no less precious than the creatures in this realm who live thousands of years. Its delicate mortality illuminates its beauty more poignantly than we can imagine. It makes us cling to the things we are so quick to lose."

That she understood. She would mourn the loss of the butterfly and the flowers once death had paid its call upon them. Kate felt as though she understood Roan in that moment, perhaps even more than she first realized.

"Is . . . is that how you see *me*?" She stared up at Roan, who looked to be in his mid-twenties, except for his silver hair, which was pulled halfway back by a leather tie. There was something ancient in his eyes, though, that betrayed his true age. How old was he? She didn't dare ask.

Roan continued to watch her curiously. "Do I see you as more beautiful because you will one day die?"

She managed a nod.

"I will not lie to you. Your mortality adds an element to my fascination, but it is only one piece."

"What are the other pieces?"

Roan stood and pulled his tunic shirt off his body, exposing his glorious chest and his back to her view. She saw more faint scars along his beautiful skin, just above his black leather pants, and wondered what could wound a Fae king.

Roan's blue eyes turned as dark as the sea at midnight, and a shiver ran down her spine. "No more questions tonight, little one. You must pay your price for a day in the labyrinth. Not as simple as you boasted, is it?"

Pay the price? A day in the labyrinth? She couldn't remember what she'd agreed to earlier; she'd been focused on saving her little brother.

"You agreed to my terms, and those terms were that each night you would give to me whatever part of you that I *desired*."

Roan's voice was deep, smooth, seductive. Kate's stomach somersaulted, and she clenched her thighs as her body responded to his words on a primal level that she hadn't thought possible.

He towered above her as he stood at the side of the bed, his hands resting on his hips.

Kate swallowed hard, her gaze roving over his body. "What do you . . . *desire?*" she asked. The shimmering silver strands of his hair were slightly wet, and it curled at the ends, brushing his shoulders. She had the strangest urge to reach out and touch it.

"I wish to take a single memory."

"You want to take a *memory* from me? Why? And what do you mean by *take?* You mean I won't have it anymore?" She shrank back from him as he put one knee on the bed. He looked wild and dangerous, and not just because he had magic at his fingertips.

"Fear not, I shall take one you won't miss," he promised with a wicked grin as he climbed on the bed and came toward her on his hands and knees.

"Roan, wait!" Kate pressed her hands against his chest, then realized that had been a foolish thing to do. Whenever she touched him, she forgot she wasn't supposed to like it.

"It's *only* a memory," he purred as he pulled her to lie flat beneath him on the bed.

"Then why are you on top of me?" she asked, her hands still pressed against his chest.

"Because I like how you feel beneath me, little human." He nuzzled her cheek, and that simple skin-to-skin caress sent wild bolts of heat shooting through her. She felt trapped, yet safe. What a strange contradiction . . . and so intensely wonderful. His lips brushed along her jaw and up to the shell of her ear, making her tremble with a violent longing and she moaned softly as she struggled with her need for more of him. More touches, more caresses . . . *more.*

"I need to take your memory with a kiss." One of his hands brushed her bare shoulder, exciting planes of skin that had never felt this sensual before in her life. Roan could touch her anywhere and she would come alive.

His mouth gently covered hers, and the warmth of his lips encouraged her to respond.

Whenever he kissed her, she was overcome by a strange sense that this was what she had been waiting for her whole life. She should be pushing him away, slapping him, fighting him, and yet right now nothing mattered aside from his kiss. She drifted on a path of pleasure as he taught her to kiss, how to use her lips in ways she'd never thought possible. Her hands explored his face, her fingertips tracing his jaw, the shape of his ear, before she stroked her fingers to the wetness of his silvery hair.

It brought back the memory of the morgens' attack and how he'd saved her life. How he'd healed and tended to her. Roan claimed he only felt desire for her, but Kate swore that in this kiss she felt something *more.* Something her foolish heart wanted to cling to in this strange world that was so very far from home.

She opened her mouth to his tongue, her body warming up at the erotic way he thrust his tongue lightly between her lips. It made her think of how he would claim her, how he would make love to her with a blanket of stars and the wisteria hanging above them.

The ache deep in her womb was new and fierce, but Kate recognized it for what it was.

*Desire.*

Her body wanted this man—no, this *Fae.* Whatever he was, he was so harshly beautiful, even with his scars. He was enchanting. Nothing like she would have imagined a Fae would be. He was muscled and massive instead of slender, his hair silvery, not gold. And his eyes . . . Lord, those blue eyes were of a shade that escaped words.

"Kate, show me your mind . . ." Suddenly, it felt as though the world was spinning around her.

She was pulled into a memory.

*She stood on the campus lawn of the University of Nebraska. Her father and Sandra had dropped her off four hours ago, and now she was exploring. She had located the student union on a campus map, and she had her book list printed off from her computer.*

*"Hey, freshman, look out!" someone shouted.*

*Kate was tackled to the ground by a young man only a few years older than her. The breath was knocked out of her lungs, disorienting her enough that she simply stared up at the man above her. He was really hot. His shaggy blond hair matched the faint smattering of freckles along his nose.*

*"Hey there, gorgeous." The man winked at her, then realized he was lying on top of her in the grass. Trapped beneath a beautiful boy.*

*"Oh my God, I'm sorry." He sat up and helped her to her feet. "Sorry, really. I didn't want you to get hit." He nodded toward a group of boys who were throwing a football on the lawn.*

*"I'm just glad I didn't get hit." Kate's face heated as the young man continued to smile at her.*

*"You're a freshman, right?"*

*"Yep. I was on the way to buy my books for the semester." She held up her now crumpled list.*

*"Nice, need help?" he asked with a boyish grin.*

*"Oh . . ." Before she could really answer, he called out a farewell to his friends.*

*Then he took the list from her and examined it. "Abrams, huh?*

*He's nice but tends to ramble a bit," the young man said as he glanced at her schedule.*

*"You've taken his international business transactions course?" Kate asked, excitement filling her.*

*"Yeah, last year. Wait, how did you get into this class? If you're a freshman, you need to have met the prerequisites or get special permission."*

*She couldn't help but preen a little. "My advisor gave me permission based on my Advanced Placement courses from high school."*

*The young man chuckled. "So you're a hot nerd. I like it. I'm Justin." He held out a hand. "Nice to meet you."*

*"I'm Kate." She shook his hand. "So, tell me more about Professor Abrams."*

The memory quivered, the surface rippling as though it were a lake into which someone had cast a stone. As the ripples cleared, Kate blinked and Roan lifted his mouth from hers, their faces a mere breath apart. Where had she just been? She couldn't remember. Whatever she'd been thinking about . . . Had she been thinking about something? There was just a blank space within her mind. What had happened?

Roan's blue eyes glowed, and Kate stared up at him, lost in his gaze.

"You will know no other man but me," Roan said, his voice somewhere between a purr and a growl.

Caught in his trance, Kate traced his lips with her thumb, and he let her explore him as he leaned over her in the fairy bed. He was so beautiful it hurt to look at him. Was this really the same brooding king who had demanded she wait naked for him in his bed? Well, here she was in a bed with him, mostly naked. And all he'd done was kiss her in a way that had changed something within her on a chemical level. Nothing would ever be the same again now that she had tasted him.

Did that mean she was doomed? At that moment, Kate couldn't find it in her to care. Roan kissed her exploring fingers, nipping them gently with his teeth. She shivered as she imagined those teeth nipping other places upon her body.

One of his hands slid down her stomach, gliding beneath the waistband of her panties and she gasped in surprise as his large palm cupped her mound.

"Mine, little pet, all mine," he whispered roughly against her neck before he nibbled on her earlobe. The combination of his touch between her legs and the feel of his teeth biting down on such an erotic place as her earlobe sent jolts of pleasurable fire through body.

"Yes..." she panted as she lifted her hips, encouraging him to touch her more, *to do more.*

One of his fingers feathered over her clit and she squirmed against him. He chuckled, the sound dark and dangerous as he penetrated her slowly with two fingers, stretching her, invading her.

"You're so tight, my darling. Do you have any idea how mad you make me?" he demanded with a seductive growl.

"I do?" she wanted him to keep talking, to hear how she made him feel.

"Yes," Roan said as he brushed his lips over hers again. "Just thinking about pounding into you, stretching you with my cock, making you scream my name...it's enough to create the best sort of madness in a male."

He braced his one arm above her head as he moved his mouth down from her lips to her collarbone, his tongue flicking out against her skin as he continued to thrust his fingers in and out of her. A delicious building need started within her lower belly, like a fire being stoked on a dark night, sending embers and flames sparking to life.

"We shall live out every dark and wonderful fantasy,

little one. You and me," Roan said. "Just like this..." he increased the penetrating rhythm of his fingers, his hand moving so fast that Kate could barely catch her breath until... she simply shot straight over the edge into violently cascading ecstasy. Roan's mouth covered hers, silencing her scream, his tongue invading her lips, fucking her just as his fingers were.

He drew out every twitch, every spasm until her body simply couldn't take another moment of pleasure and she begged him to stop. He slowly withdrew his hand and she watched in hazy fascination as he licked the juices of her arousal of his fingers as though he was tasting the finest honey. Then he lowered his head and kissed her, letting her taste herself upon his lips. Kate melted beneath him, basking in the glow of her climax and the pure enjoyment of kissing Roan as though nothing else in the world could matter.

Above them, a breeze stirred the wisteria, and the scent of sweet night-blooming flowers filled the air. Dusk had given way to night.

"How long have we been kissing?" she asked in a whisper.

Roan gave a rich chuckle. "Not nearly long enough." He kissed her forehead. "Sleep now, and you may face the labyrinth again tomorrow."

His words swept her into a deep, dreamless sleep.

Roan held Kate in his arms until the night turned into a predawn sky. He whispered a spell and forged a crystal on a silver necklace in his palm. Kate's stolen memory slipped from his mind into the crystal, which turned a pale blue. He sat up and placed the necklace around his neck, holding it against his skin. Then he tucked the bedcovers around her.

"Sleep on. Dawn is not here yet," he whispered when she stirred as his departure from the bed.

He walked back to the morgens' pool and knelt by the sleeping kobold who lay by the edge of the pond. He gave the creature a shake, and the kobold roused with a grunt and then swung a fist at his face. Roan only had to move an inch to avoid the blow.

"Manners, kobold," Roan said.

The kobold gasped as he realized who he had just tried to clobber. "My lord!"

"Your name, kobold."

"Um . . . Patch, my lord."

"Listen carefully, Patch. You will continue to accompany Kate in my labyrinth. If you encounter any other dangers, you will summon me at once. Should anything happen to her, you will pay with your life. Is that clear?"

The kobold nodded and swallowed hard. "But I've never been deeper than this, my lord. I don't want to go any farther."

"She saved your life," he reminded the kobold with a dark scowl. "You owe her a life debt. And since she belongs to me, that means you owe *me*, Patch."

Roan hesitated, thinking. He needed to make sure that Kate would be safe and that she would go no deeper within the labyrinth. Over the centuries, the labyrinth had filled with numerous creatures besides those he had set within it. Even he did not know of them all now. To keep his little human safe, he had to keep her away from the heart of the labyrinth. Only he had ever been to its center, and that was very long ago. Kate must be kept away, for her own safety and so that she would fail in her mission. Then, by their bargain, she would belong to him forever.

In order to protect her, he'd start by removing that pool infested with morgens. He'd leave no trace of it behind and he'd kill every bloody beast as he did it. He could not take the chance that Kate would find herself drowing in those dark waters again.

He gave the kobold another stern glare. "You know those outer paths well enough. Keep her on the outskirts. She must not solve the labyrinth."

The kobold nodded. "Y-yes, my lord."

"Good." Roan released the kobold. "Now, go wait for her to wake." He swung an arm to point at the bed behind him. "Remember. She *must not* find the heart of the labyrinth."

# CHAPTER
# EIGHT

*The bride spoke softly to the trees in the dark woods, and creatures answered her call. She was unafraid of the monsters, for in them she saw they only wished to live beneath the stars like her.*

*"Join me," she urged, and the creatures followed her, bound by a magic greater than any other—love.*

—Anon., *Tales from the Twilight Court*

A GENTLE TICKLE ON HER NOSE ROUSED KATE FROM A SLEEP THAT HAD been deeper than the morgens' pool. She scratched her nose and drowsily opened her eyes, only to see a bearded, goblin-like face looming close over her.

She screamed.

"It's only me!" Patch shouted as he pulled back from her.

"Patch! You scared the crap out of me." Kate flopped back down on the bed, staring up at the wisteria as a breeze breathed through the blooms. She still had only her bra and panties on—not her favorite way to sleep—but the bra that Babbitt had made for her was soft and had no irritating underwire to poke her. She was beginning to suspect humans could learn a thing or two from the Fae.

Patch jumped off the bed, muttering darkly.

It took Kate a moment to recall everything that had happened. The attack in the morgen pool, reliving that lost memory of her mother, the way Roan had rescued her, and how he'd carried her to this bed afterward. Then something about losing a memory . . .

She touched her lips with her fingertips, still feeling the ghost of the king's exquisite kisses. He'd tasted of spice and dark hunger. She found herself missing the warmth of his body covering hers and the power of his muscles as he'd gently pinned her down. And the way he'd touched…used his hand to get her off. It had been incredible. He hadn't even asked her to do anything for him in return. He'd just given her pleasure, like Patch had said he would. A romantically selfish Fae? She wanted to laugh at the idea, but she didn't. All she thought of was the way his eyes had darkened as he'd taken care of her wounds, held her in his arms, and then kissed her senseless. If that wasn't romance, what was?

It made her miss more than just his body. It made her miss him, his voice, his words, his very presence. He'd made her feel like she was the only thing that mattered, that nothing else outside of her existed for him. Feeling like she mattered? That was something she could get seriously addicted to.

*I shouldn't miss him.* But she did. *Stupid Stockholm syndrome.*

"Where did Roan go?" she asked as she forced herself to sit up. It was tempting to just lie there in the shade, but time was slipping away from her.

"Gone. You think the king of the dark woods is going to

wait for you to wake up? *Hah!*" Patch plopped to the ground, digging through his satchel, examining his cache of rough gemstones.

"Has anyone told you that you're rude?" Kate asked. She pushed back the covers on the bed and searched for her clothing. Hadn't she left her sweater and jeans by the pool when she'd stripped down?

"Of course I am," Patch shot back. "Got no time for niceties." He glanced away. "Your clothes are over there." He pointed a knotted finger at the foot of the bed.

She found her jeans, sweater, boots, and socks beneath a gold blanket. Everything was dry and folded. She lifted the sweater to smell it cautiously. No scent of lily pads or fish monsters. Roan must have had them cleaned. Probably just snapped his fingers to do it. For a selfish jerk, Roan could be thoughtful, if only for the little things. She got dressed and stared around at the tall walls of the labyrinth.

"Patch, which way was the morgen pool?" she asked, feeling a little distressed that she had lost her way. She'd gotten turned around when Roan had carried her away from the pool, and she had no views of the palace to orient herself.

"Doesn't matter which way it was."

"Why not?"

Patch shot her an irritated look. "Because it's gone, foolish girl. His lordship was most displeased by what those slippery fiends tried to do. He destroyed the pool and killed all of the morgens. Watched him do it myself. That's why it's best to stay on the king's good side."

"Okay . . . so I'm starting from scratch . . . *again.*" She planted her hands on her hips and started forward until she reached a place where there were several paths to choose from.

*Remember, you must search for the heart of the labyrinth, not the other side,* she reminded herself.

Rather than choosing the right, she opted for the second one inward, hoping that it would take her closer to the center. Not that she had any real way of knowing at this point. If she couldn't get an overhead view of the labyrinth, she'd never really see the right path. That realization hit her hard enough to make her chest tight with rising panic. She really had been a fool to think she could solve the labyrinth and find the center. No wonder Roan had given her a month—she'd need every day of it to even get close.

Patch shouldered his bag and followed. "You're going this way too?" she asked.

"Might as well," he said. "There are a few places along the way where I can deliver my gems for retrieval by the palace."

"Oh . . . well, okay." Kate didn't want Patch to know how relieved she was to not be alone in the labyrinth.

As they moved together through the seemingly endless passageways, a sudden fluttering sound above drew their attention. A glittering flock of birds...no wait... those weren't birds, swirled like a murmuration of starlings.

"What are those?"

"Pixies," Patch spat. "Don't say anything. They're always listening. They'll tell the royal court what they hear."

The little creatures danced in the air, shimmering dust drifting down from their hummingbird fast wings. A high pitched cackling sound filled the air as the little pixies chittered wildly. They swooped down, swirling around Kate chanting.

"Kate of the Winslows...Kate of the Winslows..."

Kate, fascinated, peered at their little bodies, seeing the bright green or bright blue skinned little humanoid bodies covered in glimmering iridescent clothes.

"Shoo! Shoo!" Patch leapt up into the air next to Kate, swatting at the little creatures who began to jeer at him.

"Patchy-Patch, the Kobold cat!"

"You said they'd tell the royal court what they hear? Does that mean Roan will hear what they say?" Kate asked Patch who was still angrily swiping at the pixies now clustered around his head.

"Yes, that's exactly what the little beasts will do."

"Excuse me," Kate addressed the pixies. The parade of pixies halted their gleeful torment of Patch and turned her way. "I hear you noble creatures possess the ear of Lord Arun?" she asked them.

The pixies all exchanged curious glances with each other and then began nodding proudly.

"Please kindly tell the king that I'm getting close to solving the Labyrinth. I *will* win."

Clearly excited about this bit of gossip, the pixies swarmed upward into the skies and shot out of sight.

"There, that got them away." Kate laughed as Patch fixed his cap on his head and double checked his gems. "By the way, I thought you said no one could travel through the labyrinth. But the pixies flew through just fine."

Patch scratched his beard before replying. "Pixies and sprites can fly over the labyrinth. For some reason, they aren't controlled by the wards, perhaps its because they aren't loyal to the Seelie or Unseelie. They are neutral."

Neutral. Kate digested that idea. So there were some exceptions with the magic that guarded the labyrinth.

They walked without speaking for a long while. Kate noticed the ivy on the walls thinned out and eventually gave way to stone. Part of the rock turned dark and wet as a light storm passed overhead, and a faintly rotting smell reached her nose.

"Do you smell that?" she asked.

Patch nodded. "There's something dead nearby. Told you, it's a dangerous place."

Kate repressed a shiver. Still, she couldn't turn back. She had to figure this thing out so she and Caden could go home. The more they walked, the darker the path became. The sound of water dripping against the stones was the only accompaniment to their footsteps, which echoed endlessly against the rock walls.

"I suppose . . . I suppose I should thank you," the kobold said as they rounded another bend.

Kate turned to him in shock.

"Don't look so surprised! You saved my life. It's only right."

Kate laughed at how utterly displeased he sounded by that admission. She stopped and Patch stopped walking as they faced each other. Kate smiled at him.

"You're welcome, Patch. You're my only friend here, and I didn't want you to drown."

"Friend?" He eyed her skeptically.

"Yeah. Friend," Kate said.

"Huh," said Patch. "So what's that going to cost me?"

Kate frowned. "Cost?"

Patch rummaged in his pouch. "Everything's got a price. I reckon I have a stone here I could part with. Not one of the best ones, mind you."

Kate chuckled. "Friendship is something you *give*, not buy. If you have to buy it, it's not worth anything."

"Now that just makes no kind of sense," said Patch, shaking his head. "Everything worth having costs *something*."

A distant rumble ahead of them caused Patch to grip Kate's arm and jerk her to a halt.

"*Wait*," he whispered.

She leaned down to hear him better. "What is it?"

"Rocks . . . that's rocks tumbling. You know what that

means." Patch's dark eyes scanned the passage ahead of them, focused on something she didn't see.

"You know full well I don't know what that means," Kate replied, her voice still low. "So tell me."

"Trolls." Patch scratched his bearded chin. "Must be trolls."

*Trolls?* Kate's stomach knotted in fear. What had Patch said? Be fast and avoid getting hit by clubs or something? She could be fast. Sure. That was something she could do.

"Let's see if we can slip around them," said Patch.

Kate tried to hide her dread as Patch led the way forward, Kate following as they ran into a forked pathway.

"Left or right?" she asked, her chest tight as she weighed her options. Left seemed quiet, safe. It was a sunlit path with smooth walls. The right path, however, shook with the tumble of rocks against one another and seemed far less welcoming by the way the walls of the labyrinth here had turned jagged and sharp-looking.

"Well, left, obviously," Patch said.

Kate breathed out slowly, letting herself calm and follow her instincts.

*Assume nothing in the labyrinth is what it seems . . .*

An idea grew in her mind. If *she* had a labyrinth, she would guard the path that led to the heart of the puzzle with the most dangerous creatures. The safer path would keep leading the person around in circles or back out.

"Left, then?" Patch prompted.

"No." She turned toward the left path with a wave of her hand. "That's what *he* wants. To keep me stuck at the edges of this thing forever." Well, she wasn't going to fall for it. "We go right."

"*Toward* the trolls? Don't be stupid, girl." Patch started to walk in the other direction, but she grabbed his arm and pulled him back to her side.

"I'm not scared of trolls." She'd had her social media accounts targeted by mean girls when she was in high school. From what she remembered of her mother's stories, there were various kinds of trolls, and these definitely weren't of the mean-girl internet variety. The ones she remembered from the tales lived under bridges and ate goats. Surely these trolls couldn't be worse than the morgens?

THEY WERE *MUCH WORSE*, AS IT TURNED OUT.

Kate and Patch huddled behind a large boulder as five massive trolls, each more than twelve feet tall with gray skin, slung stones at a sixth that was crouched against the wall opposite where Kate and Patch were hiding. The labyrinth had opened up into a wide-open space filled with piles of rocks that formed tall, unstable-looking towers of stones.

"Why are they hurting that other troll?" she asked Patch. They kept their heads down and peered through a crack between two boulders to watch the trolls.

The kobold studied the trolls for a moment. "That one's a runt, smaller than the rest. Trolls are a bit judgmental about things like that."

"A *bit*?"

The trolls were massive, thickly muscled, with round heads and black eyes. They wore leather vests and trousers, and their skin looked like it was covered with a layer of silvery fur. A few had small pairs of horns jutting from their temples.

"We might be able to get around them if we go now." Patch pushed at Kate's hip, trying to get her to move. They had a chance to escape if they stayed on the narrow path between the boulders. Kate moved along the path, peering between the stones every few steps to keep her eyes on the trolls. She saw the smaller troll fall to its knees, covering its head from the blows of the others as they threw massive rocks. She was pretty sure the others were laughing.

*They* are *mean girls,* thought Kate.

A flash of memory shot across Kate's mind. She was crouched in the corner of her bedroom, listening to Sandra complain about her to her father. Sandra had never hit her, but she'd been as cruel with her words as the stones these trolls were throwing. A stab of pain in Kate's chest made her stop. She couldn't just leave. If she had the power to stop someone from getting hurt, she wasn't going to just run away.

She caught Patch's shoulder and whispered to him. She nodded to the place where the labyrinth walls seemed to narrow in the direction they'd been moving. "Meet me at the far end of the pass."

"All right," Patch said, then halted. "Wait—what?" The kobold whirled back to face her.

"*Go,*" she hissed. Before she could talk herself out of this really stupid idea, she crawled between the two nearest boulders to a place where the trolls could see her.

Then she shouted at the top of her lungs, "Hey! Pick on someone your own size!"

The trolls slowly turned around, some still holding hefty rocks.

*Yep, that was stupid. Really stupid.* Why had she said that?

"What did you say?" one of the trolls ground out in a slow, gravelly voice.

Kate's gaze shot across the group of trolls, and suddenly she had an idea.

"I said, '*Pick on someone your own size.*'" She pointed at one of the other trolls in the group that had been throwing stones at the smallest troll. "Someone like him."

The troll in question looked shocked, wondering why he had been singled out. The other trolls seemed just as confused.

"Why him?" asked one troll.

"She said because he's our own size," said another.

"Yeah, but I'm taller than him," the first one pointed out.

"And I'm wider," said another.

"Well, what about him?" asked Kate, pointing out a different troll.

"Naw, he's not my size either," said the first.

"He is my size," said the fourth.

"Yeah, but you're twins, ain't ya?" said the first.

At least they had stopped throwing rocks at the small troll. The problem was, if Kate didn't think of something fast, they might start throwing rocks at *her* instead.

Then a thought occurred to her. If these trolls lived in the labyrinth, perhaps Roan had some control or influence over them. What if they lived here at his command? It was worth a shot.

Kate crouched down and slipped Roan's silvery dagger from her boot, then held it up.

"By the command of Lord Arun, I order you to fight each other."

One of the trolls growled, the sound like thunder, as he weighed the stone he held in his hand.

*Shit . . . this isn't going to work.*

"Lord Arun?" one of the trolls grunted at the leader.

"Yes, it is Lord Arun's command that you leave that troll alone and fight each other. May the best troll win. He promises a prize to the victor!"

*Please . . . please . . . please fall for it,* she begged silently.

The leader growled again. "What kind of prize?"

"Um . . . it's a surprise! The best kind of prize!" Kate lied.

Another slow growl. "We must hold council," the leader replied. He and the other trolls slowly moved to form a circle.

Kate didn't wait for them to decide what to do. They'd just given her an opportunity to act, and she wasn't going to waste it. She ran around them to reach the fallen troll. The poor creature was leaning against the labyrinth wall, its head still covered with its hands. When she touched the creature's shoulder, it flinched.

"Hey, it's okay. I'm not going to hurt you. You need to come with me while they're distracted." She shook the troll's hefty arm.

The beast turned a bruised face toward her, one eye swollen shut, the other staring at her in confusion.

"Oh God . . . They really hurt you, didn't they?" Kate murmured as she rubbed the troll's arm. The fur beneath her hand was as soft as silk. "Listen, I'm trying to help you. But we need to move. Now." Kate pointed in the direction she wanted to go with her dagger. Patch waved at her frantically, jumping up and down.

"Who are you?" the troll asked.

"I'm Kate," Kate whispered to the troll. "Please, come with me. Hurry!"

The troll's unswollen eye fixed on the shiny dagger in Kate's hand.

"Lord Arun wishes me to go with you?"

"Yes," Kate lied. But she wanted to believe that Lord Arun would have wanted to save this poor creature if he had been here. He was a dark Fae, sure, but Patch had said that *dark* didn't mean *evil*. It just meant his powers came from the night, from the moon. He wanted to protect his realm and all the creatures in it from the Seelie, so it only made sense he'd want to protect them from each other too, right?

*I'm probably just trying to make excuses for him.*

The small troll got to its feet and staggered a few steps. It was perhaps only eight or so feet tall, far smaller than the trolls that had been attacking it.

"Magda," the troll rasped, her voice softer than the others. "I am Magda."

"You're a girl?" Kate asked as the ring of trolls still held their council.

"Yes."

"A girl troll. That's cool." She held out a hand to Magda. "Let's get you out of here."

Magda and Kate hurried away, reaching a frantic Patch at the end of the long passageway just as the trolls finished their discussion and turned around. The beasts clearly expected to find Kate still standing where she had been. One scratched his head in bafflement before another spotted Kate and Magda, who were now quite a good distance from the group of trolls.

"Here, squeeze through here!" Patch pointed at the narrow rock walls on either side, which formed a somewhat covered roof with a small bit of light breaking through above them. "They won't be able to follow us through here."

Kate saw the trolls in the distance, lifting rocks to throw in their direction. If they didn't get deep enough into this pass, those rocks might hit them.

Magda watched Kate with dark, worried eyes.

"Take Magda with you, Patch. I'll be right behind you," Kate said, encouraging Magda to go. She stood and faced the trolls, who were slowly lumbering toward them. From here, she caught a glimpse of the distant palace above the trolls' heads.

*How did I miss that?*

"What are you doing, girl?" Patch snapped. "Do you have rocks for brains?"

The kobold's shout shook her out of her thoughts.

The ground shook from the herd of trolls heading their way. Kate raced behind Patch and Magda through the slender passage between the walls. The trolls hurled rocks at them, which shattered over the top of the narrow passage, causing debris to rain down.

"Keep running!" Kate shouted at the kobold and troll ahead of her.

A fragment of one of the smaller rocks that burst above them struck Kate's temple in a glancing but painful blow. Kate stumbled, trying to catch herself on the side of the passageway walls as her vision blurred and an intense wave of pain washed through her body.

Magda turned back, her dark eyes searching for Kate in the dim light.

"Kate? Where are you?" Magda called out.

"Here. I'm . . . *here*." Kate tried to breathe through the pain in her skull, but it was difficult. She reached up to touch the side of her head, and her fingers met a warm, sticky liquid.

Blood.

Kate stared at her fingertips. Head wounds usually were superficial, but they bled a lot, right? *Please, God, let that be true . . . because I don't feel that good.*

"Kate, are you okay?" Magda asked.

"Yes, I'm fine." Kate knew it was a lie, but she had to get a little farther inside, make sure it was safe for her friends before she sat down to rest.

Magda took Kate's hand as they moved deeper into the tunnel, deeper into the dark. She was thankful to hold Magda's hand and for a short while to feel that she wasn't alone, or that someone besides the grumpy kobold might care about her.

"Be quiet, both of you," Patch whispered somewhere up in front of her. Kate stared into the gloom, trying to spot the kobold. She thought she could make out his dark form just ahead.

The sky vanished above, and they entered a cave-like passageway. No sunlight broke through here.

"It's too dark," Kate said. "We can't go forward without a light. Is this one of the mines your brothers work in, Patch?"

"No, this is something different. Something I've never seen before." Patch stopped and faced Kate and the troll. "I don't know where we are now . . . Maybe she knows." He pointed a knobby finger at Magda.

Magda looked around and then slowly tilted her head back to look up at the ceiling. Her thick lips parted as she pointed at faint silvery swirls that covered the ceiling. Kate, her head aching, stared at them in confusion. The silvery lines glowed faintly. What would cause something like that? Nothing Kate knew of. But then again, this world had different rules, as well as creatures and mysteries that she could spend a lifetime studying.

"The Crystal Cave," Magda whispered, her voice quivering. Kate squeezed the troll's callused hand.

"Is something bad in here?" She offered Magda her dagger. "You can take this if it will make you feel safe."

"No. No danger." The troll shook her head, and her faintly silver fur shimmered in a way not unlike the light above them. Magda wasn't at all what Kate had expected trolls to look like.

"Patch, do you know what the Crystal Cave is?" Kate asked.

Patch nodded slowly, as if in wonder. "The only Crystal Cave I know is a place where a wizard was born. But that place was never in the labyrinth. It was . . . by the sea."

"A wizard?"

"Aye, but not just any wizard, *the* wizard. He found himself here. Or there. Whatever. He was one of you, in a way, but something more." Patch sounded almost reverent. "He had enough power to challenge King Bahden in the great wizard war."

"The wizard war?" She remembered Patch telling her something about Roan's father and how he'd stolen Queen Guinevere from her world. "Wait . . . you don't mean *Merlin*, do you?"

"Do not speak his name," Patch hissed in warning.

"Why not?" Kate whispered. Her head was still throbbing painfully.

"Because you might wake him."

"Wake who? Merlin?" This time she whispered the name.

Patch growled in frustration. "Have you read no tales of him in your world, girl?"

"That was a thousand years ago. He would have to be dead now."

"Nothing here that dies stays dead. And certainly not wizards with his power. He sleeps on the isle of Avalon, which is partly in your world, partly in ours."

"He's sleeping?" Kate asked.

"At the foot of the bed where King Arthur rests. Close your eyes, girl. If this is the Crystal Cave, the legends say you can hear him breathe."

Kate closed her eyes, feeling very foolish, but then she let out a breath and let her mind wander. The pain in her skull began to fade.

Then she heard it. A breath that was not her own or Patch's or Magda's. And then, within the darkness of her mind, a vision slowly bloomed before her. She saw a man with golden hair lying on a bed covered with a red velvet mantle. The man held a single white lily, whose petals shimmered in the light. Sitting upon the floor, head resting against the stone foot of the bed, was an older man with silver hair and a long silver beard. He wore robes the color of midnight, and faint silvery stars shimmered in the fabric. The man breathed in and out, and the air in Kate's lungs seemed briefly to match the old man's.

"Did you see?" Patch whispered, and the vision vanished.

Kate blinked and opened her eyes. "Could you see it too?" she asked.

"No, but I've been told mortals can . . . mortals, the Seelie and Unseelie. They all have a connection to Arthur and to the wizard, because both were born with the royal Fae in their blood. I guess these are the caves after all."

"Is . . . is Mer—the wizard bad? I always thought he and Arthur were good."

"Are they? Maybe. The Seelie think the Unseelie are bad. Are they? Sometimes good and bad depend on who is left to tell the stories. But I suppose Arthur might be as close to good as a mortal can get . . ." Patch said slowly, as if trying to figure out how best to explain this. "But it isn't time for him to wake yet. Your king . . . Arthur, he is the once and future king. We are not in the future yet, we are in the present."

"But isn't every minute of the present once the future?" Kate couldn't help but ask.

Patch narrowed his eyes. "Aye, but that isn't what I mean. Just leave him to rest. You have enough to worry about, don't you? You want to save your brother and go home. Waking the wizard and the golden king . . . Well, that wouldn't do you much good. Just stir up a lot of stuff best left *unstirred* for now."

"Oh . . ." Kate had secretly started to wonder if perhaps Merlin could send her home, but maybe Patch was right.

Kate touched the damp cave walls and felt a gentle breeze track through the tunnel. She smelled the scent of rain or near rain in the air. It was hard to describe, but it was . . . soothing, enticing. It smelled a little like Roan.

"You smell that?" she asked the others. "I smell rain, I

think." She gently released Magda's hand and walked deeper into the cave, following the thick silvery trails as stalagmites and stalactites formed a latticework pattern in the tunnel. They had just enough light now that their eyes adjusted to keep moving.

"Rain? What rain?" Patch scrambled to follow her, loose rocks sliding beneath his feet. "Wait, girl, wait!"

But Kate wasn't waiting. She smelled petrichor, the scent of rain-soaked soil. It was the smell of a place that humans could live in and grow crops in and only humans could smell it. She'd learned that in some science class years ago.

She grinned as she continued to follow the slowly glowing trails of light as they grew brighter and brighter. She slipped through a small gap and stepped into a vast opening that was as big as a football field. Beautiful crystals grew out of the stones everywhere. But it was the thousands of glowing lights around and above her that made her suck in a breath in awe. The world glowed blue and green like a thousand stars in the night sky.

"Beautiful . . ." Magda spoke behind Kate.

"Yes," Kate agreed. "Beautiful." She walked deeper into the cave and stared at the pulsing lights. She got a glimpse of one of the stars up close and she laughed. It was no star.

"These are glowworms," she whispered to Patch and Magda.

"Worms, eh?" Patch grumbled. "They good eating?"

"Probably not. They are a bit like fireflies. I've never seen them in real life." She swayed a little on her feet.

"Kate need rest," Magda said. "Kate is bleeding." The troll tried to catch her arm.

"I'm fine, really." Kate waved Magda away, but she wavered and the pain in her head grew stronger. Magda caught her, then lifted her up in her arms and carried her.

Kate felt too weak and too tired to protest. Her head lolled back as she looked up into the night sky of glowworm stars. Had Roan ever been here? Had he ever seen this? Kate wished he had. It was one of the most incredible things she'd ever seen. And she could just picture how his blue eyes would reflect the stunning light. Surely he knew about it. He was a king, after all, and this was his labyrinth.

"We have to summon the king." Patch's voice sounded so far away now.

*Roan . . . Roan could help me . . .* Kate's thoughts danced in a circle within her head, spinning out and back inward until little else made sense except that she wanted Roan to come.

Kate stared at the beauty of the stars above her as they slowly vanished into darkness.

"She's fading . . ."

CHAPTER

# NINE

*The dark woods were full of strange and wonderful creatures, like the dryads who sang to trees to make them grow and the dwarves who dwelt in the Black Hills in their palace of Vol Buldohr, where they whispered incantations over their treasures of gold.*

—Anon., *Tales from the Twilight Court*

ROAN KNELT ON THE GROUND, THE TIP OF HIS SWORD BURIED IN THE fire-blackened earth as he stared helplessly at the dying dryad before him. The beautiful creature's tawny eyes were filled with unspeakable pain.

Roan, Hagni, and a group of Unseelie Shadow Guards had traveled to the woods just moments ago from the palace and had come upon the destroyed forest and the massacre of the dryads. Fires set by Seelie warriors were still burning and caught upon the wind, blowing embers over the ruined landscape. But none of that mattered right now. All that mattered was the lone surviving dryad before him.

Lady Kyma, the queen of the dryads, had skin the color of night and hair like snow. She was an ally, a *friend*, and Roan was going to do all he could to save her.

He gathered the ancient soil in his hand and settled it in Kyma's palm, closing her trembling fingers over the soil. He opened his mind, body, and soul to the magic in his blood. His hand shook as grief and rage warred within him, and he wasn't sure which emotion would conquer him.

"Save my sisters . . ." Lady Kyma begged, her gaze starting to drift into the distance.

"They are gone," Roan whispered. "You are the last, my lady." He could barely speak the words that cut like broken glass as they left his lips. The truth, *this truth*, above all others, was one he wished was a lie.

He didn't dare take his gaze away from the dying dryad. If he did, he would be forced to look once more upon the charred remains of the noble trees that had formed the dark woods. Trees that held power and secrets too old to name. Trees that deserved to grow beneath the moonlight and give life to the fauna within.

At the base of those wrecked trunks lay the broken bodies of Kyma's sisters, the other dryads of the dark woods. Beautiful tree spirits who had caused no harm to anyone, even though they dwelt in the land of the Unseelie. If Roan dared to face that destruction again, his rage would take over and he would not be able to save Kyma's life.

*I must save her. She is the last of her people, the last dryad of the dark woods.*

Kyma's gaze returned to his as he clutched her soil-filled hand and brought it to his lips. Roan wove a healing spell with the ancient tongue of the *Sidhe*, giving her what he could of himself and his power. The energy flowed into her, seeking out the places where she was wounded. The burns, the cuts . . . so many wounds. It was nothing less than barbarism.

"Let me join my sisters, Roan." Kyma's once musical voice was now a rasp of sound.

"*No*," Roan growled as he clenched Kyma's fingers tighter.

His magic burned within his chest, that light and healing energy pushing outward. "You must fight. You must survive. Without you, the forest is truly lost." How could she not know what she meant to his realm? That her light, her beauty, her *spirit* were worth fighting for? If she lived, the trees could grow again, the forest could thrive, but without her . . . the land would remain nothing but the ashes of trees and the bones of her sisters.

Roan held her hand as he softened his tone. "You're my friend, and I will not surrender you to death."

Kyma's eyes widened. She was seeing the shine he so rarely let others see as his power grew alongside his strong emotions. She gasped and the strength in her grip deepened as she drew in a strong breath. Roan pushed more of his magic into the dryad's body until he was sure she was out of danger.

Kyma's lips twitched as though she wanted to smile but was still too weak. "You wouldn't let me die."

He brushed his thumb soothingly over her fingertips. "No, my lady. Your king commands you to live on and to one day regrow your beautiful forest."

"Then I will do my best, Lord Arun," Kyma sighed, the sound like the wind passing gently through the foliage of her forest.

It took Roan a moment to catch his breath after having used up so much of his power to save her. He would regain his strength soon enough once the moon rose.

He called for his trusted guard. "Hagni!"

"My lord." Hagni, who had stepped back to give Roan and Lady Kyma their space, now rejoined him, his face grave.

"We must take her directly to Andvari. He will be able to keep her close to the dark woods so that she may heal." Roan looked at the burned woods and what was left of her forest. Perhaps with time Kyma would find a way to grow great trees once more and rebuild the forest. And if trees grew . . . then new dryads would be born, and she would no longer be alone. He would do all that he could to help her.

"Yes, my lord."

Hagni came to Kyma's side and crouched down by her. "May I carry you, my lady?" he asked.

Kyma managed a nod, and Hagni raised her up in his arms. Roan pulled his sword from the soil as he stood, weary from his efforts. At last he turned to face the destruction, his heart shattering at the loss of such innocence.

Roan then turned his gaze toward the Seelie lands.

"Culan," he whispered into the wind. "You burned my beautiful dark woods. You murdered the dryads who cared for them. You will pay for your crimes, *cousin*."

His cousin's hunger for power, his jealous desire to destroy whatever he could not possess, was so unlike the other Seelie. Yes, the Seelie and Unseelie spent much time fighting, but even Roan had to admit that the Morning Court Fae were not without honor and decency. Most of them, anyway.

The Fae, while they lusted for pleasures and beauty, had far less obsession with destruction and power. That was a human trait. Culan, however, was almost *human* in his greed. He was far too much like Roan's father, Bahden, a king obsessed with power and territory. He had dreamed of ruling the humans by possessing their queen, Guinevere. Thankfully, he'd been stopped, but only the Unseelie had been punished for Bahden's greed. Now it seemed the Seelie were at the mercy of Culan, and they were likely unprepared to deal with the consequences of the war he was about to start. Roan swallowed a snarl of rage, knowing that his lands and his creatures would suffer because of his foolish cousin.

He and Hagni made the journey on foot into the Black Hills, flanked by the Shadow Guards. In time, they arrived at the entrance to Vol Buldohr, the underground palace of the dwarves. While they could have traveled by the Fae roads, it was considered rude to appear without warning upon the dwarves' doorstep. The obsidian entrance to Vol Buldohr was heavily guarded, but when the dwarves realized who approached, they rushed to open the tall gates to allow them entrance.

A male dwarf in golden robes greeted them. "Greetings, Lord Arun." He bore the mark of the royal dwarvish advisor to Lord Andvari, the king of the dwarves.

"Tell Lord Andvari I must speak with him at once. We have a guest in need of sanctuary."

"Of course. Follow me." The bearded dwarf rushed down the long hall, his golden robes flowing behind him. The court of the dwarves was far quieter and emptier than the Twilight Court. Dwarves, by nature, preferred to busy themselves with the making and keeping of their treasures and did not care for political intrigue as the *Sidhe* did.

No one dared to challenge Roan in his own court. He was the strongest of the Fae, and his bloodline had ruled upon the Unseelie throne for several thousand years.

The vizier led them to the throne room, where a broad-shouldered, muscular dwarf sat upon a white marble throne. Unlike many of the dwarves around him, who wore the court robes of Vol Buldohr, he wore a tunic with a silver belt around his waist that bore the hilt of a broadsword. Several others were gathered around him, speaking in hushed tones. Many carried battle-axes and were likely the dwarf soldiers that most often conducted patrols. Roan wagered that Andvari had just learned of the attack on the dark woods.

The advisor pushed between the soldiers and spoke to the dwarf on the throne. Darric Andvari, the king of the Black Hills, swept his light-brown eyes over the room until he spotted Roan. Andvari's dark hair, streaked with gray, was pulled back at the base of his neck, and a smattering of gold beads threaded his beard.

The dwarf bowed his head. "Lord Arun. I understand you are here bearing grave tidings, old friend."

Roan nodded. "Lord Andvari. I see you've just been told of the attack on the dark woods."

"Yes, we heard of the attack too late to assist them." Andvari's eyes were bright with a rage that came from the dwarves' innate dislike of injustice. They were a people who placed value on rules and order. They had always adhered to the treaties between the Seelie and the Unseelie, and the attack on the dryads would be seen as a declaration of war.

Andvari's gaze then strayed past Roan to the dryad Hagni held in his arms.

"Lady Kyma!" Andvari gasped and rushed past Roan to the dryad. "I did not know you survived!"

"Andvari, it is time," Kyma whispered. "You must tell Lord Arun…" The dryad raised a hand to touch the dwarf's bearded face with an affection born of centuries of their people living as neighbors. Andvari's eyes glistened with tears.

"Lady Kyma is very weak," Roan said softly. "I must ask that you shelter her here so she may be close to her woods— what's left of them," Roan said.

Without looking away from Kyma, Andvari nodded his consent. "Yes, of course." Andvari called one of his servants to send for their best healers and asked Hagni to carry Kyma to a bedchamber to rest. The Shadow Guards escorted Hagni and the dryad away.

Now that Andvari and Roan were alone in the throne room, the dwarf closed his weary eyes and rubbed them.

"You believe it was Culan and his guards, don't you?"

Roan nodded. "We found one dead Seelie warrior. His tunic bore Culan's royal crest. Culan's discontent is growing. He is pushing at our boundaries. I fear you may be next." Culan would have to pass through Andvari's hills to launch any attack upon the Unseelie court. If he captured Vol Buldohr, he would have a staging ground to keep his men rested and fed and somewhat protected from attack by an Unseelie army.

Andvari looked around his throne room as a heavy sigh escaped him. It had been more than fifteen hundred years in the land of the humans since the Seelie and Unseelie had been truly at war.

"If we face war, it will be unlike any war we've seen before. Culan has made it clear that he would see our lands turned to ash if he cannot control us himself . . . You will need something to stop him," the dwarf said.

Roan gave a wry smile. "Do you think I'm not powerful enough to face Culan in battle?"

Andvari's lips twitched. "We both know you are ruthless and the power you wield hasn't been seen in a *Sidhe* Fae in more than seven millennia." The dwarf hesitated before continuing. "But Culan is hungry for power like your father was. That greed can make someone desperate, and desperate Fae are far more dangerous. Also, you carry too much of your mother in you. For an Unseelie king, you have too much heart . . . too much mercy." Andvari lightly squeezed Roan's arm and smiled.

"You wound me to say such things, my friend. I am a black-hearted king." Roan chuckled, knowing the dwarf's words carried too much truth to them. He had inherited his mother's magic and he was cursed with her compassion, and his father had despised him for it. To Bahden, empathy was a weakness that could be exploited.

"What will you do if you face Culan?" Andvari asked.

"I will do what I must," Roan said simply. He was not afraid to kill to protect his lands or his people, but he didn't like to think about how many others would die when he and Culan faced each other on a battlefield.

"Then I will trust you with something that Lady Kyma wishes me to show you. Come." Andvari led Roan out of the throne room and down an empty corridor. He removed a golden medallion from around his neck and pressed the medallion into the surface of a carved piece of one of the stones in the wall. After a moment, the stones broke apart with a soft whoosh of air to reveal a doorway. The room was filled with towers of gold coins and treasures too great to count.

Andvari led Roan to a black marble pedestal, atop which was a box made of a dark silver-black metal that Roan recognized came from the heart of a star that had fallen to the earth.

Andvari passed his hands over the symbols carved into the surface of the metal in a pattern that seemed to make sense only to him. With a soft click, the box lid opened. Inside, a ring of black onyx sat upon a pile of gold dust.

"Only use it in the final hours, if you must. To wear it is to die," Andvari warned him.

"How does it work?"

"You will know when you put it on." The dwarf king produced a slender black leather pouch and folded it around the ring to safely tuck it inside without touching it.

"Tell no one of this, Roan. *No one.*" He gave Roan the pouch. "It was forged under a black moon's light."

Shock tore through Roan at the dwarf's actions. "The black moon? You dared to make a weapon in such a way?"

The black moon was the one night when the moon's power changed, during a lunar eclipse. In those times, the realm of the Fae was covered in true darkness. Enchantments made on such a night were far more powerful, but they always carried a great and terrible curse.

Andvari's broad shoulders sagged. "The day I ascended the throne, Lady Kyma came to me in a dream, telling me that I must make this. She warned me that the peace I would build could be destroyed if I did not offer the Unseelie king a weapon to protect us all. She spoke of you, old friend. I made this ring in secret, alone in my private forge. Lady Kyma somehow knew it would come to this."

Roan wanted to push the cursed ring back at his friend.

"Keep it. Defeat Culan however you must," Andvari insisted. "For Lady Kyma's sake, for all the others who will die if he is not stopped. It may be that only a great sacrifice will stop him."

Roan closed his fingers tight around the black leather pouch and thought of Kate lying dead, Culan standing over her . . . an innocent even among innocents. He gave a shake of his head, trying to dispel the terrible vision, and focused on the matter at hand.

"You will see that Kyma's sisters are properly buried? And do what you can to protect the surviving trees?"

Andvari nodded. "We will. If we come under attack, I will light the beacons. Tell your guards in the palace to watch for them."

Roan nodded. The spells around the labyrinth prevented messages from being sent between the palace, the dark woods, and the Black Hills. Only the pixies could travel across the labyrinth unaffected by the vast network of enchantments, but

Roan was not about to put the fate of his kingdom at risk by trusting pixies.

If Culan came for the Twilight Court, he would have to pass through the dark woods and the Black Hills on his way north. Then he would have to contend with the labyrinth. The labyrinth's enchantments prevented flight over it, but all the same, Roan didn't trust those safeguards alone. If Culan was determined to attack the Twilight Court, he would find a way, a hole in the labyrinth's defenses. No Unseelie would sleep easy for a while, least of all Roan.

His thoughts turned to Kate again, and her brother. Caden was safe in the palace under Eudora and Rath's watchful eyes. Kate was in the labyrinth with Patch to keep her out of trouble. In some ways, she was safer there than at the palace because Culan would come to the palace directly and avoid the labyrinth if he could. But if he couldn't . . .

Roan bid Andvari goodbye.

Hagni and his men left Vol Buldohr and resumed their patrols on the borderlands. Roan once more took to his owl form as he flew back to the palace. Warm air carried him higher, but then a distant cry from the depths of the labyrinth reached his tufted ears.

"Lord Arun?"

Roan dove toward the labyrinth, seeking Kate, but she was hidden from his view.

He reached out to Kate and searched for that ever-growing connection between him and the mortal woman.

*"Where are you?"* he asked. *"Show me."*

The whisper came back along the pathway that connected them, and he felt a power that stiffened his feathers like no other. Only one place affected him like that, a place that moved constantly in the labyrinth. The Crystal Cave. It was a place between worlds, half in his, half in Kate's. Great power was trapped within the crystals of that cave, which bled out into its pools. It was not a safe place for Kate without him there to protect her.

Roan flew faster, tracking the magic in his mind until he found the cave's entrance. He landed before the dark opening and returned to his true form. The connection to Kate was growing stronger. She was unwell, he could feel it. Her pain beat at his skull like the drums of war. The sound of his boots echoed as he walked down the glowing tunnel until it gave way to a vast cave. He halted at the sight that met him.

Patch sat upon the ground, hands knotted in his brown cap, his wrinkled face strained with concern as a small female troll cradled an unconscious Kate in her arms. Blood soaked Kate's hair by her temple.

*No . . .*

Culan couldn't have found her, not here, not in the safety of the labyrinth. It wasn't possible . . . The faces of the dead dryads blurred in his mind with Kate's, and his knees suddenly threatened to give out.

She'd been hurt, his Kate . . . The cave shuddered around them, rocks cracking above and below, as rage filled his blood.

Roan grabbed Patch and lifted the kobold in the air. "What have you done?" Patch tried to respond but couldn't get any words out as Roan shook him. "You little *fool*!" Roan snarled. "I'll kill you and every kobold who's ever breathed your name—"

"Lord Arun," the troll interrupted, her voice tremulous. "I am to blame. Kate is brave. Kate saved *me*."

Roan dropped the kobold with a thud, and Patch scampered away, cap still clutched in his hands. Roan turned to the troll, his temper still roiling. His hands itched to touch Kate, but he had to calm down first or his magic could harm rather than heal her.

"Tell me what has happened, troll." Roan crouched down in front of the creature, who held Kate protectively in her arms.

In a slow but competent tale, the troll explained how Kate had rescued her, and their flight from the other trolls. She explained how Kate had been struck by a rock, but that they couldn't stop moving until they were safely away from the danger of the other trolls. That was how they'd ended up in the Crystal Cave.

So Culan hadn't found her. Roan felt he could breathe again, but only just. Kate had been hurt. He had told that damned Patch to keep her near the outer sections of the labyrinth away from all of the dangers that existed deeper within.

"Give her to me," Roan said, holding out his arms. He was calmer now and ready to heal her.

The troll handed Kate to him. Roan brushed the hair back from Kate's face, then glanced around to ensure they were alone. He was still weak from healing Lady Kyma and would need to use the healing magic of the crystal pools instead. There was a pool just across the cavern. Roan stood and carried Kate to the water. This water was safe, untouched by dangerous creatures, and it glowed softly with bioluminescent swirls that came from the silk webs of glowworms, which dripped into the water. The healing magic was, in part, due to these tiny glowing creatures.

He cradled Kate's head and lowered her wound beneath the surface of the water. Dried blood softened around the injury, and soon the blood swirled away as the water healed the spot. It took Roan a long moment to calm himself, and be reassured that she would be all right. That was twice now that he had almost lost her, and both times he'd been so desperate to rescue her.

"Why do you matter so much?" he whispered to the unconscious woman.

He received no answer. He knew only that the moment he had crashed into her world and into her arms, he'd been forever changed. And he was a creature who was *never* supposed to change.

"Wake up, little one." He bent his head to press his lips to hers. He let some of his own magic escape in that kiss, unable to control himself.

Kate's lashes fluttered open. She gazed around in confusion. Her brown eyes were still cloudy, but they grew brighter as she continued to heal in his arms. For a moment, he was lost in the soft, warm color.

"Roan?"

His body tightened at the way she spoke his name. Roan pulled her even closer in his arms, tucking her against his chest.

"I have you," he promised. "I have you, Kate."

Kate's head was foggy as she gazed up at Roan's concerned face. His electric-blue eyes reflected the shimmer of the cave's light, making him look more ethereal than ever. Where was she? Her head throbbed, but the pain slowly began to fade. Dizziness hit her momentarily before it too slowed down and she could focus without getting sick. She took in the cave and the cold sensation of being wet.

She was cradled in Roan's arms, his body wonderfully warm compared to the cold water. This was a dream, wasn't it? This wasn't the Roan who had forced her into the labyrinth to save her brother. This Roan was keeping her safe. She wanted to wrap herself around him and enjoy being held like this. She wouldn't drift away again, not so long as he held her in his arms. But then she came back to herself as he moved her body in a slow spin in the water with him. This wasn't a dream. This was real. And she was really wet. *Again.*

"Why are we in the water?" she asked. "There aren't any morgens here, are there?"

Roan chuckled. "No. These are healing pools."

"Thank God . . . You know, this labyrinth of yours keeps trying to kill me," Kate grumbled.

"You, little human, were never supposed to get this deep into my labyrinth. Instead, you somehow were injured saving a troll, or so I am told."

"Oh! Magda!" She tried to get out of the pool. Was Magda okay? The last thing she remembered was being in the cave and the troll calling her name in fear.

"No, no. Not yet, little one. You still need to heal."

"But Magda was hurt."

"*Your* injuries were far greater. Don't you *ever* worry about yourself?" Roan asked. "It is no wonder that your family thinks little of you. You don't demand it of them." He got out of the pool carrying her, and Kate fought her instinct to try to get free. Roan holding her felt too nice. And she did feel woozy . . .

"I think about myself all the time," she argued. "And my family *does* care . . ."

"There should be no lies between us, little mortal. And we both know *that* is a lie."

"You can be such a jerk," Kate muttered. Every time he mentioned her family, it felt like a slap, but deep down she feared he might be right. Only Caden cared about her, and that was because he was a little kid who didn't know better. Sandra hadn't corrupted him into forgetting Kate existed. Yet.

The Fae king's lips twitched, but his expression was still stern.

"I am not the king of niceties, Kate. I am king of all that is dark and wonderful."

She looked up into his face. "What does that mean? All that is dark and wonderful?" She still couldn't understand the things he said sometimes even if his words sounded beautiful enough to make her heart ache for things so far out of her reach.

"What does that mean?" Roan smiled, the expression dangerous. "It means that every forbidden desire, every sinful dream, *every* willful thought you've ever had . . . I can grant." He chuckled. "Tonight you will think of no one except yourself . . . and me."

Kate strained to see where her friends were. "Where did Patch and Magda go?"

"Their presence is inconvenient. You will not see or hear them, nor will they you. Not tonight. I wish to have no interruptions." Roan stopped and set her down on her feet while keeping one arm wrapped around her waist.

"But, Roan, I—"

"You are *mine*, Kate. Mine tonight, mine *forever*, and I will not share your attention right now. They know that you are safe, and that is enough." There was an edge to his voice that scared her a little, not because she feared him, but because she didn't. Not the way she used to. But she sensed that something terrible had happened to him before he'd come here.

"Roan, what happened? Something happened to you . . . I can feel it."

His eyes darkened. "I nearly lost a dear friend today . . . and she lost all of her dryad sisters," he breathed, fury lighting his eyes. "It has reminded me all too clearly that I have precious things to lose, and that includes you, little one." His tone warned her not to ask any more questions, but Kate's heart clenched at the thought of who he might have lost . . . and what that meant in a world of beautiful beings and dangerous magic.

She pushed at his chest, but he captured her chin and lifted her face up to his. His eyes still glowed, and the hard lines of his beautiful face frightened her for a brief instant. Then, without warning, he kissed her so hard that it made her dizzy and she swayed in his hold.

The world seemed to tilt, and then she was on her back on the softest surface she'd ever felt. Roan's mouth moved over hers roughly, hungrily, but his hands were more gentle as they explored her body.

"Roan . . . what are we doing," she moaned as he nibbled her earlobe. Without thinking, she wrapped her arms around his neck.

"Don't fight me, Kate. Love me, adore me, worship me. Be my treasured pet," he growled against her skin. "Let me hang a necklace of stars around your throat, and give you the universe...all you must do is surrender to me...to your own desires."

Kate's desire was so strong right then that Roan's words set a fire inside her rather than angered her. She could picture herself . . . *Sitting at his feet in a beautiful gown of midnight-blue silk, letting him feed her fruit that was sweet beyond words. A necklace of pure silver hung around her neck, and on it glittering diamonds forged in the heart of newborn stars. His hand would stroke her hair as she gazed up at him adoringly, worshipfully . . .*

Then she saw herself naked in a bed beneath him, his body moving above hers, and the erotic fantasies spun on endlessly until an ache that hurt between her thighs made her beg Roan for more, for anything to ease the ache.

She wanted that fantasy, she wanted to be his, to know his pleasure, to know that he wanted only her . . . forever.

"Forget the world, Kate. Remember only me and how much I *desire* you." Roan's words spun a spell that erased everything beyond him. She tugged at the white tunic shirt he wore, and he sat up, pulling it off his body. She wanted to touch him, to explore him, to feel like he was *hers*.

God, he was beautiful, even with the faint scars on his skin. She wanted to kiss those scars. But he didn't give her a chance. She stared around them in confusion as she saw they were still in the cave, but somehow he'd made a bed out of stone. Stalagmites and stalactites had risen up to form bedposts, and glowworms above them looked like a blanket of stars. The rock beneath her had turned into a soft feather mattress.

Kate stared at Roan, once more enraptured at the sight of his body as he stripped out of his clothing. It continued to amaze her that he could be so singularly beautiful, yet undeniably masculine. The breadth of his shoulders, his towering height, the roped muscles, slender hips, and powerful thighs. Everything about him was seductive, right down to the large, rigid cock that was stiff with his arousal. He'd said he was bigger everywhere, she just hadn't fully believed he meant *everywhere*.

*Oh boy* . . . She raised her gaze to his face and didn't miss the satisfied smirk on his lips before he turned serious again.

He came toward her in his full naked glory, stalking toward her like a jungle cat. When he reached her, he pulled her to him and began to undress her. She had a fleeting thought that she was forgetting something important, but as the cool air caressed her bare skin, she found herself unable to care. She wanted Roan. Wanted to finally taste what it meant to belong to someone like this...to share herself with him in the most intimate way possible.

Her jeans hit the floor. She gasped when Roan's fingertips tugged at the edges of her panties. She squirmed as he peeled them down her body. She closed her legs instinctively, but he pushed them apart with his palms on her inner knees. No man had ever seen her down there. She held her breath as Roan knelt between her thighs, simply gazing at her before his eyes moved up to the rest of her body.

"You are beautiful, Kate," he breathed. "And tonight, you are *mine*." His possessive words sent a shiver of excitement through her.

He reached up and tugged the cups of her bra down, setting her breasts free as he brushed his fingertips over her nipples, stiffening them into peaks. Desperate to be free of the bra, she unclasped it and tossed it away.

Roan's eyes lit with sensual mischief as he captured her mouth once again, before his lips moved down her body toward her breasts. He took one nipple in his mouth, sucking at the tip. The erotic tug went straight to her womb and she arched into him, trying to push her breast deeper into his mouth. A groan escaped her as the weight of his body pinned her down. All she could do was relish whatever he chose to do to her. She clutched his head, her hands fisting in his silvery hair as he continued to suckle.

She'd never known, never *imagined* that Roan's mouth could elicit such exquisite feelings in her. It was like waking up to a world with brighter colors, sweeter tastes, and richer sounds. He nuzzled his way to her other breast, and all she could do was gasp and writhe in encouragement.

Her breasts felt deliciously heavy, and he moved to her belly, where his tongue teased her navel before he moved farther south. He pinned her legs open to gaze at her lower body, and she struggled to escape his gaze but failed.

"I've been dying to know how your honey tastes, little

human." Roan's voice was gruff with desire. He bent his head and kissed her mound, then his mouth moved lower between her legs.

Kate shouted his name in surprise as he licked her. The sensitive folds of her sex were wet, and she felt hot all over as he used his tongue to stroke patterns along her opening. She'd always blushed at the thought of a man going down on her before, but she'd never thought it would feel like this . . . feel so good that she never wanted it to stop.

She panted as a deep trembling within her body turned painful from need. "Please, Roan, please . . . I . . . oh God . . . *yes*." She lifted her hips as he pushed a finger deep into her, penetrating her. It almost hurt to feel him pushing his long, elegant finger into her body and fucking her with it.

She thrashed her head on the soft pillows as he introduced her to her first climax at his touch. It knocked the breath from her lungs, and her body went rigid, every muscle straining before she sank back limp in the bed. Her eyes closed as Roan's deep chuckle filled the cave.

"You cannot fall asleep on me," he warned. "Not yet."

Kate opened her eyes as Roan knelt between her spread legs and fisted his cock. She stared at it and swallowed hard. She wasn't sure that he was going to fit inside her. Maybe they should talk about the logistics first?

"Roan—"

"Hush, little human. It's *my* turn."

Roan lifted her bottom up as he leaned over her, bracing his forearm beside her head as he nudged at her entrance. She was wet, throbbing, and aching as he pushed into her. The head of his cock sank in a few inches, creating an intense pressure that made her whimper.

He hushed her with soft kisses on her lips, cheek, and jaw. Before she expected it, he thrust deep and hard. Something within her twinged with pain, and she bit instinctively into Roan's upper arms. His hips jerked, and then he stilled above her and breathed against her cheek.

"It will never hurt again." Roan's tender promise wrapped a cottony warmth around her heart. "There will only be pleasure from now on."

*Only pleasure. Yes. Pleasure.* That was all she wanted now. All she needed. To be Roan's pet, to receive his pleasure, to be his everything. The thoughts were so unlike herself, but she couldn't deny that they felt right. It was her choice after all. She wanted this.

"Give me your mouth," Roan demanded.

Kate gazed up at him, feeling delightfully, blissfully rebellious because she liked it when he conquered her. It thrilled her to defy him, to make him take what he wanted. It made everything hotter and somehow sweeter too.

"Take it, if you're so powerful," she challenged.

His eyes narrowed. "I'd rather you give it to me, little pet."

She pressed herself against him, teasing him. "I'd rather you give me another orgasm." She had to fight hard to stop from giggling at his darkening look. He lowered his head again so that their lips were inches apart. His dark lashes lowered as he gazed at her lips.

"Then I *will* take it, and any other part of you I wish. Never doubt that."

He kissed her, open-mouthed and raw, thrusting his tongue between her lips as he withdrew his cock from her body and then sank it back in. Nerve endings zinged to life at each hard thrust. This was what she wanted, this feeling of challenging him so she could surrender and feel the sweet bliss of his sensual dominance. It made everything so much hotter, so much *wilder.*

Kate never imagined sex could feel so life-changing. It was

no wonder people went mad with lust and longing. She'd wanted to feel this her entire life. Each time Roan thrust into her, she felt like she belonged to him, that they were connected in a way that could never be broken. After everything she'd been through in the last few days—nearly being drowned by the morgens, getting attacked by the trolls—she just wanted to be right here in Roan's arms, getting what *she* wanted. *Him.*

"Yes," he growled. "*Mine, forever.*" Those simple words were her joy and her doom as her body burst apart in a fierce orgasm that nearly killed her.

She lay limp, smiling dreamily. The cave shook as Roan roared her name, followed by silence. The glowworms' light winked out before they cautiously lit themselves again. Heat filled her womb, with Roan's hard shaft still buried deep within her body. Kate had just enough strength left to tighten her thighs around Roan's hips, desperate to hold him inside her.

"Please don't go . . ." She buried her face against his shoulder, fighting tears. She didn't want to lose that sense of connection to him, and she feared that now he had gotten what he wanted from her, he would abandon her.

"I'm not going anywhere," Roan assured her. He gave a low chuckle that sent a delicious shiver down her spine.

CHAPTER

# TEN

*The king of the dark woods kept watchful eyes upon his precious bride. She made no cry for help, not even when she faced the worst of his world. She kept her head high and let nothing keep her from the path . . . the path that would lead back to him. He held his breath . . . waiting . . . hoping.*

—Anon., *Tales from the Twilight Court*

Kate felt loose all over. Every muscle had been worked to exhaustion by Roan's lovemaking, and now all she wanted was to drift to sleep in the arms of the man who had introduced her to such bliss. She rubbed her cheek against Roan's chest. The smattering of dark hair that grew between his pectorals fascinated her. It was soft, even silky. Her lips curved in a drowsy smile. Sex had been everything Kate hoped it would be.

Roan lay stretched out on his back, an arm folded beneath

his head. His other palm rested on her bare hip, while his thumb slowly rubbed back and forth on her skin. Kate studied his face beneath the glowworms that still gently pulsed with blue-green light above them.

She wanted to touch Roan, explore him, feel how *real* he was in that moment to her. He was not something ethereal—he was more than feathers, magic, and moonlight. This was a virile, muscled sex god. She'd grown up hearing such hyperbole from her friends, talking about famous movie stars or popular boy bands, but there was no exaggeration here.

She reached up to gently cup his cheek, and Roan angled his face toward her. The cleft in his chin called for her kiss. Just as his furrowed brow, with its permanent sternness, made her want to snuggle close and steal his worries away. She wondered what a Fae king would even worry about, then remembered that this was not a safe land he ruled over. Patch had told her something of the fighting between the Seelie and the Unseelie. Was Roan always worried about war? His lips parted when her fingers traced his mouth and caressed the cleft of his chin.

"What are you thinking about, little one?" Roan asked.

"Me?" She wasn't used to being asked that.

"Yes." His rough chuckle sent delicious shivers through her. He wanted to know what *she* was thinking. Her thoughts were all over the place one minute, and then they'd suddenly snap back to being here with him.

"I honestly don't know. I was thinking that this is surreal, being with you. Impossible, even. But you're so very real, aren't you?"

His smile deepened. "Yes. How does that make you feel?"

"Like I'm dreaming . . . but awake. Like *anything* is possible." But that barely touched how she felt. How could she explain it? Letting down her guard with him, thinking about herself for once . . . it had set part of her free that she'd never realized had been trapped.

*I've never felt like this with anyone,* she realized. Of course, she'd never had a chance. She'd worked too hard during high school on her grades and extracurricular activities to have time to truly get to know the few boys she'd dated. She'd been so burdened with worries about Sandra, her father, and failing their expectations. And when she got to college . . .

Had she met anyone in college? She had, hadn't she? Kate swore that she'd met someone during her first semester. Why couldn't she remember who? It was like that part of her memory was just . . .gone.

A faint cry of alarm rose up in her. She shouldn't have a blank space for something like that. Forgetting car keys, sure, but not whole relationships. Her hand swept down Roan's body as she started to sit up, brushing over his cock, which had become stiff again. Roan caught her wrist, holding it against his lower belly, stroking his fingers over the back of her hand. It was sensual, intimate, and she was mesmerized by the feel of it.

Her straying thoughts, whatever they'd been, faded, and she reveled in this moment with the very real, very dangerous, and *very* attractive Fae king lying beside her.

"Are you mine?" The question, meant only for herself, slipped out, and she winced as a wave of mortifying heat swept across her face.

It was a ridiculous thought. Roan couldn't belong to anyone. He was a dark Fae king with powers she had no under-standing of. And she was just Kate, a powerless human woman who was here to temporarily entertain him.

"Kate." Her name was a low rumble on his lips. He captured her wrist and gently brought her fingers to his mouth, where he kissed her knuckles.

"Sorry. Forget I said anything." Kate tried to pull her hand away, but Roan only pulled her closer, until their bodies were skin to skin. His gaze pinned her in place, and that string of thoughts that had made her so unhappy faded away. The spell in his eyes refused to let her think about anything except how good it felt to lie here against him.

"I *am* yours," he said. His words sent a jolt of joy through her so strong that she felt like she was flying. But it came crashing down a moment later as she realized he couldn't mean it. This was just pillow talk. She could hold part of this man, this Fae who was in her life for a while, but only a while. He was as unattainable as the distant stars.

"You do not believe me," Roan mused, his sinful smile turning to a frown. "Why?"

Because her desire for him, wanting to claim him on a deeper level, terrified her. She'd never done that before with anyone, and she also didn't trust that it would be true. Why would a Fae king care about her? This, this moment right here, was all she'd really have of him, moments where she could pretend that he was hers.

"Kate, I crave you in a way that I've never craved anyone. The things you make me feel puzzle me, even frustrate me, yet you make me feel all of these emotions I'm so unaccustomed to feeling. You own me in a way no other ever has. That you must believe." His eyes seemed to search hers, for what she didn't know.

She peered up at him in wonder. How could she ever hope to keep him? "But . . . but you . . ." she stammered, trying to find the right words. "Tell me something, *anything*, something no one else knows. Give me a part of you no one else has."

He kissed her fingertips again, then moved to lie on his side facing her. His large, muscled body was outlined by the glowing of the cave's bioluminescent light.

"Just as you do not belong in your world . . . I do not fully belong here. My father was an Unseelie warrior, but my mother was a princess of the Morning Court. Her powers came from the sun." He paused for a long moment. "I know what it means to grow up knowing that those who brought you into the world did not want you. My father believed I would never be strong or ruthless enough to succeed him."

Kate held her breath, not wanting to reveal that she knew some of this because of Patch. In a strange way they were alike, and that broke her heart.

Roan's blue eyes seemed to frost over as he spoke again. "But I *was* ruthless, Kate. More ruthless than my father could have imagined." His voice deepened with a cold rage. "He told me that with his dying breath as my dagger pierced his heart."

Kate's heart skipped a painful beat. "You . . . killed your father?" The words were barely above a whisper.

The Fae king's grip on her wrist was firm but gentle as he stroked the inside of her wrist. It made her heart jolt in her chest.

"Yes. He was determined to break the barrier between your world and mine for his own selfish reasons. It would have destroyed both worlds in the process. Someone had to stop him. And you are the only one who knows what I've done. Even my sister believes our father was killed by a Seelie warrior. The day after he died, we made a treaty for peace. I swore that my father's death would go unavenged because it brought about peace."

Beneath his determined, steely gaze, she glimpsed sorrow so deep that it could carve oceans out of the earth. "The truth was, I knew he must die. He had caused too much harm as king. Too much that couldn't be forgiven. It cost me greatly to do what had to be done."

Kate, strangely unafraid, moved closer to him and placed her head on his arm.

"What happened?" she asked.

"My mother left after my father's death. When she did, something inside me withered. The parent who had actually cherished me left, and I could tell no one what I'd done. It would throw the Twilight Court into chaos, and others would vie for the throne. I am a fair ruler, no matter how I came to be king, but I knew others would not see it that way." He paused, letting out a slow breath. "My power comes with a price—my solitude."

*He has no one to belong to and no one to claim as his own. Just like me.*

"Is there no way your mother could come back?" Kate asked. "Is she truly lost forever?"

She swore she saw Roan's expression shutter closed, blocking out any other displays of emotion. It was clear he didn't want to talk about his mother anymore. Kate understood that need to curl into a defensive ball against the world, but she had hoped, perhaps foolishly, that Roan wouldn't shut her out. Still, he had told her something no one else knew, something dark and sorrowful.

Roan leaned in close to her, his lips brushing over hers. "It could always be like this, if you wished."

She took in the sweet scent of him, letting it briefly cloud her good sense with heady desire. Would it be so bad to just lie here and kiss him until the stars fell from the sky?

Roan kissed her deeper. "We could stay in this bed forever."

The touch of his wicked, wonderful lips was simply too much for her. Kate slid closer, opening her mouth to his, letting his tongue play with hers. His tongue traced the softness of her mouth as he persuaded her with slow, drugging kisses, willing her to forget the world outside, to forget all but him.

She lingered in that moment, and when he rolled her onto her back beneath him, her legs opened around his hips, ready to experience heaven with him again. She'd gone from having no understanding of her body or its desires, to the woman she was now, a creature who craved pleasure, who knew what true pleasure was.

"Mine," Roan whispered fervently. "My little Kate." He lifted her arms above her head, pinning her wrists together in the bedding with one of his hands. A moment later, he removed his hand from her wrists, but they were pinned in place now by some invisible force.

Then he eased his other hand down to his cock and guided himself into her. She moaned at the sore stretching of her body as he entered her, sinking so deep that their hips were pressed tight together. There was no end to her and no beginning to him. They were simply . . . *one*.

"The way you grip me . . . " Roan growled like an animal, his blue eyes glowing like a summer sky even in the darkness. "It's like you never want to let me go."

Kate nodded desperately. It was true. She never wanted to feel unconnected to him. Perhaps they could stay here forever in this bed, making love beneath the light of these cavern stars. He withdrew and surged deep, making her cry out with pleasure. Her arms strained against the invisible grip on her wrists.

Roan flashed her a wicked smile. "My pretty human pet," he teased. "I rather like you helpless beneath me. Perhaps I will keep your wrists bound to the bedposts in my room in the palace and spend all night and the next day bringing you to climax over and over." He thrust deep again, driving his words home.

She submitted to his control, letting him fuck her. Her body was his to tease, to torture with pleasure. Yet even at his mercy like this, she felt safe. Somehow, her body knew that he wouldn't hurt her. Kate shook with excitement as Roan took her. In that moment, she could have vanished into the blue sky of his eyes.

It was both terrifying and exciting to let him take what he wanted of her, to submit, but it also made her feel desired . . . cherished. He was tender and cruel at the same time. His thrusts were hard, deep, almost punishing, but the look in his eyes, the way he focused on her every little reaction was intoxicating. He seemed to only think of her and what he could give to her and how she was feeling. The heady rush of that intimate connection was undeniable. She would never trust anyone else the way she trusted this dark Fae king.

*He sees me,* all *of me.*

And yet he seemed to want her even more . . . and Kate felt the same about him. He had shared his dark and terrible secret, and she was unafraid of him. She understood him and why he had done what he had and didn't judge him.

"Do you trust me, my little mortal?" Roan asked.

Kate nodded.

"Good." He moved then, pulling out of her, and she wanted to weep at the empty feeling between her thighs. But Roan distracted her as her wrists were suddenly free from that invisible hold, and he urged her to sit up.

"Face the wall. Put your hands flat on it." He nudged her to turn around and place her palms on the cave wall above the nest of pillows at the edge of Roan's cavern bed.

She did as he commanded, and he knelt behind her, his hand sliding up her belly to cup her breast and lightly pinch her nipple.

"Ah!" She jerked at the tender peaks being tugged and played with and arched her back, her bottom pressing against his thighs. He chuckled low and rough.

"So little—I keep forgetting." He pushed more pillows up

beneath her knees, which raised her height so that her bottom nestled against his groin.

"Oh yes, that's it," he growled as one of his hands parted her ass cheeks and slid down to stroke the opening of her sex from behind with questing fingertips. She wriggled when he penetrated her with his fingers, playfully spreading the wetness of her arousal more fully around her opening.

"I'm going to take you just like this, little pet. You will thank me for your pleasure when you come. Understand?" He gave her bottom a light smack. The order created a rush of fresh wetness between her legs, and her body quaked with the need to come. She nodded eagerly.

"Roan . . . oh please . . ."

"See how pretty you sound when you beg?" Roan gripped her hair in his fist, tugging her head back so she could see his cold, beautiful eyes burn like winter fire. She whimpered, writhing against the hand that still teased her down below. One fingertip swept over her clit, causing her to jerk toward him and away from him each time he brushed it.

"Beg me to take you, Kate. I want to hear the words come from your lips." Roan's voice had become guttural, primal, promising dark, delicious things.

Kate rubbed her bottom against his hard cock. She couldn't say the words; it would make her weak, give him too much power when he already owned so much of her.

"*Beg me*, little one." Roan's demand sent shivers through her as he eased his cock inside her once more. He sank in a few inches, promising to give her what she wanted before he withdrew and then teased again.

Kate wanted to scream at being denied the bliss that hovered on the horizon. The hand on her hip slid up to tease her breasts once more, and his warm breath tickled the back of her neck. Then he thrust in hard and deep, sinking in so hard that his balls smacked Kate's bottom, and she moaned in utter bliss at the stretching sensation from this new angle. He moved in and out, slowly, sensually, just enough to keep her hovering on the edge of where she wanted to be. She closed her eyes, enjoying each little sensation. But she needed more. She thrust her bottom back against him harder, chasing the orgasm she so desperately wanted.

Kate cursed out loud when she couldn't get what she wanted—and what she wanted was him, fucking her wildly, taking control. She wanted to give her trust to him in the most intimate way possible.

*Choose him . . . ask him . . . trust him.*

Panting breaths escaping her lips. She felt the rough scrape of Roan's fingertips on her skin, felt him deep inside her, filling her. Her inner walls clenched around his cock, trying to hold him inside her. All around them, the glowworms made their shadows dance on the cavern walls.

Was it truly surrender if it was what she wanted? Giving herself to him was *her* choice. She saw that now. Surrendering to his seduction was *her* power move, not his.

"Fuck me, Roan, please," she gasped. "I want to be yours."

Roan felt the instant something changed between him and the little mortal. The wall that existed around her, the barrier that kept him out of her head unless he was kissing her, crumbled away. He could see every memory, every triumph, every failure, every moment where she'd thought she was all alone in the world and soldiered on in the face of that loneliness.

Then he saw the child, Caden, the child she'd once wanted

to hate, the child who'd stolen her place in her father's heart. Yet Kate could only love the boy, despite Caden being the wedge that had driven her and her father further apart. The one thing Kate couldn't see but Roan could was that the child adored her in equal measure. The boy's love for her was there in every memory, but Kate had missed the clues, her heart too broken by the years of her stepmother's belittling and her father's cold distance.

Roan delved deeper into her memories, pulling out the ones that filled him with rage, memories no one should have. He would take them all, keep them away from his precious Kate.

*I will guard you, even against yourself,* he vowed.

The crystal that hung around his neck shone bright with the memories he had taken. Memories that would free Kate from the pain of her past.

"Roan . . . I feel . . . *strange,*" Kate said.

He held her tight as he made love to her, distracting her from what he had done. She turned her head to the side, and he kissed her neck hungrily, as she dug her nails into the cave walls. He took her harder, driving so hard that she screamed with pleasure, and the sound was muffled by his kiss and the sound of his hips smacking into her bottom.

"Oh . . . my . . . God . . ." Kate groaned as he continued to pump into her before his body seized with the rush of his own climax. He pressed deep into her, emptying himself into her. His breath escaped in a harsh gasp as he grew dizzy with pleasure. Taking her like this had been so intense that he didn't feel like himself at that moment. He felt like he had been separated from his body as he basked in the heat that flooded his chest and made him want to hold her close to him and never let her go. If she'd asked for his kingdom right then, he would have handed it to her and a dozen stars from the sky along with it.

As he breathed hard against her neck, sweat dewed on his body. Still deep inside her, his body relaxed as he let the pleasure of holding his sweet prisoner soothe his possessive spirit.

Why did she affect him like this? Pleasure such as this had always been enjoyable . . . but this was so much *more*. That elusive peace he'd felt, that he'd been chasing since he'd first met Kate and she'd cared for him, was finally within reach.

Holding her in his arms, comforting her, pleasuring her, giving himself to her and telling her about his past had somehow given him a sliver of that blissful peace he'd craved.

But he also felt alive, right down to the last fiber of his being. Making love to Kate had electrified him, and that feeling of excitement didn't fade. It lingered like the scent of spring flowers as twilight descended on the royal gardens after the rain.

"Thank you." Kate kissed his cheek, then the crown of his hair. She had remembered to thank him for the pleasure he had given her, as he had commanded. Yet it wasn't the worshipping whisper of a mortal woman craving his desires. No . . . this was different. Kate's thanking him was sweet, full of tender affection and something deeper than he ever could have imagined he'd hear from a lover.

He gently pulled out of her body, hating to disconnect himself from her. He wanted to press his lips all over her skin, to taste every part of her. Roan wanted to imprint in his mind the memory of her just as she was at this moment forever. Sweet, vulnerable, yet brave enough to trust him.

A voice whispered in the back of his mind that he was not worthy of her, that he was a selfish creature, like all Fae, but he didn't want to face that truth.

"Sleep, my little Kate," he urged. He caught her up in his arms and settled her gently on the bed that he had made in the

Crystal Cave and held her close, more covetous than any dragon with his gold.

She was his now. All that he had to do was keep her away from the center of the labyrinth for a few more weeks. The labyrinth itself would do most of the work, leading her down false trails, but he also planned to use his seductions as a way to keep her distracted.

And then . . . then she would be his. *Forever.*

# ELEVEN

*The bride discovered that the trolls, creatures without beauty, had the voices to sing and make the dryads weep at their sonorous songs.*

*—Anon., Tales from the Twilight Court*

A song woke Kate from sleep, and the voice that sang was soft and deep. She reached instinctively for Roan, but he was gone, just like last time.

Kate drowsily sat up, her eyes taking in the rhythmic pulse of the glowworms and cave crystals as a beautiful, melancholy tune continued. The words were in a language Kate did not understand and somehow filled her mind with the image of the bright and beautiful moon high in the sky.

She pushed back the blankets, dressed quickly, and wandered through the cave in the direction of the song. She found Patch sitting on a rock that was low to the ground, a spellbound expression on his face as he watched Magda.

The troll was the source of the intense, beautiful song.

Kate sat beside Patch and listened as the song's deep notes vibrated the air around them. She felt such peace just sitting and listening to the troll sing. Magda held her arms up to the sky, even though they were in a cave, but a brightness glowed from above, lighting her upturned face.

Kate looked up and saw hundreds of glowworms, their glow keeping time with the song. Magda spun in a slow circle, rocking back and forth on her booted feet as she sang. Kate once more saw images in her head, but this time they played out like a movie.

Magda was facing the other trolls, frozen in place as they began to hurl stones at her. She had accepted her fate. She was too small, too unlike the others of her clan, and she deserved to die.

Then sunlight flashed across the blade of a dagger. A dagger belonging to King Arun. The rain of rocks stopped.

Kate gasped as she saw herself through Magda's eyes. A tiny human who challenged the trolls and then, while they were confused, came to Magda and held her hand out to her. It was a gesture of friendship and trust, so sacred among the Fae that Magda was overcome with emotion. A stranger had saved her and offered her the precious gift of friendship. Then that new friend had been hurt.

The troll's song deepened as rage, sorrow, and fear for Kate's safety colored the visions the song produced.

Kate's lips trembled. She felt what Magda had felt when they had entered the cave. Magda's desperate need when she'd called for Lord Arun's help. Her hope and fear as she guided him to the cave to save Kate.

*So that was how he knew I was hurt.*

Magda ended her song, and her arms dropped back to her

sides. She turned toward Kate, a solemn look of relief on her face.

"Kate is back," Magda said in her slow, solemn voice.

Patch gave a start as he only now realized Kate was sitting next to him. "Oh! Glad to see you back, girl. After Lord Arun took you to the healing pools, you both vanished. Magda said she felt you close by, but neither of us could see you. We hoped you would show up at some point." He turned away from her to wipe a tear from his eyes, then clapped his hands together as he stood, trying to act like everything was back to normal.

Kate smiled at Patch, still shaken by the power of Magda's song. "Does that mean you missed me? *Worried* about me?"

"Me?" Patch scoffed. "Hardly. But I promised Magda I would wait to see if you came back. She rather likes you and doesn't want you to get hurt."

Kate hid a smile. She had a feeling that Patch liked her too but didn't want to admit it. "I actually didn't go anywhere. Roan made us invisible to you."

The kobold's eyes narrowed slightly. "Well, what do you expect from a Fae king? You finally figured out pleasing him wasn't so bad, *eh*?" He snorted as he retrieved his bag of gemstones from the ground.

Kate's face burned with a hot blush. "Um . . ."

She glanced between him and Magda, trying to change the subject. "So, do either of you know the way out of here?" The moment the question left her lips, she saw the glowworms pulsing strangely above her, as if forming a tunnel of light that was darker where she, Magda, and Patch stood, and grew brighter down in the distance.

"The glowworms . . . they're showing us where to go!" Kate realized as she pointed in the direction of the brightest light.

"So we're asking worms for directions now?" Patch grumbled as Kate and Magda started toward the well-lit tunnel.

As the three of them walked in silence, Kate felt intensely grateful that she was not alone. She had friends. Patch could have left her a long time ago but hadn't. And Magda was a lot like her, an outcast. She smiled a little at the thought of how her two friends had stayed with her.

It made her think of home and her friends in high school. Those relationships had remained superficial. Whenever she'd felt herself looking forward to seeing someone too much, whenever her joy at the sight of their face became too noticeable, she'd pull up her walls. It was better—safer—so she couldn't get hurt again. Like with her mother. And then her father.

*I kept myself from making real friends because I was afraid.*

It seemed so silly to think that she'd feared her friends would simply abandon her. They *had* left after graduation, but she hadn't actually lost them as friends. They had even called her every week to see how college was going. Yet she'd always convinced herself she was alone, even when that hadn't been the truth.

Life at home had been so easy in some ways, and she'd been so blind to that fact. She had faced death at least twice here, and she was beholden to the rules of a dark Fae king who desired her. It kind of put her situation back home in perspective.

Heat rolled through her body when she remembered how much Roan had desired her last night and how much she'd wanted him too. She was still sore, but it felt good in a way she couldn't explain. Maybe it was because she'd let nothing hold her back last night. She'd finally felt free.

Her thoughts turned from Roan back to the labyrinth. Here everything was beautiful and dangerous. Here she could lose everything, including her life. But she had to continue, for Caden's sake. He needed her.

A sudden thought pierced her like a dagger. She'd been so worried about others leaving her that she hadn't realized she'd done the same thing to her brother when she'd made that wish for Roan to take her away from her life. She'd willingly left Caden behind, at least in her own secret wishes, without a thought as to how that would make him feel. She fought off the wave of sickness in her stomach. And then she'd managed to get him stuck in this realm with her. Now she had to find a way through the labyrinth and get him home, no matter how scared she felt.

*I can't let fear stop me.*

She hadn't let fear rule her when she had saved Patch from the morgens or when she'd rescued Magda. She had refused to let fear take over because someone had needed her.

*When I got hurt, they were here for me. They called Roan to help me. They waited for me, even though they weren't sure I'd come back. That's what friendship is.*

Her affection for the grumpy kobold and the quiet troll only deepened. They really were her friends, no matter what Patch may grumble in disagreement.

The tunnel widened slightly now, and Magda gestured for Kate and Patch to wait as she scouted up ahead. The faint scent of sea salt tingled Kate's nose. Were they near an ocean? She thought she remembered Patch mentioning that the Crystal Cave was by the sea. Surely they hadn't traveled so far across the vast labyrinth so quickly . . .

"Magda, do you see the ocean?" Kate asked. The glow-worms' light began to fade, and a natural light slowly grew brighter ahead. She could see Magda already returning to them.

"Yes, the ocean is ahead," Magda said.

How was that possible? The sea was far north and east of

the labyrinth, based on what she'd seen when she'd first entered the towering gates.

They followed Magda back toward the surface. Soon, they all stepped around a bend in the tunnel as it opened to face the sea.

Kate stared in awe at the dark-blue waters crashing along the rocky shoreline, which sent a cascade of foamy water up into the air. The cave gave way to a beach with fine white sand for about fifty yards until it reached the rocks in the water. To the right, the coastline continued for miles, with tall cliffs beyond the sand and the beaches. But to the left was the palace . . . Roan's palace . . . where Caden was.

"Patch, how did we get here?" she asked the kobold.

Patch stared up at the towering edifice of the rocky base that led to the palace of the Twilight Court with surprise.

"I don't know. Must be wizard magic. This cave led to the sea in the northeast where the Twilight Court is, but when we entered it, we were on the fringe of the labyrinth to the southwest . . ." He scratched his beard, deep in thought.

"We go to the palace?" Magda asked Kate.

"Yes!" Kate exclaimed at the same time Patch shouted, "No!"

"*Yes.*" Kate shot the kobold a look. "We are. My brother is in there, and I need to see him. Roan had him locked up in the dungeons the last time that I was here."

Patch wagged a finger at Kate. "Lord Arun wants you in the labyrinth, girl. He—"

"He won't know I'm here. I'll just sneak in."

Patch groaned. "You don't *sneak* into a fortress, girl. That's what this is. *A Fae fortress.* It has spells to ward off those who wish the palace and its inhabitants harm. You won't make it through."

Kate studied the palace a moment. "Well, I don't mean anyone in the palace any harm, do I? If anything, I care about the welfare of someone inside, which is like the opposite, right? I should be able to walk right in."

Patch glared at her. "Just wait until Lord Arun hears about this . . ."

Kate clasped a hand around Patch's mouth, silencing him. "He won't find out because *you* won't tell him. Got it?"

The kobold glowered. His dark eyes sank into his wrinkled face with displeasure and his pointed ears twitched beneath the edges of his black cap.

"*Please*, Patch. I need to see my brother. He's only a kid. He doesn't belong here. He's terrified and just wants to go home. Roan locked him up in the dungeons before he sent me to the labyrinth. I need to know he's okay."

The kobold crossed his arms over his chest, and Kate slowly lowered her hand from his mouth. When he didn't yell to summon Roan, she let out a sigh of relief.

"Well, you are on your own, then. I'll not give Lord Arun a reason to put my head on a pike on the ramparts. He threatened to kill me after a stupid troll beamed you with a rock." Patch glanced at Magda. "No offense, Magda."

The troll shrugged as a breeze drifted off the water, stirring the silver fur on her body.

It took a moment for Patch's words to sink in. "He threatened you . . . because of what happened to me?"

Patch rolled his eyes. "Oh yes, girl. He was mad with rage when he saw you were hurt. I thought for sure old Patch was done for. You must never underestimate a Fae's anger, girl. It don't come easy, but it comes strong."

Roan had been upset to see her hurt? Her chest tightened as she recalled the almost reverent way he'd stroked her skin last night, the tenderness in his voice as she'd woken in the healing pool in his arms. A flutter of treacherous hope spread warmly through her chest.

Yet it was blacked out by a shadow of a dark voice that whispered in her ear: *That's not love. That's ownership. You are not a lover to be cherished; you are a toy to be possessed.*

She remembered the words he'd tossed so carelessly at her. She was a pet to him, a toy, said with the arrogant assurance that there could be nothing between them but physical desire occurring at his convenience, as if she had no will or purpose of her own outside of his bed.

Even if he did care about her, that wasn't enough. She needed more. She needed *love*. But could a dark Fae even know the kind of love that she needed?

It was foolish to entertain the thought, because she wasn't going to be here forever. The dark whisper grew until that flutter of hope was smothered, and Kate resolved not to think of it again.

*I'm not staying. I will solve this labyrinth, take Caden, and go home.*

If the thought of home made her feel strangely empty, she took strength in her decision and forced her gaze back to the palace. Her determination left her feeling strangely empty. Kate turned back toward the palace and the rocky walls she'd have to climb to get to it. If she could get in and find Caden, then perhaps she could find a way to send them both home. If she failed in that, her plan was to return to the cave and go back into the labyrinth once more with Roan none the wiser. It was possible the glowworms might even show her the way to the center or at least point her in the right direction. Maybe even Merlin's magic could get her there.

"You should both wait for me here by the cave," she told her friends. "It'll be easier if I sneak in on my own. I'll come back soon."

"Be careful, Kate," Magda replied.

"I will," Kate promised. She rolled up her sleeves and started toward the rocky base that rose up out of the sea, holding the glittering palace far above.

"I'm coming, Caden."

A GOLDEN FALCON ROSE HIGHER ON A THERMAL CURRENT OF AIR FAR out on the sea, staying just out of reach of the faintly shimmering barrier that kept him from the shores of the northern kingdom of the Unseelie. It was shielded, as was his own kingdom, from being breached by the enemy.

But that didn't stop him from flying as close as he could. His keen hawk eyes now spied three figures walking along the shore. One of them broke away and started toward the palace.

But that figure was no creature born in the land of the Fae. It was a human. A *human*. No human was to be brought into the Fae realm by the Unseelie. But apparently, Roan had done it.

So the treaty agreed to after King Bahden's death had been broken? This was better than he could ever have hoped. Now the Seelie had their chance. He would return to the Morning Court and tell his subjects what he had seen, and they would have no choice but to declare war.

The fire of greed and desire filled the falcon's chest. His little side attacks were no longer necessary. For the first time in centuries, Culan truly felt joy.

KATE CURSED HERSELF FOR NOT GOING ROCK CLIMBING THAT ONE TIME she was invited by some friends. Every muscle in her hands was strained or stiff or scratched from stretching to reach for gaps in the rocks to hold on to. She wiped blood away on her jeans, wincing, but she had to keep moving.

*I'm making progress, even if it's slow.*

Once she had started climbing, she realized that the rocks that served as the base for the palace formed tiers like on a wedding cake. As long as she could navigate up a level, then she could take a bit of time to catch her breath and rub at her muscles before she had to move on to the next level. She glanced down, which was a mistake given how high she was. She saw Patch and Magda waiting near the mouth of the cave, two tiny figures standing out against the cave's dark opening.

She shut her eyes as a wave of nausea nearly buckled her knees. What was she thinking? She *hated* heights. When she had climbed down from Roan's bedchamber balcony that first day here, she'd been focused on the rope and avoided looking down. This was different. She had no rope this time. If she missed her footing, she'd be crushed on the rocks below.

"Breathe . . . just breathe. You've got this." Kate shut her eyes and took a moment to collect herself before facing the rocks again.

Tipping her head back, she stared at the remaining two levels she had to get to the base of the palace. The sun hung low in the sky by the time she finally reached the place she wanted to get to. The rocks pitted by the sea spray changed to a smoother material somewhere between marble and mother-of-pearl. She stroked a finger over the surface while catching her breath. It was beautiful.

"This must be what causes it to shimmer in the sunlight and glow under the moonlight." She couldn't help but wonder what it was made of. Patch would probably tell her if he was in a good mood when she got back.

Crawling carefully along the wall, she tried to work her way inward from the sea. Kate saw the dying sunlight kiss the tops of the labyrinth walls to the southwest as she came upon a door. It was a shorter door, barely big enough for her to go through without hunching over. She turned the ornately carved latch, and a wave of delicious smells hit her nose as the door opened. She took a step into the room and found herself in a vast kitchen. Hundreds of lit candles were above her head, illuminating the ovens and counters, but they weren't held by chandeliers. They simply *floated* in place by magic.

The brownie chefs were suddenly disappearing and reappearing before her as they raced about preparing trays of food. Once they seemed to have a full tray, they would simply vanish with a *pop!* Others stood on step stools to reach large copper pots to stir ingredients. Fresh-cut herbs like rosemary and lavender hung in bouquets above several of the stovetops.

Kate's stomach growled. When was the last time she'd eaten? It had been a few days ago when she'd been at the palace. She'd had that little bit of bread. Had it really sustained her *this* long? She would try to sneak some food out to the cave to her friends after she found Caden.

She took a step deeper into the kitchens, and one of the brownies materialized right in front of her, almost colliding with her. Kate gasped and the brownie shrieked. All of the work in the kitchen ceased, and she found herself being stared at by every brownie in the room.

"Mistress Kate!" a voice squeaked as Babbitt rushed toward her.

"Hey, Babbitt!" She was so relieved to see a familiar face. A second later, she realized the brownie might tell Roan she was here.

"What are you doing here?" Babbitt asked. "The pixies said you were in the labyrinth."

*Pixies. Right.* She would have to remember that those little creatures saw everything, which meant sooner or later Roan would know she was here.

"Er, yeah, but I just returned to visit my brother before I go back." It wasn't exactly a lie. She had to let the brownie assume that Roan knew she was here. "Actually, could I have some food? Maybe some bread and something to drink? I haven't eaten since . . . well, since you last saw me. Which, honestly, I'm not sure how that's possible."

The brownie chuckled. "Our food has healing powers, and it will fill you up for days at a time. Doesn't your food do that?"

"Um, sort of, but I normally have to eat three times a day."

The brownie's eyes widened. "Three times a day? It's a wonder you have time for anything else besides eating!" Babbitt exclaimed.

She began to pile slices of bread on a plate for Kate, who sat down on an empty stool and gratefully accepted it. Then Babbitt prepared a bowl of some steamy soup and a goblet of pale-blue liquid.

"Word is you survived the morgens." Babbitt chattered as she watched Kate eat. "Pesky creatures, aren't they?"

"Yeah, that was pretty scary. I almost drowned." She shivered and pushed down the terrifying memory of that cold water filling her lungs as she sank deep into the darkness in the arms of one of those awful creatures.

"And I heard you saved a kobold from them. *That* was

brave." Babbitt beamed. "The palace kobolds who watch over Lord Arun's treasury hold you in high esteem."

"They do?" Kate blinked and swallowed more of the soup. It was some kind of flavorful potato leek soup that she really liked.

"Then you rescued a troll from being killed by the wild trolls in the labyrinth. We have troll guards who maintain the palace gardens, and they speak your name in reverence because of the kindness you showed to one of their kind."

"Really?" Kate couldn't figure out why the trolls would be talking about her.

Babbitt leaned in close. "The trolls in the labyrinth aren't like the trolls at the palace. Most of them are brutal beasts, backward and cruel. Not like the trolls here in the palace. You're a hero to them."

Kate almost choked on the last of her bread. "A what?"

"A hero, miss. You put the lives of others before your own. The Shining Ones . . . they don't do that. Well, Lord Arun, Lady Eudora, and Lord Rath do, but not many of the others would. They are the ruling class of Fae, and we are considered beneath them."

"Babbitt, I was only doing what anyone would do."

Babbitt's eyes shimmered. "You must come from a wonderful land if that's the case." The brownie cleared her throat. "Now eat up."

When Kate finished the last of the sweet drink in her goblet, she felt refreshed and energized. She was ready to find her brother.

"Can you tell me where the dungeons are?" she asked Babbitt.

The brownie nodded. "You simply close your eyes and imagine the space you wish to jump to, and then you will appear where you want."

"Babbitt, I can't jump to wherever I want like you can."

"Oh, right . . . you're human. I forgot." The brownie wrinkled her nose as if thinking hard. "If you follow the corridor outside to the right, take the last staircase on the right to the dungeons."

"Thank you." Kate stood and then on impulse bent over to hug the little brownie. She really had been so helpful and sweet, and Kate appreciated that more than she could say.

Kate went out the door and found herself in a dim hallway that was lit by sconces of fire. No, that wasn't it. The sconces didn't have any flames. They just . . . glowed. She moved closer to one and stared closely at it. The light was spherical and didn't seem to give off any heat.

"What are you made of?" she murmured as she reached up to the silver sconce. The ball of light suddenly bobbed up out of her reach, wound its way over her head, and flew down the hallway. Fascinated, Kate followed the light as it danced in the air like a glowing firefly. Then it started to drift away from where Kate wanted to go. She stopped in front of the staircase that led down to the dungeons, but that ball of light was so tempting and pretty and it beckoned her to follow it . . .

Caden's tearful face flashed before her eyes. Jolted out of the odd, dreamlike feeling that the light gave her, Kate forced herself to go down the winding stone staircase into the dungeons. She braced her hand on the wall as she navigated the narrow steps.

She halted when she got to the cells. All of them were completely empty.

Caden wasn't here.

"Oh God . . . Caden." Kate covered her mouth to hold back from crying. He was here when she'd left. What had Roan done with him?

Kate had dared to trust Roan with her brother's safety.

She'd given herself to him and opened her heart to him, and he hadn't kept his promise. Her brother was missing in this land of dark and dangerous creatures.

She'd been such a fool. Roan was Fae. Her mother's stories had always said they weren't to be trusted. She'd not only trusted Roan, but she had fallen in love with him.

She gripped the iron bars of the nearest cell. Her legs gave out as she was overcome with a numbing sense of despair. Would she ever see Caden again?

# CHAPTER
# TWELVE



Eudora sat on the floor upon a mountain of silver and gold cushions, the human child named Caden beside her. Spread before them were plates of food and goblets of periwinkle punch. The blooming flowers in dozens of vases throughout the room filled the air with a thousand wondrous scents. The lamps and chandeliers glowed from the light of a dozen will-o'-the-wisps. Rath leaned against the wall in the corner of the room, his hand resting on his sword hilt as he guarded them.

The little boy listened with rapt attention as Eudora told him tales of the Flower Fairy.

"And you went to live with her?" Caden asked.

"Yes, I lived with the Flower Fairy for ten short years. There I learned more about my powers and my fairy graces. Before I returned home, she gave me the gift of my wild Fae form."

It was a tradition for Fae princes and princesses to study magic under the Flower Fairy, whose home was on an island just off the coast, between the Seelie and Unseelie lands. The young Fae royal would receive a gift from her when they departed.

"What about your family? Did you miss them?"

Eudora exchanged a glance with Rath, who moved to a chair and continued watching them. He crossed his arms over his chest, a bemused smile contrasting the intensity of his focus. He did not understand her fascination with human children, but he said nothing as she doted on the little boy. It had been far too long since she'd been around a child.

Long ago, they used to dance with children in fairy circles beneath the full moon. She missed those days. Eudora turned her focus back to the child's question.

"There were many days where I missed my family desperately and my gardens and my home. There is quite a bit of power in a place where one puts one's head to sleep, where one finds comfort and rest. But what makes a home a home is one's family and friends. I had no one but the Flower Fairy for counsel when I lived with her. She is a solitary fairy, you see."

"What's a solitary fairy?" Caden asked as he scooted closer to Eudora.

"A fairy who lives alone. I am a trooping fairy—I love being around others. Their energy gives me strength. Solitary fairies find both power and solace in being alone; their minds are allowed to contemplate life's deeper mysteries. The Flower

Fairy knows so much about our world because she spends so much time alone thinking about it. It is what makes her wise."

Eudora drew in a breath as she realized what it was about this child and Kate that tore at her heart. They were in a world that was not their own, a place that was not home, and they'd been separated. It was cruel of Roan to do such a thing, but her brother often did things that puzzled or frustrated her.

"Does she get lonely?" the boy asked. "The Flower Fairy?"

"I believe that is why she brings the young Shining Ones to her home to give them gifts. It banishes her occasional melancholy away. And she was certainly there to aid me in the same way. She could often chase my sorrows away whenever I missed my brother and mother."

"*And* me," Rath added with a wicked wink. Eudora's heart skipped a painful beat as she saw the heat in his eyes conveying a promise that both excited and frightened her.

She rolled her eyes at him. "Rath, surely you have something *else* to occupy you." She was not in the mood to be teased. Fear of an approaching war with the Seelie had most of the Twilight Court on edge. As a Fae who took in the energy of those around her, she was weakened by their fears and anxieties. It didn't help that those who would seek to take Roan's place were now vying for loyalty amongst the courtiers.

The presence of the human child was a welcome distraction from her worries. His bright-eyed hope and keen interest in her world refreshed her. When the palace brownie Babbitt had brought the boy to her, she had been annoyed at first, and then she'd felt the boy's energy and it soothed her. Human children carried a type of magic that did not exist in the Fae realm.

"Now, let me tell you about the Holly King—"

Eudora halted her tale as a will-o'-the-wisp flitted into the room, glowing brightly.

Rath eyed the wisp warily. Roan and Eudora both held the loyalty of the wisps, which provided light to the residents of the palace, but Rath didn't trust the watchful little creatures as much as she did.

Eudora held out a hand to the wisp, which drifted down to land in her palm.

"What have you seen, little wisp?" she asked.

Within its glow, she saw a vision of the mortal Roan had taken as his pet. According to the palace pixies, she was wandering the labyrinth, where Roan visited her, but the vision this wisp presented showed the woman in the palace. The dungeons, to be precise. How on earth had she gotten there?

Rath crouched beside Eudora and gazed into the light over her shoulder. "I wager that Roan has no idea his little pet is in the palace," he said so only Eudora could hear him.

"Is that Kate?" Caden asked, also staring at the vision within the wisp's glow.

"Yes. It would seem your sister has returned to the palace."

The child got to his feet, grinning. "I *knew* she'd solve the labyrinth. I knew it."

"So it would seem," Eudora said reluctantly. "Though I would imagine that if she had, Roan would be with her, because he would have to bring her here from the center of the labyrinth. But he is not with her. Instead, I see her in the dungeons alone. Weeping." Why was the human woman weeping? She was not trapped in one of the cells.

"She's crying?" Caden's voice pitched in alarm. "Is she hurt? Did Roan hurt her?"

"What? No. Roan would never hurt your sister. But I can't understand why she's in the dungeons."

At this, the boy's eyes widened. "Because I was there. I was in a cell when he sent Kate away to the labyrinth. She doesn't know that he brought me to you after she left."

Eudora tapped her chin, thinking. "So she hasn't spoken to Roan. Somehow, she got back into the palace and found her way to the dungeons without passing Roan's challenge directly." Eudora was quite impressed. "Clever creature. Would you like to see her?"

Caden nodded eagerly.

"Then we shall devise a way for you to see her without my brother finding out," she told the boy.

Caden beamed at her and Rath. "Really?"

"Really?" Rath said in a very different tone, one full of skepticism.

"Yes, really," said Eudora.

"Princess, now isn't the time to anger your brother," Rath said, his tone filled with warning.

"I shall not *anger* him because he shall not find out. Instead, I will please him by distracting his anxious royal court with a ball. We haven't had a true one of those in years."

Rath rolled his eyes. "Oh yes, that will be *just* what Roan wants when we are on the eve of war. Why on earth do you think this is a good idea?"

Eudora lifted her golden skirts and stood. "Don't you see? A ball will keep Roan *away* from the palace. He does so despise such things."

Rath raised an eyebrow but conceded her point.

Eudora continued. "His absence will give us a chance to let Caden see his sister, and the ball shall be a cover for us to reunite these two. It shall also have the benefit of distracting the rest of the court." She bit her lip. "You will help me, won't you?" she asked Rath as she placed a hand upon his arm and smiled at him.

The First Lance's eyes focused on her mouth. "You know

full well I'll do anything that you wish." When she moved away to take the child's hand, Rath captured her other wrist, gently bringing her back to him. "And you will gift me a kiss, Eudora. A *true* one. No more sisterly pecks upon the cheek."

Eudora's body heated, but she couldn't look away from Rath. They had danced around each other for centuries, never daring to address their mutual attraction directly. Eudora feared to do so, because she would be irrevocably changed if she admitted how much she loved Rath, and Fae were afraid of change, even while being fascinated by change in others. But change meant that you were not the same as you once were, and Fae by their very natures feared that fate greatly for themselves.

Rath's fingers rubbed Eudora's skin gently, forging a sweet fire beneath it. The impending war and the sense of urgency it brought with it only heightened her reaction. But there was also something else stirring inside her, something that felt very human, and she believed that her proximity to Kate was to blame. The young woman's emotions were so strong they reached Eudora even here. Humans felt everything intensely, and she'd always been drawn to humans and their wild range of emotions.

"A kiss, then," she agreed, suddenly breathless.

But a kiss between Fae could also be a promise, and she wasn't sure if she was ready to make a promise to Rath. But her pull toward him had been undeniable her entire long, enchanted life, and the threat of an impending war pushed her to agree because it was quite possible that neither of them would get the chance again.

"Then tell me what you wish me to do," Rath whispered. "And I shall see it done."

"Prepare the palace for a ball. The brownies will know

what to do. I also need you to watch the child while I find Roan's wayward mortal."

Eudora closed her eyes, delving deep as her wild form came forth.

Kate wasn't sure how long she'd been in the dungeons, but her body was stiff from sitting on the floor. She forced herself to get up and wipe her tears. Despite the desperate nature of her situation, crying had released some knot of tension deep inside her that she hadn't known was there. She could breathe easier now and focus on what mattered.

*Caden needs me. I can't give up.*

She tried to approach the problem logically.

Caden wasn't in the dungeons, but she had to believe Roan wouldn't hurt him. She had a month to solve the labyrinth, so he would not have returned Caden to the human world. That would be outside the scope of the deal they'd struck. Keeping him in this world would keep the pressure on her, and having him in this castle would keep him safe.

Ergo, he was still in the palace somewhere.

And if Roan had moved him, *someone* in the palace would have noticed.

Babbitt had said that the kobolds and the trolls liked her. Perhaps they could help her. It was a small chance, but one she had to take.

She was halfway back up the stairs when a fluffy white cat appeared in front of her. The cat's blue eyes were large and luminous, and its long hair looked as soft as angora. The cat twitched its plumelike tail as it watched her.

*A white cat* . . . Something about that stirred her memory, but she couldn't quite put a finger on it.

The cat turned away with a meow, keeping its gaze on Kate over its shoulder, its tail twitching.

In a place where everything was magical, why not the cats as well? Kate nibbled her bottom lip and took a chance. "Do you know how to find someone in the palace?"

The cat nodded.

"Great. So you're some kind of magic cat, huh?"

The cat hopped up the steps ahead of her and meowed in the affirmative.

"I'm looking for a boy, a human one, eleven years old. He has blond hair . . ."

The cat was already moving. Kate followed it out of the stairwell and back into the palace corridor. The cat glanced around, then started to trot away.

"Wait!" Kate whispered, running after the cat. "Will you help me?"

"Mreow—mreow." The cat paused long enough to make sure Kate was following. They hurried down a series of halls together, pausing only a few times to hide in alcoves as other Fae passed by them. Kate pressed herself flat against the wall each time, praying that no one would see her. She wasn't exactly sure what kind of trouble she'd be in if she was spotted and would prefer not to find out. The brownies didn't seem to be dangerous, but the others like Roan . . . She had a feeling it wouldn't be good to be caught by them.

When the most recent batch of guards had moved on, the cat darted forward, and Kate chased after her. The feline ducked through an open doorway and leapt onto a lavish bed. Kate glanced around the room to get her bearings. It was a bedchamber, much like Roan's, but decidedly more feminine. The bed was made of the same type of white wood, but more slender in build. The coverlet and sheets were awash with gold and purple hues.

"I don't think we should be here." Kate moved to pick up the cat, but in a flash of blinding light, the cat vanished and the most beautiful brunette woman she'd ever seen sat on the edge of the bed. Her features were unmistakably familiar, especially her blue eyes, which were so like Roan's.

It was a trap! Kate scrambled for the door, but it shut and bolted before she reached it. Kate turned and gaped at the woman. She looked to be in her mid-twenties, and the gown she wore was made of silver-and-gold satin. Pearls were threaded into her hair, and a diadem of silver stars and moon-flowers adorned her brow.

The woman chuckled. "Kate of the Winslows. We meet again."

"We've met before?" Kate asked.

The Fae's blue eyes sparkled with mischief. "We certainly have. Not that you would remember. I'm afraid you were unconscious at the time. Traveling through the realms can be overwhelming to mortals. My brother landed in the middle of his throne room with you in his arms."

Kate let that sink in and then she gasped. "So Roan is your brother?"

"Yes, my elder brother. I'm Eudora Moondove."

"Not Eudora Arun?" Kate asked curiously.

"Among the Fae, females have equal standing. We female Fae keep our matrilineal names, and the males take patrilineal names. My mother was Thalia Moondove, and my father was Bahden Arun."

"Men and women are equals here?" The irony didn't escape her that she'd had to travel to a land of myth to finally find more equality between the sexes.

"Oh yes." Eudora smiled softly. "Now about my brother . . .

He can be so delightfully broody. He said very little of his plans for you and simply shooed me out of his bedchamber. And then the next thing I heard is that he'd put you in the labyrinth, and he gave me charge of your little brother."

"Caden is here?" Kate spun around, hoping she'd find her brother in some corner of the room waiting to shout *surprise*, but deep down she knew he wouldn't be there.

"He is with Rath, who is Roan's dearest friend. You can be assured that he will see to Caden's care."

"Oh please, can't I see him? I've been so worried—"

The Fae princess tutted and waved Kate over to sit beside her on the plush bed. Kate sat down, and the woman grasped one of Kate's hands, gently squeezing it.

"You mortals. Always in such a hurry. He's all right, my dear Kate. I swear it."

Kate's chest tightened as her panic flared again. "But Roan left him in the dungeons . . ."

"No, he didn't. My beast of a brother only wanted you to *think* that so he could make you do what he wished. He would never have left the poor boy down there."

"But I did do what he wanted . . .sort of." She didn't want to tell Roan's sister about how foolish she'd been to fall for him and sleep with him. That he somehow captivated her so completely when she was with him that it was impossible to think of anything or anyone else.

"Well, you wouldn't be the first female to bend to his wishes, just the first human one who made it far more difficult for him to get what he wanted. I imagine it must be an unsettling thing to have to obey my brother's whims. I can quite understand why you resisted. Males always believe they have a right to us, don't they? And always, they are quite wrong and try to force us to do as they wish."

Kate hadn't really thought about it like that, but Roan had

just thrown her into the labyrinth on a whim because he wasn't pleased she didn't want to stay and be his little human pet forever. It almost made her laugh to think of Roan throwing a Fae king–level tantrum when she'd refused his order to wait naked in his bed. Kate wasn't someone who felt smug very often, but she did in that moment. She'd rejected Roan's demands and had made love with him on *her* terms.

"Now . . . Please do not be offended, but I wish to fix your clothes," said Eudora. "All that mud is bothering me and . . . Is that blood?"

Kate glanced down at herself. Her jeans were torn at the knees, and she had wiped her bloody hands on them during her climb, which left reddish-brown stains in places. Her sweater and part of her jeans had mud streaks.

Eudora marveled at her appearance. "Good gracious, what on earth have you been up to, little mortal?"

"I . . . um . . . climbed the rocks by the sea to get into the palace."

Eudora gasped. "You *what?*"

Maybe Kate shouldn't have said anything, but she wanted to trust Eudora. "I climbed," she repeated.

"I hadn't actually given any thought to how you got inside the palace, but climbing? You could have died, Kate. Even in our land, death is quite permanent."

"I had to make sure my brother was safe." Kate realized what she'd done had been very risky, but making sure Caden was okay, seeing that he was safe and well cared for with her own eyes? That was worth it.

Eudora lifted Kate's hands, turning them over and frowning when she saw the cuts and abrasions.

"Well, that won't do, will it?" She closed her eyes, and a warm tingling moved through Kate's body. The cuts healed and the scrapes vanished.

Eudora nodded in satisfaction. "Much better. Now, what do you think of attending a ball with me? You would be the first human in centuries to see an Unseelie ball in the Twilight Court."

"I really just want to see my brother. And I don't want Roan to find me here, since technically, I didn't find the center of the labyrinth yet. I found a cave that led here instead."

Eudora's brows rose. "He would be displeased that you found a rather clever way to defy him, I'm sure. Then again, you are where he originally wished you to be, aren't you? Here in the palace? Maybe he would not be as angry as you think."

Kate blushed as she remembered *exactly* where Roan wanted her to be. In his bed, naked and waiting for him. "We sort of made a bargain, or an agreement. I'm not sure what to call it. He said if I could solve the labyrinth, he would send Caden and me home."

"You made a bargain with Roan? That is quite binding in our world."

"I know that . . . now," Kate sighed. "My plan was to see Caden and go home if I could find a way. If not, my second plan was to climb back down the way I came in and go to the cave and find my way into the labyrinth again. I don't think that cave is meant to be part of the labyrinth, and just because I made it to the castle doesn't mean I solved the labyrinth. I'd lose on a technicality."

"Yes, Fae bargains are nothing if not riddled with such things. In your world there are humans who also revel in technicalities. I believe they're called . . . lawyers?"

Kate chuckled. She had briefly considered going to law school after college but had decided she liked business way more than she liked arguing with people.

"Well, in any case, I don't see how attending one little ball first would hurt. You could stay for a short time, then I could fly you down to the cave you mentioned."

"Wouldn't Roan see me at the ball?" Kate asked. "Doesn't he have to attend those sorts of things?"

"Oh, every time I have thrown a ball, my brother manages to vanish for the entire evening, much to the dismay of all the young female courtiers. He knows he is a highly sought-after dance partner, but he is not the most social of creatures. I assure you, he will turn into an owl and fly far away just to avoid a single dance."

This didn't sound like a good idea. "I really don't want to risk it. What if he does stay?"

"Well, in that very unlikely possibility, he won't be able to see you if he can't recognize you. It's going to be a masquerade, and I shall disguise you." Eudora clapped her hands together, delighted at the prospect.

"I don't think putting a mask on my face will be enough."

The Fae princess tutted. "We don't just use masks. We also use glamour, Kate of the Winslows. The balls have a certain excitement and titillation that comes with the idea of deception and illusion. You dance with someone, but they may not be who you think they are. They may look exactly like someone you desire but end up being someone else entirely. I shall place a strong spell over you, and no one will recognize you except me."

Kate wasn't sure she should agree to this plan. Too many things could go wrong. It would be her luck if Roan decided to stay, and surely he would see through a spell, even Eudora's, wouldn't he?

"Lady Eudora . . ."

"Please, call me Eudora. I wish for us to be friends," the princess said with such honesty that Kate felt an instant warmth and connection. She hoped it wasn't because of some glamour Eudora was using. She genuinely wanted to like Roan's sister.

"Eudora, I can't risk upsetting your brother if he finds me at the ball. Please, just let me go see Caden."

"Darling Kate, there is but one lesson you must learn as a woman in the land of the Fae: *never* refuse a chance to dance at a royal ball. Our balls are legendary, and one never knows what magical opportunities they might afford. Even the humans know of fairy balls, do they not?"

Kate remembered reading about fairy dances and balls, and she reluctantly nodded.

"Good, then it's settled. You shall dance at least once at the ball—after you see your brother, of course. Then I promise to fly you to the cave you came from to get back to the labyrinth before my brother realizes you are missing."

"Did you say you would *fly* me down to the cave?"

"Yes. All Shining Ones can fly." She stood up from the bed and suddenly spun in a circle. A pair of iridescent wings appeared behind her. They were silvery with hints of pale seafoam green with slender tail parts like a luna moth that draped down in an elegant way.

"You have wings," Kate gasped in awe. "Does Roan have wings?"

"Oh yes, but we rarely show them, except when in court. Think of them like court dress. So Roan hasn't shown you his when he visits you in the labyrinth?"

"No, he simply shows up and we argue . . . or he is rescuing me and then we just end up in a bed he conjures out of thin air. I try to get him to talk to me, but . . ." She halted when she realized how pathetic that sounded. The last thing she ever wanted to be was a stupid damsel in distress who couldn't save herself. She'd always hated those parts of fairy tales. What she wanted was for Roan to see her as a strong person, to value her, to open himself up to her like she was doing with him.

"Roan is guarded, even from Rath and me. Don't lose hope, Kate. You are closer to him than you realize." Eudora said this so gently, yet her words were filled with hope, a hope that Kate held on to as well.

Kate tried to shrug off the pain of knowing that she and Roan were still strangers to each other. It was foolish to want more when she wasn't going to stay here after she solved the labyrinth. But that didn't stop the little flame of hope burning within her that they would someday share everything between them . . .

"I should hate him, you know," Kate admitted. "He took me away from my home, and he stole Caden too. Then he tossed me into the labyrinth just so I would agree to sleep with him, and now—"

Eudora took her hand again. "Now you fear you might love my stubborn brother, and you worry what loving him will mean for you."

"That's it in a nutshell," Kate replied, her tone soft and full of an ache that burned in her throat.

"*In a nutshell.*" Eudora chuckled. "You humans have such amusing sayings. Do you know the funny thing about nuts? When planted, the seed within will grow into a mighty tree— like an acorn turning into an oak."

"I'm not sure I understand what you mean."

Eudora's wings fanned out as she smiled. "Love grows from something small into something infinite. You must give it time to see what grows between you."

"It's a little hard to do when I'm in the labyrinth and he's doing . . . whatever Fae kings do." Kate couldn't believe she was having this conversation with Roan's sister, let alone a Fae princess. "Besides, there's no future to any of this. I'm just human. He sees me as a pet, a thing, and I won't be staying." Kate had been afraid to say those words aloud, but now they were spoken. Her mother would have said she couldn't unring that bell.

Eudora bent down to face Kate, who still sat on the edge of the bed. Her wings fanned out, shimmering and beautiful. "You know what the Fae think of humans?"

Kate sniffled and wiped away tears with a furious hand. "What? We grow old and die and—"

"Kate," Eudora cut in gently. "Your mortality isn't the fascination for us. It's something far more valuable. You *change*. Strength comes from changing. A human woman who has lived all of her life stages and sits with weathered skin and white hair . . . that woman has experienced more life than I will in many ways. Change requires choices, new paths, new adventures, and lessons to be learned. The Fae cherish stories about humankind because it teaches us about things we might otherwise miss."

"You mean, like how we have fairy stories about you guys?" Kate wiped away a stray tear that had crept down her cheek. "My mom loved fairy tales. She said they weren't actually for children but that children were the only ones smart enough to understand them."

Eudora smiled. "Your mother sounds like a very wise woman."

"She was." Kate smiled through her tears. The old pain in her chest was almost unbearably agonizing at that moment. "I miss her so much. I try so hard to act like I'm okay, as if losing her didn't destroy everything inside me." Kate sucked in a breath. "But it did. I thought my stepmother, Sandra, would want me, that I'd matter to her, but I . . . I was just in the way, taking up space."

Eudora curled a slender arm around Kate's trembling

shoulders. "Never let anyone in your life make you feel like you're not enough. You are Kate of the Winslows. You are perfect as you are, and what is wrong with taking up space? Think of the space your mother took up in your life. The depth and vastness of your grief demonstrates the incredible space she took up in your life. You deserve to be that for someone else. Let yourself grow inside someone else's heart . . . perhaps someone like Roan."

"You think I should stay here in your realm and fall in love with your brother and abandon my life and my home? Like it's that easy?"

"Nothing worth having is ever easy. Sometimes, the most important journeys we make start with a single step away from all that we know." Eudora brushed a lock of hair back from Kate's face in a motherly way. "The question is, are you brave enough to take a journey?"

"I doubt I'll have a choice," Kate sighed. "I doubt I'll solve the labyrinth, which means I'll be stuck here forever."

The Fae princess chuckled. "There is *always* a choice."

"Is this your way of telling me that I should choose to go to the ball?" Kate almost laughed. It would be like a fairy tale.

"Yes, exactly." The princess grinned. Eudora looked her over. "But you will need a dress."

"Fine. I'll let you fairy-godmother me or whatever. But I want to see my brother first."

"Fairy-godmother you? Well, I don't exactly have the credentials for such illustrious work, but I could certainly try. The Fae chosen for such professions are rare and powerful," Eudora said so seriously that Kate actually believed what she was saying.

"Never mind," Kate said. "Can you take me to Caden?"

She decided to trust Eudora. Each time she looked into the

other woman's eyes, she couldn't help but feel like it was Roan watching her.

Thank God he hadn't seen her turn into a blubbering mess about her mother just now. Kate caught herself. No, she wouldn't apologize for having emotions, especially about her mother. If anything, Roan might actually understand. He had lost his mother as well, and it was rather clear she had left a gaping wound in his heart.

She was certain Roan would be furious if he found out she'd reached the palace unfairly, but part of her wished that he was here now, offering comfort to her. Despite his brooding intensity, he could be wonderfully comforting when she needed it most.

She couldn't forget how he'd held her in his arms, kissing her so sweetly after she'd survived the morgen attack, even as he healed her. It hadn't felt selfish, hadn't felt like he was healing her for his own needs. He'd touched her so tenderly, the concern in his eyes so deep, so real, that even that memory of it made her shiver with a need to be back in his arms.

Maybe Eudora was right. Maybe what she felt for Roan was worth taking a risk for. But was it worth leaving her entire world behind?

Eudora pulled Kate to her feet and tucked one of Kate's arms in her own as they left the bedroom.

The Fae princess grinned impishly. "Now then, let's see your brother. Then we will fashion you a dress worthy of a princess."

CHAPTER

# THIRTEEN

"Kate!" Caden flew into Kate's open arms, nearly knocking her over. She pressed her cheek to the top of his head and held him, smelling that familiar clean scent children always had after baths. She let out a shaking breath, suddenly homesick, then pulled back a little to examine him. He looked happy, healthy, and unhurt. Kate let out the tight knot of a breath she'd been holding on to. He was okay.

"Kate of the Winslows," a deep voice said. Kate looked up

223

to find a man as tall as Roan with a similar build standing behind Caden. His arms, armored at the shoulders and forearms, were crossed over his chest as he returned her scrutiny. His dark-silver armor glinted dimly beneath the light of the room.

"Kate, this is Lord Rath Ender, First Lance," Eudora said. Kate didn't miss the affectionate way the Fae princess spoke about the handsome warrior or how she looked at him.

"It is a pleasure to see you awake and conscious," Rath said to Kate.

"Did *everyone* see me unconscious?" Kate muttered.

"Most of the primary court," Eudora said. "Roan landed in the middle of the throne room with you in his arms."

"Great, that's not humiliating at all," Kate sighed. It was mortifying to think that everyone had seen her passed out in Roan's arms. Caden lifted his head, confused. Kate tousled his blond hair, trying to distract him.

"Have you had enough to eat?" she asked her brother.

"Oh yeah—the fairy food is so good here." He smiled, more confident again. "Did you solve the labyrinth? Are we going home now?"

"Not yet. I'm still working on it."

"It's pretty cool here, don't you think?" Caden said. "Rath told me that he can turn into a black dog, Eudora turns into a cat, and Roan becomes an owl. He's the owl that you saved, you know. That's one of his special powers." The boy seemed quite proud of himself for learning so much about their situation and the Fae realm.

Kate looked at Rath, curious about his Fae form.

"The Flower Fairy, you see," Caden said, still excited. "She grants special powers to them before they become a grown-up fairy. Isn't that awesome?"

"We've been keeping young Caden amused with stories about our world," Eudora said with an indulgent look at Kate's brother.

"And Rath took me to meet the goblins!" Caden exclaimed. "We saw them making swords!"

"I hope Rath kept you away from them," Kate said with concern.

Caden's brows knitted together. "The goblins?"

"No, the swords. I've seen you play with stick swords enough times to know you'd hurt yourself."

"I assure you the lad was quite safe," Rath said.

"Rath is gonna teach me how to play chess while you're at the ball," Caden said, then leaned up to whisper into Kate's ear, "but I know he'd much rather be dancing with Lady Eudora, because he *likes* her."

Kate held back a smile. It wasn't hard to notice the heat that sparked whenever Eudora and Rath looked at each other.

The boy looked back at Rath. "I'm sorry you can't go to the ball, Rath."

Rath waved dismissively. "I shall simply have to entice Eudora to throw another," Rath said with an amused smile.

The ball. Kate really didn't want to go to some dance, but it was hard to tell Eudora because the princess seemed so excited about it. In comparison with everything going on, it seemed so frivolous to Kate, but then again, the way the Fae viewed things, perhaps it wasn't frivolous to them. Caden had taken a different view of things while being here. He'd dived into their world, wanting to learn all he could about it, while she had been focused on just the labyrinth . . . and Roan. Maybe if she changed her thinking into learning more about the Fae, she could understand this world better and it would help her find a faster way out of this mess.

"It is time that Caden and I leave," Rath said. "I imagine

Eudora has much she wishes to do to prepare you for this evening."

"Do you have to leave right now? I was hoping to spend a little more time with my brother."

"I know," Eudora sighed, "but the ball will be starting soon, and we must get you ready."

Kate held on to her little brother's shoulders for a long moment, wishing he didn't have to leave. But a bargain was a bargain.

Kate pulled Caden close for one more hug. "Have fun with Rath."

"It's okay for you to have fun too, you know," Caden whispered. "I know Dad and Mom don't really let you have fun at home, but this is such an amazing place. You should have fun too, okay?"

Kate shut her eyes and squeezed Caden tight before she finally let go. Rath led the boy out of the room, leaving Eudora and Kate alone.

"You . . . you will send him home if I . . ." She swallowed hard. "If I fail to solve the labyrinth." She didn't make it a question. She needed Eudora's word. "Because Roan never said what would happen to my brother. I was so convinced I'd win that I overlooked what would happen to Caden if I failed."

The Fae princess looked puzzled. "Yes, but—"

"*Promise me.*" Kate grasped Eudora's hands, pleading. "He doesn't belong here. He needs to go home. If I die . . . or if I have to stay here with Roan, I need you to promise that Caden will go home."

She felt strangely desperate asking this, but her mind seemed more and more quiet, emptier of late. When Roan was around, she couldn't seem to think about anything else but him. That had to be the Fae magic at work. She feared that if she didn't solve the labyrinth, she might forget Caden altogether.

"Very well, I promise," Eudora said. "Now, come with me. I must fashion a dress for you and craft a glamour that would fool even my brother."

They returned to Eudora's bedchamber, and the Fae princess simply began waving her hand in the air, and in a matter of moments she'd conjured up a dozen different dresses.

"Did you just make these?" Kate couldn't help but reach out to touch the dresses that had materialized on the bed. They seemed to cover the rainbow of colors. She touched a pale-blue gown of watered silk that was embroidered with moonflowers.

"Oh no, I simply transported them from my official wardrobe, which is down the hall." Eudora sorted through the dresses. "Ooh," the princess cried out in delight, "perhaps something like this." She held up a deep-purple dress of fine-spun silk. "We'll have to change a few things, of course." Eudora waved a hand, and the gown floated in the air as though it suddenly settled on an invisible mannequin.

"It needs sleeves, I think . . ." Eudora whispered, and two gossamer purple open-ended sleeves suddenly appeared at the tops of the shoulders. They draped down the sides of the gown, but Kate could tell from the style that they weren't actually sleeves.

"Now to touch up the bodice . . ." The bodice was a plain purple bit of fabric split down partway so that it provided a tempting glimpse of skin down the breast line in a V-shape. The sweetheart neckline then grew into swirling patterns of silver embroidery that covered the purple fabric in Celtic patterns down the plunging neckline in the most beautiful way. The skirts then billowed out, the fabric creating an iridescent shimmer. It was sensual, powerful, beautiful.

"What do you think?" Eudora asked.

"It's the most beautiful thing I've ever seen," Kate confessed.

"Yes, I suppose it'll do." Eudora pointed at Kate. "Strip down and let's get you fitted properly."

Kate removed her clothes and lifted her arms as the dress magically floated down over her body. Eudora shortened the length of the skirts but left a three-foot train and the draping medieval gossamer sleeves, which fluttered down by Kate's side.

"Hmm . . . your hair. That simply won't do." Eudora tapped her chin, then pointed a finger at Kate's head. Kate turned to look at the mess of hair in the mirror, and her lips parted in shock. Her hair was now glossy in soft waves with a hint of curl. Threaded in her hair were pearls and glittering jewels on fine silver threads.

"I can't believe it. I've never been able to curl my hair like this before. Believe me, I've tried." Kate sighed dreamily at how perfect her hair looked.

"Oh, it's easy. You simply tell your hair what to do and let it think it was its idea," Eudora replied. "I've never understood why humans always try to use the most complicated methods when there are simple solutions." Eudora laughed. "Now shoes and jewelry. What about these?" She held up a pair of slippered kitten heels embroidered with stars against an icy-blue fabric. Kate took them and set them on the floor. She lifted her skirts and slid one foot inside. The slippers fit perfectly and were shockingly comfortable. Next, Eudora turned to her dresser and opened a rosewood box, sorting through glittering gemstones.

"Yes, this is what you should wear." Eudora held up a diamond-studded necklace with a silver crescent moon.

"Lift your hair." Eudora guided Kate to turn around and lift her hair up. Eudora settled the necklace around Kate's throat and tightened the clasp.

"There. Now all we need is a glamour to hide you from the prying eyes of the court. Close your eyes, Kate."

Kate did so, and felt a warm wind surround her, tickling her skin and stirring her skirts and sleeves. Then it faded away.

"Open your eyes," Eudora said.

Kate opened her eyes, and what she saw in the mirror stole her breath. Two iridescent purple wings trimmed in black edges, like those of a giant butterfly, formed behind her back. She had *wings*. More importantly, she didn't recognize her own face. She knew it had to be her face, but when she looked at herself directly, she saw only a mystery.

"Now, don't try to use your wings. They are simply for show. And this will help as well. We use the masks mainly as a tease, but all the Fae tonight will be wearing glamour." Eudora placed a silver mask over Kate's face and tied it with black ribbons.

"Now you're ready for a Fae ball."

Kate, lost in butterfly dreams, stared at herself in the mirror, still not recognizing her own face, and wished she didn't have to hide from Roan. What if he could see her being a part of his world and not just as some pet? Would he fall in love with her then? A tear dripped down her cheek, and Eudora gently wiped it away.

"Don't cry, Kate. *Please.* Mortal tears are too powerful to waste, and they will give you away if any of my kind see them."

"I'm sorry, you've been so nice."

Eudora's gaze softened with infinite gentleness. "Magic is easy when it's done for others. At least, it is for me."

Kate smiled through watery eyes. "You really are a princess. You're how I imagine a real princess should act."

"I shall take that as the compliment I believe you intended

it to be. Now dry your eyes, Kate of the Winslows. It's time to conquer the Twilight Court."

Her only wish at that moment was to capture Roan's heart.

A BALL. ANOTHER DAMNED BALL. NOW OF ALL TIMES.

Eudora was either mad or brilliant. Word of the burning of the dark woods and the murder of Lady Kyma's sisters had sent the Unseelie court into a spiral of terror and fear, and all were on edge. The murder of trees and their guardian dryads was unthinkable. Not in a thousand years had such a crime been committed in his lands. Even the Fae in his realm who possessed the darker gifts were haunted by the actions Culan had taken.

Only Eudora would have had the foresight to throw a ball to distract his courtiers. Roan hated balls, hated dancing with women who vied for the position of his queen consort and the power that came with it.

Eudora adored the romance and intrigue that accompanied events like these, but Roan had never cared for such things . . . until Kate. He now found himself wanting the strangest things, saying the strangest things . . . and she'd penetrated the armor around his heart like no one else ever had.

He'd intended to be far away from this nonsense, but pragmatism and something else had held him back from his usual flight. He told himself that by attending tonight, he could gauge the disposition of his court, something he would need to know once he and the war council declared war upon the Seelie. But there was something else he couldn't quite explain.

It felt like an invisible nudge that kept him here, and he could not pull away.

Roan lingered in the shadows of the ballroom, half hidden from view as he watched the Fae lords and ladies spin across the black-and-white tiled floor. Will-o'-the-wisps illuminated the room, and pixies flitted through the silver chandeliers, teasing the wisps.

A Fae named Clinda strummed a harp, filling the air with music. Several others held string instruments or flutes and joined her in creating a symphony of enchanting sound. Clinda blew Roan a kiss when she noticed him watching her. The kiss became a shimmering flash of light from her lips and turned into a bright-blue bird that flew overhead and circled Roan before flying out the nearest open back door. One of Clinda's gifts was the ability to take affection within her soul and turn it into wild and beautiful birds to fill the skies with birdsong. She also was gifted with the ability to play enchanted music that would inspire mortals and Fae alike to dream impossible, wonderful dreams. Many of humankind's greatest works of art had been painted by a mortal listening to Clinda play.

Turning his back, Roan slipped out the balcony door and faced the great labyrinth that surrounded and shielded the palace from harm. Moonlight rose above the windswept walls below him, casting black shades in a dizzying pattern. Kate was out there with her troll friend and that grumpy kobold. He wanted to go to her right then, to have her in his arms. He wondered what she would say this time, given their last encounter. Would she continue to be guarded? Would she beg to be released, demand yet again that he let her brother go yet again? Or perhaps she would try to woo him in the hopes of gaining some advantage? Or perhaps she would simply open her arms to him and he would take her straight to bed?

He grinned at the possibilities, then caught himself. It

seemed she had a strong hold over his emotions. Stronger than he'd ever expected, because he wanted her any way he could have her. He would take her quarreling with him, he would take her wiles and her wit, he would take her tears and her need to be held. He would take her kisses and give his own, and he would listen to her talk all night, every night.

From the moment he'd met her, Kate had exceeded every expectation he'd had of what it would mean to keep her here with him. She'd touched him—deeply—to the point that he couldn't think unless those thoughts included her.

She was not some simple human to collect from the human realm as a prize and keep as a lover. She was Kate—*his* Kate—in a way that seemed far too infinite to define with words alone. He wasn't even sure what that meant. He was the ruler of the Unseelie, master of the labyrinth. Whatever he desired, he claimed. And yet he realized he could not claim Kate unless she wished for it. Tapping into and unleashing her desires was easy and enjoyable . . . but he was no closer to what he truly desired from her. He wanted all of her, not just her body. He wanted his little mortal's heart, her soul, and he would battle whatever he must to prove to her that she could trust him.

Roan gripped the white marble railing as he gazed out at the labyrinth. Long ago, he'd visited the heart of the labyrinth. It had been a quiet place, a peaceful place . . . a garden where anything could bloom. He had not been able to stay long. The peace and the quiet had unsettled him greatly. It had been too tempting to stay in that place where he felt safe and quiet. He had never returned.

Kate felt like the center of the labyrinth. Was that why he was so drawn to her? She possessed violent storms of emotions and heartbreaking memories, some of which he'd stolen to give her the same sort of peace that she gave him. Even now, those memories glowed from inside the crystal that hung around his neck.

He could never tell her what he had done. She would never forgive him. He'd stolen some of those memories because he'd been jealous . . . and he'd wanted to protect her from the things he'd seen in the memories that hurt her. He'd done it because she'd become precious to him. Humans were so outspoken when they believed themselves to be wronged, even if it was for their benefit.

He conjured a silver orb of light, which glowed in front of him as he sought out a vision.

"Show me Kate," he whispered. The cloud within the orb did not change. "Show me Kate," he repeated, more harshly. Again, nothing. Curious. Worrying. He looked out at the labyrinth. "Show me the kobold and the troll."

The troll and the kobold sat in the sand beneath the moonlight, a cave entrance at their backs and the vast dark sea before them. Kate was not with them. Fear struck Roan's heart like a mortal blow. Where was she? He peered more closely at the beach in the vision of the orb.

"The sea . . ." he murmured. They were by the sea, which was outside of the labyrinth, which meant Kate was not in the labyrinth. The orb could not show her because of the magical wards he'd placed upon the palace to prevent them from being spied upon, which meant she must be in the palace.

Roan dismissed the orb. He turned to the ballroom full of dancing courtiers. He needed to find his little human and make sure she was safe. He also needed to know *how* she'd found her way inside. It should have been impossible for any creature that was not Unseelie to enter. If she could breach its defenses, then the Seelie might as well. He left the darkness of the jasmine-scented night and entered the ballroom. Dancers moved out of his way as he crossed the room. He alone among his people was uncloaked. It was the custom to disguise oneself with a Fae glamour for a ball, but he was not hiding tonight because he was not here to play games with the ladies of the court.

At the opposite end, the great doors leading into the ballroom opened. A young Fae lady stood alone in the doorway, a silver mask covering her face. The curve-hugging bodice of her purple gown was embroidered with silver Celtic knots, and loose, flowing sleeves hung from her shoulders. Her purple wings, tipped with black, shimmered behind her. She glowed with a light unlike any silvery opalescent shine the other *Sidhe* possessed. He let the wild form of his owl creep into his eyes.

"Show me the truth," he whispered as the owl's vision changed his blue irises to the near black of a barn owl.

The glamour around the Fae woman shimmered brightly, falsely, but Roan saw her true face beneath the spell.

A slow smile spread across his lips. What a wicked game this pretty creature wanted to play . . . Well, he was the wicked king of a wicked kingdom. If Kate thought she could win this battle of wills, she was wrong. He'd been too lenient, too gentle with her before. It was time to show her that he was the lord and master of this realm, and she *would* dance to his tune.

He released the owl form in his eyes and moved slowly toward the woman who stood uncertainly at the edge of the doorway. The dancers kept out of his way as he approached her. He glimpsed another woman in the crowd watching him, and he knew it was Eudora. She wore no glamour, only a silver mask. His sister wanted him to see her . . . because she was the reason Kate was here tonight in front of him. Eudora was clever indeed. He spoke silently to his sister within her mind.

*"You found my little pet wandering the palace?"*

Eudora's laughter rang in his head. *"I did, and I rescued her, poor thing. She climbed the walls by the sea, Roan. She could have been hurt. So here I am delivering her back into your care. Do not be cross with her—I assured her you would not hurt her if you discovered her here."*

*"I would never hurt her."*

*"Good. Then show her what it is like to be adored by a Fae king. Dance with her."*

Perhaps his cunning sister was right. He could dance with Kate and show her that he could be charming, he could be adoring, and he could let her taste the world that would be hers, if she would only agree to belong to him.

"Dance with me?" Roan offered Kate his hand.

She hesitantly put her hand in his, and he escorted her out onto the floor. High above, the pixies shed their magic dust, and a glittering cloud rained down like a gold-and-silver mist upon the dancers below.

"I can't stay long," she said, glancing at the grandfather clock that towered in the back of the ballroom. All around them, the dancers whirled like rare jewel-winged butterflies.

"Then how long will you be mine, lady fair?" Roan pulled her gently against him, taking in the scent of lavender and starlight that clung to her skin. "Because I would harness the winds of time to own you forever." The clock's hands began to rewind, spinning slowly but then moving faster as the dancers around them seemed to freeze in place, and he had Kate all to himself. The musicians still played, unaware of the time spell Roan used on the rest of the room.

Kate's eyes widened as he led her into a waltz. Her gaze flew over the finely dressed men and ladies who stood frozen as they danced by. Roan had eyes only for her. His sweet human love held the power to enchant him with spells even stronger than his magic. In a room full of Fae who would have seen her as nothing more than a treasured pet, this woman stood alone, unrivaled.

"You truly are the most beautiful creature I've ever seen," Roan said as he spun them in another circle across the floor.

"I'm not—"

"Look at yourself." He faced her toward a wall of mirrors. "See your beauty. Tell me again you are not."

She gasped as the wall of mirrors flashed with images, not of her and Roan dancing but of moments from Kate's life.

*She was swimming in the dark waters of the morgens' pond . . . She was defiant in the face of trolls . . . She held her head high as Sandra and her father confronted her in the kitchen. And again when she wept in the darkness of her bedchamber.*

"You see—you *are* beautiful." Roan swept her out onto the balcony, feeling her shiver as he drew her closer in his arms. Inside, the dancing resumed as the clock ticked on like it had never stopped.

"You knew . . ." Kate breathed.

Roan caught her chin and lifted her face up to his as he removed the mask with his other hand. "I would know you in every lifetime, Kate. There is no world where I would not see you just as you are. No spell can hide you from me."

The majesty of her humanity was laid bare in her dark-brown eyes as he lowered his head and kissed her. He wrapped his arms around Kate, his fingers digging into the purple silk of her gown. He sought to hold on to her so tightly that time would fold in on itself and there would be no moment when she was not here with him like this . . . his forever.

Kate breathed against his lips as he kissed her deep, hard. The moonlight kissed her skin and made the pearls and diamonds in her hair shine. Aching to touch her, Roan buried his fingers in her silken tresses and gave himself over to the utter stillness in his aching heart.

This was peace. This was joy. This was *Kate.*

At that moment, Roan knew he would break his vow even if

it destroyed him. He would never send her home, even if she found the heart of the labyrinth. He would break the bargain he had made and keep her for all time. Because he could see no future, no way forward without her. There was only one way he could be certain she would not resist his desires.

Roan kissed her again and stole Caden from Kate's mind. He saw the child's life through Kate's eyes, when he'd been such a tiny thing in a bassinet . . . how his little hand had curled around Kate's finger . . . his laughter when she'd pretended to hide behind her own hands . . . the weight of his little body as he fell asleep against Kate when they sat on the couch . . . the fear on his face when Kate planned to leave on Christmas Eve . . . her pain as she realized she might never come back to him . . . his frightened face in the dungeon, Kate's fear for his safety, and the reunion between Kate and Caden that Eudora had so carefully hidden from Roan when she'd discovered Kate in the castle. He could feel Kate's relief and joy at holding the child in her arms, knowing he was safe . . . and how she'd learned that Roan hadn't hurt the child. He'd cared for Caden by taking him to Eudora. He lingered over the memory of Kate accepting the truth that Roan wouldn't hurt her or her little brother and the peace that followed. As he experienced this through Kate's memory, the emotions were so intense that he caught his breath.

*She trusts me—even after all I've done—and yet I am wicked. I have taken so much from her, and she will never know.*

*But at least she will no longer remember the life that caused her so much pain. Not like me...* His own memories weighed him down, threatening to drown him. An unwanted son, a lonely prince, a king with a dark and terrible secret...and now he was a thief of memories for the woman he cherished above all others.

Every last memory of Caden became trapped in the crystal

that hung from his throat. Roan almost staggered under the weight of all those memories. No, that wasn't it. As the gravity of what he'd done sank in, he realized Kate would never forgive him should she ever learn the truth. Out of sheer selfishness, he had taken the memories of the one person she had left in her world to love her, all so she could be his.

His heart darkened as he could hear his father's voice from beyond the mists of time and death. *"You truly have no mercy, no heart . . . Perhaps you are my son after all."*

CHAPTER

# FOURTEEN

*The greatest weapon one can forge is the strength to love. Love renders all other enchantments harmless. It mutes the songs of morgens and breathes fire into the chest so that one can fight on against trolls and basilisks.*

*—Anon.,* Tales from the Twilight Court

**K**ate bathed in the moonlight-drenched world that held the aroma of jasmine, night-blooming flowers, and music that was half dream. She twined her arms around Roan's neck and kissed him.

*My twilight lover, my secret dream.* She learned the shape of his lips and memorized the taste of him. There was something so exquisite about feeling the heat of his body pressed to hers while they were bound together as music filled the air. It felt as if anything was possible. She no longer had that sense of anxiety deep in her chest. She was relaxed and at ease for the first time in as long as she could remember.

Funny, she couldn't even recall why the labyrinth had been so frightening or why she'd even been there. She remembered arguing with Roan, getting upset. But of course, this was a strange new world she was in, and he'd taken her without asking. But it all seemed so silly now. She could have been right here, in Roan's arms, where she belonged, where she felt cherished. That urgent sense of having to leave was just . . . gone.

*I don't have to leave,* she realized. *Nothing is holding me back. Nothing.*

She couldn't remember why she'd wanted to leave Roan or this beautiful place. She felt blissfully free in a way she couldn't explain.

"Come with me," Roan said as he led her back through the ballroom.

Kate was aware of hundreds of eyes upon her, but she couldn't look away from Roan. The music followed them even as they left the ballroom. Roan stopped before a door and opened it. It was his bedchamber, the room where this strange and exciting adventure had begun. She recognized the beautiful bed with its magic headboard that showed slowly moving figures in the white wood.

Everything was like a dream, yet it felt more real than anything she'd ever experienced. Colors were brighter, sounds clearer. Even the fabric of her dress and the whisper of her sleeves became an adventure for the senses. Roan closed the door behind them and came toward her, tenderly cupping her face. God, he was so tall, and yet she liked the height difference. She felt delicate and feminine in a way she'd never felt before.

"You make a beautiful Fae, Kate, but I will always prefer

you as you truly are." He kissed her forehead, and a strange sensation moved over her skin. She glanced at the tall mirror close by and saw that her lovely wings were gone and she recognized her face once again. She was just Kate Winslow again. Human. Mortal.

She looked to Roan, his blue eyes bright and clear as he stared into her soul. He brushed his thumbs tenderly over her cheeks. He could have anyone he wanted. How was it possible that he truly wanted *her*? Yet, she could see something deeper than desire filled his gaze.

"Would you show me your wings?" she asked.

Roan arched a brow. "My wings?"

Kate nodded. He looked dangerous and yet so handsome. Unlike the other Fae in the ballroom, who wore the tailored waistcoats and frock coats of nobles, Roan looked like a pirate with his raw, muscular beauty barely concealed by a half-open shirt, fitted trousers, and black boots. She touched the silver of his hair, letting it slide between her fingertips as she searched his face.

"Please let me see them," she asked again.

Roan stepped away from her, his hands dropping from her face as he tugged the billowy shirt from his trousers and pulled it over his head. He tossed the garment to the floor and stood bare-chested before her. He slowly faced away from her, and with a shimmer of bending light, two wings appeared from his back. They were partially translucent like Eudora's, but rather than carrying a hint of seafoam green they were the palest blue and silver with draping tails.

Kate gasped at their sheer stunning beauty. "Can . . . can I touch them?" *Please say yes.*

Roan looked over his shoulder at her, a small smile curving his lips. "Yes, little one, you can."

She approached with a hesitant hand and touched the

closest wing. The texture of the blue surface was soft to the touch, and she drew a circle with her fingertip around the white circular spots that made him resemble a luna moth. Roan closed his eyes.

Kate held her breath as she explored his wings a moment longer. Then he turned to face her, catching her by the waist.

"Stay in this dream with me, Kate."

"I . . ." She was supposed to say no, that she couldn't stay with him. But for the life of her, she couldn't remember *why*.

"Stay here with me, where you are free." His mouth closed in, until it was only inches from hers. "Kiss me, Kate."

His words were made of a midnight magic that held her in place, until all she could do was kiss him. Something bittersweet tugged at her heart as she claimed his mouth. Kissing him was something she could do for the rest of her life.

*Make me forget . . . Take me away from here . . .* Those words had brought her to this world. They seemed like a lifetime ago. Why had she said them? She couldn't remember.

The old Kate was gone. That girl was nothing more than a dream that vanished like mist at midday.

"Take me to bed, Roan," she pleaded.

Roan swept her into his arms and carried her to his bed, setting her upon the edge of it. Then he leaned in and captured her lips, stoking the embers of her desire into an inferno.

Roan brushed his thumbs along her cheekbones, tangled his tongue with hers, and rubbed his hard cock against her soft belly through the fabric of her dress. As if tuned to her senses, he caressed her face with that singular tenderness only he was capable of. He drew her in, teased her mouth, and set her body afire with desire hot enough to scorch her.

Kate ached for all he had to offer her, for all the pleasure he could give her. Why had she ever resisted him? She remembered those first few hours after meeting him, that night when he'd been naked in that bathing pool when she'd seen every inch of his rock-hard body. She hadn't been afraid of him then, but she had been afraid of what it would mean to say yes to him, to surrender. Now she knew just how good it could feel to trust herself, to let herself experience passion with him.

Still holding her head in both hands, Roan now abandoned her lips and moved to her chin, then her earlobe. He trailed kisses down her neck. With each tiny bite or sinful graze of his teeth on her skin, Kate sank deeper into a haze of wicked pleasure. She held on to his broad shoulders as her knees trembled. If she'd still been standing, she would have buckled in his hold, her desire was so potent. She scooted closer to him on the bed, loving that it placed her hips at an equal height to his.

With a growl of sensual hunger, he grasped her bottom and jerked her to him, urging her to wrap her legs around him as he thrust his hips forward. When they locked eyes, his reflected the inferno now raging inside her. With a smug smile, Roan glanced down between their bodies.

"You're overdressed," he said, licking the shell of her ear.

"Then do something about it." Kate wanted to be bold with him, to entice him to take what he wanted and give her what she wanted too.

Roan slid her off the bed so she was once more standing on her feet, then twirled her in his arms so that he was standing behind her. His cock pressed against her lower back through the fabric of their clothes. He was so tall, dwarfing her in size, yet that somehow made things hotter between them. Roan had the power to do anything he wanted to her, but rather than force her, he seduced her sweetly, wickedly.

Goosebumps covered her skin as his large hand settled upon her lower belly, covering it with his elegant fingers as he clenched the fabric of her gown. Then those fingers slid to the slit in the bodice of her gown, sliding underneath the fabric to cup one of her breasts, tugging at her nipples.

"Oh God . . ." She dropped her head backward against his chest, savoring the rush of sensations that flooded her sex.

He chuckled darkly. "I believe my name is Roan . . . my darling Kate." He rolled her nipples between his fingertips until she moaned his name. His free hand pooled the fabric of her dress against one hip, lifting it up to bare her leg. Then that hand slid between her legs, cupping her mound before exploring it with long, questing fingers. He parted her slick folds and sank one inside of her. She arched into his hand, rubbing herself against him, desperate for more than just gentle penetration.

He leaned down behind her. "Who makes you wet, little one?"

"You . . . only you," she promised him, still urging her hips against his hand. He continued to play with her, fucking her with two fingers now, until she was almost embarrassed at the way her wetness was coating his hand and her inner thighs.

He sucked a spot under her earlobe and whispered, "Your heart's beating fast as a pixie's." His groin rocked against her backside again. "And you're gripping my fingers, craving my cock, aren't you?"

She bit her lip to stifle an answer. Shame burned her cheeks.

"Tell me, Kate. Do you want me?"

"Yes, oh please, yes, I want you!" Her words came out in an achy groan as her body vibrated wherever he touched or even mentioned. Why was he torturing her like this? He could just bend her over the bed and take her, but he was teasing her until she wanted to weep with her need to come.

He curved his fingers on her chin, turning her face to him. He covered her lips once more with another bone-melting kiss.

Roan broke their kiss, stepped back, and unlaced the back of her gown. She stood there in nothing but her panties, waiting for his next move, listening to his ragged breathing. When he didn't say or do anything, she glanced over her shoulder. Tall and impressive, his muscled body almost seemed to vibrate with his barely controlled hunger as his eyes raked over her. But it was the all-consuming desire in his stare that took her breath away. He desired her with the same madness that she did him. They were locked together in this world of lust.

She turned to face him, a little scared to realize how much she wanted him. It made her feel reckless, ready to do *anything* with him in his bed. He closed the distance between them, pulling her against his rock-solid chest and invading her mouth once more with his probing tongue.

Kate gripped his shoulders, then buried her fingers in his soft hair. She removed the leather tie that kept it bound, and his hair fell like a silvery waterfall around his face as he bent his head to hers. He sucked her tongue, sending ripples of desire through her, scorching her soul. Her nipples and her clit hardened as she moaned.

He straightened, his lips swollen from the rough kiss.

"Do not move. Do not glance behind," he ordered, side-stepping her.

She heard the whisper of soft fabric and wondered if he was undressing.

He wasn't.

"Arms above your head," Roan commanded.

She obeyed, and he fastened the end of a long silk scarf to her left wrist. He'd tied the other end to the upper part of one of the tall posts at the foot of the bed. Then he bound her right wrist next to her left above her head. The hard but beautiful lines of his face softened as he glided his palms down her arms to her breasts. He could touch her at his leisure, and that only excited her more.

She had nowhere to go, and to her surprise, that didn't freak her out.

*What's wrong with me?*

Roan didn't give Kate time to dwell on that as he ripped her panties at the seams, dropping the shreds of wet lace to the ground.

"Splendid," he said, gliding his tongue over his lips as he gazed at her completely bare body.

She sank her teeth into her bottom lip to avoid moaning. His searing gaze ignited her flesh and melted her bones. A cool breeze caressed her, but she burst into flames whenever he sucked on her nipple. She squeezed her thighs together, afraid her sex would overflow. Roan suckled her breast as though it were a rare piece of fruit. As he feasted on one breast, he rolled the other nipple between his fingers.

"Roan!" The word tore out of her throat, full of need and desperate longing for him to possess her.

He chuckled as he switched to the other nipple, repeating his sweet torture. Her body responded. Her mind floated as pleasure built, but release lurked just beyond her reach.

Roan crouched in front of her and bound her ankles with additional strips of silk, binding her to the posts like an ancient sacrifice.

Kneeling, he held her gaze hostage and gripped her hips. He covered her sex with his mouth, groaning when he tasted her pleasure. She shivered and dropped her eyelids, shielding herself from his scrutiny as she realized he was watching her as his mouth moved over her clit.

He lifted his lips away from her body long enough to speak. "Do not look away."

She obeyed, despite her embarrassment.

He gave a sinful grin. "Don't pretend you don't enjoy this. Keep watching me, Kate. I want you to see how much I enjoy your taste."

She didn't doubt him, so she stared as he licked the folds of her flesh, swirling his tongue in a way that nearly made her eyes roll back in her head. Her flesh quivered under his lips, tongue, and fingers. He sucked at her clitoris while two of his fingers stretched her to that threshold between pain and pleasure. His other hand found a breast and kneaded it gently. Bright spots turned her sight hazy as blood rushed through her veins. She licked parched lips and heaved as a powerful orgasm coiled deep inside her.

"Fuck! I'm going to come," she gasped, her voice husky in the cool night air.

"Not yet you aren't," Roan growled.

She gaped at him. "I can't stop it, Roan. Not once I get too close . . ."

He knitted his eyebrows, gazing up into her eyes. "Hungry little thing. If you come without permission, I will leave you wanting over and over again until you learn to come when I say you can."

Roan resumed sucking her flesh with fresh enthusiasm.

She clawed at the silk binding her to the post, biting her lip as waves of ecstasy threatened to pull her under.

*Don't think about him, think about anything else . . .* She tried and failed.

"Please, Roan," she whispered.

His tongue floated over her clit in various rhythms, leaving her guessing as to his next move, then stopped. "Please what?"

She twisted in his grip, but he dug his powerful fingers into her hips to stop her. The slight bite of pain helped her focus.

"*Please* let me come," she said through gritted teeth, not ashamed to beg, but still trying to obey his command.

His hands covered her breasts, which hung heavy and aching after his attentions. He tugged at her nipples, and she cried out at the stimulation of such an overly sensitive spot.

Molding his mouth to her folds, he pressed his tongue to the sweet spot that sent her heart rate skyrocketing.

She shook, head to toes, with the effort to keep her release at bay.

He whispered against her, "Come for me now, my little Kate. Give me your screams of pleasure."

Her body exploded, brighter than a supernova, and her soul soared. Her flesh quivered around Roan's tongue, gripping it with viselike strength. Her ears rang, her muscles twitched, and her heart thundered. As the waves of pleasure ebbed, Roan sucked harder, and the cycle began again.

She thought she couldn't take it anymore, but didn't say anything. He'd proven her wrong the last time.

Roan rose to his feet and kissed her. Such a decadent idea, tasting her own pleasure on his lips. Yet, it turned her on.

He drew back. "You taste divine, don't you think? Have some more." He dipped two fingers inside her mouth. "Suck them dry."

She did, holding his gaze as she licked his fingers. His wings fluttered behind him whenever her tongue explored the pads of his fingers.

He smirked. "Good girl."

Her body quaked under that praise. God, she wanted to be his good girl, to feel proud that he liked how she was with him like this.

Then he released her from the silk bindings.

"Do you want to taste me?" he asked in that subtle, dangerous voice, and she found herself nodding.

"Then kneel." He put a hand on her shoulder but didn't

force her down. She understood, then, that this was her choice. He wouldn't force her.

She knelt into the soft white carpet that covered part of the room.

He opened the front of his trousers and freed his erection. Her heart skipped a few beats at the sight of his thick cock throbbing. The mushroom-shaped head glistened with his pleasure, and thick veins pulsed farther down. She knew what he wanted her to do, but she'd never done this before. Still, she wanted to try. She leaned close to him in silent encouragement for him to show her what to do next.

He traced her lips with the head. The softness of his skin surprised her.

As she took him into her mouth, he fisted her hair, making it impossible for her to move her head.

Unsure what to do, she glanced up at him.

He smiled down at her. "Lick and suck it. I shall do the rest."

She flattened her tongue as he fucked her mouth with slow thrusts in and slower withdrawals out. With each pass, he grunted and pulled her hair tighter. She whimpered as her sex pulsed in sync with his shaft.

Kate hollowed her cheeks, sucking him until he released. She swallowed, tasting him, and his eyes filled with pleasure, giving silent praise as he gazed down at her.

He smoothed her hair with gentle fingers before he slid out of her mouth. "Your mouth feels better than I could ever have dreamed, little one."

"Are we . . . ?"

"Done?" He laughed. "Not yet, my darling Kate. Not yet." He raised her to her feet and scooped her once more into his arms, setting her down on the bed as he stripped his trousers off. He then climbed onto the bed, moving toward her. She lay back, already worn out, hoping he would do whatever he wished now, and she would lie there and enjoy it, even if it killed her with pleasure.

Roan now loomed above her, his body covering hers, his wings shimmering in the muted glow of the wall sconces. He kissed her lips, her closed eyelids, the shell of her ear, and her throat in soft, hot kisses. Her body warmed as though she lay beneath a summer sun. Her hands roamed over his chest and shoulders, until she fisted a hand in his hair. She moaned softly as his lips teased one taut nipple.

He explored her body as though they'd never been together before, and Kate basked in the heated glow that Roan's mouth and hands created. He nibbled on the sensitive parts of her hips and then rolled her onto her stomach so he could explore her back, her shoulders, and the dimples above her bottom. Wherever he kissed, it sent sharp jolts of arousal through her.

He lifted her hips, placing a pillow beneath her, and raised her bottom in the air. She moaned as he stroked her wet folds. His knees nudged hers apart as he knelt behind her and entered her, slow, gentle, but deep. His cock seared her channel with heat as he stretched and filled her. He felt even bigger from this angle, and she writhed beneath him, her fingers digging into the lavish bedding as he continued to have his way with her.

"You'll *always* be mine, Kate." Roan's voice was soft but carried a hint of a growl that she was coming to love. He gripped her hips, driving into her and out again, building his thrusts to a furious rhythm.

She could barely think past the exquisite pleasure of him taking her. This dark dance between the sheets held them both prisoners of their desire. He seemed to go for hours, torturing her with near climaxes over and over as he drove her to the edge and then slowed before starting over again. When she could not take it anymore, Kate's voice grew hoarse with begging for her release.

Roan at last moved to bend over her, his hands grasping her wrists as he lay above her, his chest pressing against her back as he hammered his hips against her ass. Then she flew apart, her body spiraling in exquisite pleasure. He shouted her name, his body becoming rigid as he followed her over the precipice. Heat filled her as she welcomed his release. His breath, warm and sweet, covered her neck as he took a moment to catch his breath.

"What have you done to me, little one? *What have you done?*" Roan's voice was full of wonder as he pressed kisses to her shoulder. Kate couldn't speak, but she smiled as he stayed buried within her a moment longer. He withdrew and rolled her to face him, curling his arms around her to tuck her into his body.

"You fill me with such madness," he whispered against the crown of her hair.

In his eyes, Kate saw thousands of years of life with him at her side. She saw herself exploring everything this universe had to offer. She saw an infinite stretch of time that could be hers to live, to love, to discover her truest dreams and her deepest desires. Roan could give her all that and more.

Her gaze shifted to stare at the distant labyrinth. Strange . . . she could not remember why she'd ever wanted to walk through its dark and winding passageways. Her memories were like a melancholic dream that filled her chest with an ache that had no name.

A light from far beyond the vast labyrinth caught her eye. It was like a single flame upon a dark sea of midnight that glowed bright.

"Roan, what is that light?"

Roan rolled to face the balcony doors to see where she

pointed. He cursed and threw himself out of bed. "No . . . no . . ." In a matter of seconds, he simply snapped his fingers and was dressed.

"Roan, what is it?" Kate clutched the bedsheets to cover herself.

"The beacon fires of the dwarves of the Black Hills. Culan has attacked Vol Buldohr." His wings were gone, and he was sheathing his sword in a scabbard at his hip.

She scrambled to get out of bed. "Culan . . . the Seelie king?"

"Babbitt!" Roan bellowed.

The brownie popped into the room.

"Dress Kate at once and take her to Rath and my sister." Roan glanced between Kate and Babbitt, his blue eyes burning with kingly rage. "Tell Rath that Kate is his mission now. He must see her safely out of danger."

"Roan—" With the sheet wrapped around her body, Kate ran to him as he stopped at the bedchamber door. "Roan, please, tell me what's happening." She grasped his arm, feeling the taut muscles beneath her fingers.

"The war I have dreaded has begun. We are about to engage the Seelie army. Follow Rath's orders and remain by my sister's side." He pulled Kate into his arms, kissing her one last time. A moment later he was gone, leaving her and Babbitt alone. The brownie snapped her fingers, and Kate was back in her jeans and sweater, clean and untorn.

"Mistress Kate, come with me at once." The brownie tugged on Kate's arm. "We will find Lord Rath and Lady Eudora. They will know what to do."

CALLS TO ARMS FILLED THE PALACE AS THE TWILIGHT COURT FELL into chaos. His soldiers met him in the throne room, where Roan instructed them to fortify the palace and prepare for an assault. Dozens of Fae women joined his warriors. They were dressed in slender but strong battle armor, and many carried bows with elf shot arrows or blades. Even though they were ladies of the Twilight Court, they were not defenseless. He commanded them to guard the windows and the key entry points of the castle.

"My lord!" One of the ladies pointed to a shooting star of light that, rather than fall to the earth, was flying upward into the night sky.

"Hagni . . ." Roan recognized the distress call of his trusted friend. He reached out, opening a single Fae road in the direction of that light. The air shimmered around him, and a figure burst into being before him. Hagni fell to his knees, an elf shot arrow buried in his back. Roan knelt beside the loyal warrior who had fought alongside him over the centuries. Hagni looked up at Roan, his eyes full of sorrow and pain.

"My king . . ." Hagni swallowed hard as he struggled for breath. "The dwarves are fighting, and the Lady Kyma has been taken to safety deep in the keep. But they cannot hold the line."

"Hold still. Let me remove the arrow." Roan tried to get a better look at the arrow embedded in the guard's back, but Hagni shook his head. "Too late . . . my king. Too late. Andvari said to use the ring. He said . . . you'd know what he means."

Impossible. He couldn't use that cursed ring. The battle could not be that lost already, could it?

"Defend . . . the court . . . Roan." Hagni's eyes clouded with death as his last breath drained from his body. Roan stared at his old friend in shock. Death was so foreign to a Fae. It was unnatural. It was *agony* to even consider.

"Rest in the starlight, old friend," Roan whispered as he lowered Hagni's body to the ground.

"Lord Arun, the labyrinth is burning!" a maiden shouted from a window. Roan rushed over and stared out into the night. The distant boundary of the labyrinth to the south glowed with a vermilion edge that stood stark in the night. A swarm of pixies burst into the throne room, fluttering around the ceiling, their tiny voices crying out what they had seen.

"Fire sprites aid the Seelie," they shrieked. "They will burn us all!"

Fire sprites were not creatures that Roan guarded his labyrinth against. Sprites of all kinds were considered neutral in the battle between Seelie and Unseelie. The labyrinth would not keep them out, just as it did not keep out the pixies that roamed the passageways. But the fire from the sprites should not have been able to harm the labyrinth. Something was wrong with his wards and spells.

Roan bellowed orders to those nearest him to guard the palace. Then he rallied his Shadow Guards to follow him. He opened a Fae road and leapt out of the window, instantly reaching the southern part of the labyrinth, his guards right behind him. The acrid smell of smoke choked him as he landed a quarter of a mile from the burning walls.

"What are your orders, my lord?" Toran, the new head of the Shadow Guard, asked as he unsheathed his sword.

"Defend the land. Kill if you must."

"Even the sprites?" Toran asked in a low voice.

"Even the sprites," Roan said. "They have chosen their side

and will feel the consequences. Somehow they have helped break apart the very enchantments that guard our lands."

Toran gave a solemn nod and spread the orders among the Fae. Roan stared out across the vast walls that were lighting up with fresh flames. Somewhere behind those fires was Culan.

Roan tightened his grip upon his sword as a flurry of fire sprites rounded the nearest tall ivy-covered walls. He threw a bolt of power from his palm, sending the majority of them careening backward until they crashed into stone. A sudden cry had Roan and his men spinning around to face a battalion of Seelie warriors, flanking them from the other side.

"To me!" Roan roared and plunged into the fray.

Screams arose from Roan's right as a massive snakelike creature slithered out of the nearest passageway and barreled into the Seelie fighters. Several of them turned to stone the moment they gazed upon the basilisk. It whipped its tail, lashing out at others before striking out and biting those in front of it with its long, venomous teeth. It charged left after half of the Seelie soldiers.

"To the right!" Roan roared. The basilisk would kill the Seelie in front of it, leaving Roan and his guards free to attack the right flank of Culan's army.

The labyrinth was fighting back.

CHAPTER

# FIFTEEN

*The king of the dark woods paced his moonlit palace, fearful that his
bride would be hurt in the dark world that he'd brought her to, but
she dared to shine on in the shadows, defying every evil curse that
lingered in his woods.*

—Anon., *Tales from the Twilight Court*

Babbitt and Kate materialized by the sea, the sand shimmering like diamond dust around them as the waves rolled in.

"Stay here, Mistress Kate!" Babbitt vanished, leaving Kate to stare up at the towering palace of the Twilight Court.

"Kate?" A deep, familiar voice had her spinning around. Patch and Magda were rushing across the sandy beach toward her. She embraced the troll and even hugged the ever-grumpy kobold.

"What happened, girl? The earth is speaking to me . . . it

screams of blood and death," the kobold said. "Something bad's happened, hasn't it?"

"The Seelie attacked the dwarves," said Kate. "Roan sent me with Babbitt. I was supposed to hide with Eudora and Rath, but—"

The brownie reappeared on the beach, but she wasn't alone. Lady Eudora and Rath were with her. Behind them was a small boy with blond hair and large, worried eyes. The child unsettled her. There was something about him that Kate didn't like.

"Kate, where is this cave you spoke of?" Eudora asked.

"Over there." Kate pointed to the cave entrance, half hidden in the distance.

"Everyone inside the cave, now," Rath ordered. He scooped the child into his arms, and they all ran for the shelter of the cave entrance. Eudora clutched a silver bow, and a quiver of arrows was strapped to her back. Gone was the princess's beautiful crown and dress. Instead, she wore a white shirt tucked into black trousers, along with a slender silver chest plate. A fierce light filled her eyes. She was a Fae warrior princess.

"I should be at Roan's side," Eudora said, her usually soft voice now steeled with resolve. "But he has commanded us to protect you and Caden, which means keeping far away from the battle."

"Caden?" Kate said the name, not knowing who the Fae princess meant.

Eudora's eyes narrowed. "Yes, Caden. Your brother." She pointed at the boy Rath had been carrying, now back on his own feet. The boy was staring at her, just as confused as she was.

"I don't have a brother," Kate said. "I don't have . . ." She was certain she had no brother . . . she was certain she didn't even have a family. She had no family, no one . . . except Roan. But that didn't make sense. Surely she'd had a father. A mother . . . Was she an orphan? Why couldn't she remember her parents . . . or even the lack of them?

"Kate?" The little boy reached for her hand. "You don't remember me?"

Kate jerked away from the child and stepped back. "No. I don't know you . . . I mean . . . please leave me alone." She didn't want to look at those eyes staring at her with such pain.

A sudden throbbing in her head made her wince and close her eyes.

"How could he do this?" Eudora hissed at Rath. "He's robbed her of her memories."

That didn't make sense. Roan wouldn't do that. It wasn't even possible. Was it?

"We have no time to worry about that now. Follow me, everyone. We need to put distance between us and the palace," Rath said. The glowworms above them began to shine, pulsing as they pointed inward, away from the cave opening.

The tall Fae warrior led the way, following the glowworm trail that lit a winding path through the cave. They walked in single file, but Kate fell behind, looking back at the distant cave entrance one more time. She couldn't just leave Roan like this . . . but there was no way to get back. It would take too long to scale the cliffside again, and most likely he wasn't even in the palace anymore. War had come to the land of magic.

"Roan, be careful," she breathed.

When she turned back to follow the others, they were gone. She was alone in the dark caves.

"What? How?" Kate asked. She'd only looked away a moment. They couldn't have gotten that far. She cupped her hands around her mouth and shouted, "Eudora! Patch!

Magda!" The silence was punctuated by the sound of dripping water from a great distance.

"No," she whispered. "No . . . no, no . . ." She looked back toward the cave entrance, but it had vanished as well. She was lost . . . in the dark.

Kate ran blindly through the caves, shouting their names. Her hands got scraped whenever she collided against a wall in the dark or stumbled over the jutting crystals. Their once vibrant green glow had faded to a dull milky white and was barely visible.

"Help!" Kate shouted until her voice grew hoarse. When she stopped, her legs shook hard enough that she could barely keep moving. Had she been here for hours? Days?

She lost all sense of time as she leaned against one of the walls and sank down to sit on the floor. Despair filled her, making it hard to breathe. She was alone, with no way out and no way to help Roan. Even the glowworms had abandoned her, their lights so dull far above her that she wondered if she'd ever see them shine again.

*This way,* a voice whispered in the dark. *This way . . .*

The glowworms above her began to pulse brighter, like newborn stars in the night sky. As if in a dream, she moved in the direction of the voice. The dark world around her transformed into a silver forest of ghostly aspen trees and a mist that reflected shimmering mirages of herself in every direction.

Where was she? The cave was gone. She was alone in a forest she'd never seen before. Was this part of the labyrinth?

A gentle, melodic voice echoed in the mist around her. "We meet at last . . . Kate of the Winslows."

Kate stood still, holding her breath as a figure made of starlight appeared. The figure who came toward her was so beautiful it hurt to look at her. She glowed with a light that made Kate think of sunlight rather than moonlight. The blue gown she wore was the color of a perfect summer sky. It was the color of Roan's eyes when he smiled.

"Who are you?"

The woman stopped a short distance away from Kate. "My name is Thalia." She smiled as she took another few steps in Kate's direction. Kate gasped. A trail of brightly colored flowers bloomed in the wake of the woman's footprints.

"Thalia . . . you're Roan and Eudora's mother." Kate looked around at the silver woods. Was this a place out of space and time, as Roan had said? Goosebumps broke out on her arms as she realized this place did feel strange. It felt as though nothing moved or ever *changed* here.

"I am." The woman held out a hand. For reasons she couldn't explain, Kate instantly trusted her. She placed her hand in Thalia's. Something about her gentle grip stirred feelings within Kate's chest that made her heart ache. She was supposed to remember...but remember what?

"Roan needs you." What compelled her to say that, Kate didn't know, but part of her feared she might upset Roan's mother. "You have to come back."

Thalia didn't seem upset. "My son has always been alone. Born with the magic of Seelie and Unseelie, he has never felt he could be accepted . . . just as you have felt most of your life. Standing alone made you both strong. You share that same strength of people born to such vast loneliness. But you cannot survive alone forever. Even the mightiest of trees still grow strongest when in the midst of a forest. You and Roan are stronger together."

Kate shook her head. "I'm not strong. I can't fight at his side. I can't protect him. I have no power here. I'm just . . . *human.*"

Thalia shook her head. "He doesn't need you to carry a

sword. You possess far greater weapons, greater ways to protect those you care about."

Thalia began to walk and Kate followed, still holding the woman's hand. The fear and anxiety she'd felt in the cave were long gone. She was safe in the silver woods with this woman who felt so much like a mother to her. If she'd had a mother . . .

"What weapons do I have?" Kate asked.

"Love," Thalia said. "It is the first magic, the *truest* magic . . . and it can be wielded by anyone. Come with me. I wish to show you something."

They stopped beside a river that ran through the woods. Kate watched the clear water rush over the smooth river stones. It was strange, but she seemed unable to conjure up any worries or fears.

"Before I show you, we must discuss what's happened to you." Thalia placed her hands on Kate's shoulders, peering into her eyes.

Kate blinked. "I don't understand."

"My son has done something to you. Something many would see as unforgiveable."

That was impossible. He'd only ever shown her pleasure and taken care of her. She couldn't imagine what he'd done to her that would be unforgiveable.

"In his misguided attempt to protect you, he has stolen something precious from you."

"He hasn't, he—"

Eudora's voice came back to her. *He's robbed her of her memories.*

At the time she'd been so worried about Roan and the battle with the Seelie that she hadn't stopped to process what Eudora had said.

"Yes," Thalia said gently, as if she'd heard Eudora's voice in her head. "He took away everything dark and sorrowful. Everything memory he believed you would be better off without. He also believed that if you couldn't remember your life, your brother, that you'd choose to stay with him forever."

He'd taken away something that had hurt her. How could that be unforgiveable? She didn't want memories that hurt her. Why would anyone? And he'd done it to keep her here with him. She should be angry about that, that he'd do something like that control her emotions, but...he'd taken away the pain. How could she be angry at him for that?

"Is that such a bad thing? I don't feel any different." In fact, Kate had never felt clearer, freer. She wasn't certain that the memories were worth anything but pain.

Thalia lifted Kate's chin so that she met the woman's eyes. "He took from you everything he wished someone else would take from him, but he does not understand, and he does not have that right. I will return your memories to you—"

"No!" Kate jerked her chin free of Thalia's grasp. She didn't want to feel any more pain or sorrow. "I don't want them back." She turned to flee, but Thalia's voice halted her.

"Without the pain of life's worst moments, you can never truly know the value of your greatest joys. He took all of it from you, not just the bad, but also the good. What we experience, the good and the bad, teaches us the most important lessons in life. We must look inward and ask ourselves who we want to be. Without those lessons, you would never know what matters to you, what you would move heaven and earth to protect and love. To love my son, to save him, you must accept all of who you are, Kate of the Winslows. The good and the bad. You are the sum of all your dreams, your memories, your desires, your grief, and your joys."

Kate turned, her heart filling with hope. "You think he loves me?"

Thalia smiled. "In a thousand years, my son has never let

anyone close to his heart, except you. You have traveled where others have tried and failed. You have gone deeper into the labyrinth than anyone else, and the dark paths have remained clear of most of its dangers. You, the woman he loves, have shown courage within those walls. Because of who you are, you not only survived, you stood strong. You got back up on your feet whenever you were dealt a blow."

Kate shook her head. "But I was afraid."

"Courage isn't the absence of fear, it is persevering in spite of it. It's facing the darkness within your soul and realizing it has no true power over you. It comes from those moments where your memories have guided you and reminded you what made you the woman you are."

*The darkness . . .* Kate had been in the dark for years, the darkness of not having enough love, of an uncertain future, of not trusting herself or believing she was enough. When Roan had sent her to the labyrinth, she'd faced darkness and she hadn't let her fear rule her.

Was Thalia right? Was she brave and she simply hadn't realized it?

"Do you trust me, Kate?" Thalia spoke, but Kate heard Roan's voice when his mother spoke. She saw *his* eyes through his mother's as Thalia held out her hand once more.

Kate stared at her hand. Her instincts made her want to run away from the pain, from the memories she knew would be agony. Then she thought of Roan and the look in his eyes as he'd danced with her. He'd seen her that night, all of her, just as he had the other nights he'd been with her. He'd wanted her, but not because of desire alone. He'd wanted something more.

"I can save him?" she asked.

"You can. Let your heart guide you. You will know what to do when the time is right."

Kate placed her hand in Thalia's. Pain shot through her body as memories struck her like bolts of lightning and visions flashed across her mind's eye, forcing her to relive *everything* in an instant.

*Her mother spun her around the yard with her hands, both of them laughing . . . her mother's body lay in a coffin, her features waxen . . . dirt covered the coffin as it was lowered into the grave . . .*

*Sandra taking her father's arm and kissing him . . . Sandra pushing Kate farther and farther away from her father . . .*

*Little Caden in a cradle, his chubby hands grasping the teddy bear that Kate had snuck into his crib . . . her standing apart from her family at Caden's birthday party . . . thinking of how her own birthdays had been forgotten . . .*

*The college campus, vast, beautiful, exciting . . . the face of a cute boy who knocked her down on the grass . . . the sunlight of his smile . . . the promise of the life that had its own adventure if she ever returned home.*

So many memories, so many parts of herself that she didn't know she could ever want back, but now that she had them . . . as much as some of them hurt . . . they were *hers*. They belonged within her heart. Thalia was right. She felt deeper, richer, even with the agony of her mother's death and her father's distance. She was herself again in a way she'd never thought she would need to be.

But Roan was not and could never be a part of her previous life or a part of that other world. The weight of her life encapsulated in a thousand memories buried her like an avalanche . . . but one thought rose to the surface.

*I have to save Roan.*

No matter what she chose about her future or what Roan had done to her, she had to save him. Thalia was right. Those memories, the ones that Roan had taken to protect her, she needed them. Even the hardest, most painful ones. They made her who she was. Losing her mother, growing up so alone, connecting to Caden and then being brave enough to start a new life at college. All of those things had made her the woman she was, the woman who had braved the labyrinth to save her brother, the woman who'd fallen in love with Roan.

Thalia watched her with a penetrating, all-knowing look.

"What must I do?" asked Kate.

Thalia pointed to a flowing river just beyond where she stood. "Time is a river here. Where we stand, we are beyond its reach. To join my son, you must step into the river."

Kate started forward, but Thalia stopped her. "You will need this." She held out a slender dagger, the one that she had stolen from Roan's bedchamber.

"Where did you get that?" She thought she'd lost it climbing up to the palace.

Thalia placed the dagger in Kate's hand. "Where I found it does not matter. What matters is that this blade can wound a Seelie warrior . . . even a king."

"Culan," Kate breathed in understanding.

"Be brave, Kate. Be true to yourself."

Kate swallowed hard. It was difficult to leave this place, which felt so calm and safe. No wonder Thalia had dwelled in these silver woods for so long.

"If this is the river of time . . . is it possible to see my mother? To go back to a moment when she was still alive?" The need to see her mother had been buried so deep, but now it was clawing its way to the surface.

"It is possible. You could return to a time when she lived." Thalia's tone was quiet. "But it comes with a cost."

"What cost?" Kate would give anything to see her mother again.

"Once you step into the river, you cannot return here. The way will vanish. The mists of time will drift far out of reach, and my son will be lost to you. You will be a child once again and live the past with your mother, starting over. Your mother will still die, your father will still move on. All that has happened will happen again. None of that is within your power to change. But if you go back, you will never remember *this* world. This future will never come to pass. Before you choose, you must see Roan's world as it will be if you never set foot in the realm of the Fae." Thalia waved a hand, and the woods around Kate filled with muted sunlight that cast images in the mist.

Patch drowning in the morgens' pool because she was not there to save him. Magda perishing beneath the stones hurled by her own kind because Kate was not there to stop them. The walls of the labyrinth growing taller, the passages darker . . . the endless lives lost in the winding darkness as the labyrinth stretched forever and ever, covering the land. Roan sitting upon a throne, his eyes cold and vengeful as he watched his lands destroyed by the Seelie. Eudora, Rath, even Babbitt all lay dead, Seelie weapons having taken their lives. All because of a war that never should have come about.

Kate swallowed back a sob as the grim future tore her heart in two.

"No," she gasped, and the visions vanished.

"You cannot save your mother or change the past . . . but you can change the future."

Thalia pointed at the river. "Make your choice, Kate of the Winslows."

On shaky legs, Kate approached the water. Within the diamond glints of the rushing flow, she glimpsed her mother's smiling face.

"I miss you . . ." Kate whispered to the reflection of her mother within the fairy river. "I miss you so much, it feels like I'm dying inside." The desire to choose her mother, to choose her past, was so strong. She wanted to leap into the water, to go back to a time when she hadn't lost anything in life yet. Even knowing she'd lose her mother all over again, she wanted those few precious years back.

The enchanted water showed her mother's face as she spun Kate around in the backyard. Fireflies glowed in the warm green night. *"And he shall say, 'Kiss me, Kate.'"* Her mother's voice drifted up from the water as she spoke of the dashing man that Kate would someday know was her destiny.

*Roan.* He was her destiny.

Her mother wouldn't want her to return to the past, to lose herself in it. Not when she could save not only the man she loved but the world that had shown her she was strong, that she was worthy.

"The winds of time will shift soon, Kate. You must choose . . ." Thalia's voice came from a great distance now. Kate dove into the water, dagger gripped in her hand as she chose her fate.

Roan swung his broadsword in a large arc, slicing the nearest Seelie warrior in half. The labyrinth's passageways were now filled with the dead—both Seelie and Unseelie. Friend and foe alike stained the soil with their blood. But Roan could not stop, could not grieve, until he killed his cousin and ended this.

He spotted the Seelie king across the arena of fighting warriors. "Culan!"

The Seelie king turned to face him with a savage grin. His fair looks held a darkness that reminded Roan so much of his father. "At last."

The two men charged at each other, swords raised. They connected in a clash of ringing steel.

Culan sneered. "Where is your human pet, cousin?" Culan shoved hard with his blade, pushing Roan back. "The one you violated our sacred treaty for?" Culan continued. "Perhaps when you are dead, I will take her as my prize. She would suit me well, wouldn't she?"

Roan knew his cousin was baiting him, but that didn't mean Culan's threats didn't burn like a fire sprite's rage in his chest. He jerked his blade free and swung at Culan from a different angle. His cousin barely leapt aside, nearly losing an arm.

Around them, the warriors from both lands fought on, their cries a cacophony in Roan's ears.

Suddenly, a figure appeared in a burst of light just behind Culan. The clash of steel slowed as everyone struggled to regain their sight. Too late, Roan recognized who the figure was. It was Kate, standing mere feet from Culan.

"Kate!" he bellowed.

Her eyes grew wide as she took in the hundreds of dead Fae around her, petrified. Before she could react, Culan grasped Kate by the throat, lifting her up. She dropped the dagger she held as she clawed at Culan's hand, trying to free herself.

"So you are the tempting mortal my cousin broke our ancient laws for." Culan's gaze swept over Kate, whose face turned red as she struggled for breath. "You are the reason for this war."

"Let her go, Culan. Your battle is with me."

Culan laughed. "Oh, but this is far too amusing, Roan. To see you squirm with fear. Beg for her life on your knees and perhaps I will let her go."

Roan met Kate's gaze, and she tried to shake her head. She would rather die? But he couldn't let that happen. Roan would give everything to save Kate. His land, his people, his palace, his power, and his life were forfeit if it would save her.

Roan eased down on one knee, and Culan's eyes widened, as if he hadn't expected Roan to capitulate.

"Culan, let her go. *Please.*" The words came out a growl because he feared Culan wouldn't release her no matter what he did. Just then, a great and terrible idea struck him. He knew how to stop Culan. He knew what he must do.

Roan reached into his trouser pocket and pulled out the cursed ring Andvari had given to him.

He slipped the ring onto his left ring finger. The curse hit him like a thunderclap. Exquisite power surged through him, expanding his control over the universe. He harnessed the winds of time, reversing the deaths of his men. His soldiers, once lying still upon the battlefield, now rose, taking their arms up again, outnumbering Culan's soldiers as they dove back into the fight. He wasn't sure how long his hold on time would last, if he'd be able to keep those men alive. The ring's power was more a mystery to him than he wished it to be.

The veins on his hand turned black. With a curse, Roan used his powers over time itself to hide the deathly spell that was crawling through his body. Culan could not see that, could not know what would be the end. He dug his hands into the earth, holding himself up on his knees when he felt ill enough to collapse.

"What was that?" Culan demanded as he spied the ring. "A trick? What magic are you hiding from me, cousin?" He glanced around at the newly risen soldiers, who were staring at him, their weapons raised as they fought once more for the Twilight Court.

"I hide nothing from you," Roan lied. He fought against the black moon power, but soon it would take him. All he had to do was last just a little bit longer, hide the deadly effects of the ring just for a few moments more.

"Give it to me!" Culan threw Kate to the ground, forgetting her. She lay on her side, gasping but alive. "If you won't give it to me, I'll take it."

Culan surged forward, kicking Roan in the chest. Roan fell onto his back, and Culan crushed Roan's left wrist with his boot as he bent down and pried the ring off Roan's finger. His cousin stared at it, his eyes dark with hunger.

"No! You are not worthy of its power," Roan said, his body weakening as the poison from the dark moon continued to move through him. He knew that if he let his cousin think the ring was a thing to be coveted, it would entice Culan to take it from him.

"And you are? I think not." Culan slid the ring onto his finger and grinned as he raised his sword. "Such power," he rasped, his eyes glowing overbright as fire burst from his free hand in a ball of flame. "I will harness the power of the sun," he roared with triumph. Then he slung the flames as though throwing a spear of light toward the battle. It struck the earth, rippling outward with fire. Men, Seelie and Unseelie, screamed as they were devoured by flames.

Culan swung back to face Roan. "You always were the weaker of us. You cannot stop me, not with your silly tricks of time."

"Ahh . . . but you forget, cousin . . . time comes for us all . . . in the end." Even an immortal could not hold back the fate of the end if it was destined to come. And the bells of time were tolling now for Culan, the silver ringing sound a painful blow to Roan's cousin.

Culan's eyes flashed with pain and confusion, and he stumbled, his grip on his sword faltering momentarily.

"What magic is this? What have you given me?" Culan

stared at Roan, his eyes wide with shock and agonizing pain. "I hear bells . . . I . . ." He glanced around, seeking the source of the sound that only he and Roan could hear. "No . . . it can't be . . . I am king . . . I . . ." Culan's face took on a fierce but frightened look full of madness. He was still dangerous, still a threat to Kate if he realized she was close by. Roan knew Culan would kill her if he had the chance.

He struggled to get back up on his knees. The cursed ring would slow Culan down, but what if it didn't slow him enough and he went after Kate again?

Kate climbed to her feet, retrieving her small dagger. She looked between Roan and Culan, then burst into a run straight toward Culan. Everything around Roan seemed to slow as he reached out with his magic to stop time, to protect her, to stop her from doing what she was going to do, but he could not harness the winds of time for long—they jerked free of his hold. Roan had never felt so helpless in his life. He'd used up most of his strength earlier on, trying to slow the advance of the Seelie forces, giving his soldiers a chance to regroup. And the ring had taken almost all of what he had left within him to wield in Kate's defense.

"No, Kate!" Roan bellowed as she leapt at Culan's back and thrust the dagger between his armor plates. It sank in, but it wasn't a fatal blow.

With a roar, Culan threw Kate off his back. She landed beside Roan on the ground with a hard thud.

"Is that the best you can do, you damned little—" Culan lunged for Kate, his blade held aloft.

With the last of his physical strength, Roan knelt and stabbed his blade up into Culan's chest, just below the edge of his armor.

Culan stumbled back, the sword in his hands falling to the ground. Kate and Roan watched as he collapsed, black spiderwebs crossing his skin as the cursed magic moved through him. The bells within Roan's mind grew louder, tolling of doom, of death . . . of the end of time . . . for Culan . . . for himself. He'd always feared the sound of silver bells, they were painful for a Fae to hear, but now . . . He could not outrun the sound, and despite what they would bring, he could hear the beauty in the ringing notes. The purity of them. He glanced once more at his cousin.

Culan's eyes were still, the light within them gone.

"Kate . . ." Roan managed to get onto both knees. The fighting slowed around them. The Seelie, seeing their king dead, began to throw down their weapons. Kate threw her arms around his neck and covered him with frantic kisses. But he could scarcely feel her lips anymore. How strange, this feeling of losing his senses, slowly, bit by bit. Black shadows began to bleed in at the corners of his vision. He strained his gaze, trying to chase them away.

"Kate . . ." he said again as he gently held her back so he could see her face.

Kate gasped. "Roan . . . your skin. It's . . . ." She looked between him and Culan, noting the similarity of their appearances. "What's happening to you?"

"I don't have much time," he said. The pain was growing. How strange it was for an immortal to feel the pain of death. It was like nothing he'd ever felt before. Like an eternal shadow was passing over the moon, blocking out the light and, with it, stealing away everything he was. He'd always wondered why mortals feared death so much. Now he understood. It was an ending, and endings were such dark and lonely things, weren't they?

"No." Kate grasped his arms, holding on to him. "I won't let you go. I—"

Roan shook his head. "It's too late . . ."

"I don't understand." Kate moved her hands up to his face, holding him between her palms. "This whole world is magic! Someone can heal you. Eudora can, she . . ." Kate's words were breaking as she tried to speak.

Roan turned his face to kiss one of her palms and managed a small smile. "This is but a dream . . . and all dreams must end. It's time to send you home."

"No! I won't go. I'm staying with *you*." Kate cupped Roan's face as that beautiful and often frightening intensity started to fade from his gaze. It terrified her. She was losing him. Just like she lost her mother . . . her father. And she couldn't go with him; the faraway look in his eyes warned her of that bitter truth.

"We're in this together," Kate said, her voice breaking. "I'm yours. You can't just leave me . . . You *can't*."

"It's all right," Roan whispered. "You will be all right, little one. You are brave and compassionate. There is no realm you cannot conquer with your love. Whatever happens next, you will be all right." Roan held her wrists as he held her gaze. "Forgive me . . ."

"Forgive you?" Kate's heart was fracturing like a sheet of ice. Each word he spoke sent deep cracks echoing through her.

"I stole your memories." He touched a pink crystal that hung around his neck. "I thought you would be happy if you no longer had that darkness within you . . . because I didn't want that darkness within me. I thought...if you had no one else to love...you might love *me* and stay..." Roan's eyes held a thousand years of sorrow. "But it was wrong to take them from you, wrong to take your choice away. I've never been worthy of you..."

"I know what you did, Roan." Kate stroked her fingers along the lines of his jaw, trying to soothe him. "Your mother told me, right before she gave them back."

Roan's eyes widened in shock.

"My mother?" His focus on her broke as he looked around the battlefield, but she wasn't there. She still dwelt in the mists of time. "Where is she?" He looked so young then, as young as a Fae king ever could, as his face lit up with a moment of hope.

"I was separated from Eudora and the others in the Crystal Cave. She brought me to her, in a silver forest covered with mist," Kate said. "She said it was a place out of time. She told me what you'd done . . . but I forgave you. I chose to come back for you, even knowing what you'd done." She hated admitting that, but she wanted only truth between her and Roan.

"I never should have taken them from you. They belong with you . . . they are part of you. That is what makes you strong. I didn't realize that until now." The pain and regret in his beautiful blue eyes nearly tore her very world apart. If she'd ever doubted a dark Fae king could have a heart, this was her proof that Roan did.

He let out a weary sigh, and the glow of his eyes dimmed a little more like a star's light fading out.

Kate felt so helpless; just as she could not aid a dying star in the distant sky, she could do nothing to help Roan now. It didn't stop her from trying, though. She'd believed Thalia when she'd said that Kate could save Roan. She just didn't know *how*.

"You can't go. Your mother said I could save you. I came back to save you." Kate could barely speak—her throat felt like she'd swallowed glass shards.

"You have already saved me." Roan's words were breathless, like an ancient forest breathing in soft sighs.

Only now did she realize that Eudora and Rath had arrived, standing behind Babbitt, Patch, and Magda. And clutching Eudora's hand was Caden . . . her brother. She wasn't alone. They were all here when she needed them the most.

Remembering how she'd forgotten Caden, even for so brief a time, was strange and painful. How she'd pulled away from him, not wanting to touch him, not wanting to remember. Now her hands ached to hold him close.

Caden pulled free of Eudora to come kneel beside her. "What's wrong with him, Kate?"

"I don't know . . ." Kate looked up at Roan's best friend and his sister, wishing they had answers.

Rath had his arms around Eudora now. Tears stained the princess's face, and Rath looked as if his sorrow would forever leave its mark upon his face.

"Is there nothing we can do?" Kate asked them.

Roan smiled sadly and answered for them. "There is not, my darling Kate. I used a cursed ring to draw Culan to his death. It is a magic too dark for even your light. It won't be long now . . ." He managed a wry smile. "I never imagined what it would be like to die . . . But if it meant saving you, I would do it again in every life I am given."

He steeled himself and grasped her hands. "I have just enough power left to send you and Caden home."

"No. Save your strength. I'm not leaving you." She pressed her forehead to his. "I'm *not.*"

Roan closed his eyes and Kate pressed her lips to his, soft and sweet as she fought off a sob. She belonged right here with him.

Roan's lips trembled against hers before he pulled away.

"That is why you must go. You have a life, and now you must live it. I should never have stolen you and brought you here."

Kate remembered what Thalia had shown her, what would have happened to his world if she had never come here. He was wrong. By bringing her here he had given her a chance to save this world and him. She just had to find the way. His eyes closed as he drew in a shallow breath.

"I have no regrets, Roan. *None*," she promised him. "If I had the choice, I would ask you to bring me here all over again. You don't need to hide your true self from me, Roan. The light or the shadow. I love you for who you are. I always have."

His eyes opened and he stared at her. "I will love you to the beginning of all there is and back again. No matter what happens, my love for you will stretch beyond time. Now, kiss me, Kate, before you go, so that I may leave this life with the memory of your lips."

Roan reached up and threaded his fingers through her hair at the nape of her neck and held on to her as he slanted his mouth over hers. The kiss was lightning from a summer storm, crashing waves upon a rocky shore. It was the flutter of a butterfly's wings upon one's skin. It was the beginning of everything, and yet it tasted so bittersweetly of the end.

*Kiss me, Kate . . .*

The world began to spin around her. She felt herself being ripped away from Roan. The battlefield and the labyrinth became a wild blur. Streaks of colorful light shot past her, the roar of the winds of time deafened her ears, and she could barely breathe. She screamed Roan's name, but he, and the rest of his world, was already gone.

# SIXTEEN

*The bride came upon an enchanted pool in the dark woods. To look into the pool was to see one's fate and then have one's memories erased. The bride, unknowing of this curse, peered into the depths of the enchanted waters and saw the king's death. Her king . . . the one she had grown to love as she learned to love his creatures and his forest. But just as soon as she realized she would lose her beloved king, all memory of it was taken from her.*

—Anon., *Tales from the Twilight Court*

Kate woke up, her bedsheets twisted, pillows scattered everywhere. The tattered strands of a vast and terrible dream hung at the corners of her mind. What had she been dreaming about? Her heart was pounding hard enough to bruise her ribs. Kate caught her breath and stared around the moonlit bedroom. She took comfort in the sight of her familiar textbooks, the jewelry music box her mother had bought for her, the photos of her friends she'd taped to the edges of the mirror on her desk. She was home. She was safe.

Yet she couldn't shake the strange feeling that something was missing. Something was wrong. It was like she'd gone to bed without locking the front door, or perhaps someone had left the oven on? It was that sense of something left unfinished, something out of place.

She climbed out of bed and walked down the hall to Caden's bedroom. Her little brother was asleep, one arm curled around a dinosaur stuffed animal. Kate let out a breath of relief.

He was safe.

But why wouldn't he be? There was no reason he wouldn't be safe in his own room in his own house. Yet for a moment, she'd been certain that he'd been in danger.

It must have been tied to whatever she'd been dreaming about. The threads of that dream had pulled loose the moment she'd woken, and she could not recall anything about it. Only the feeling that she'd lost something. Something precious that she could never get back.

Standing on the threshold to her brother's room, she realized part of what it was. She felt as though she was in between worlds, neither in his room nor out. Yet the sense of this *in-between* was vast, as though she'd stepped out of time itself. It reminded her of those moments she'd had when she didn't feel like herself, as though she was a stranger in a strange body and nothing around her seemed to feel right.

Desperate to rid herself of the unsettling, out-of-place feeling, she closed her brother's door. The house was quiet, and the grandfather clock ticked away in the hall downstairs. She went back to her room, standing barefoot beside her bed, unable to shake that sense that she'd forgotten something important. But what?

She noticed a book lying on the floor by her bookshelf. Curious, Kate walked over and picked it up. It was her mother's favorite book of fairy tales.

"*Tales from the Twilight Court . . .*" She read the faded gilt title on the spine and traced the lettering with a fingertip. It was an old book, based on the style of its binding. She thumbed through the pages, her eyes taking in the lines of the fairy tales and their half-forgotten stories.

*The path through the dark woods led to the center of the forest. The bride turned every which way, seeking a continuation of the road . . . but the road was at its end.*

*"So you found me at last . . ." The king of the dark woods emerged from the hollow of a rowan tree.*

*The bride gasped. "Why are you here?"*

*The king smiled and replied, "Did you not know that your path always led to me? And I have loved you as you have cared for my trees and my dark and wonderful creatures. You have been my queen all along . . . and I would give you the world if you would ask it of me."*

*The bride shook her head. "If you love me, then that is all I would ever wish for."*

The words choked on Kate's lips, tears blurred her eyes. She couldn't continue to read. Why did this little childhood story tear at her soul? As she closed the book, something white and gold fluttered from the pages and fell to the floor.

It was a feather.

Kate picked it up, running her fingertips over the delicate thing. How long had it been inside the book? Where had it come from? It was clear by its size it was a feather from a large bird. It shimmered faintly as she examined it.

*Kiss me, Kate.* The words that echoed in her mind were not

from the childhood story her mother used to tell her. No . . . she'd heard these words spoken by a deeper voice, a voice that held a universe of love within it.

"Kiss me, Kate . . ." She covered her mouth with her hand to stifle a sob. Those words seemed to rip apart the universe around her as a tear fell from her face, landing upon the feather. She was supposed to remember something very important.

"I wish I could remember . . ."

She had a right to remember what she couldn't, but a voice whispered in the back of her mind that it would hurt. Hurt more than anything else in her life. Whatever it was she desperately needed to remember, it would be worth all the agony that came with it.

"Give me back my memories!" she demanded of the night, and she could feel the magic winding its way around her. "They are *mine*."

The feather suddenly sparkled, as though dipped in diamond dust. Kate's heart stopped. Moments later she gasped as images, voices, sensations, and emotions whirled around her, engulfing her in a torrent of joy and grief. When the storm of memories subsided, she sat alone in the thick silence of her bedroom, a river of tears flowing down her cheeks.

"I *remember*," she whispered, her fingers clenched around the feather. "I remember you . . ."

She could see his face so clearly now. The long silver hair half pulled back from his face. The bright-blue eyes that burned with such fire. The sensual lips she had first thought so cruel, then come to love more than life itself as they'd whispered words of adoration across her body.

She had failed to save him, her Lord of the Labyrinth. Thalia had lied to her. The queen had promised Kate she would be able to save him, and she hadn't. He'd sent her away as he died so she would not be trapped in his world without him.

But Roan *had* left her trapped. Her without him was a fate just as cold and numbing as any prison. He'd had no right to send her away.

"I made my choice," she said in the moonlight. "I *chose* to stay with you. Nothing else should matter."

She got to her feet and walked over to her desk, setting the feather down. When her gaze lifted, she stared at her face in the mirror. Her skin was splotched with red, and her eyes were bloodshot and swollen. She was just Kate again . . . no longer Kate of the Winslows, no longer the love of a dark Fae king.

A breeze drifted through the room like music from a summer night when the world was new and life held every possibility.

"Is that *all* you are?"

In the reflection of the mirror was a woman clothed in starlight and silk. She stood behind Kate, glowing softly. Kate spun around, but no one was in her room except her. When she looked back in the mirror, Thalia Moondove was still there, staring back at her.

"You are more than just Kate," the woman said. "You have *always* been more. The moment you were born you had the wild within you, as all humans do. But like so many, you've forgotten that deep and most ancient magic that you were gifted with. It's time that you remember."

"The wild?" Kate asked, her body trembling. She wasn't quite sure she understood.

"Yes. You may know it by its other name. *Love.* Not all magic is love, but all love *is* magic."

Kate wiped at her tears as she glared at Thalia.

"You lied to me! You said I could save him. But love couldn't bring Roan back."

Thalia's summer-blue eyes were solemn. "In our realm, a great many things are possible, if one has the strength to believe in them. The question is . . . do you believe?"

"Do I believe in Roan?" Kate asked.

"Do you believe in *you*? You must believe in yourself. We are all here waiting . . . hoping that you do."

Thalia's face faded from the mirror. Kate stared at herself for a long moment. She jumped when her bedroom door suddenly opened. Caden stepped inside, rubbing a fist at his sleepy eyes.

"Kate? Who are you talking to?"

"Go back to sleep. I was just talking to myself." The last thing she needed was her brother hearing her talk about fairy queens. He would think she was crazy, because there was no way his memories would be left if hers hadn't been.

"Are you going to go back?" the boy asked.

Kate's mouth parted. "Back? Back where?"

Caden gave her a puzzled look. "To save the king."

"You remember?" Kate was stunned. She hadn't remembered, not until she found the feather and made the wish. Why had he left Caden's memories but taken hers?

Because if she had remembered . . . the pain would be worse, and she would try to find her way back when he didn't want her to. The only way he thought he could control her, even in death, was infuriating. He couldn't keep doing this to her. She had a right to remember, had a right to feel every moment of joy or pain that came from loving him.

Caden stared at her in concern. "Of course I remember. You don't?"

"I do now," Kate admitted.

"So, are you going to go back?" he asked again.

Kate swallowed hard. Going back meant leaving Caden and her family forever. She hadn't even considered that until she found herself staring at her little brother for perhaps the last time.

Caden's smile quivered as he came over to her. "It's okay, you know. It's okay for you to leave."

But how could she leave him? He was her brother. He needed her.

"If I left, I don't know if I could ever come back, Caden. It might be forever."

Something shone in her brother's eyes. "Forever is okay as long as you're happy, right?" he asked. "Because you were happy there, I think. You were different."

"Different?"

Caden nodded. "You seemed . . . I don't know . . . just *better*." He shrugged. "Happy. I think if the king made you happy, then you should go back."

Kate bit her lip to keep from crying. "Would you miss me?"

"Of course I would," Caden replied. "But that doesn't mean you should stay. You're always so sad here."

"How did you get to be so wise?" Kate asked, her voice trembling.

Caden's eyes were serious. "I have a really smart older sister."

Kate threw her arms around the little boy, hugging him against her chest. She breathed in the scent of him and pressed her lips to his golden hair. She would carry the memories of him with her always like a shield into every battle.

"I will miss you more than you know." Her words were barely a whisper, because if she said them any louder, she might lose the strength to go.

When at last she let go of him, he smiled, but his eyes were full of tears.

"I believe in you, Kate. *You* just have to believe in you too."

Then, without looking back, he left and closed the door behind him.

Kate glanced around her bedroom once more. Her home, her clothes, her books, everything would be left behind. But that was the old Kate's life. She didn't need any of it anymore . . .

Except her mother's book of fairy tales.

She retrieved it from the floor and pressed it against her chest, shutting her eyes.

*How do I get back to you, Roan? Are you even alive?*

"Show me the way back . . ." she murmured to the night.

She didn't know if it would work, but she had to try. She couldn't live the rest of her life not having taken the chance to go back.

Nothing happened.

Kate opened her eyes, still in her room. She closed them again. "Take me back, *please.*"

She waited. Still nothing.

"Damn it . . ." She stifled a sob, but she refused to give up. Roan had said he opened roads to travel between worlds. Roan could open those roads as he pleased, but she wasn't Roan. So how . . .?

Lightning crashed outside and rain poured from the skies. Just like the night when she got into her car and . . .

"Oh my God . . ."

She remembered driving through the storm past the edge of the woods, where Roan in his owl form had crashed into her car. It was a liminal place between worlds, according to the fairy tales. She remembered her mother telling her that places "in between" could help a person find their way to the land of the Fae.

Kate scrambled to change out of her PJs and into her jeans and a sweater. She then pulled on a raincoat and tucked the book in one of the pockets, along with the feather. She left her house and slipped into the night. The clouds above shuddered with thunder, and a bolt of lightning tore across the sky.

"I'm coming, Roan. Hold on." She ran down the street, straight toward the dark outline of the woods.

*I wish to return to the labyrinth. I wish to go home.* She repeated the words in her mind like an incantation, praying it would work.

Lightning struck a tree at the edge of the woods. Fire sparked through the leaves and shot down the trunk, breaking the tree clean in half. There in the center of the split tree was a shimmer of light, bending and refracting in a way that was not of this earth.

She ran toward that sliver of light. Ignoring the fire that now wreathed the area, she leapt through.

The tides of time carried Kate away from the place she'd once called home. Blinding colors and flashes of light pulled Kate across thousands of universes. All she could do was hold on to the image of Roan in her mind.

*I wish to go home. To Roan.*

It was night, with a full moon overhead, yet Kate couldn't recognize where she was. She only knew that she was no longer in her world. Was this the right place? Nothing looked how she remembered it. The ivy-covered walls of the labyrinth had fallen into ruin. The once intricately carved towering gates lay in pieces on either side of the entrance. Charred evidence of fires blackened the once pale stone.

The air was thin, as though nothing grew here anymore.

What had happened to this place? She remembered how deeply parts of it had smelled of flowers, where others smelled of darkness and decay, but the scents had been rich and real. Now the place smelled stale, empty, lifeless. It was as though all the dark and beautiful things that had lived within the labyrinth were but a dim memory. Kate got to her feet and removed the book of tales from her raincoat as she stared at the labyrinth and the pale moon far above. Where had the bright moonlight gone?

Kate slapped a balled fist against her chest as fresh agony sliced through her heart. She was too late. Roan's world could only look like this if Roan was no longer here to see it grow and flourish.

The air around her suddenly crackled with energy, as though lightning was about to strike. Then in a blinding flash of light, a figure appeared before Kate. She shielded her eyes until they adjusted. The woman in front of her wasn't Thalia Moondove, but she was a familiar face that gave Kate a burst of hope.

"Eudora?"

Lady Eudora didn't smile. Her blue eyes were so filled with grief that it seemed like they would never carry joy again. She wore a court gown of deep purple and silver, and on her brow was a circlet of glowing pearls and diamonds. She looked just as beautiful as she always had, yet she seemed to have aged from the grief in her eyes.

"I had hoped after all these years that you would come back."

Kate drew closer to the other woman. "What do you mean, 'all these years'?"

"It has been a hundred years since the battle of the labyrinth . . . a century since you left . . ."

"A hundred years?" The words punched Kate in the stomach.

Eudora shook her head. "Time is less stable here than it once was. The years speed up and slow down without control compared to your world. Roan always held time in place, mastered it better than any of us."

Kate felt ill. It had only been a short time in her world, half an hour at most?

"Much has changed since you left," said Eudora.

"What about Roan?" They were the only words that Kate could get out right now.

"He is frozen in a deathlike sleep. After Roan sent you home, our mother appeared. She cast the most powerful enchantment I've ever seen upon him. She laid his body to sleep in the heart of the labyrinth, and Rath chose to stay with him until he wakes. I haven't seen either in a century."

Kate didn't understand. Rath and Eudora were in love . . . and they'd been parted for that long? "Why didn't you go visit him?"

"The labyrinth grew far more dangerous after you left. I tried many times to find the center, but I always lost the way." Eudora paused to clear her throat. "Mother left the mists of time and returned to us. She gave me the right to rule the Unseelie, and she returned to the southern lands to rule the Seelie court." Eudora's voice quivered. "But I have no desire to be queen. I only wish for my brother to return."

Kate placed a hand on her arm. "Can Roan be saved?"

"I don't know. Mother said only you would know the way." She glanced around at the dim and dying world. "We need him. All of us, from the *Sidhe* down to the smallest pixies, need him. This world is nothing without his light." The Fae princess spoke, her heart in her eyes. "You must bring him back to us."

"Can't you show me the way?"

Eudora shook her head. "I only know he lies in the heart of the labyrinth. It opened briefly at my mother's command to allow Rath to carry Roan in and just as quickly closed behind them. Now, the heart is just as impossible to find as it's always been."

Kate turned toward the gates, taking in the dark path that was half filled with stones and shadows. She had failed to find the center before—how could she do so now?

After a moment, she opened her mother's book and stared at the story on the page. "The Ballad of the Bride of the Dark Woods."

*The bride put her hand in the king's, and she smiled at her husband. "You know I've uncovered your secret. You are the woods, and the woods are you."*

"The woods are you . . ." The hairs on Kate's neck rose as she realized that all this time she'd had the key to solving the puzzle right before her. How had she not seen the connection before? She was the bride and Roan the king of the dark woods.

Only here, Roan was the *labyrinth*. The labyrinth was Roan. Therefore, the center of the labyrinth was and always had been the *heart* of its king.

"You've found the way?" Eudora asked as she joined Kate at the gates.

"Yes . . . I think so."

Eudora embraced her with a fierce hug. "Then we shall arm you to fight whatever dark creatures you may meet on your way. Babbitt!" Eudora summoned the brownie, who appeared instantly in that way only brownies could.

"Mistress Kate!" Babbitt cried in delight and hugged Kate's hips like a small child. "You're back!"

"She is, and we need to prepare her for battle, Babbitt," Eudora said as she touched the brownie's little shoulder.

"Battle, yes." The brownie studied Kate, and with a snap of

her fingers, Kate's clothes changed before her eyes. She now wore a lightweight chest plate intricately carved with Celtic knotwork over dark-colored trousers and a comfortable white tunic top. Her arms were shielded with adjusting plates like dragon scales.

"And food, you'll need food!" Babbitt provided her with a bag to sling over her shoulders that had fairy bread wrapped in cheesecloth and a bottle of something blue that had a cork stopper in the top.

"Eat only a bite and drink only a sip as you need it," Babbitt advised.

"Take this." Eudora offered her a dagger that she remembered all too well. Roan's dagger.

"What, no sword?" Kate tried to joke.

"Without training, you are more likely to hurt yourself with a sword," Eudora said. "For now, this will be your weapon."

Kate tightened her grip on the dagger's hilt. It felt familiar, comfortable, as though she'd carried it for decades.

"Good luck, Kate of the Winslows. The sister of my heart," Eudora said.

Kate held the book out to her. "If something goes wrong . . . if I don't make it, can you make sure Caden gets this?" Her brother would treasure one of her mother's gifts if he knew Kate had sent it to him.

The Fae princess accepted the book, and Kate faced the gates again. The roots and fallen trees seemed to draw closer together, preparing to stop her from entering. Drawing a deep breath, she nodded to herself. She could do this.

Kate burst into a run. She flew across the ground as if she had wings, passing through shadows, leaping over fallen trees. The more she thought of Roan, the stronger her instincts seemed to know which way to go. No hesitation whether to go left or right, just a certainty of the path ahead. She no longer feared the darkened paths. If Roan was the labyrinth, she would trust herself to find the center, his heart, because she loved him.

She could still remember the taste of that last kiss between them and the tears that had flowed down her cheeks as she stopped denying how much she loved him and wanted to be here with him. The walls began to crumble away, revealing straighter, truer paths toward the center of the labyrinth, toward the heart of the man she loved.

# SEVENTEEN

*The birds, the rocks, the rain, the pixies . . . . all of Faerie came to the dark woods, singing to the bride of her journey, giving her courage to find and save her king. They helped her remember all that she had conquered and brought back the light that shone within her. The enchanted pool's curse was broken by her love for her king.*

—Anon., *Tales from the Twilight Court*

Kate could feel a strange pulsing, like a slow but steady heartbeat deep in her chest, but it was not *her* heartbeat. It was Roan's.

*"Find him . . ."*

Whispers came from above Kate as she ran. Glancing up, she spotted glittering green and blue pixies swirling like a murmuration of starlings above her head.

"Find him, Kate of the Winslows. Find the king. Wake him."

Their voices were like the chatter of birds after a storm. Eager and hopeful, despite the gloom of the decaying labyrinth around them.

As she moved through the darkened space of tunneled archways and entered a courtyard, she spotted a tall, silver-haired beast at the far end of the open lawn that was strewn with dead grass. Her heart leapt with joy. It was Magda. She would recognize her friend anywhere.

The troll turned, a holly leaf crown resting on her horns. She wore silver armor and held a deadly axe in one hand. Several other trolls stood around Magda as she gave orders to them. They bowed respectfully and checked their weapons before splitting up in different directions.

"Magda!" Kate cried out once the troll was alone.

The troll's mouth opened, and she lowered her head to see Kate better as she approached. "Kate?" Magda had changed since Kate had last seen her . . . but she reminded herself that for Magda it had been a century. Her silver fur was thicker, her body stronger, bulkier. She held her head higher.

"I'm so glad to see you, Magda." Kate said her friend's name again, suddenly uncertain if things had changed for Magda in the last hundred years.

"You've come back."

"I didn't know I would be gone so long. It took me a while to find the way back," Kate said. "Do you know where Roan is?"

Magda tipped her head up to the moonlight. "No one does. Be careful, Kate. He is lost deep inside this maze of walls. None have seen him since Queen Thalia laid him to rest. She opened a path for Rath to carry the king to his final resting place, and once the path closed behind them, it was lost forever."

"What are you doing in the labyrinth?" Kate asked. "And who were those trolls?"

"Lady Eudora put me in charge of the palace troll guard. We fight any wild creatures that stray out of the labyrinth."

Kate couldn't stay and talk to her friend, no matter how much she wanted to right now. The pulsing inside her was growing more insistent, more desperate. Time was running out.

"I have to go . . . I've got to find Roan."

Magda opened her arms, and Kate hugged the troll. "You will find him. I know you will. Be safe, Kate."

Magda hadn't lost faith in her, even after all these years.

"Thank you for believing in me." Kate's throat tightened. "I never knew how much I needed a friend like you."

"You saved my life, Kate," Magda said quietly, her dark eyes luminous. "I had no one to believe in me, no one but you." She squeezed Kate a little tighter before she let her go. "But you must go—you have to save the king." The troll gave a sad smile. "Find him. Bring him home. I will be here for you, waiting."

Kate managed a shaky nod. "Wish me luck."

"You do not need *luck*. You have love, and that is infinitely more powerful." The troll let Kate go, and once more Kate was running as if her life depended on it. The pulsing kept pushing her forward.

The first sign of trouble was the sight of a cloud of fire sprites in the sky as dawn crested the horizon. She had just passed through a glen of trees when a bunch of the blinding orange creatures darted around her, screeching and spitting flames. Kate gasped as embers fell around her, burning her hands and face like the sting of wasps.

Hissing sounds like laughter filled the air as she scrambled backward. The sprites flitted about her hair, and she feared they would set her on fire. It seemed the armor that she wore kept her clothing from burning, even when several of the little creatures shot flames at her chest. With an inward moment of thanks to Babbitt and Eudora, she pulled the dagger from her belt and shouted at the creatures.

"If you don't stop, I will make you."

One of the little creatures laughed, and its high, tittering voice gave a mocking cry. "Who are *you* to make us do anything?"

Kate stared at the creatures as they swirled in the air, leaving behind dizzying, glowing patterns of embers. She let out a slow breath, trying to calm herself. The labyrinth was Roan, and Roan wouldn't hurt her.

"Chase them away," she whispered as she reached out to touch the nearest wall of the labyrinth. The once beautiful, dangerous ivy was gone, and the rough-hewn stone was cold to the touch. *Hear me . . . help me.* She sent the thought out as loudly as she could within her mind.

A distant roaring sound came from the north, a violent rush of wind that traveled through the passageways with the force of a tornado. Kate flattened herself against the wall, shutting her eyes as the wind ripped past her. Shrieks and screams from the fire sprites were soon drowned out beneath the train-like torrent of wind.

Kate dug her fingers into the stone, hanging on for dear life, praying she wouldn't get swept away as well.

And then . . . just as quickly as it had risen, the wind died away, leaving silence and the faint scent of burning things lingering in the air. The sprites were gone. Exhausted, Kate sank to the ground, her legs shaking as she caught her breath. She closed her eyes briefly before she dragged herself up to her feet again. She had to keep moving.

Next, she entered a canyon-like part of the labyrinth. She had the terrible sense that a thousand eyes in the dark shadows of the caves lining the canyon were watching her. Her steps quickened and she kept hold of her dagger, ready for anything, or so she hoped.

She was halfway through the vast passage when she heard the strains of eerie music. It was no melody she recognized, yet her feet itched to dance. She paused, listening, and began to sway, feeling the rhythm move through her. A melancholy pleasure rippled through her as she spun in circles, humming along with the now familiar tune.

Figures slithered out of the darkness from the corners of the canyon and came toward her. Women in white flowing gowns, their dark and pale-blonde hair as loose and flowing as their dresses. Barefoot, they danced with her, eyes glowing red in the dim light. The music swelled, making every cell of her body vibrate. The women drew closer, their full red lips gleaming as they watched her with hungry eyes.

*Baobhan sith—Vampire Fae* . . . The words drifted through her mind, disrupting the relaxed state she was in like a stone cast into a still lake. It was Patch's voice she was remembering, warning her of the creatures who would dance her to exhaustion and then drain her of her blood.

Panic lanced through her dazed mind. She had to get away, find a way to stop them. But the music . . .

A vision of Roan at the ball flashed across her eyes. Yet it wasn't just a vision. She had conjured a ghost of him here in the canyon.

"Dance with me," he said, his voice an echo of the real Roan. The shining vision of the man she loved stood before her, hand outstretched.

Kate placed her palm in his, allowing the spectral form of Roan to lead her into a waltz. She couldn't feel his touch, and it made her ache that much more for him. He was so beautiful, so masculine and powerful. Yet he'd always been tender with her, compassionate and loving, even when he had believed he wasn't capable of it. He was everything she had never known she wanted in a man. But what she wanted most was to be in his arms, to feel his heartbeat again and know that he loved her. It was his love she could not live without.

"Will you show me your shine?" she asked the vision, the memory that lived so brilliantly within her head.

His lips spread into an amused smile as they swirled around and he began to shimmer . . . then shine. The bright starlight of his glow was almost too much for Kate to bear, but she held on to him, not wanting to let go.

The women dancing close to her screamed, their suddenly clawlike hands covering their faces as they fled into the shadows.

The music stopped, the danger ebbing away, but she didn't want to let go of him.

"Stay with me?" she begged this vision of Roan. "Please . . . don't leave."

Roan lifted her hand up to his lips, kissing her knuckles. "Find me, Kate. I'm waiting for you. *Find me.*"

The vision faded, the starlight dying away. Kate choked on a sob.

She glanced around, her feet aching, but she couldn't stop. "I have to keep going."

The next thing she came across as early evening approached was a marshland. Vast, sweeping patterns of thick grasses formed narrow places where she could tread through the dark, murky water. A foul stench rose from the marshes, and as she walked deeper along the path, she glanced down once and froze.

Bodies lay beneath the glass-like surface of the water, their milky-white forms visible despite the darkness of the waters. Men and women . . . kobolds, goblins, pixies, even a few trolls . . . their bodies here forming a silent graveyard. How had they become trapped beneath the water?

Kate glanced around, looking for any sign of a deadly creature, but all she saw were distant glowing lights that bobbed in the gloom. The pale sunlight above them had vanished as night had come over the labyrinth. The mesmerizing lights had become a beacon, showing her a way out. Kate tried to keep her eyes upon the lights ahead and glanced down to where she put her feet with each careful step, but soon she was gazing straight ahead in a trance.

*Sploosh!* Her foot sank into the water as she stepped off the safety of the thick grassy path.

She screamed and fell forward into the water, which closed in around her up to her chest like quicksand.

*Oh no . . .* She knew in that panicked moment how the other creatures had died. She looked toward the lights in the distance.

"Help!" she shouted. "Help!"

But no one came. The water grew thicker, pulling her slowly downward. Despair threatened to drown her.

No, she'd come too far to let some stupid bog defeat her.

Kate shut her eyes, no longer looking at the lights. Instead, she stretched her hands out toward the grass that was so close she could feel the thin, crisp stalks brush her fingers.

"I don't need the light to follow . . . I have my own." She thought of all the moments in the last week where she had proven that she was strong. That she was enough. That she had a right to be here. It made her feel warm and bright inside.

The grasses tickling her fingertips began to thicken and the water around her moved, becoming more fluid, and she dared to kick her legs in a powerful stroke.

Her hand grasped a thick knot of grassy soil, and with a cry of triumph, she opened her eyes. She was holding on to the narrow earthen pathway that she'd fallen off of. She dragged herself onto the bank, her clothes drenched, her armor feeling as though it weighed a thousand pounds. When she got back onto solid ground, she sat on her heels and took a moment to catch her breath.

Glaring at the distant lights in the darkness, Kate got to her feet, checked that her dagger was still at her hip, and continued her trek through the marshes. But this time she followed her feet and her instincts, not letting the tempting lights trick her.

For the next two weeks, Kate braved the vast span of the labyrinth. Each time she turned down a new path, she battled her way through creatures or dangerous elements, striking out with her dagger, drawing blood when she had to, evading when she could. With each deadly encounter, she lost more and more of her fear.

The paths she followed grew darker, the rocks sharper, the smells more rotted and decayed, as though death lingered in every shadow. But Kate wasn't going to give up. Nothing could stop her.

Except, perhaps, a basilisk.

She came to a stop thirty feet from the entrance to a tunnel that called her name. *Roan. Roan is in there somewhere.* A vast serpentine creature lay coiled before the entrance, sleeping. Kate cursed under her breath. Her dagger would be of little use against something that big.

A raspy voice came from her right. "Close your eyes, girl! Close 'em!"

Patch stood rooted to the spot, his hands half raised as if to indicate she should be silent. A bag of what she guessed were gems hung at his hip, which meant he'd been visiting the mines within the labyrinth, far deeper than he used to go. Her relief at seeing her friend was cut short as she had to face the fact that they were in grave danger.

"Patch?"

"Shut up and shut your eyes, girl. *Now!*" he urged.

The basilisk's long body twitched, its tail flicking. From where it lay, it could see them easily, but not at the same time. Kate had to find a way to distract the basilisk if it woke up.

She took a step to the left, away from Patch, her blade clutched in her hand, even though it was useless against such a beast. Out of the corner of her eye, she could see Patch waving frantically at her not to move, but he didn't understand. The snake was going to go after one of them . . . unless she could find a way to stop it.

Suddenly, she had an idea. She carefully, slowly removed the breastplate of her armor. If she could get the basilisk to stare at the armor, maybe the reflective surface would rebound the snake's deadly, hypnotic gaze and freeze the beast. She raised the armor like a shield, moving toward the creature, her eyes careful not to make direct contact with it.

The snake's eyes were closed, but suddenly the head lifted and its eyes opened. Despite trying to be ready for it, it still startled her and she glanced right at its eyes. Yellow slitted pupils stared at Kate before she could clamp her eyes shut. A slow lethargy stole over her limbs as the snake uncoiled and came closer to her. She was almost frozen now as the snake's forked tongue flicked out into the air as though tasting her scent.

*Sleep . . . sleep the long sleep of death. No more pain, no more anything.*

The words circled around her, then slid deep within her.

The basilisk . . . it was the basilisk talking to her, Kate realized.

*Such peace, little human. Don't you wish for it? For quiet? For the end? I can give it to you.*

Kate tried to move, but it was as though her feet had grown roots and trapped her in place. She tried desperately to remember what Patch had said about the basilisk and its poison. She couldn't possibly fight this snake with a dagger and had no way to use its own poison to kill it.

Off to the side, she could hear Patch muttering. "Come on, old boy. Just bloody move. You can save her. You've lived a good life, and it's worth giving up for her." He was trying to convince himself to move, to draw the basilisk away from her. Kate's heart ached at the sweetness in the grumpy kobold's voice, and it only deepened her resolve to keep him safe.

*Surrender to me, little human. Let go of your fears. Let go of your worries. I shall take them all away . . .*

The basilisk's words struck something within her. *Let go of my fear . . .*

The longer she gazed at the beast, the more she realized she recognized it. The yellow slitted eyes turned blue, vibrant like a summer sky. *Roan's eyes.*

This snake came from Roan. It was a manifestation of him, a part of him, one of the most dangerous parts. But she wasn't afraid of Roan. She wasn't afraid of his darkness.

"You have no power over me," she said. "You are but a piece of the labyrinth . . . a piece of Roan. You cannot control me. Leave us and go."

The basilisk blinked. For a long second it stared at her intensely, then it turned its head and slithered away, unblocking the path to the tunnel beyond. Kate, free of the spell that had held her frozen, crumpled to her knees, her arms shaking. Patch rushed over, staring at her with wide eyes.

"Took you long enough. Where have you been, girl?" Before

she could speak, he'd wrapped her in a hug. Kate laughed to keep from crying.

"Sorry I'm late," she replied.

"Better late than never coming back at all, I suppose." He let go of her and fixed his lopsided hat. "You've come here to save him, haven't you?"

"Yes. Do you know the way?"

He shook his head. "No, 'fraid not. No one does. Everything's changed, it has."

"What are you doing so deep in the labyrinth?" she asked. "You said you always kept to the outskirts."

"My brothers started digging deeper and deeper inside, moving their mines farther in because gems were becoming scarce. I warned 'em, but they wouldn't listen. I had to follow."

"I saw Magda," Kate said.

The kobold grinned. "Ah, she's done well since you left, girl. Very well. Got herself respect among the palace trolls, and now she leads them without fear into the labyrinth." He was quiet a moment. "That's because of you, Kate."

Kate's heart clenched as a wave of emotion swelled within her. "And how about you, Patch?"

"What about me?" he asked.

Kate wasn't sure exactly what she was asking, but she didn't dare admit that she'd missed him. He seemed to understand, and he grinned again.

"There'll be time for you to hug me later, girl. You have a king to save. Now, concentrate. You'll find the way."

"You said I'd never find the center," she reminded him, trying to tease him. But this time his gaze turned solemn and his smile faded as he reached out and gently clasped her hand.

"That was then," he said. "Things change. *You've* changed. You're Kate of the Winslows now. You just stopped a basilisk from killing us both. If anyone can find the center, it'll be you."

He said it with such sincerity that Kate had to stop herself from hugging him again. He believed in her. *Everyone* believed in her.

"You know the way. Just trust yourself." He gave her a gentle push toward the tunnel she'd been trying to reach before she'd encountered the basilisk.

It was much like the one that led to the Crystal Cave. A tremor of hope clenched in her chest. If this was the same cave, perhaps it could help her like it did before. She had to believe.

"Don't fail me now," she whispered as she stepped into the darkness. She held on to the memory of Roan as he let her glimpse his shining form, the light that glowed around him like the most powerful starlight ever seen. The memory of that light kept the hope within her burning on.

Her hands became her eyes as she felt for the closest wall and took careful steps forward. No glowing crystals or luminescent glowworms yet. It felt like hours passed before the darkness gave way to something that shone with a distant light.

She began to peel away her armor, piece by piece within the dark as she walked toward the light. It had protected her, but now she was certain she did not need it any longer. She no longer feared the labyrinth, because she didn't fear Roan.

When the tunnel ended and she left the vast darkness behind her, she found herself in a courtyard. Decaying, wilted flowers covered the beds that she guessed must have once been filled with wildflowers. An elegant stone fountain covered one wall of the courtyard, but it was empty and a century of dust covered everything that Kate could see. Her heart broke at the thought of how beautiful this place must have once been before Roan had . . .

She shook herself free of that painful thought.

What lay in the center of the garden was what held Kate's

attention most. A four-poster bed stood alone, far from everything else.

Kate knew with certainty that this bed was the very center of the labyrinth.

It pulled her closer with the force of cosmic gravity. The bedposts were laced with a thick draping of spiderwebs, concealing whatever lay upon the bed. But it could only be one person.

Kate took another step. She saw a statue of a gray dog lying beside the bed. Its head lay on its paws as if asleep. The dog suddenly moved, sounding like stone grinding upon stone as it looked at her.

It wasn't a statue. It was alive. A growl of warning came from the dog, then died away. The dog cocked its head at her as though it recognized her. She recalled what Eudora had said, that Rath had gone with the queen to guard Roan in his enchanted sleep. Rath's wild form was that of a black dog, wasn't it? Wasn't that what Caden had said?

"It's me . . . Kate," she whispered to the dog, then nodded to what lay hidden beyond the cobwebs of the bed. "He's in there, isn't he? "

The dog stood, shaking his fur. A century of dust floated into the air, changing its color from gray to black. Then the dog slowly came toward her, his paws making no sound upon the soil. Kate held her breath as the dog nuzzled one of her hands. Then he pressed his nose into her palm.

A sudden wave of images filled her mind.

*Roan collapsed as Kate vanished in a blinding beam of light. Rath held his friend in his arms as Thalia appeared on the battlefield. Thalia cast an ancient enchantment over Roan, falling like golden dust on his skin, halting the progress of the cursed magic in his body but unable to cure him.*

*The years passed. The walls crumbled, flowers withered into dust, water vanished, trees decayed and fell to the earth. The ivy shrank into dry husks and fell away. All that had once made the labyrinth a dark and beautiful place vanished as the century rolled forward. This place that had once been untouched by time had now been conquered by it.*

Kate's lips parted in shock as the vision faded. The black dog changed before her eyes into the weary form of Rath.

"Eudora hoped you'd come . . ." he rasped, his voice hoarse after a century of silence. "We all did." He placed a trembling hand upon her shoulder. "Please, bring my friend back to me," he pleaded. "And I will owe you a fairy's debt."

Kate nodded. She had to. She would find a way.

With careful fingers, she pushed the delicate layers of webs away from the bed, revealing Roan's sleeping form, still as death upon the bed.

Her love's skin was pale, his eyes closed. A faint patchwork of black veins could still be seen on his neck and hands. His fingers were folded around the pommel of a sword that lay lengthwise upon his body, a warrior king lying in death's bittersweet repose.

Even now, he was still beautiful to her, still filled her heart with such a deep longing that could fill up centuries with her need to be with him. How could it be that her virile, strong, stubborn love had been asleep for a hundred years?

"I came back," she whispered to him, thinking foolishly that her words would wake him. But he didn't stir.

Kate lifted her face to the moon. Its gentle power, weaker than it had been before, still soothed her skin. She unwound Roan's fingers from his sword and brought one of his cold hands up to her cheek. It took her a long moment to find the strength to speak past the pain in her throat.

"You're the reason I'm here, Roan. I chose to stay, even as you forced me to leave you. I would choose you over all the lives I might've lived in my world. If there's one thing I learned about being human while I've been here, it's that my stubbornness and my determination can be one of my greatest strengths. And if I have to sit here at your side for a thousand years to bring you back, that's what I'll do." She kissed his knuckles and gazed at his serene face. The proud, beautiful Fae king had become her world and had given her his heart. She just had to find a way to save it.

"I found the heart of the labyrinth. Keep your bargain with me, Lord of the Labyrinth. You promised to send me home. Keep your promise."

*You are my home,* she thought with all her heart. *Come back to me.*

The world was quiet. Nothing moved, not even a breeze rustling the dead flowers.

"Please . . . show me how to save you," Kate whispered. *"Please . . ."*

A single drop of rain fell upon her nose. Dozens of other drops followed as rain clouds eclipsed the moon.

*Rain . . . rain like tears. Tears!*

She sucked in a breath. Tears carried magic. It was what she'd been told so many times. Tears held *love,* and love was magic.

Kate leaned over Roan, and the tears came so easily to her. They flowed in rivers down her cheeks, coating her lips even as the rain fell all around them.

When her lips touched Roan's, the world seemed to stop except for the rain, which turned into a torrent as an ancient, invisible fire kindled between her mouth and Roan's.

*Come back to me, my Lord of the Labyrinth.*

The rain suddenly slowed around them, drops hanging like frozen dew in the air before they began to slowly fly back up into the clouds as though time itself was turning back, like the hands upon an ancient clock.

Kate lifted her head and stared down at Roan. His lashes fluttered, and the shimmer of a century-old spell rippled over his skin and then was gone. The black veins on his skin faded away. Kate held her breath, waiting . . . hoping.

At long last, her king opened his eyes. And the rain once more poured down from the skies around them, and the air flooded with the smell of petrichor and growing things . . . of life.

Blue eyes no longer clouded by death or pain burned bright, like diamonds infused with fire. Those eyes . . . they were what her dreams were made of, and she couldn't live another moment without losing herself in them.

Roan's lips parted as he stared at her in endless wonder.

"Kiss me . . . Kate. Kiss me or I'll believe this is yet another dream . . ." Roan whispered.

A joy brighter than any Shining One could create filled her body and soul as she kissed him. Roan was awake, *alive*. He was *hers* again.

Kate curled her arms around his neck as he sat up, and he pulled her onto the bed with him. Laughing, she buried her face in his neck as they held each other beneath the wild rainfall that coated their skin, washing away the dust and darkness of a century.

"You did it," Rath said to Kate as he joined them at the bedside and clapped his hand on Roan's shoulder.

"My friend." Roan gazed up at Rath, his eyes dark with emotion. "You stayed with me, didn't you?"

"I would stay with you until the very end of everything," Rath promised.

"How long was I . . ." Roan didn't finish.

"A hundred years," Kate said. "I didn't know it would take me so long in your world to get back here."

"What of my sister?" Roan asked his friend.

"I haven't seen her since you were laid to rest. The way here was closed to all. I do not know if . . ." The First Lance swallowed hard and looked away.

"She's waiting for you, Rath. Go to her," Kate said, then glanced at Roan. "Open a Fae road for him, send him home to her."

Roan closed his eyes, and a blinding portal of light burst forth behind Rath. "Go, my friend. Delay not another moment. Life, even for us, is too brief to miss those we love."

With a rakish but weary grin, Rath leapt into the road and vanished as the light from the gateway faded.

Kate and Roan looked at each other again, and then she leaned in, pressing her lips to his, tasting the magic that filled each tender, passionate caress of their mouths.

Kate wasn't sure how long she and Roan were lost in each other, but when they finally took a moment to catch their breath, Kate realized the smell of death and dying around them had faded. Dozens of intoxicating aromas now mingled in the air with the clean scent of rain. She gasped as she saw the blooms of a thousand flowers in a thousand hues covering the ground. The wildflowers had come back. Wisteria hung in draping boughs above their heads.

"You brought it all back to life, Kate of the Winslows," Roan chuckled. "You brought *me* back to life." For the first time, she glimpsed faint crinkles at the corners of his eyes when he smiled. Had he changed?

Roan placed his hand on the back of Kate's neck as he pressed his forehead against hers. He closed his eyes and held her tight, as though he feared she might vanish.

"You're mine, Kate. Mine now . . . mine *always*. I'll never let you leave me."

Her heart felt like it was going to burst. She was exhausted, so tired she could no longer move, but she didn't need to. She was right where she wanted to be. With him.

"I'm not going anywhere," Kate promised him. "I'm yours, remember?" She kissed the tip of his proud nose, which earned a smile from her dark king. Then she stroked a finger over his lips as their gazes held.

"How did you come back? Did Eudora come find you?" he asked after a long moment. "I used the last of my power to send you away."

Kate feathered her lips over his and whispered, "Love."

It was only one word, but it was the only word she needed to say.

He smiled back at her. "Love," he echoed in wonder.

There was no greater force in the vast reaches of the universe. Even the Fae knew that.

"Once I realized that *you* were the labyrinth, it was easy to find you. Because I *love* you, even the darkest and scariest parts of you." She traced his lips with a fingertip. "That meant I could always find my way to the heart of the labyrinth . . . to the heart of you."

He touched her cheek and she flinched, rubbing one of the wounds she'd suffered during her journey. "Somehow, I suspect it's more complicated than that."

"I'll tell you the very long and crazy story later. Right now, I just want you to hold me." She nuzzled him and breathed in that unique scent of his that in the past had driven her wild with lust, but right now simply made her feel like she'd come home. His arms tightened around her, and he feathered kisses on her forehead and the crown of her hair.

"You will tell me what you've been up to, Kate of the

Winslows, because I'd like to hear it before the blasted pixies tell everyone else."

She started to laugh so hard it made her stomach ache. When she finally stopped, she was wiping tears of joy from her eyes.

"All right, I'll tell you, but only after you do something first."

Roan's blue eyes burned intensely. "Name it, my darling."

She was cradled on his lap and really didn't want to leave, but it was time. "I found the center of the labyrinth. It's time you kept your promise to take me home."

His dark brows rose in surprise. "Home?"

"To the palace," she added with a cheeky grin. "It's our home now, isn't it?"

"My home is wherever you are," Roan said as he brushed the pad of his thumb over her bottom lip, "my love." His deep voice carried those last two words with such power that she shivered.

His smile promised Kate that she was well and truly loved by the dark and powerful Lord of the Labyrinth. Just like the bride of the dark woods in her book of fairy tales, she was no longer afraid. She had set foot upon her path, and that journey had changed her. Here in the land of the Fae, she had learned to believe in fairy tales and happy endings again.

After all, she was living in one.

# EPILOGUE

*The bride danced in the arms of her dark king. The curse that had haunted him was washed away by the power of the bride's love for him. The bleak future that she had sought to prevent never came to pass. All was well in the land of Faerie after many long years.*

*"I knew the moment I first saw you that you would be mine . . . mine to love, mine to worship," the king whispered against the lips of his bride.*

*She smiled up at him, trembling with joy. "We fought so much darkness to be together. Now even the stars cannot match the light of our love."*

*And thus, as this tale began once upon a time, it now must end as the bride and the king of the dark woods lived happily ever after . . .*

*—Anon., Tales from the Twilight Court*

Kate plucked nervously at her silver-and-purple gown as she waited to enter the throne room. She could scarcely believe it had been a month since she'd woken Roan from his deathlike sleep.

So much had happened since then. Her head was still spinning. The palace had thrown parties every night for an entire week upon Roan's return. Then there had been countless meetings between Roan and his mother as the Seelie and Unseelie forged new treaties, *better* ones. Ones that promised someone like Culan could not sound the horns of war so easily ever again.

The labyrinth was no longer a barrier against the Seelie. The enchantments that had kept everyone unable to travel over it had vanished the moment Roan had woken up, and the dark and dangerous creatures within had disappeared as if they'd never been there. Kate believed that the labyrinth had been created by the most powerful of Roan's magic after his father died because he wanted to protect his lands and his people. He just hadn't been aware of it. It was why he alone had the power to travel across it and why no creatures within dared to defy him. But now that peace reigned, the labyrinth was still there, but it was a beautiful endless garden full of delights and treasures rather than danger and fear. Lady Kyma had claimed the ruins of the most crumbled parts of the labyrinth to build a new forest for her kin, and soon new dryads were born from the tiny seedlings she planted in the ground

Andvari, the king of the dwarfs, had new gates to the labyrinth built, ones that would remain open, a beautiful passageway between the two Fae kingdoms rather than a barrier.

Perhaps the biggest change came a few nights ago, when Roan had asked her to be his queen. *Queen.* It still didn't seem quite real to her. She'd gone from worrying about finals for her business course to running a kingdom side by side with Roan.

Kate smiled. Her mother would have loved that her daughter had dared to leave her own world behind to find love and a life in another. To find the life she was meant to have all along.

After she'd told Roan about how she'd returned to his world and how she'd searched for him, she told him that she had a choice when she'd met his mother deep in the cave. She'd chosen him, rather than return to a time when her mother had been alive.

Roan cupped her face and stared deeply into her eyes, recognizing the sacrifice she had made to be with him. That was the moment he'd gotten down on one knee and asked her to be his wife. His queen. His *forever*.

She never would have considered getting married so young in her world, but in this world she truly knew herself and believed in her fate and her future. It was easy to say yes. Yes to love, yes to the man she'd claimed as her own. Love made that single word so easy to say.

Behind her, Babbitt finished arranging the long train of Kate's gown. "You look magnificent, Mistress Kate."

The train was a fine chiffon of purple embroidered with silver stars in the shapes of constellations she was still learning. Roan had thought of the idea himself, wanting her to wear the night sky. She blushed at the memory of how he'd explained all of his plans while they lay in their vast bed, bodies entwined and sheets tangled. His deep voice had shared all his hopes and dreams with her and what he believed their future together would hold. He had drawn the constellations on her skin with a fingertip, tickling her and making her breathless before he'd rolled her beneath him and claimed her yet again. She had felt *treasured* beyond words.

Now she was facing the moment they had talked about, planned for, and it didn't ease her nerves in the slightest.

"I'm still not used to wearing dresses," Kate grumbled. She missed her jeans and sweaters, but Babbitt had assured her that once today was over, she could change back into whatever she felt like. It had amused Kate to learn that several of the Fae ladies were adopting a more human approach to fashion when not in their court dress.

"Oh, Babbitt, she looks perfect!" Eudora exclaimed. She joined them just outside the towering doors. "But you're missing one thing." Her future sister-in-law lifted up a crescent moon necklace.

"I can't take that. It's yours." Kate had learned that the crescent moon necklace she'd worn the night of the ball had belonged to Roan and Eudora's mother, and she had given it to Eudora before she'd left the Twilight Court long ago.

"I must insist." Eudora helped put the necklace around Kate's throat. "It belongs to you now. Its magic matches your own." Eudora touched the chain, settling it against Kate's neck. She smiled. "It was made for my mother by her mother under the light of a newborn star."

"The light of a newborn star?" Kate stroked the crescent moon pendant, and a bright vision flashed across her eyes. It felt as though she'd seen far back into space and time, to the moment when that star had been born.

"Just as making weapons and objects under a black moon can infuse an object with a curse, creating something under a newborn star blesses it. And you have indeed been blessed."

Kate's throat tightened with a dozen emotions, and she took hold of Eudora's hands in her own. *Hope.* That word held more power for her than any other . . . except perhaps *love.*

"Thank you," Kate whispered.

"For what?"

"For everything. You've been the sister I always wished I had. You made me feel loved, and you made this place my home. You didn't let me give up."

Kate glimpsed what she thought just might be tears in the Fae princess's eyes. Could Fae cry? She didn't dare ask.

"When our mother left, it was Roan who taught me not to give up, to carry hope within me, to believe that all would be well someday," Eudora said. "When I saw how my brother held you, how he looked at you . . . I knew you were the one who would have the power to change an unchanging Fae king. I couldn't give up on you, not knowing what you could mean for Roan. What you could mean for all of us."

The little brownie stared between the two women in concern. "Please no crying, Mistress Kate. We must keep your face from getting splotchy."

Kate burst out laughing as she wiped her eyes. Babbitt was right. She was still human in this world and still had some very human qualities, like puffy eyes and red skin when she cried.

But she didn't mind. She *was* human, and she wasn't going to ignore that part of herself. Being human was what had made her strong enough to save Roan. She also knew that now when she cried, they were going to be tears of joy, not sorrow. And tears held magic, *wonderous* magic. Magic that could save a life.

"Has your mother arrived yet?" Kate asked Eudora.

"She should already be inside with the others."

Kate let out a sigh of relief. Ever since Thalia had taken the Seelie throne, the two factions of the *Sidhe* were once again in harmony, just as the sun and moon were. With luck, the new treaty between the two courts would keep the peace for another thousand years. The families of the warriors who had perished a century ago in the battle had been honored by both courts. It would take time to heal the wounds from the battles and the losses, but Roan and Thalia were determined to make it work.

Despite the role she'd played in this peace, Kate was worried that Roan's people would not accept her as Roan's queen. She was a human, an outsider. However, she'd heard whispers in the halls, whispers of respect and admiration rather than scorn and derision. It seemed the pixies had spread the story of Kate of the Winslows far and wide. Champion of the labyrinth, some called her. It had embarrassed her at first, but she had to admit, it was true. She had conquered the labyrinth, taking on every challenge, every fight, and not backing down.

Yet she still couldn't believe that the Unseelie would want her as their queen.

Rath had explained to her the true reason she was held in such esteem. It was because of her power. It was believed that nothing was strong enough to break a black moon curse. The hope for Roan to wake had been utterly lost by most of the court. Even Rath had resigned himself to spend eternity by his king's side.

Yet Kate had saved the king with a kiss and human tears.

It was a magic so powerful that she'd earned the respect of all the Fae who lived in the Unseelie lands. She had conquered death itself with her love for Roan, and among the Fae there was no greater accomplishment.

Trumpets heralded, and the two silver doors opened in front of Kate. She squared her shoulders as she entered the throne room. Roan sat on his tall obsidian throne, waiting for her. Rows of *Sidhe* lined the path that led to the man she loved.

She kept her head high until she stopped at last in front of Roan. He stood from his throne, towering over her. She felt a shiver of excitement and desire that this beautiful king was hers, now and forever.

She admired the black trousers and the gold waistcoat that tucked in at his narrow waist. He wore a few pieces of ceremonial armor across his chest, the silver glinting as though he was still prepared for war. But Kate knew that they would have peace for many long years to come.

"My queen," Roan announced to the room. He flourished his fingers in the air and conjured a silver circlet, patterned with clusters of diamonds and pearls. As he held the crown above her head, his eyes twinkled with mischief.

"I stole the moon and stars for you, my love," he whispered as he placed the diadem upon her head.

Kate's gaze never wavered from his as he took her hands, raised them to his lips, and guided her to his side so she could face the crowd.

"Welcome my Queen of Starlight," Roan commanded, and the crowd burst into a cheer that nearly deafened Kate.

Among the throng of Fae she spotted Lady Kyma, the beautiful dryad Roan spoke of so fondly. Next to the towering dryad was Andvari, king of the Black Hills dwarves. And at last, Thalia Moondove, whose shining presence in the back of the room made this moment perfect. As Roan led Kate out of the throne room, her arm tucked in his, Kate saw the Seelie queen smile, making her shine as bright as the sun.

*Live long and live well, Kate of the Winslows,* Thalia's voice said inside her head.

*Thank you, Queen Thalia,* Kate replied.

She and Roan left the Twilight Court behind, which struck her as curious. She had expected a party or celebration to be next.

"Where are we going?"

"Somewhere I can have you all to myself, little one. The others can wait."

Roan shot her a wink, and Kate laughed. This Roan, the

smiling and teasing male, was the one that filled her with sheer joy.

"Take me away from here, my lord."

"With pleasure." Roan turned and scooped her up into his arms. "You are mine, now and forever. My Queen of Starlight."

Then he kissed her, showing her the stars and the universes beyond their own. And in each and every one, his love for her was endless.

CADEN STARED AT THE GLOWING ORB THAT HOVERED JUST A FEW inches above the carpet on his bedroom floor. He watched his sister turn to face a crowd of courtiers with a glittering crown upon her head.

"So cool," he said. "My sister is a *queen*."

A grumble came from behind Caden. "I suppose, if you like all that silly pomp and circumstance."

He turned to look at the creature who called himself Patch, who had conjured the orb for him. He had shown up in Caden's bedroom just a minute or so after Kate had left.

"So you see, your sister is fine, lad," said the kobold. "Now, it's off to bed with you. Otherwise, the Holly King won't be able to sneak into your house to leave you Christmas presents." He waved at the bed, and Caden got up with a sigh and jumped in.

"Wait . . . the Holly King? You mean like Santa Claus?"

Patch scratched his black-bearded chin. "Aye, I forgot that's what you mortals call him."

"Santa Claus is a fairy?" Caden asked.

"Course he is. He'd be dead by now if he wasn't, wouldn't he? Now, in bed with you."

The kobold hopped up beside Caden on the bed and tucked him under the covers.

Caden tried to fight off a yawn. "Will you tell me a story, Patch?"

"Tell you a story? Hmm . . ." Patch's funny wrinkled face turned pensive. His lips twitched, making his beard quiver as he almost smiled. "How about 'The Ballad of the Bride of the Dark Woods'?"

Caden nestled deeper under the covers. "Does it have adventure in it?"

"Aye, of course, but even better, it has the strongest sort of magic in it—love."

"Love?" Caden blinked drowsily. "Love is magic?"

The kobold tucked up the covers to Caden's chin in a most fatherly way. "It is. And *everyone* deserves a little bit of *magic*."

THANK YOU SO MUCH FOR READING *THE LORD OF THE LABYRINTH*! **If this book swept you away and gave your day just a little bit of magic, please tell your friends!**

**Post on social media! Show off the cover, make your own character art, be inspired! Help send other readers on the magic of this journey! You have my love and gratitude, dear reader, for all that you do!**

**If you want more Emma Castle content:**

**Join my private Facebook group at** https://www.face book.com/groups/429283600812685

**Join my Patreon to get advance ebooks, signed print books, teasers, merchandise, audiobooks and more! Join here:** https://www.patreon.com/c/LSandECBooks

# HONEYMOON EPILOGUE

Kate's heartbeat spiked with the rush of adrenaline as she closed in on her goal. One more turn and she'd find her way to the tunnel that led to the courtyard at the center of the labyrinth. She was certain of it. Heart thudding against her ribcage, she cleared that last bend.

And cursed as she saw a dead end. "I swore it was this way. I could feel it, I . . ." She stilled and closed her eyes, sensing what she was seeking. Roan. Where was Roan? Then she grinned as she could feel the pull of him deep in her chest, in a different direction. He'd moved! Her tall, sexy Fae lover was teasing her by moving.

"You're cheating, Roan!" she yelled at the ivy-covered stone walls around her.

"Remember, if you fail to find the way out . . . you will be punished." His words came from everywhere in every direction, making it impossible to determine where his voice really came from.

"I'm not trying to find my way out," she muttered. "I'm trying to find *you*."

Kate walked toward the nearest wall and grasped the ivy. No stinging thorns pierced her this time, so she climbed up to the top of the wall and then sat down straddling it for a moment. She was glad that Babbitt had supplied her with tons of trousers that fit her well and let her move. Dresses were nice, but when she was adventuring in the labyrinth, she needed pants. Rolling up the sleeves of her dark-blue tunic top, she studied the mazelike pattern that stretched out before her. And that's when she spotted the barn owl circling around the labyrinth.

"Cheater!" she called out to the owl as it flew her way. She stood up and watched the bird's flight before he ducked down below the walls.

*Hah!* Now she had him. Kate jogged carefully along the top of the wall toward where she'd seen the owl disappear, and then she spotted what she was looking for. A courtyard. Not the center of the labyrinth but another place very much like it. And there perched on the top of a gazebo was the barn owl. He swiveled his head at her as she made eye contact with him. She climbed down the ivy, and when she reached the ground she turned around again.

Her eyes took in the white gazebo in the expansive center of the maze. Wisteria hung from the edges of the gazebo, and beneath the wooden structure was a bed made of ash trees and covered with pillows of a dozen shades of green and purple.

The owl took flight, and suddenly Roan was there in its place.

The Fae king stood, hands behind his back, by the king-size bed placed beneath the gazebo. His gaze sparkled with dark satisfaction. "I remember challenging you to find your way out, little one. But it seems you are so eager to jump into my bed that you took that wrong turn on purpose?"

"I was honing my skills at tracking missing Fae kings, and I think I did a decent job," Kate replied with a grin. "Soon I'll be able to find you anywhere in here, and quickly too." She didn't tell Roan that she wanted to have a skill, something that made her special in this world where she was still so very human in so many ways. If she could make finding Roan her talent, she'd feel useful somehow. And it didn't hurt that each time she found him, they *always* ended up in bed.

He made a little tsking sound at her, and in the blink of an eye, his tall frame towered over her as she strained her neck to look up. Faking a defiant expression that didn't match the butterflies inside her belly, she held his probing gaze. This man had the ability to rob her of all thoughts when he was close.

A dark eyebrow arched as he scanned her face. "I'd buy your challenging stance if that vein didn't beat like a drum in your neck." He dipped his head until his nose stopped a hairsbreadth from hers. "Question is, how shall I punish you, little human?"

His lips brushed hers with each word he uttered. Air burned her lungs with her shallow inhales and exhales as she held still. There was nothing more satisfying than prolonging the moment before they kissed.

"Take off your pants," he commanded against her lips.

"Make me." She flicked her tongue against his mouth, teasing him back. "*Husband.*"

Roan smirked. "Very well, *wife.*"

He motioned with his wrist. In a mix of amusement and shock, she watched her own hands unbutton the jeans, slide down the zipper, and push the denim off her curvy hips to pool on the ground. He'd bewitched her into stripping down!

Roan pressed her against the ivy wall, which cradled her body. Then he slanted his mouth over hers in a wicked, raw, tongue-filled kiss. For long moments she was lost in that kiss and the way it seduced her into an almost trance. Then he trapped her lower lip between his teeth, nibbling her while his hand cupped her sex. The feel of his large palm possessively touching her there made her moan helplessly.

Dragging his teeth to free her lip, he smirked. "I think my wife needs a proper fucking."

His tongue glided along her lips, his teeth nibbled her skin, and his fingers teased her flesh, making her want more, but denying her what she really needed.

In her mind, Kate screamed commands for her body to shut down, to slow the way he tortured her with her own desire. But her traitorous body melted under Roan's touch.

He lifted her tunic top up and off her body, letting it fall to the ground, leaving her standing there in nothing but her panties.

With his free hand wrapped around her neck, collaring her, he kept her face tilted up while he invaded her mouth with his tongue in slow, thrusting motions. He moaned inside her mouth as their tongues tangled. Despite her best efforts to resist, her blood pounded in her veins, pooling in her sex, hardening the tight bundle of nerves of her clit as Roan's fingers tapped over the thin fabric of her panties.

"Interesting . . ." he mused with dark pleasure. "Just kissing gets you going like this," he murmured against her lips. He licked a trail to a spot on her neck, and his tongue pressed down the throbbing vein there. He rubbed his groin against hers, his erection nudging her soft belly. "I wonder how wet you'll get with a long, hard fucking, my sweet little wife?"

Without warning, he stepped away and gestured to the bed in a silent order.

Desire so potent that she almost couldn't walk had her struggling to move. Her legs quivered beneath her as she stumbled toward the bed. When she trusted her voice, she turned to face him and whispered, "*Please*, Roan."

"Please fuck you long and hard or slow and gentle?" he replied with a smug smile, then patted the bedding in invitation as he moved to stand beside her.

Aware that he'd use magic again if she didn't comply, Kate climbed up onto the bed and knelt on the soft feather mattress, her eyes glued to Roan's. He was watching her with a deep, carnal hunger that she loved so much.

"Good girl. Lie down, put your head on the pillows, and wrap your fingers on the headboard."

She settled her body as instructed and gripped the metal bars above her head, still holding his stare.

He lifted the right corner of his full lips in a satisfied smile and cuffed her ankles with leather belts tied by metal chains to the feet of the bed.

"Where did those come from?" she demanded, her voice breathless.

"You have to ask, little one?" He wiggled his fingers in the air, and magic sparked from his fingertips.

After climbing onto the mattress, he knelt between her spread thighs, and his heated stare scorched her skin as he zeroed in on her sex. She feared he would see her flesh tremble under his gaze, but her desire for him was too great.

"Roan . . . what are you going to do?" she asked.

He ignored her, crawling over her body until his face aligned with hers. When she tried to use her hands to push at his broad chest, Kate found out the headboard had shackled her wrists with delicate branches.

She frowned. "What the hell? Since when do beds do that?"

Roan chuckled as he kissed the top of her nose. "My beds are made of trees from the dark woods, and as the king of said woods, those trees always do what I want."

He swooped down to seal her mouth in another searing kiss.

Adrenaline pumped her blood faster, stealing her breath away as his lips consumed hers. Trapped, at his mercy, she fought the waves of pleasure that washed over her.

And lost.

When his fingers pushed to the side the drenched bit of silk that covered her sex, she gasped. Roan left her mouth to nip her chin and a sensitive spot under her earlobe. Her bones melted as new sensations coiled inside her.

"I'll fill you up and fuck you until you cry out my name over and over. Would you like that? Would you like to come all over my cock, my pretty little pet?"

She shook her head, wanting her hands free to touch him, but he misunderstood her head movement.

He bit her earlobe, chuckling, making the fine hairs on her skin stand up.

"Yes, Kate. You will. First, I need to get you ready for me." He added a second finger, stretching her, reaching deeper as he curled his fingers and hit some spot deep inside her that made her see stars.

He covered her mouth again, stroking her tongue in the same rhythm he rubbed his palm against her folds. As he sped the movements of his fingers, he sucked her lips harder.

Heaving, she embraced the sensations he wrung out of her, swiveling her hips when he pinched her clit. A loud drumbeat filled her ears as blood pounded through her veins. His touch ignited her body, branded her skin, and scorched her muscles.

"Come for me," he murmured, flicking her hard nub. "Scream my name, little one."

Her body exploded in a mind-boggling series of orgasms that Roan stoked. Each time the quivering in her flesh ebbed, he intensified the rubbing of his hand against her folds, triggering renewed pleasure.

Squeezing her eyes shut, she groaned, "Please, enough. I can't take it."

He kissed the tip of her nose again. "Yes, you can."

With bright spots flickering behind her eyelids, she thrashed her head and arched her back off the mattress. "*Please . . .*"

Consciousness threatened to slip away, and she didn't fight to hold it. She'd never thought one could pass out exhausted from too many orgasms. As Kate sank into oblivion, Roan rolled her onto her side, freeing her from the magical and physical restraints and pulling the covers over her sated body. Her last thought as she drifted to sleep was how wonderful it was to be in the shelter of his arms, deep in the labyrinth where no one would find them.

***

With a glance ahead, Kate recognized the waterfall over pale stone to her right. That way would take her to the outskirts of the labyrinth. She exulted at the discovery and lunged left at the fork in the path. When she'd woken that morning, she'd discovered that Roan had left her another note, challenging her to find the way out or else. She had grinned at the "or else," knowing it would end up in sweaty, naughty sex that would leave her limp and sated. But she adored this game with him, the running, the chasing, the hiding, the seeking. It was *fun*, and she loved having fun with her husband.

She paused at the edge of the waterfall and cupped her hands beneath the spray, filing her palms with clear, cool water. Then she lifted her hands to her lips and drank deeply. The water in this place always satisfied her thirst in the most magical way. Then she continued on, going in the direct opposite way that she could sense where Roan was. Because he would wait in the center of his labyrinth, like a sexy spider tugging on his web, waiting to see what silly, fuckable little fly got caught, like her. Chuckling at the mental image of her lying naked on a vast web as Roan came toward her, she took another turn around a towering cluster of trees and followed a new path.

"Damn!" she growled as she turned a corner and was met with the sight of a bed beneath the swaying canopy of a willow tree.

"Glad to see you too, little one," Roan chuckled, fists digging into his hips as he stepped out from the willow's draping branches.

Sneaking a peek over her shoulder, she calculated her chances of escaping before scowling at him.

"You wouldn't make it five feet," he warned with his uncanny ability to read her like a book. "You found me, and now I get to take what I want from you."

She arched an eyebrow, pretending her knees didn't turn to jelly at the way his voice wrapped around her like a silk shawl. Smooth, soft, and sexy as hell.

"You're tricking me, I just can't figure out how," she replied.

"Such a feisty little thing you are. I can't wait to have you begging for my cock." His grin matched the increasing heat in his gaze. He tilted his head as he lifted the draping willow branches out of the way to let her see a better view of this new bed. When she stopped a couple of feet away from him, Roan closed the distance, cupped her shoulders, and whispered, "Let's see how much you can take this time."

Kate defied him with a pointed stare.

He squared his shoulders, eyes gleaming now with suppressed mirth. "I'm not tricking *you*." He stepped into her personal space. "It's designed that way. Otherwise, it wouldn't be fair."

She stepped back as he strolled toward her. Then, they

moved around in a wide circle, opponents sizing each other up. She braced herself for an attack, knowing he would never hurt her. It was part of their game. Still, her shrieks reverberated through the maze when he wrapped his hands around her waist, hoisted her up, and threw her over his shoulder like she weighed nothing.

Kate kicked.

Roan fastened an arm around her legs.

She punched his back, screaming, "Let me down."

He tossed her on the bed. "There. You're down." He laughed, his eyes holding hers as they glowed like bright sapphires. "Stay down," he barked when she scrambled up the bed on her elbows and heels.

"I'll never go down without a fight," Kate retorted with a grin of her own.

She heaved with her back against the massive headboard of the bed. The acorns, branches, and leaves carved on the oak panel bruised her skin under the light loose top of her tunic.

His lips curved in a humorless grin. "Suit yourself."

She gasped when his fingers cupped behind her knees, pulling her down onto her back on the mattress until her head sank into the feather-filled pillows. Her eyes rounded at the sight of his erection tenting his pants. Desire spiked her pulse, but she shoved the X-rated images to the side as she debated how best to resist him until it was too much to resist. She turned her face to the side and lightly bit his forearm where it was braced next to her head on the pillows.

"My adorable little pet likes to nip, does she?" he grunted as he sat back, pulling himself out of nipping range, but it gave him the opportunity to remove her boots, tossing them off the bed, and soon her trousers joined them on the ground.

Suddenly, he slammed his body against hers, thrusting one thigh between hers and raising her arms above her head. He held her wrists with one hand while the other pinched her chin, jutting her head up until their eyes met.

Out of breath, he whispered, "I claim you, little one, as my love . . . my very life . . . my darling wife."

Oh God, he melted her to pieces when he called her *wife*. She'd never imagined she'd be okay getting married young, but with Roan, she'd needed no time to think. She knew she was his and he was hers. It was the easiest decision she'd ever made.

Roan's mouth claimed hers, while his fingers kept their steely hold on her face. He rubbed his cock against her belly as his tongue invaded her mouth. It wasn't a rough kiss. But it wasn't a sweet one either.

To Kate, it was like a branding. Roan assaulted her senses with his scent, his taste, his power. Her body betrayed her mind as it molded her curves to his hard planes. Her head screamed for her to resist while her flesh quivered under his touch.

He flipped her to lie on her belly. One arm across her back pressed her down, and she turned her head to the right to be able to breathe.

His other hand hooked around her panties, pulling them down around her knees. She heard him fumble with his pants seconds before the head of his cock nudged her ass.

"God," she groaned, because despite his rough treatment, her sex quivered.

His fingers penetrated her from behind, stretching and probing. His teeth grazed her shoulders. "You're fucking drenched, darling."

She lost his heat when he knelt between her legs.

Swatting her ass, he ordered, "On all fours." When she hesitated, another smack landed on her butt. "Don't make me repeat myself."

Kate assumed the position, while her thighs trembled as the sting of his slaps connected to her clit, sending shocks through her muscles.

"My little pet likes it rough—I can smell your excitement."

With two more blows, one on each cheek, he sent her libido into overdrive. And her good sense into outer space.

"Such a brave Fae king, taking on a woman half your size," she taunted, mock glaring at him over her shoulder.

Their gazes dueled. His, simmering. Hers, defiant.

His fingers dug into her cheeks as he whispered, "Remember, you've asked for it."

He kissed her hard, but briefly.

Reaching between them, he rubbed the head of his cock along her sex, coating himself, poising his shaft at her entrance. He gripped her right hip and left shoulder, anchoring himself as his erection parted her folds.

"So fucking tight," he grunted, thrusting deeper.

She fisted the covers as he didn't give her body time to adjust to his girth. His shaft pressed on, as Roan plunged to the hilt.

In one swift movement, he pulled all the way out of her. "Let's see how long it takes for you to cave."

He hammered his cock in and out of her without mercy. The friction turned her initial discomfort at the sudden, hard invasion into shocking pleasure. Her torso collapsed on the bed, and she buried her face in the pillow, biting the soft cloth of the pillowcase to avoid wailing his name as ecstasy gripped her chest in an iron fist.

"Fuck, Kate. You're killing me." He covered her back with his chest, grazing her ear with his lips as her sex clamped around his cock.

Lacing an arm around her waist, he surged upward, bringing her with him. The new position allowed his shaft access to different sweet spots. She hooked one arm around his neck, seeking support on his chest and moaning.

She caved. "Roan, please."

His fingers tweaked her clitoris, and her body shattered under the weight of a tsunami of pleasure. Hot jets filled her as he came too. She found his lips and kissed him with abandon, trying to show him the feelings she didn't know how to translate into words.

Roan groaned, withdrew from her tight sex, and turned her around in his arms. Burying his fingers in her hair, he held her captive for a kiss that held enough heat and life that she felt the flowers around them growing taller, their blooms brighter. It was one of a thousand things she loved about making love with him. Together...they made entire gardens within the labyrinth.

He covered her lips again, in a tender kiss this time. He waited for her to open up for him, sliding his tongue against hers. As she kneaded his shoulders, he squeezed her ass. They drank each other's chuckles before Roan dragged her lower lip between his teeth. The sensual gesture ignited her blood, and she hummed inside his ear, licking its shell.

Pushing her to lie on her back, Roan straddled her thighs. He leaned down and pecked the corner of her mouth. She licked his lower lip. He evaded her attempt to deepen the kiss.

She smiled into his eyes, arching her back and raising her arms when he pulled her tunic top off her, tossing it over his shoulder.

His gaze traveled along her body, desire burning bright, scorching her skin. Adrenaline sped up her heart rate and she chest heaving with panting breaths. Her body begged for his attention.

She laced her fingers behind his neck, gliding her tongue over dry lips. "Roan, please. I *need* you."

His grin turned sinful.

With superhuman speed, he got rid of his clothes, returning to kneel between her thighs. His member jutted up. She ached to taste him again, but her body throbbed for the feel of it spreading her.

Roan propped himself on his left forearm, hovering above her as he hooked his right hand around her knee, pushing it out. She gasped when he penetrated her a couple of inches and stopped. She exhaled in a sigh as he moved another couple of inches in, smiling. Returning the grin, she inhaled when he fed her hungry body another small part of himself. Droplets of sweat gathered on his brow as he waited for her walls to accommodate his length. With a subtle nod, she indicated she was ready for more. He thrust forward until their hip bones collided.

Roan rested his forehead against hers. "Are you alright??"

She smooched his lips. "I'm better when you make me come."

He shook his head. "What am I going to do with you, my darling wife?"

She chuckled. "Make me come, my wicked husband?"

He winked. "Remember, you've asked for it."

Her heart swelled at the playful tone he used, appreciating the full circle. Then her mind checked out, leaving her senses in control. He set a lazy rhythm to his movements as he drove in and pulled out of her. Each time he did, he created a new turn in the coil of desire building inside her.

Moaning, she matched his thrusts with her own, wrapping her legs around his hips, crossing her ankles at the small of his back.

"Yes, deeper," she begged as his shaft sank inside her.

Roan swiveled his hips, tweaking her nipples, sucking her neck.

She dug her heels into his ass, urging him on as her body gripped his throbbing cock. She arched her back off the mattress when the first waves hit her. Panting, she nibbled at his earlobe. He sped his movements up, increasing the friction, and she shattered.

Dropping her arms to the mattress, thrusting her hips up, she screamed, "Roan! Oh . . . my . . . God!"

His chuckles rang around them, but she was too high on pleasure to process thoughts. His mouth covered her nipple and he slowed down inside her sex, allowing her soul to float back to her body.

She traced his lower lip with her index finger. "You haven't come."

He trapped her finger between his teeth. "Yet."

"What . . . ?"

She never finished her question because Roan's hands grabbed her legs, folding them against her chest, exposing her to his searing gaze. Instead of vulnerable she felt empowered, because she was the reason for the bone-melting hunger in his expression.

Holding her in place, he sheathed himself in her tight sex in one swooping movement. Sealing their lips together, he kissed her until he reached her soul. She welcomed the torrent of feelings his body poured into hers as he grunted, moaned, and hummed.

She smoothed his hair and shoulders, reaching down to cup his ass. He sucked at her tongue, his cock twitching inside her. When he let go of her legs to brace himself over her, she kept them folded, riding the high tide of orgasms he gifted her. His body quivered, but he went on sliding in and out of her in a maddening sluggish speed.

She framed his face, making him stare into her eyes, and repeated the words he kept saying to her. "Come for me."

He filled her as he shouted, "Kate! Kate!"

When she thought he had finished, he smiled against her neck and started over. She lost count of the orgasms until she passed out in his arms.

Again.

When she woke up expecting to see a cloudless sky, the arched ceiling of Roan's bedchamber in the palace surprised her. Snapping her head to the left, she found him sound asleep on his side, an arm cinching her waist.

Leaning over, she showered open-mouthed kisses on his chest until she reached a nipple. She closed her lips around it, flicking the hard nub with her tongue.

He hissed.

She chuckled, doubling her ministrations.

"I could get accustomed to this waking up like this," he groaned, combing her hair with his fingers, his voice thick with sleep.

With a wicked grin, she murmured, "So could I, husband."

Laughing, he rolled her beneath him, teasing her with the sweetest words she could ever hear.

"I promise we'll always have this, Kate. For the rest of our very, very long lives . . ."

"I just need you, Roan." Kate traced his lips with her fingertips. "Just you."

"Forever, my darling wife. *Forever*."

# The Lord of the Labyrinth Playlist

I write best when I have a playlist. Many authors feel the same. There is something intangible about the way music can affect one's brain and emotions as they write. Words, or even just patterns of notes can be enough to stimulate some of the most evocative, emotional or powerful scenes of my stories.

This is my list for the songs which helped shape The Lord of the Labyrinth. It's not always about Lyrics, but often just the sound from these songs which moved me to reach emotional places for Kate and Roan.

- The Twist by Frightened Rabbit
- The Letter That Never Came by Thomas Newman
- Love and War by Fleurie
- Underneath the Covers by Priscilla Ahn
- What it is by Kodaline
- Madness by Ruelle
- Tessa by Steve Jablonsky
- Breathe by Fleurie
- Hurts like Hell by Fleurie

- Time by Hans Zimmer
- So Far by Ólafur Arnalds
- Calling by Wolf Saga
- Shock to Your System by Tegan and Sara
- Give me Everything (Stripped) Bridgerton Edition by Archer Marsh
- Roads Untraveled by Linkin Park
- Hoppipolla by Wenzel Templeton and Robert Pegg
- Signs by Bloc Party
- Daddy's Gone by Glasvegas
- Fresh Feeling by Eels
- Wicked Game by Theory of a Deadman
- Bears by Sam Isaac
- Ordinary by Alex Warren
- The Law of Surprise by Sonya Belousova and Giona Ostinelli
- Here's Your Destiny by Sonya Belousova and Giona Ostinelli
- Everytime You Leave by Sonya Belousova and Giona Ostinelli
- Bumblebee Captured by Steve Jablonsky
- Fellowship by Thomas Newman
- The Cottage by Abel Korzeniowski
- Mother by Abel Korzeniowski
- Forever by Labrinth
- Einaudi: Experience by Daniel Hope, I Virtuosi Italiani and Ludovico Einaudi
- In This Shirt by The Irrepressibles
- Arcade by Duncan Laurence
- Outro by M83
- The Night We Met by Lord Huron
- Star Wars (Epic Main Theme) by Samuel Kim
- Too Sweet by Hozier

- Cold Lamb Sandwhich by Thomas Newman
- Like a Prayer (Choir Version from Deadpool and Wolverine) by I'll Take You There Choir and Madonna
- Richter: Spring 1 (2012) by Max Richter, Daniel Hope, Konzerthaus Kammerorchester Berlin and André de Ridder

# ONCE UPON A TIME...
# WHY WE LOVE FAIRY TALES

Every reader has at least once in their life read a story that began with those four powerful words...*Once upon a time...* Those words hold the power to change our lives, to inspire us, to teach us a lesson, to offer a portal to a world where we can, for a brief time escape the ever present pressures of our current reality.

If you're like me, you get goosebumps the moment you hear a voice slowly, deeply breath out those words *Once upon a time...* And you know in most cases that the story will probably end with *And they all lived happily ever after...*

These words are so powerful that romance became a genre built entirely around that beautiful promise of a happy ending for people dwelling within the worlds of those stories. And for me, the best part of romance is finding a way to retell a fairy tale or a popular story in our modern world that has in a way become a fairy tale. If we look to pop culture, many stories have become iconic and are fast on their way to being identified as what I consider modern day fairy tales.

If you approach younger readers who grew up when these

immensely popular stories were already out for several decades, there is now a built in awareness for this younger generation of these stories on an almost mythic scale. Take for example Star Wars, or even Indiana Jones and maybe even Back to the Future. These are modern movies that released in the last thirty or so years but they have become legendary stories to audiences. Harry Potter is another great example. These stories will outlast many of the other stories that came out at the same time. These stories are built...different. There is something about them, something epic that leaves us breathlessly wanting to return to that world again and again.

For me, the 1986 movie Labyrinth was one of those movies, and I know based on the internet posts and social media engagement that I am not alone in my complete obsession with Sarah's battle through the Labyrinth and the enigmatic Goblin King Jareth. I've found an immense pleasure in being able to take elements of these modern fairy tales and recreate a new but hopefully inspired story that will speak to a more adult audience while still capturing that fantastical adventure of first love.

### _A brief history of fairy tales..._

In another life, I was a history and political science major. Research is in my blood and bones. So naturally, when I turned my mind to writing _The Lord of the Labyrinth_ I wanted to get my fairy facts straight and my mythology figured out. For copyright reasons and for my own enjoyment of creating something new, I didn't want to copy the movie. I wanted this story to be a tribute to the movie. With that goal in mind, I knew I wanted to build a fairy kingdom that was more in line with true fairy mythology so I turned my research towards fairy lore and its history.

No one is quite certain where fairy tales first originated.

Many scholars believe that these stories came from oral traditions dating back thousands of years. And arguably the first mythologies about gods and goddesses in ancient societies like Greece and Rome were essentially fairy tales. They featured gods, monsters, wild lands, and mortals tossed into adventures in those elements.

As the oral tradition of fairy tales progressed into written forms, there was a societal division with regard to whether fairy tales were for poor peasants to tell around the hearth at night, or if they were stories to be relegated to the Victorian nurseries. Perhaps only in the last seventy-five years has this division weakened and fairy tales have once more become acceptable across all classes and all elements of society.

There are still critics who argue that literary fairy tales are too sentimental, kitsch or escapist, to which I would argue, is exactly the point of reading them. Many people lose their love of reading in their high school or college years when they are required to read texts that are dry, boring, uninspiring or banal. They forget that they can simply walk into a bookstore, a library or even pick up their phone and access a story that is worth reading simply for their own pleasure. The power of fairy tales is that they are exactly that, an escape for all of us, from whatever we need escaping from. That is a fairy tale's truest power.

When you turn the page of a fairy tale, you know you will be encountering a fantastic world, possibly a supernatural one, it may be whimsical or dark, it may be playful or simply wondrously strange, but it will be worth reading. These tales will be some of the most entertaining, astonishing, or inspiring stories that have ever been dreamt up by writers.

Some fairy tales will offer political arguments that relate to the age and area in which they were first written, some will tackle the balance between cultural concerns and advancing economics of an ever changing world. But the way these stories are written, these issues are handled delicately within the framework of the story itself so as to still remain enjoyable while imparting a message to the reader.

### ***What do fairies have to do with fairy stories?***

As has been pointed out by literary scholars, most fairy tales or fairy stories do not include actual fairies as we think of them, with little tiny shimmery bodies, wings and often reckless behaviors. We think of fairies like Tinkerbell from J.M. Barrie's *Peter Pan* but those are not the fairies which originally were dreamt up in the oldest stories we know. The Seelie and Unseelie Courts and the *Sidhe* lore are particularly striking in this regard because the *Sidhe* species of fairy creature are considered to be far taller than humans and yet they look human. There is no mention of pointed ears, and not all of them are blond and beautiful, although *most* are described to be beautiful and captivating.

So where did fairies began to fit into our sense of fairy tales? I believe that like with ghosts within horror stories or spooky stories, fairies as creatures became a sort of mascot for the genre of fairy tales. Many of the now more obscure tales in fairy tale collections do not contain fairies in the traditional sense, but may possess fantastical creatures. However, the more popular stories, like those of the Brothers Grimm include fairies as prominent characters.

What is it about fairies that attract us? C.S. Lewis that fairies brought out an overarching medieval picture of the world with a wonderful element of mystery to it. Fairies were creatures who could be defined by several categories all at once, yet they defied being pigeon-holed into box or another. Sometimes they were good, sometimes they were evil, and always they seemed to come as emissaries to us from a wilder, more fantastical world than our own.

The birth of the modern fairy like the Tinkerbell sort of fairy within fairy tales began in the Victorian era where the folklore of old transcended into a true literary art form. The writers of this golden age of fairy tales saw themselves as bringing readers back to their childhoods, back to their ancient roots of those oral traditions, albeit with a touch more wonder and magic infused within their words, than the old stories. It was clear that these Victorian writers were in love with the idea of these 'other worlds' and the stories that could be told within them for not just children but adult audiences as well.

At the height of Industrialism, with coal residue coating much of England, and children workers in factories as business men pushed for the economic advancement of England, fairy tales grew in importance for audiences. As if driven by the need to combat their very opposite nature, these fairy tales, which had existed long before technology, and likely will exist after all technology is gone, remain the way for all of us, to travel back childhood, to connect with nature and magic again on a soul deep level that has been inherit in human nature for thousands of years.

These stories have the power to teach, to provide children with their first discoveries of intertextuality. These stories are known, loved, and even when mocked by others who have forgotten the way back to magic, they stand strong and tall in our literary traditions.

J.R.R. Tolkien, author of the famous Lord of the Rings series even penned and performed an essay famously titled 'On Fairy Stories' where he said that there is no necessary connection between the child and the fairy tale. What he means is that these stories are for *any* audience, not just necessarily children. Simply because the stories involve child-like trust, open-heartedness and wonder that often fill a child's mind, it does not mean that these are not worthy feelings to be embraced by adults.

In an age where we are judged for everything we do, everything we post, everything we wear, read or even listen to, there has been a grassroots movement to defend what you love to read and make no apologies. That to me is one of the gifts of fairy tales. Now, if you tell someone that you love fairy tale retelling romance novels, no one will judge you, in fact you find you might make a new friend with similar interests. We don't have to leave the wonder and beauty of childhood behind, thanks to the everlasting magic of fairy tales. These stories provide us a way to connect once more with the 'wild' within us. The ancient magic of believing in something mysterious, unexplainable and beautiful. Reading fairy tales is a lot like falling in love. I can't imagine anything more perfect than romance novels that have a fairy tale feel to them because it's like falling in love twice.

I hope you enjoyed my little journey into fairy tales and I hope that Roan and Kate let you feel that magic of falling in love both with them and with fairy tales.

# CREATURE GLOSSARY

Here is a quick guide to some creatures mentioned in the story. These are all based on hundreds of years of fairy lore and you'll find that some like Brownies will remind you of house elves in the Harry Potter novels. Some of the creatures have been taken from lore in countries other than the British Isles.

### Banshee

- Harbinger of death
- Shows up at the home of the person who is about to die
- Appears as a crone with long hair and glowing red eyes wearing a gray mantle over a green dress
- Some families have their own personal banshee that wails for a death

### Baobhan Sith

- Vampire-like fay

- Takes the form of beautiful man or woman looking for hunters or men walking along in the woods at night
- It dances with its prey until they are exhausted and then drains them of blood
- Can be killed by iron

## BASILISK

- Highly poisonous so lethal it can kill by looking at you
- Body of a massive snake
- Can be killed by a blade covered in its own venom

## BROWNIES

- assist people with domestic chores, very shy but very sweet
- Usually work when people are asleep
- Benevolent
- Three feet tall
- Tidy up kitchens, mow grass, run errands, cook
- Wear ragged brown servants clothing, males sport shaggy hair and beards
- If you try to give them new garments they can get offended
- Very social, hold conferences among themselves where they meet on remote rocky shorelines

## DEMOTED DEITIES

- Descended from ancient gods and goddesses
- Had dominion over the earth, heavens and all inhabitants
- Govern night and day, land water, the seasons, growth of plants, wild and domestic animals – just about everything

- Two categories: Those who guard and guide the natural world and those who deal with destiny and fate of humankind
- Fate fairies
- Bring gifts to newborn humans such as courage, beauty or cleverness
- Always dazzlingly gorgeous, gossamer wings that for dark fae can look silvery or shadowy depending on the mood and can vanish entirely - more female fae show their wings than males
- Sidhe – pronounced "shee" – ancient and powerful group of spirits also known as 'people of the hills'
- Once lived in fairy mounds and rings which are entrances to the Fae realm
- Human-like, exquisitely beautiful with powers far exceeding those of mortals
- Can fly through the air at great speeds, transform into creatures
- Nearly immortal
- Extremely beautiful, youthful in appearance, give the impression of being aristocratic, mature, powerful, not just in mind but in ability and mind and body
- Generally skilled artisans but were considered experts and excelled in baking, crafts, dancing, hunting, metalwork, music, spinning, weaving
- Held beauty, fertility, generosity, love, loyalty, order and truth in very high regard

## Dryads

- Forest fairies once served Artemis and her companions and attendants
- Live in oaks, willows and other trees and protect the woodlands

- Usually playful and harmless to humans
- Appease them with wine, olive oil and honey


**DWARVES**

- Short in stature
- Live underground in magnificent structures hidden beneath the hills
- Excellent at metalsmithing
- Possess great wealth
- More solitary than other races, focus on their mines and gold


**GOBLINS**

- Ugly and sometimes mean-spirited, small creatures often travel in groups and wreak havoc
- Love money and other goodies, not above trickery to get what they want
- Have no real home and take shelter where they can in the roots of trees or in cracks between rocks


**KOBOLDS**

- Small in stature and ugly in appearance, they dwell in mines and search for gems
- Relatives of brownies
- They aren't evil just mischievous
- Like playing tricks


**MORGENS**

- Brenton and Welsh water fairies, will sit mermaid-like upon the rocks combing long hair.
- Have sharp teeth
- Use their voices to lure fishermen and sailors toward them to wreck ships
- Survivors glimpse a happy memory as they are drowned and then morgens drain them of blood


**PIXIES**
- Tiny, child-like beings who once lived beneath the stone circles and fairy mounds in and around the British Isles
- Been linked with Picts- race of mysterious, small people who occupied Ireland and northern Britain in ancient times
- Enjoy a bit of mischief now and again
- Can steal horses and love to horseback ride during the night – will braid the manes and tails of horses
- Arched eyebrows and slightly winged ears
- Glittery green or blue with wings


**SIDHE (THE SHINING ONES)**
- Prounced as "Shee"
- Evolved from the Tuatha de Danann
- Human like in size and shape
- Can be invisible or change shape in the blink of an eye
- Handsome and aristocratic in bearing
- They organized into tribes or clans- ruled by fairy kings and queens
- Called the Gentry out of respect
- Live in magnificent castles made of gold, jewels, pearls or marble

- Hold lavish feasts and celebrations, complete with music and dancing

- When they cry their tears turn into pearls


### SOLITARY FAIRIES

- Prefer to live alone and eschew gatherings of any kind

- While trooping fairies govern the society of the fey, solitary fairies guard fields, forests and lakes and streams

- Reclusive, nature-loving beings making their homes in forests or underwater

- Generally speaking ominous, outcasts, malicious renegade fairies who wear brown, grey or red clothing

- Usually one of kind beings associated with a certain place

- Quick to anger, have sense of entitlement

- Do not join in fairy dances, prefer to interact with humans one on one

- Lord Roan Arun is a solitary fairy whereas his sister Lady Eudora is a trooping fairy.


### SYLPHS

— sylphs (air), sprites (earth) and water nymphs (water), fire sprites (fire)

- Air Sylphs can fly, manipulate the winds, influence air quality and help earthlings breathe

- Earth Sprites are tree guardians, gnomes, dryads, some pixies and elves (wood elves)- aid the growth of flowers, trees and plants

- Water nymphs – mermaids, sirens, nourishing life on earth, regulating tides, inspiring poets and artists, protect fish and aquatic life, guide humans on sea voyages

- Handsome or Beautiful, male or female. Can be human sized or as small as pixies

**TROLLS**

- Can be friendly and helpful
- Can also be thieves, sinister and dangerous
- Many are slow to move or speak, but are incredibly strong. They have power over stones and rocks.
- They like music and dancing and kidnap humans to entertain them
- Live underground in burrows and caves where they guard vast stores of teasure
- Large, dull-witted, lumbering hairy
- Can be ferocious if you taunt them

**TROOPING FAIRIES**

- They travel in long, elaborate processions throughout the countryside
- Aristocracy of the Irish fey, they deck themselves out in elegant garments for their parades and play trumpets, harps and flutes
- Some of them mount horses; others ride in splendid chariots
- They like to dress in medieval clothing or renaissance styles with rich fabrics and adorned with gorgeous gems
- They live and travel in groups
- They love getting together for feasts in their grand castles, single and dancing near ancient stone circles or in groves of trees

. . .

**Will-o'-the-wisps**

- If you stray near a bog on a dark, stormy night, you may glimpse small lights flickering over its surface, half hidden among the reeds

- Lure unwary travelers to their deaths

- Sometimes they can mark the location of buried fairy gold

- Dark Fae use them to light the palace sconces and they can show visions of what is happening somewhere else to the Fae

# ABOUT THE AUTHOR

Emma Castle has always loved reading but didn't know she loved romance until she was enduring the trials of law school. She discovered the dark and sexy world of romance novels and since then has never looked back! She loves writing about sexy, alpha male heroes who know just how to seduce women even if they are a bit naughty about it. When Emma's not writing, she may be obsessing over her favorite show Supernatural where she's a total Team Dean Winchester kind of girl!

If you wish to be added to Emma's new release newsletter feel free to contact Emma using the Sign up link on her website at www.emmacastlebooks.com or email her at emma@ emmacastlebooks.com!

facebook.com/Emmacastlebooks

x.com/emmacastlebooks

instagram.com/Emmacastlebooks

amazon.com/default/e/B07F2KRG7W?redirectedFromKindle-Dbs=true

bookbub.com/authors/emma-castle

tiktok.com/@laurenandemmabooks

threads.com/@emmacastlebooks